Emmanuel Guibert   Marc Boutavant

ARIOL

A Nasty Cat

PAPERCUTZ™
New York

ARIOL Graphic Novels available from PAPERCUTZ™

ARIOL graphic novels are also available digitally wherever e-books are sold.

Graphic Novel #1
"Just a Donkey Like
You and Me"

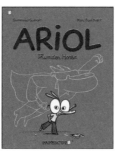

Graphic Novel #2
"Thunder Horse"

Graphic Novel #3
"Happy as a Pig..."

Graphic Novel #4
"A Beautiful Cow"

Graphic Novel #5
"Bizzbilla Hits the
Bullseye"

Graphic Novel #6
"A Nasty Cat"

Boxed Set of Graphic
Novels #1-3

Coming Soon!
"Where's Petula?"

ARIOL graphic novels are available for $12.99 only in paperback, except for "Where's Petula?" which is $9.99. The ARIOL Boxed Set is $38.99. Available from booksellers everywhere. You can also order online from www.papercutz.com. Or call 1-800-886-1223, Monday through Friday, 9-5 EST. MC, Visa and AmEx accepted. To order by mail, please add $4.00 for postage and handling for first book ordered, $1.00 for each additional book and make check payable to NBM Publishing. Send to: Papercutz, 160 Broadway, Suite 700, East Wing, New York, NY 10038.

papercutz.com

A Nasty Cat

To Monsieur Brichard,
– Emmanuel Guibert

ARIOL
#6 A Nasty Cat

Emmanuel Guibert – Writer
Marc Boutavant – Artist
Remi Chaurand – Colorist
Joe Johnson – Translation
Bryan Senka – Lettering
Noah Sharma – Editorial Intern
Jeff Whitman – Production Coordinator
Michael Petranek – Associate Editor
Jim Salicrup
Editor-in-Chief

Volume 6. Chat mechant © Bayard Editions, 2011

ISBN: 978-1-62991-157-1

Printed in China
February 2015 by O.G. Printing Productions, LTD.
Units 2 & 3, 5/F, Lemmi Centre
50 Hoi Yuen Road
Hong Kong

Papercutz books may be purchased for business or promotional use. For information on bulk purchases please
contact Macmillan Corporate and Premium Sales Department at (800) 221-7945 x5442.

Distributed by Macmillan
First Papercutz Printing

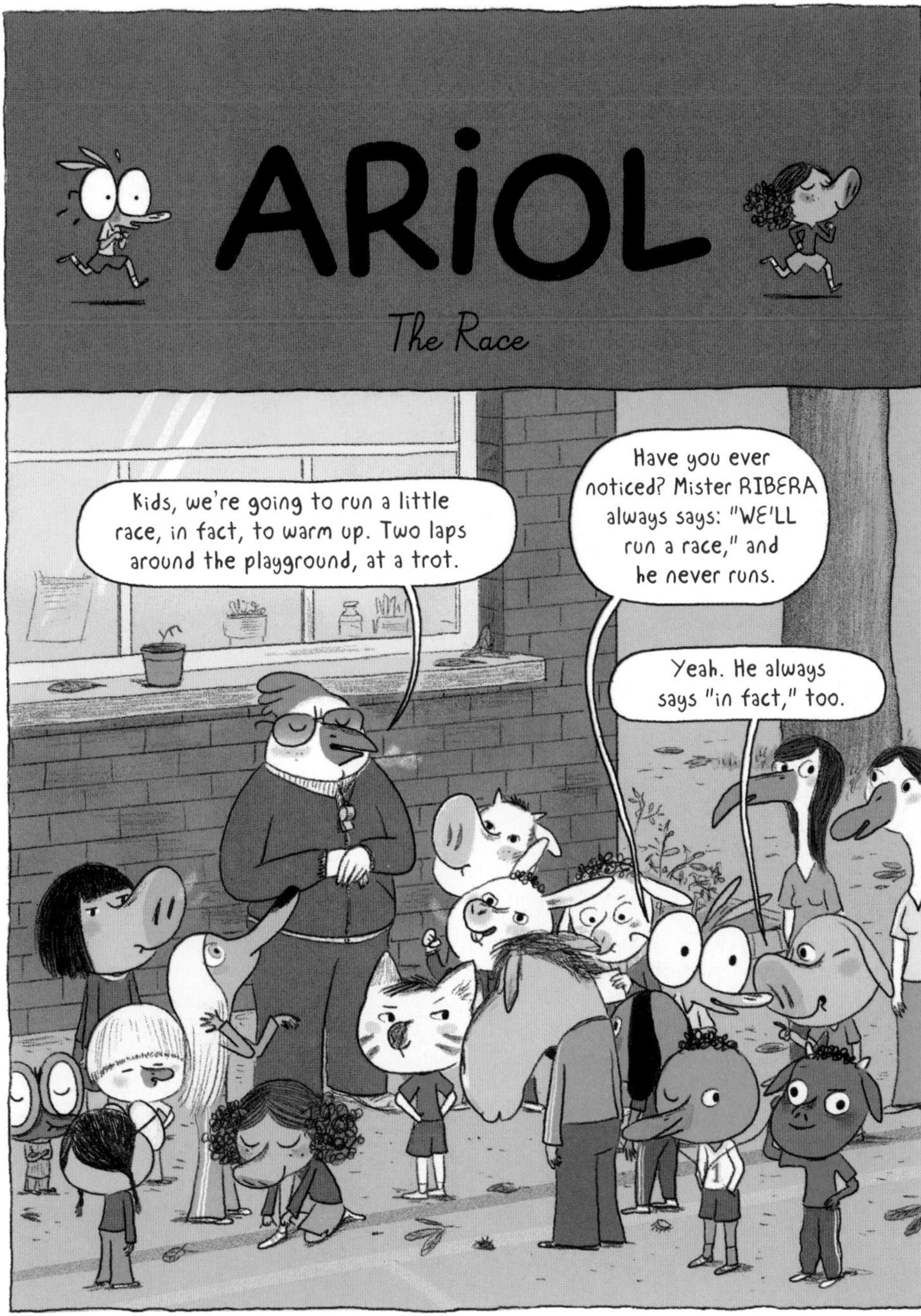
ARiOL
The Race
Kids, we're going to run a little race, in fact, to warm up. Two laps around the playground, at a trot.
Have you ever noticed? Mister RIBERA always says: "WE'LL run a race," and he never runs.
Yeah. He always says "in fact," too.

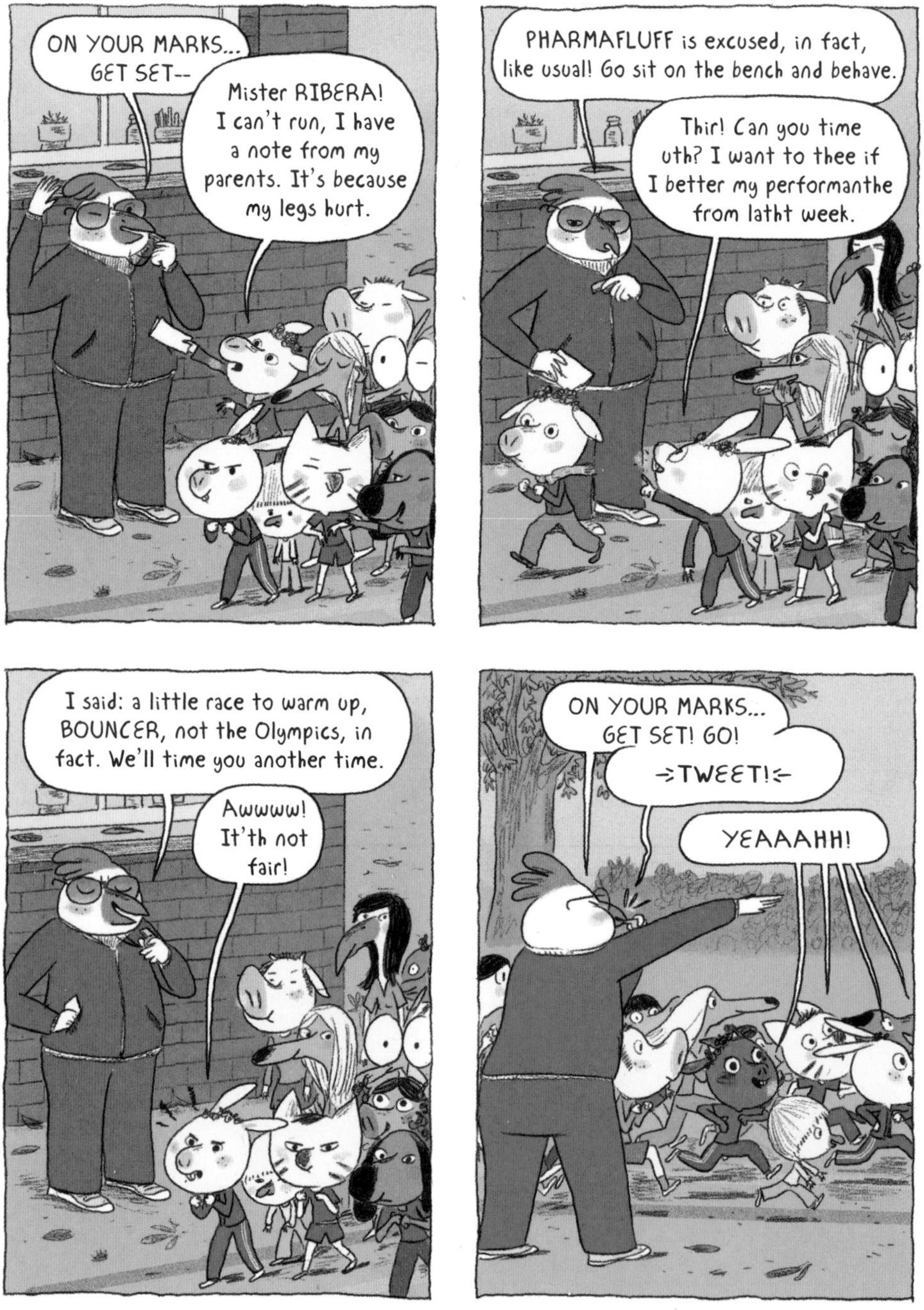
ON YOUR MARKS... GET SET--
Mister RIBERA! I can't run, I have a note from my parents. It's because my legs hurt.
PHARMAFLUFF is excused, in fact, like usual! Go sit on the bench and behave.
Thir! Can you time uth? I want to thee if I better my performanthe from latht week.
I said: a little race to warm up, BOUNCER, not the Olympics, in fact. We'll time you another time.
Awwww! It'th not fair!
ON YOUR MARKS... GET SET! GO!
TWEET!
YEAAAHH!

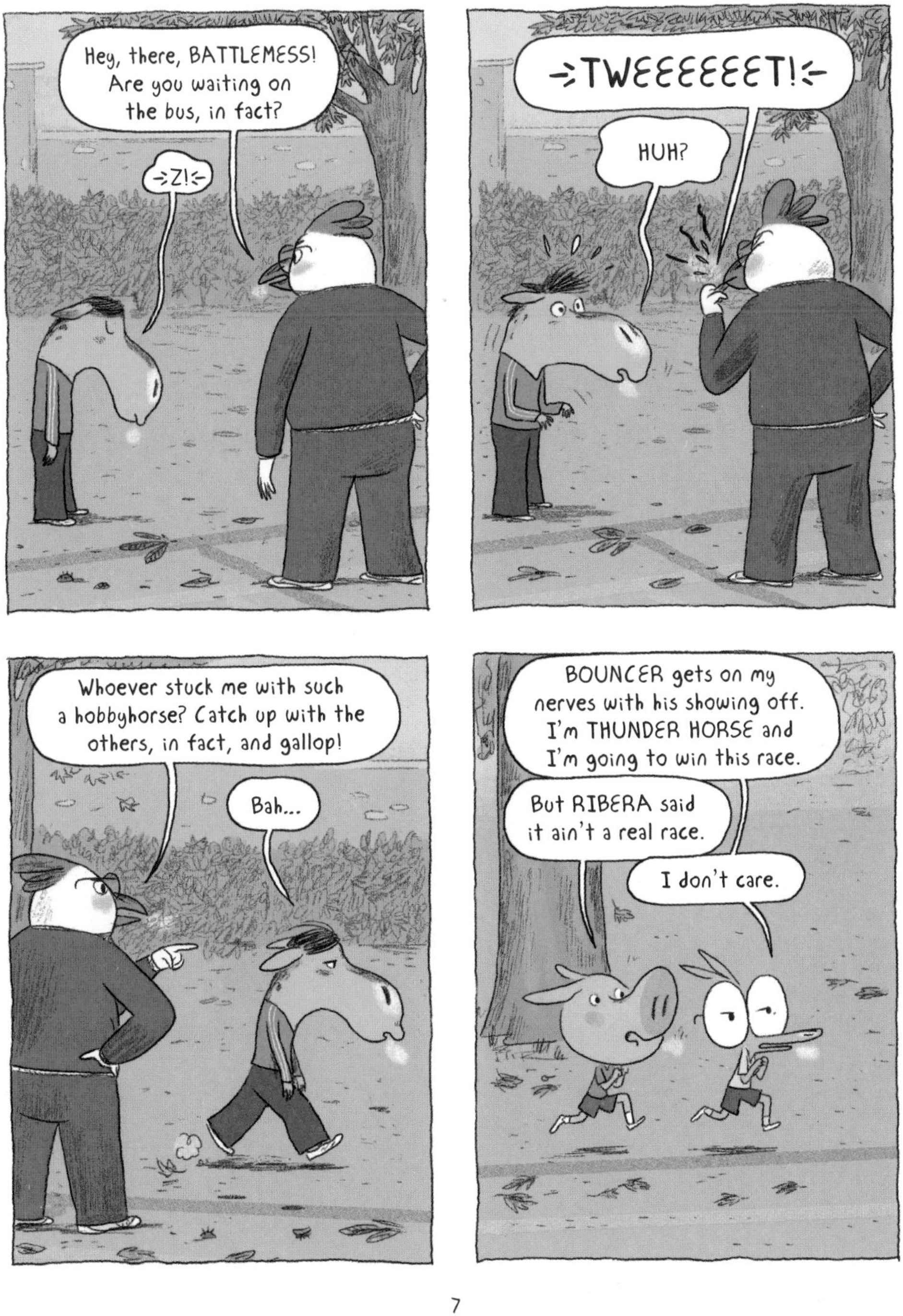
Hey, there, BATTLEMESS! Are you waiting on the bus, in fact?
Z!
TWEEEEEET!
HUH?
Whoever stuck me with such a hobbyhorse? Catch up with the others, in fact, and gallop!
Bah...
BOUNCER gets on my nerves with his showing off. I'm THUNDER HORSE and I'm going to win this race.
But RIBERA said it ain't a real race.
I don't care.

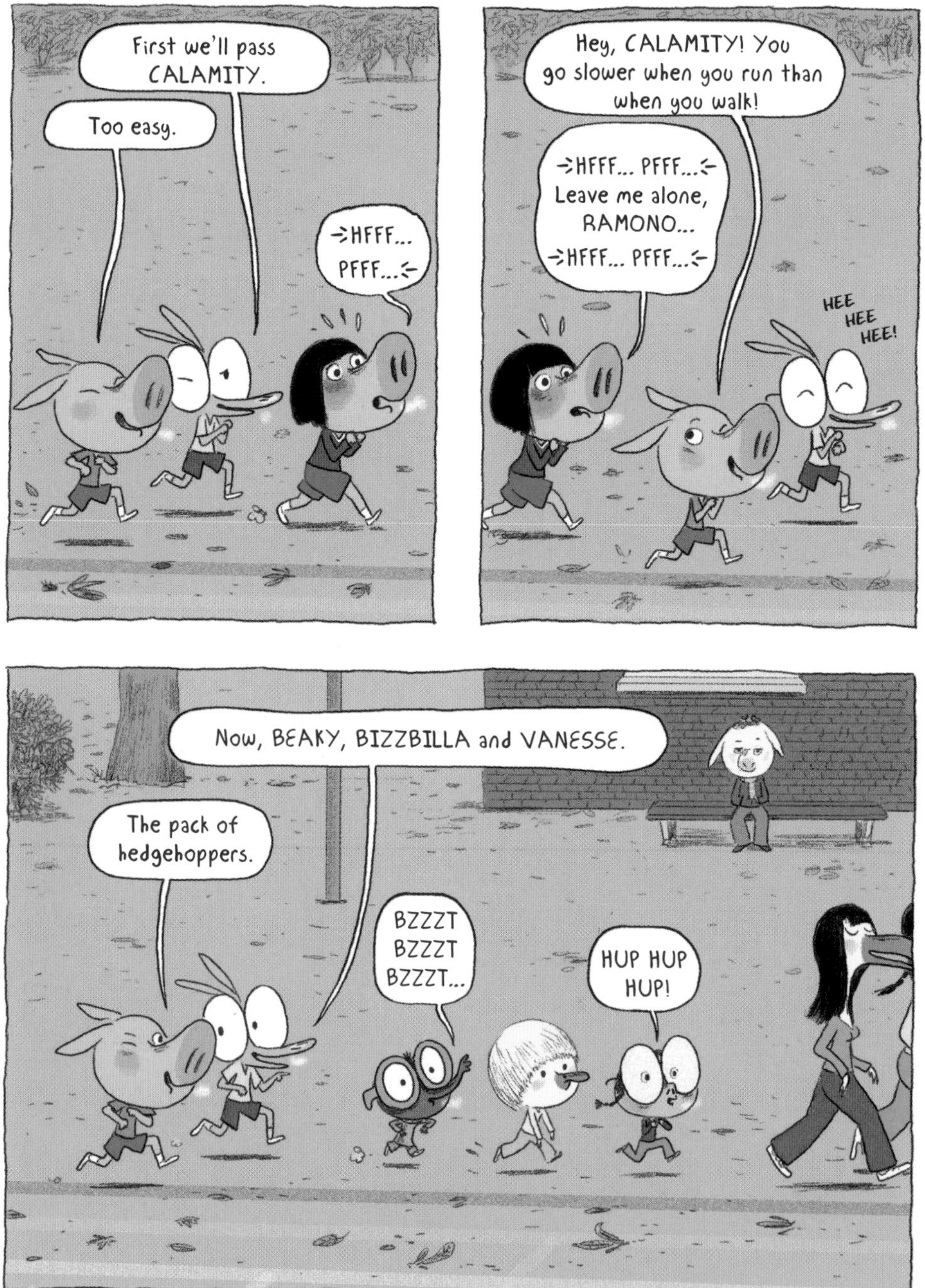
First we'll pass CALAMITY.
Too easy.
HFFF... PFFF...
Hey, CALAMITY! You go slower when you run than when you walk!
HFFF... PFFF... Leave me alone, RAMONO... HFFF... PFFF...
HEE HEE HEE!
Now, BEAKY, BIZZBILLA and VANESSE.
The pack of hedgehoppers.
BZZZT BZZZT BZZZT...
HUP HUP HUP!

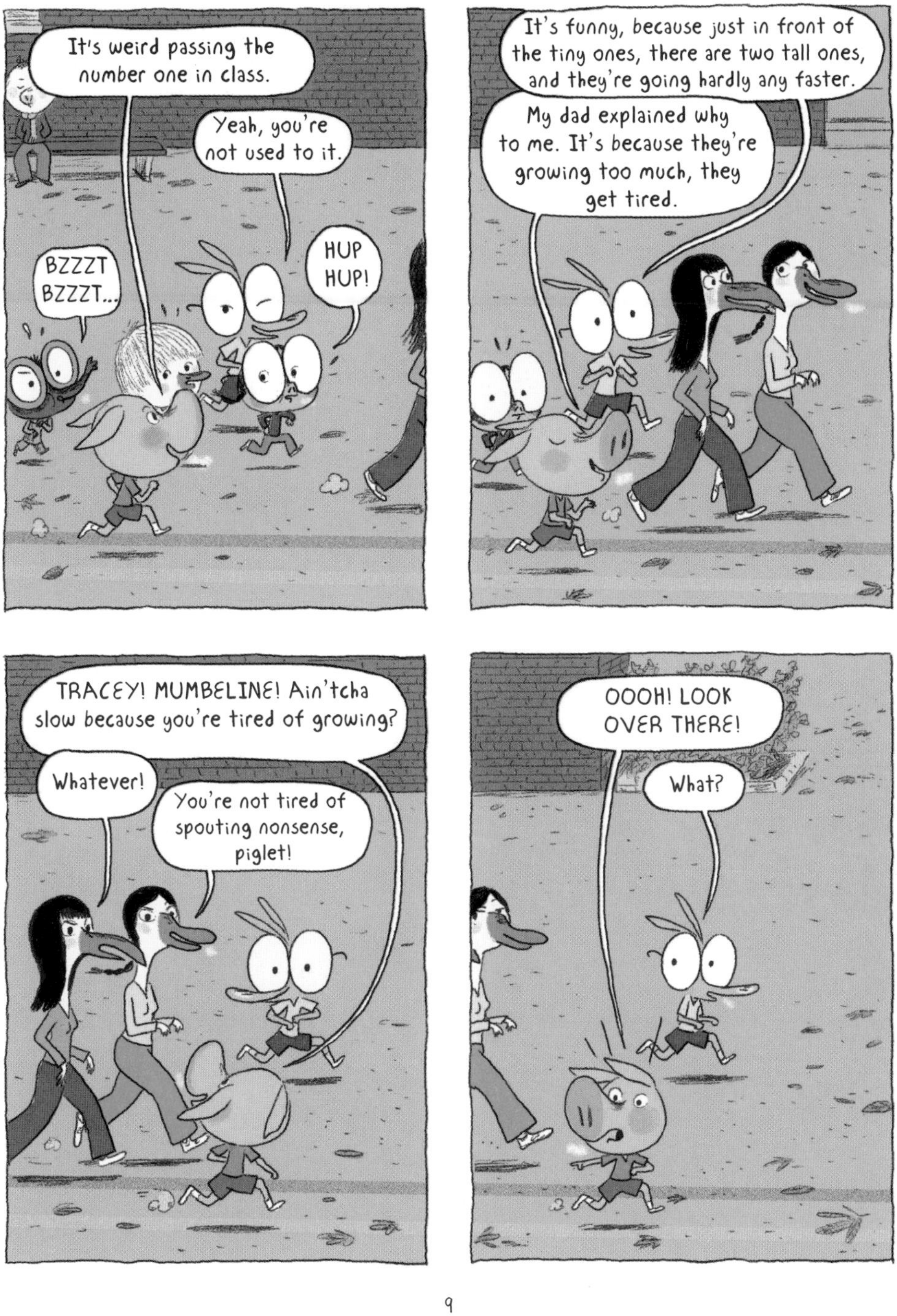
It's weird passing the number one in class.
Yeah, you're not used to it.
BZZZT BZZZT...
HUP HUP!
It's funny, because just in front of the tiny ones, there are two tall ones, and they're going hardly any faster.
My dad explained why to me. It's because they're growing too much, they get tired.
TRACEY! MUMBELINE! Ain'tcha slow because you're tired of growing?
Whatever!
You're not tired of spouting nonsense, piglet!
OOOH! LOOK OVER THERE!
What?

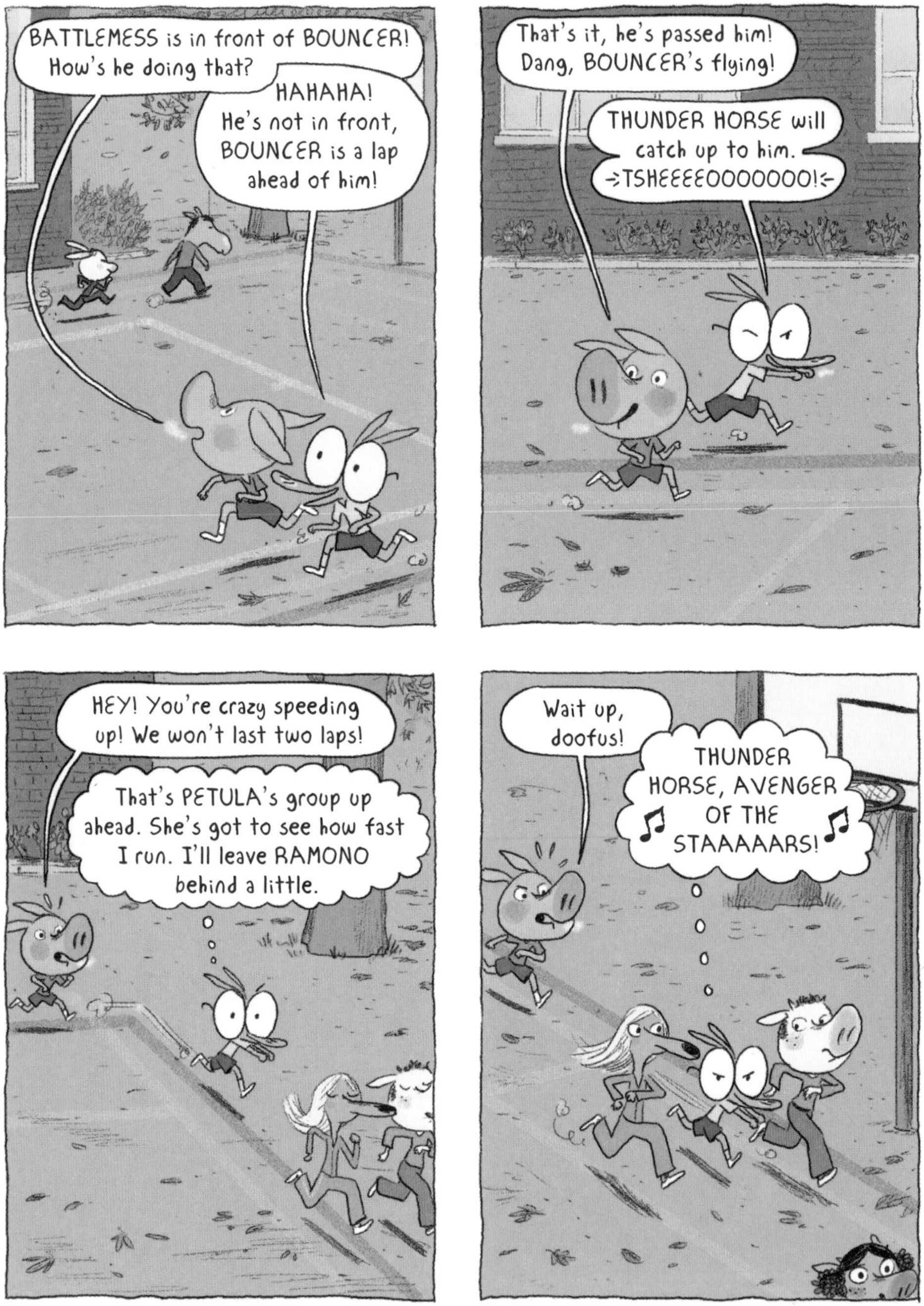
BATTLEMESS is in front of BOUNCER! How's he doing that?
HAHAHA! He's not in front, BOUNCER is a lap ahead of him!
That's it, he's passed him! Dang, BOUNCER's flying!
THUNDER HORSE will catch up to him. TSHEEEEOOOOOOO!
HEY! You're crazy speeding up! We won't last two laps!
That's PETULA's group up ahead. She's got to see how fast I run. I'll leave RAMONO behind a little.
Wait up, doofus!
THUNDER HORSE, AVENGER OF THE STAAAAARS!

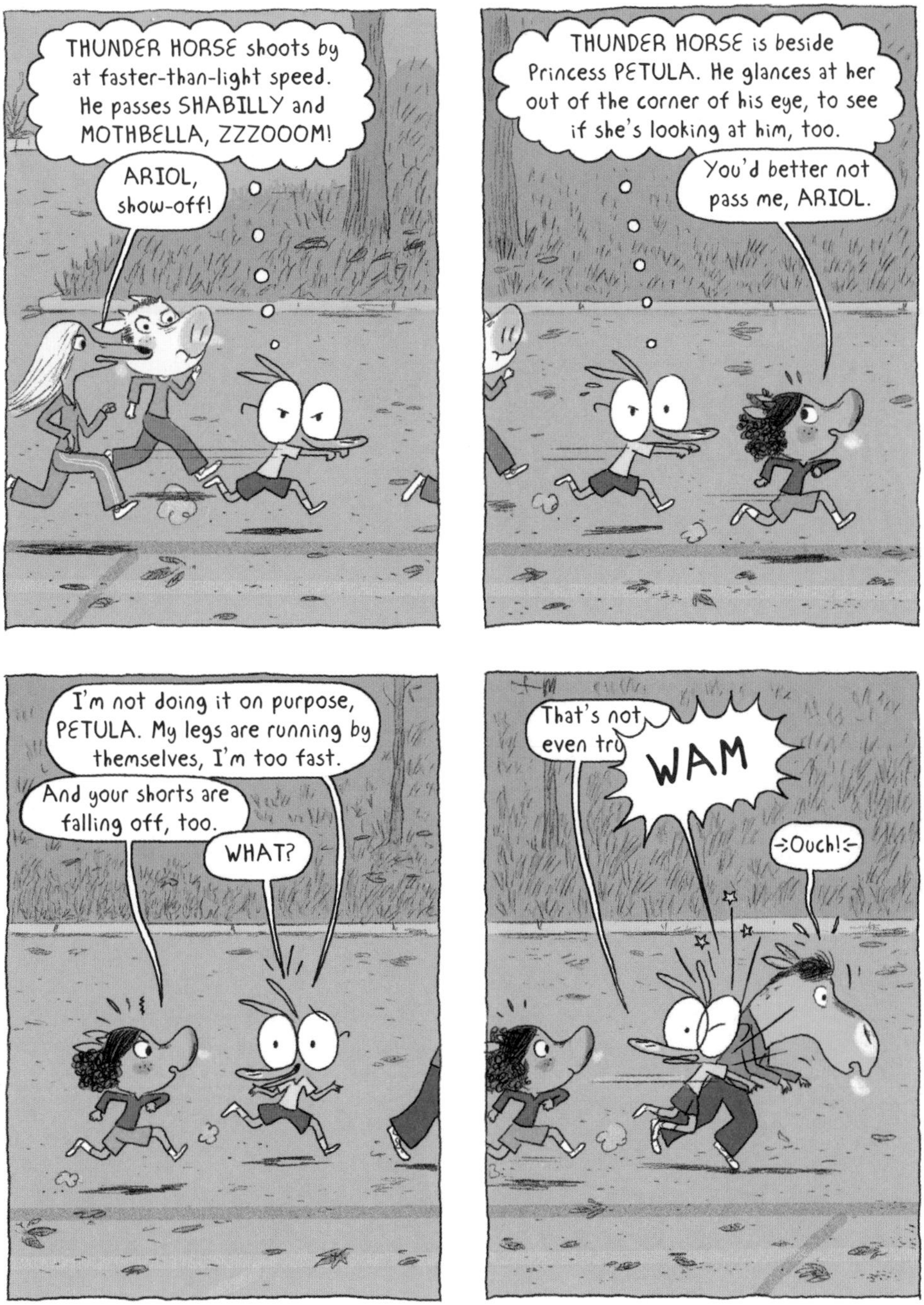
THUNDER HORSE shoots by at faster-than-light speed. He passes SHABILLY and MOTHBELLA, ZZZOOOM!
ARIOL, show-off!
THUNDER HORSE is beside Princess PETULA. He glances at her out of the corner of his eye, to see if she's looking at him, too.
You'd better not pass me, ARIOL.
I'm not doing it on purpose, PETULA. My legs are running by themselves, I'm too fast.
And your shorts are falling off, too.
WHAT?
That's not even tru
WAM
Ouch!

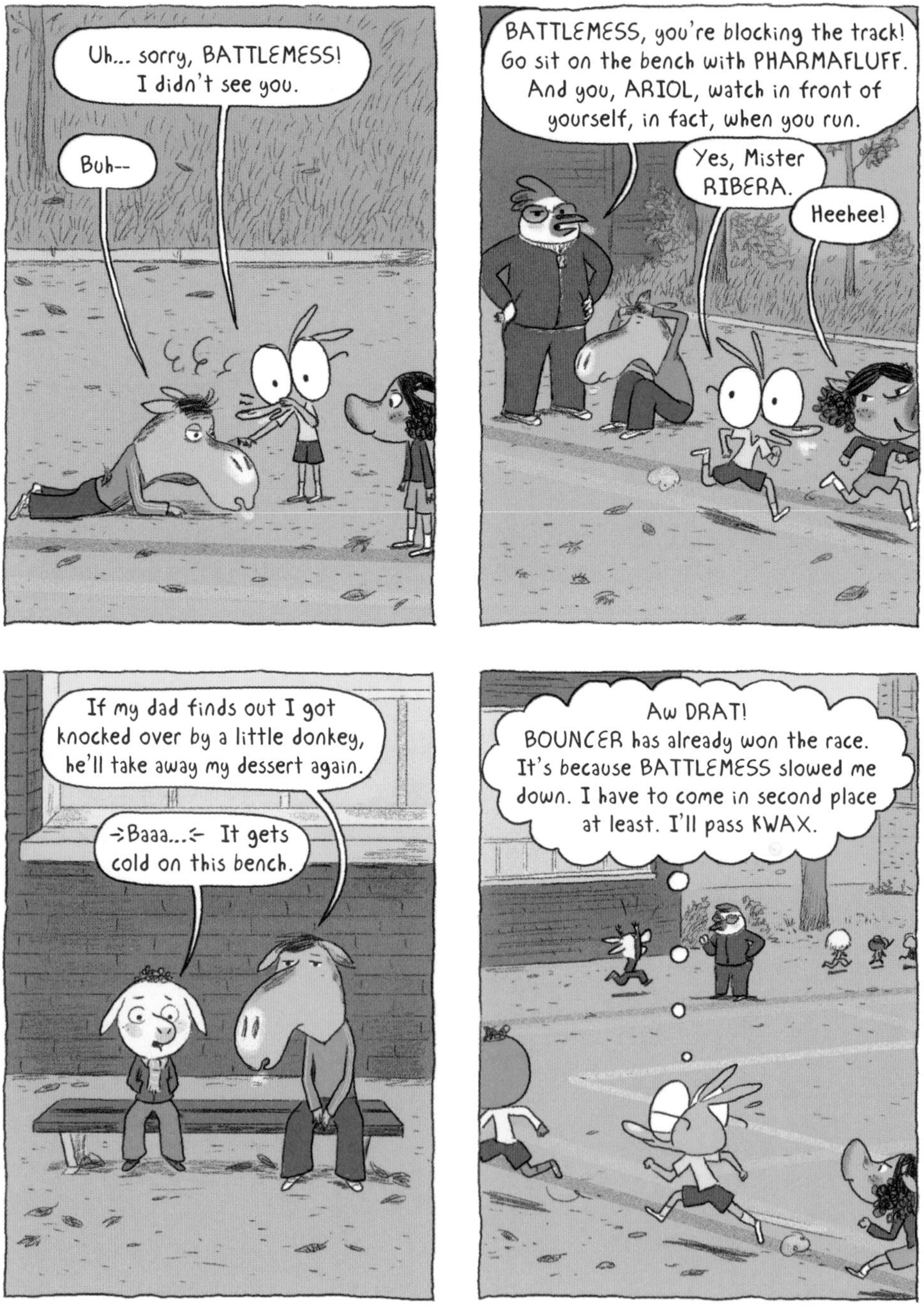
Uh... sorry, BATTLEMESS! I didn't see you.
Buh--
BATTLEMESS, you're blocking the track! Go sit on the bench with PHARMAFLUFF. And you, ARIOL, watch in front of yourself, in fact, when you run.
Yes, Mister RIBERA.
Heehee!
If my dad finds out I got knocked over by a little donkey, he'll take away my dessert again.
Baaa... It gets cold on this bench.
Aw DRAT! BOUNCER has already won the race. It's because BATTLEMESS slowed me down. I have to come in second place at least. I'll pass KWAX.

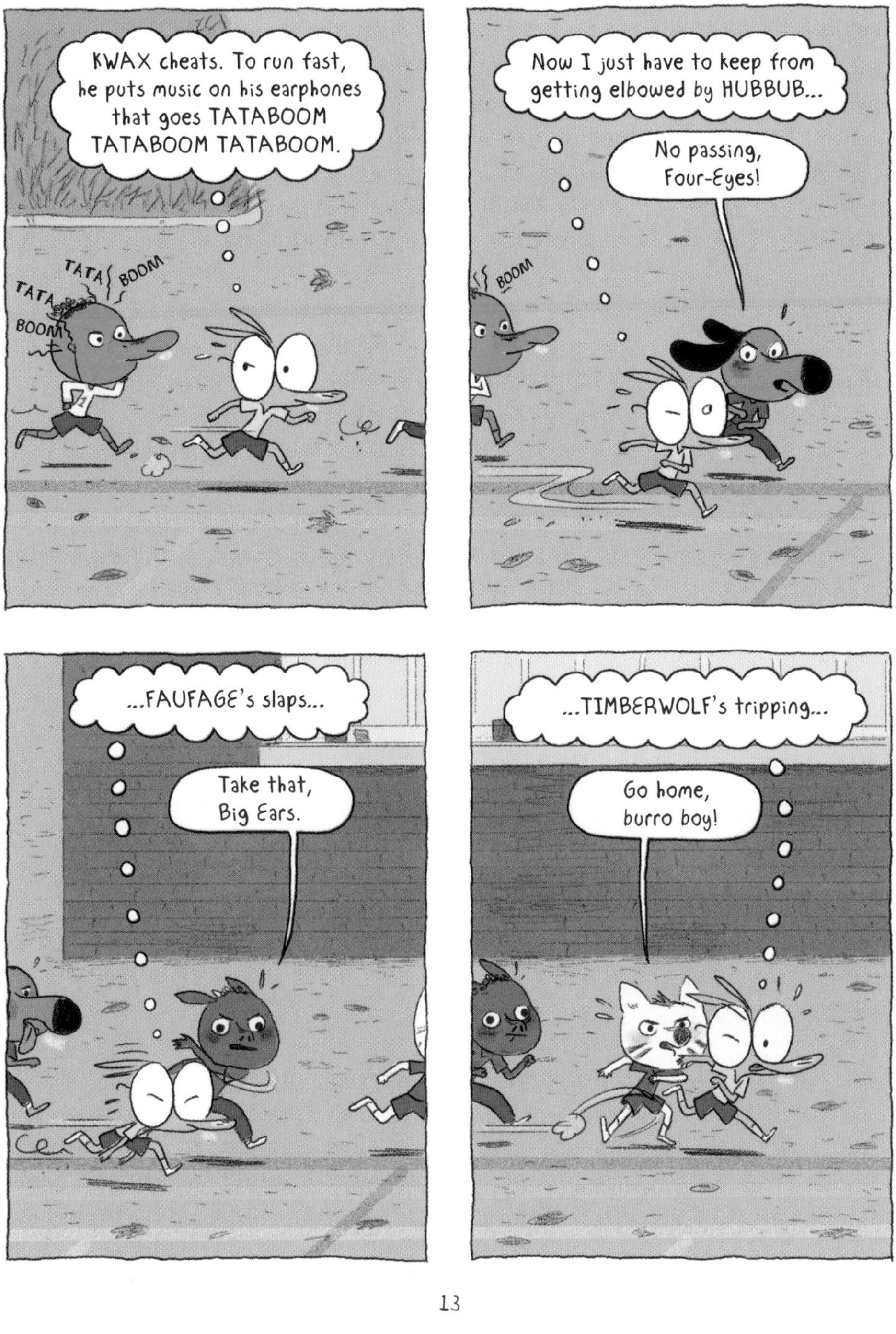
KWAX cheats. To run fast, he puts music on his earphones that goes TATABOOM TATABOOM TATABOOM.
TATA BOOM
TATA BOOM
BOOM
Now I just have to keep from getting elbowed by HUBBUB...
No passing, Four-Eyes!
...FAUFAGE's slaps...
Take that, Big Ears.
...TIMBERWOLF's tripping...
Go home, burro boy!

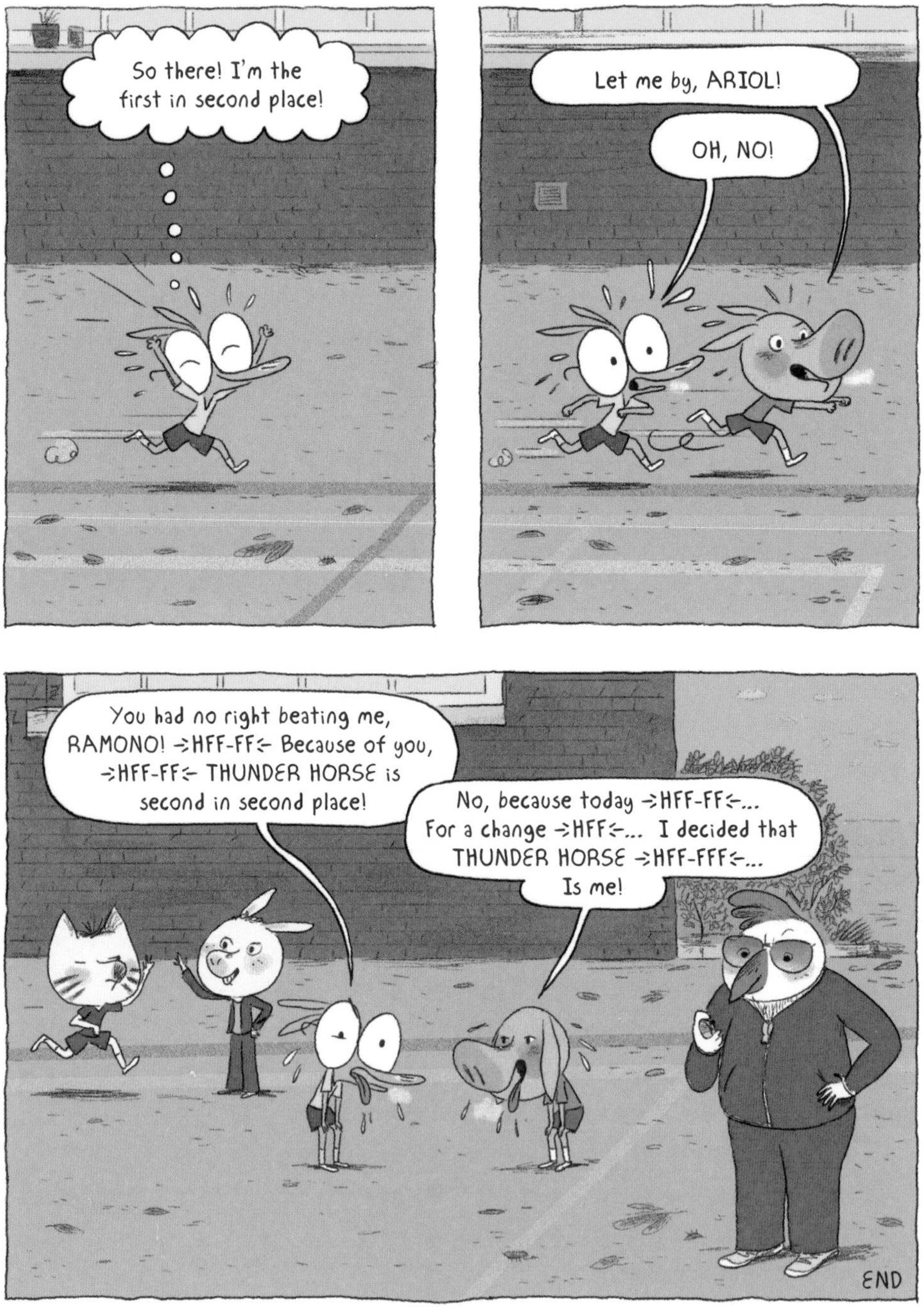
So there! I'm the first in second place!
Let me by, ARIOL!
OH, NO!
You had no right beating me, RAMONO! ->HFF-FF<- Because of you, ->HFF-FF<- THUNDER HORSE is second in second place!
No, because today ->HFF-FF<-... For a change ->HFF<-... I decided that THUNDER HORSE ->HFF-FFF<-... Is me!
END

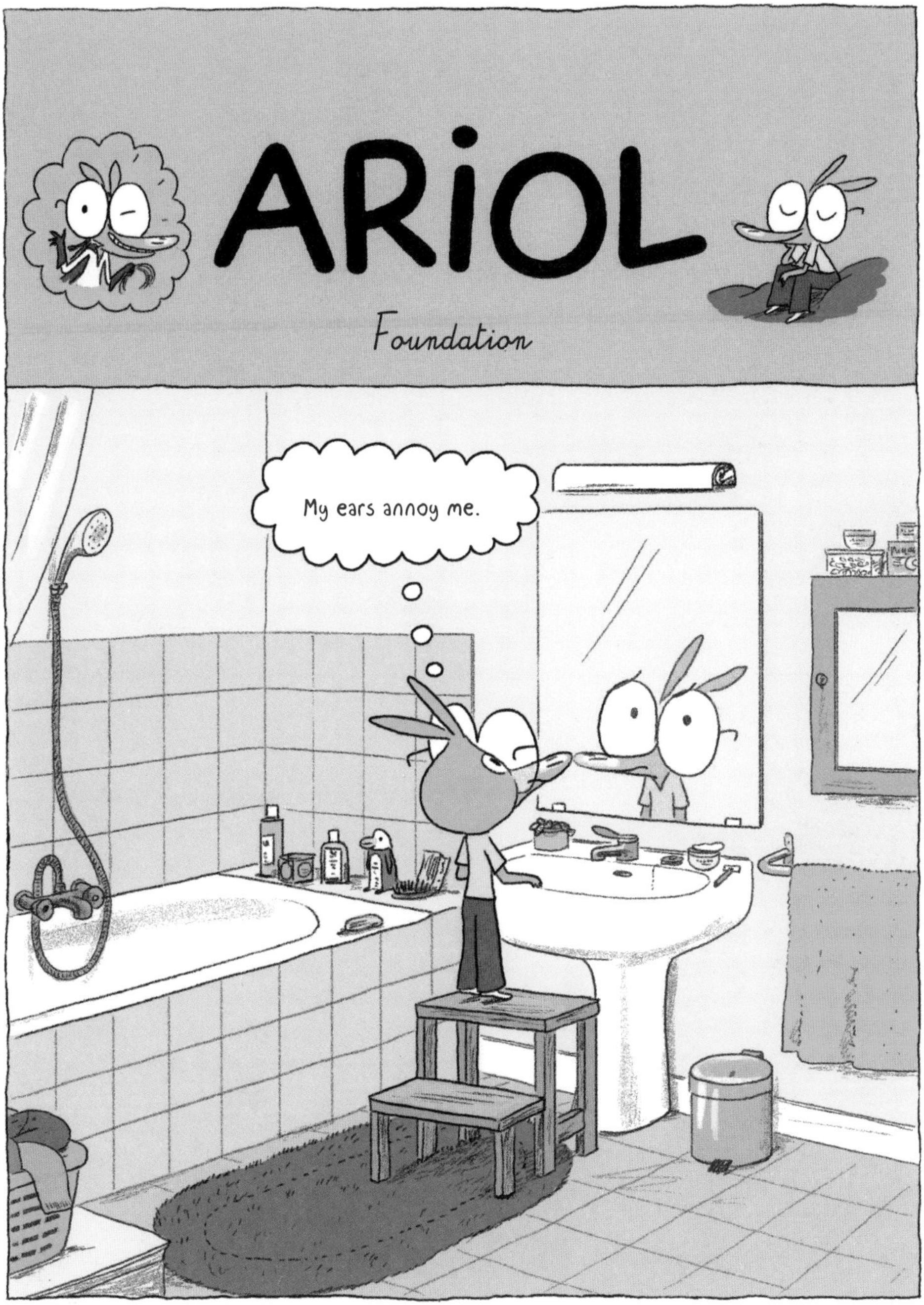
ARiOL
Foundation
My ears annoy me.

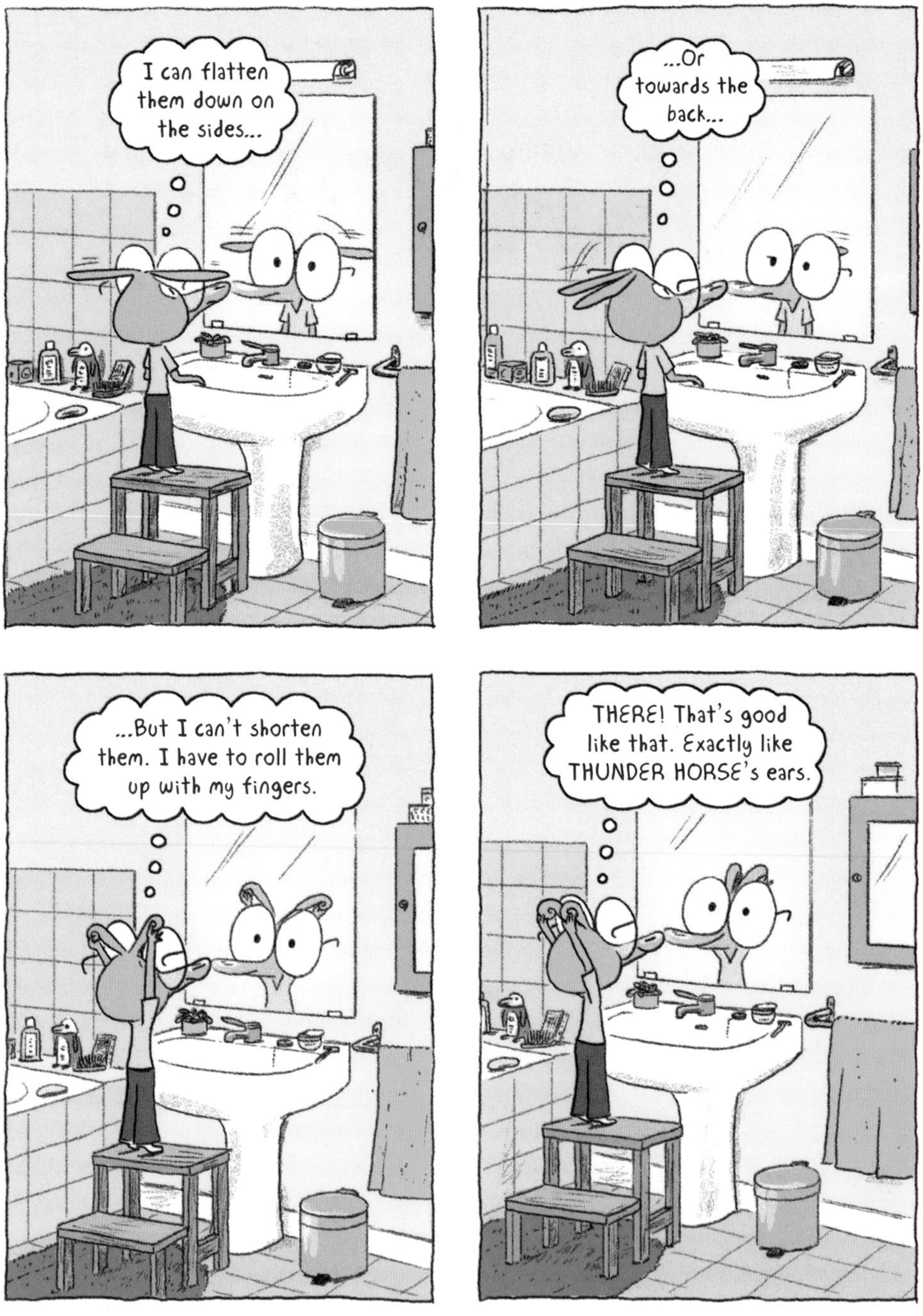
I can flatten them down on the sides...
...Or towards the back...
...But I can't shorten them. I have to roll them up with my fingers.
THERE! That's good like that. Exactly like THUNDER HORSE's ears.

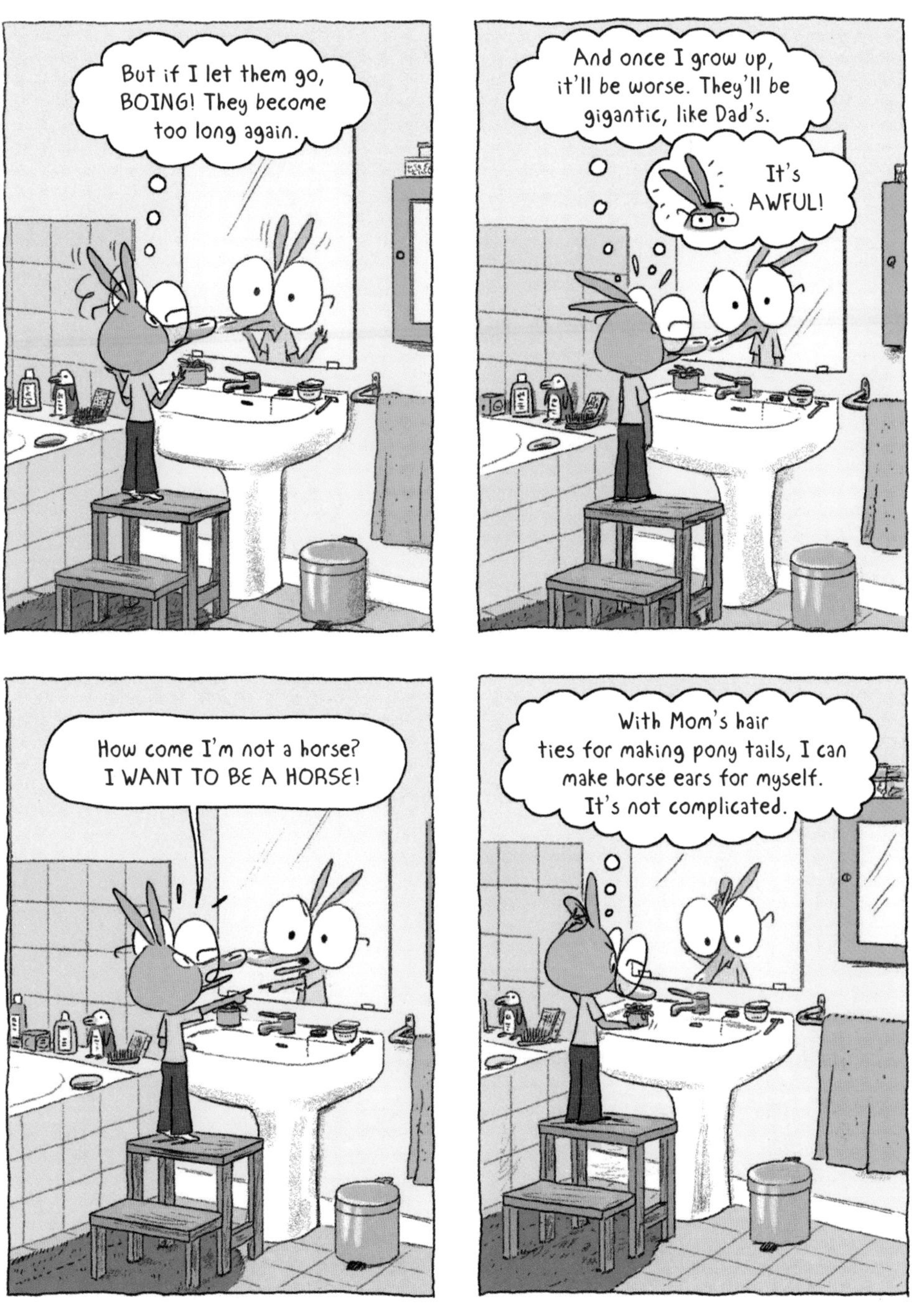
But if I let them go, BOING! They become too long again.
And once I grow up, it'll be worse. They'll be gigantic, like Dad's.
It's AWFUL!
How come I'm not a horse? I WANT TO BE A HORSE!
With Mom's hair ties for making pony tails, I can make horse ears for myself. It's not complicated.

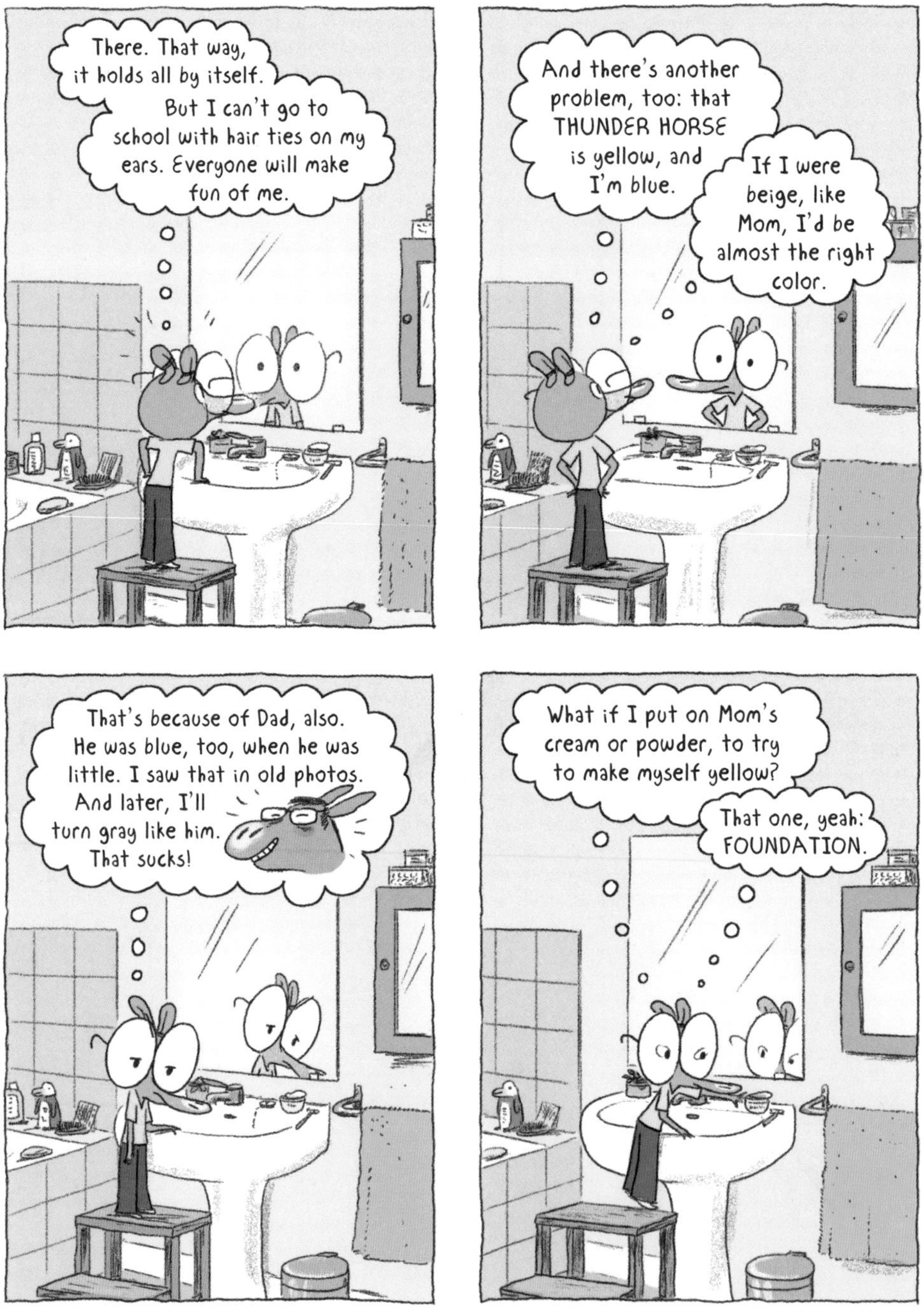
There. That way, it holds all by itself.
But I can't go to school with hair ties on my ears. Everyone will make fun of me.
And there's another problem, too: that THUNDER HORSE is yellow, and I'm blue.
If I were beige, like Mom, I'd be almost the right color.
That's because of Dad, also. He was blue, too, when he was little. I saw that in old photos.
And later, I'll turn gray like him. That sucks!
What if I put on Mom's cream or powder, to try to make myself yellow?
That one, yeah: FOUNDATION.

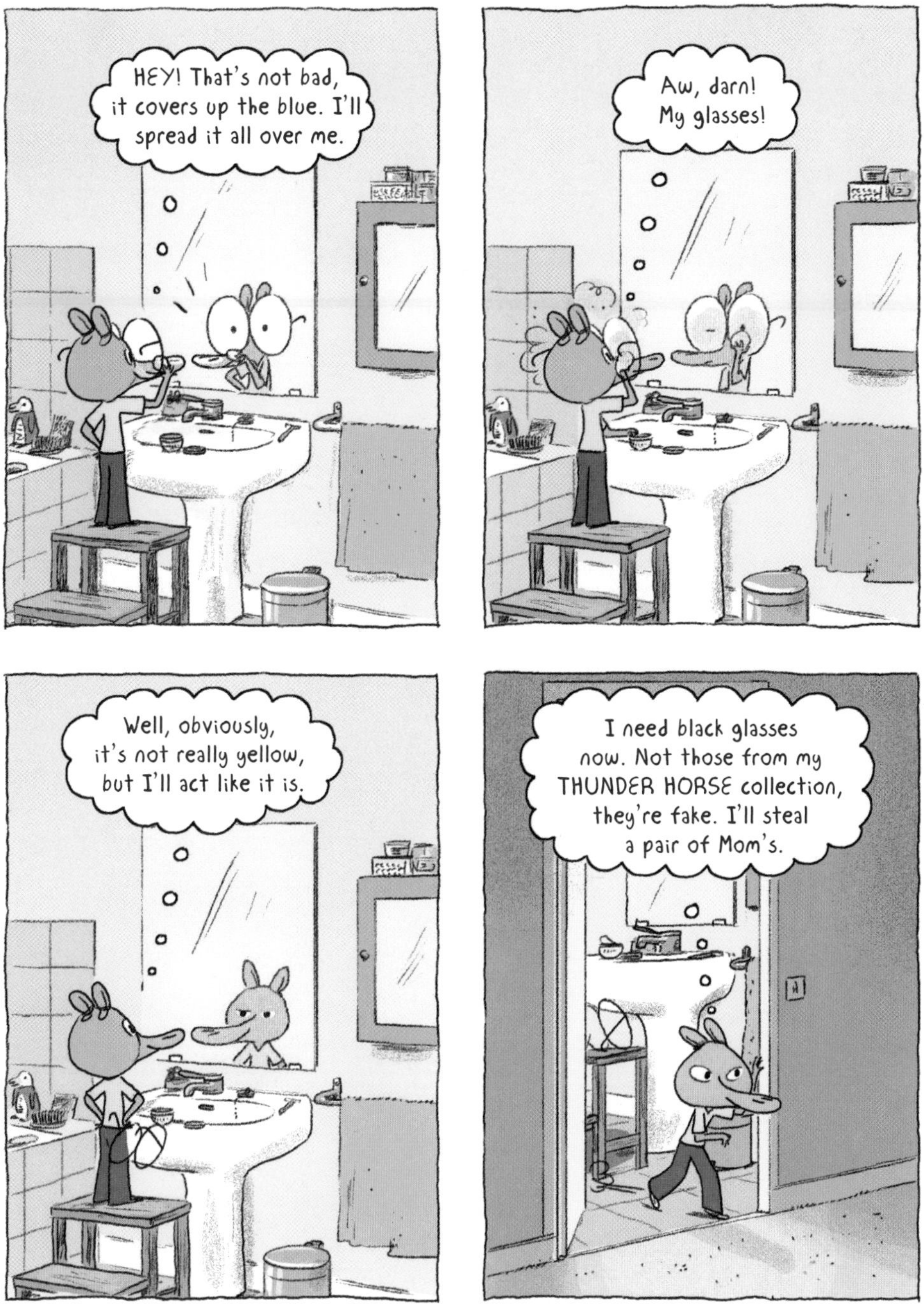
HEY! That's not bad, it covers up the blue. I'll spread it all over me.
Aw, darn! My glasses!
Well, obviously, it's not really yellow, but I'll act like it is.
I need black glasses now. Not those from my THUNDER HORSE collection, they're fake. I'll steal a pair of Mom's.

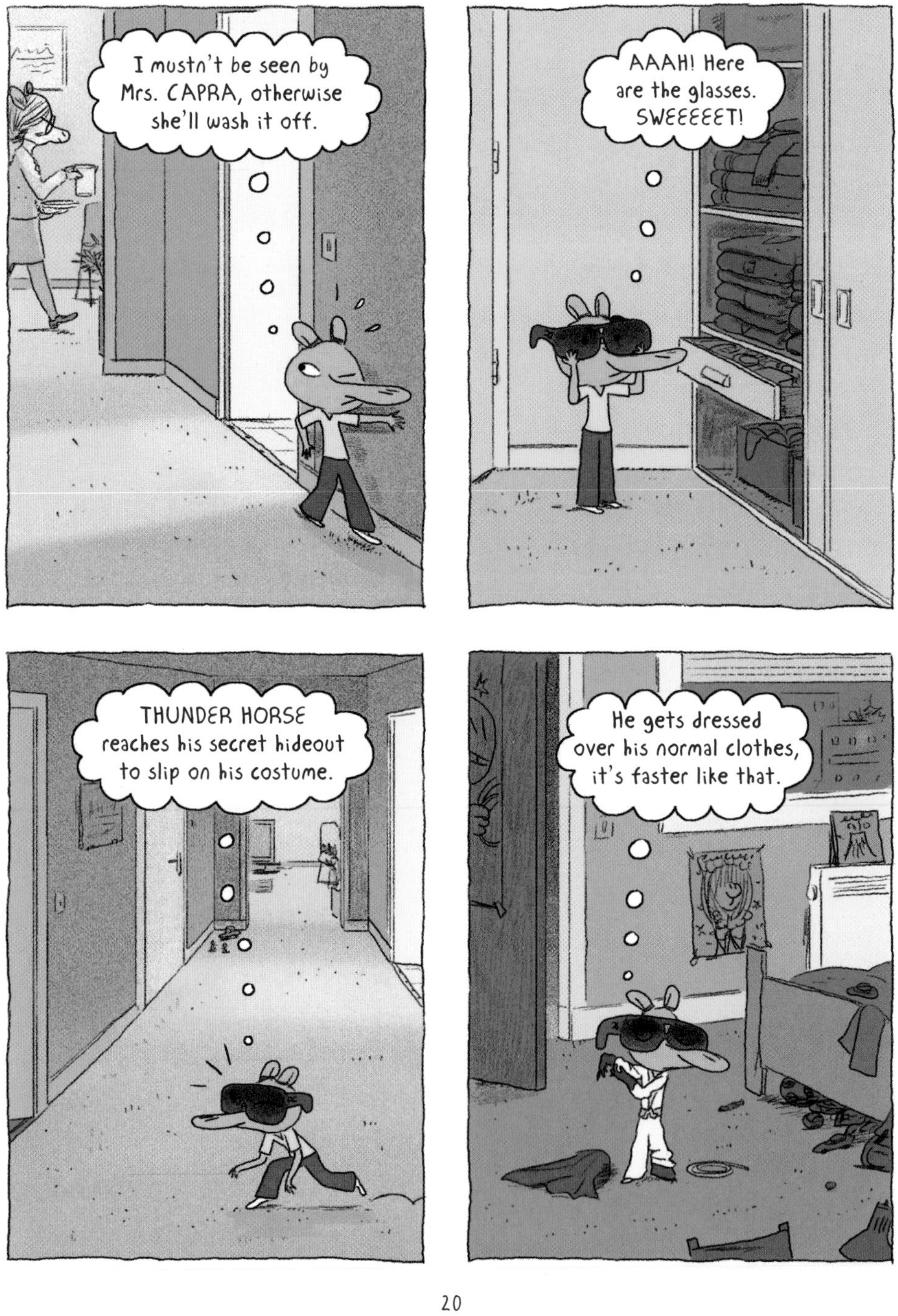
I mustn't be seen by Mrs. CAPRA, otherwise she'll wash it off.
AAAH! Here are the glasses. SWEEEEET!
THUNDER HORSE reaches his secret hideout to slip on his costume.
He gets dressed over his normal clothes, it's faster like that.

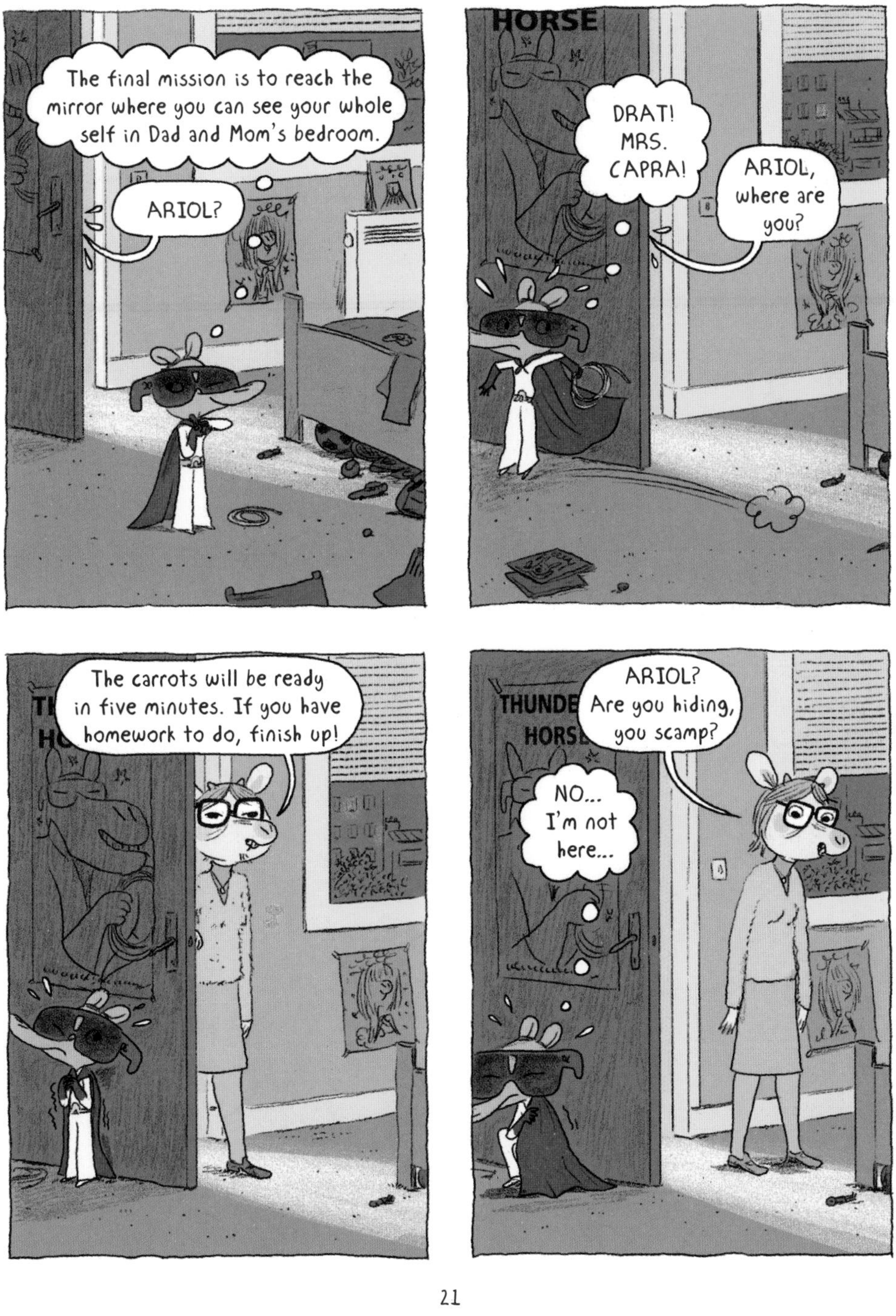
The final mission is to reach the mirror where you can see your whole self in Dad and Mom's bedroom.
ARIOL?
HORSE
DRAT! MRS. CAPRA!
ARIOL, where are you?
The carrots will be ready in five minutes. If you have homework to do, finish up!
THUNDE
HORSE
ARIOL? Are you hiding, you scamp?
NO... I'm not here...

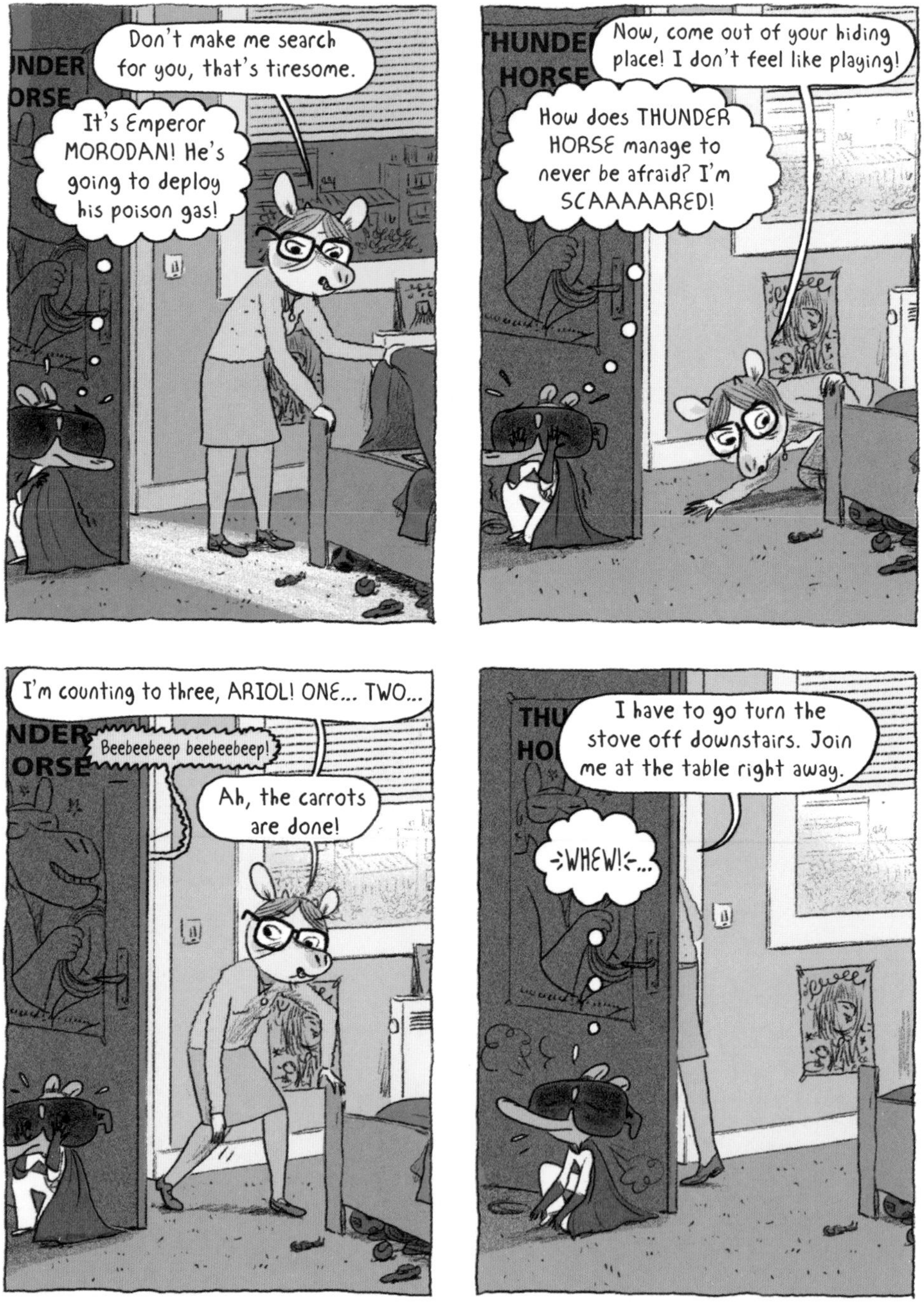
THUNDER HORSE
Don't make me search for you, that's tiresome.
It's Emperor MORODAN! He's going to deploy his poison gas!
THUNDER HORSE
Now, come out of your hiding place! I don't feel like playing!
How does THUNDER HORSE manage to never be afraid? I'm SCAAAAARED!
I'm counting to three, ARIOL! ONE... TWO...
THUNDER HORSE
Beebeebeep beebeebeep!
Ah, the carrots are done!
I have to go turn the stove off downstairs. Join me at the table right away.
WHEW!...

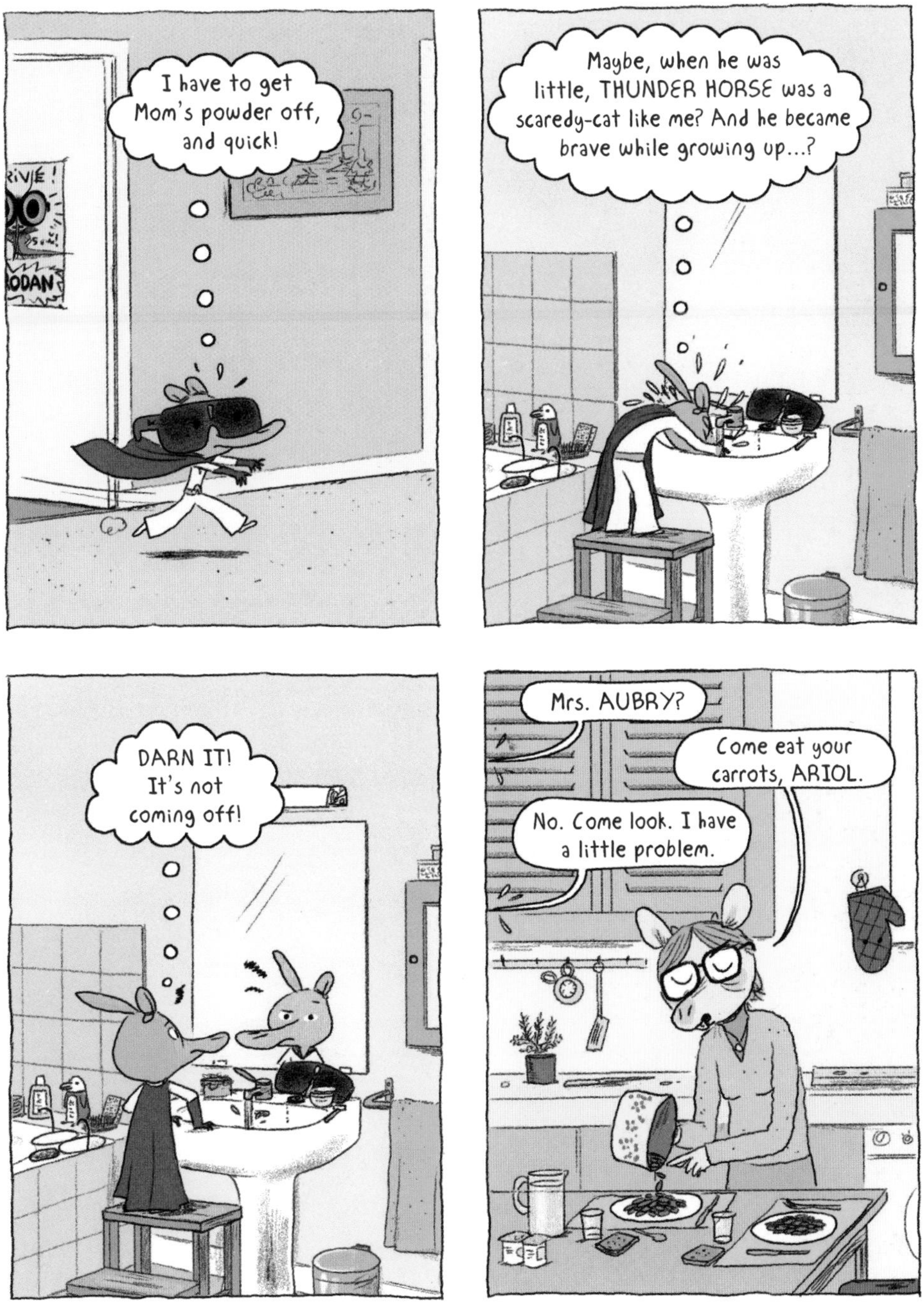
I have to get Mom's powder off, and quick!
Maybe, when he was little, THUNDER HORSE was a scaredy-cat like me? And he became brave while growing up...?
DARN IT! It's not coming off!
Mrs. AUBRY?
Come eat your carrots, ARIOL.
No. Come look. I have a little problem.

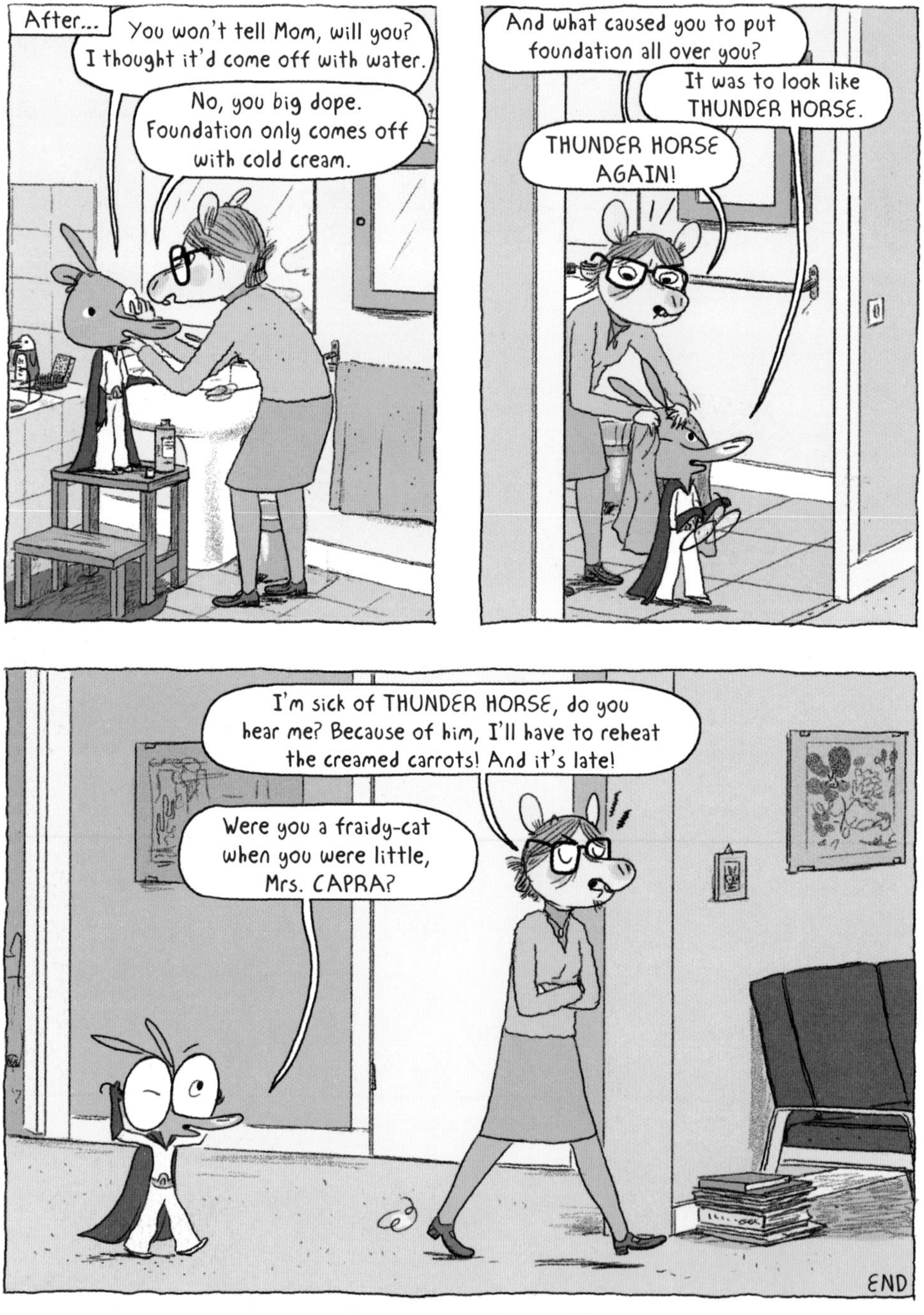
After...
You won't tell Mom, will you? I thought it'd come off with water.
No, you big dope. Foundation only comes off with cold cream.
And what caused you to put foundation all over you?
It was to look like THUNDER HORSE.
THUNDER HORSE AGAIN!
I'm sick of THUNDER HORSE, do you hear me? Because of him, I'll have to reheat the creamed carrots! And it's late!
Were you a fraidy-cat when you were little, Mrs. CAPRA?
END

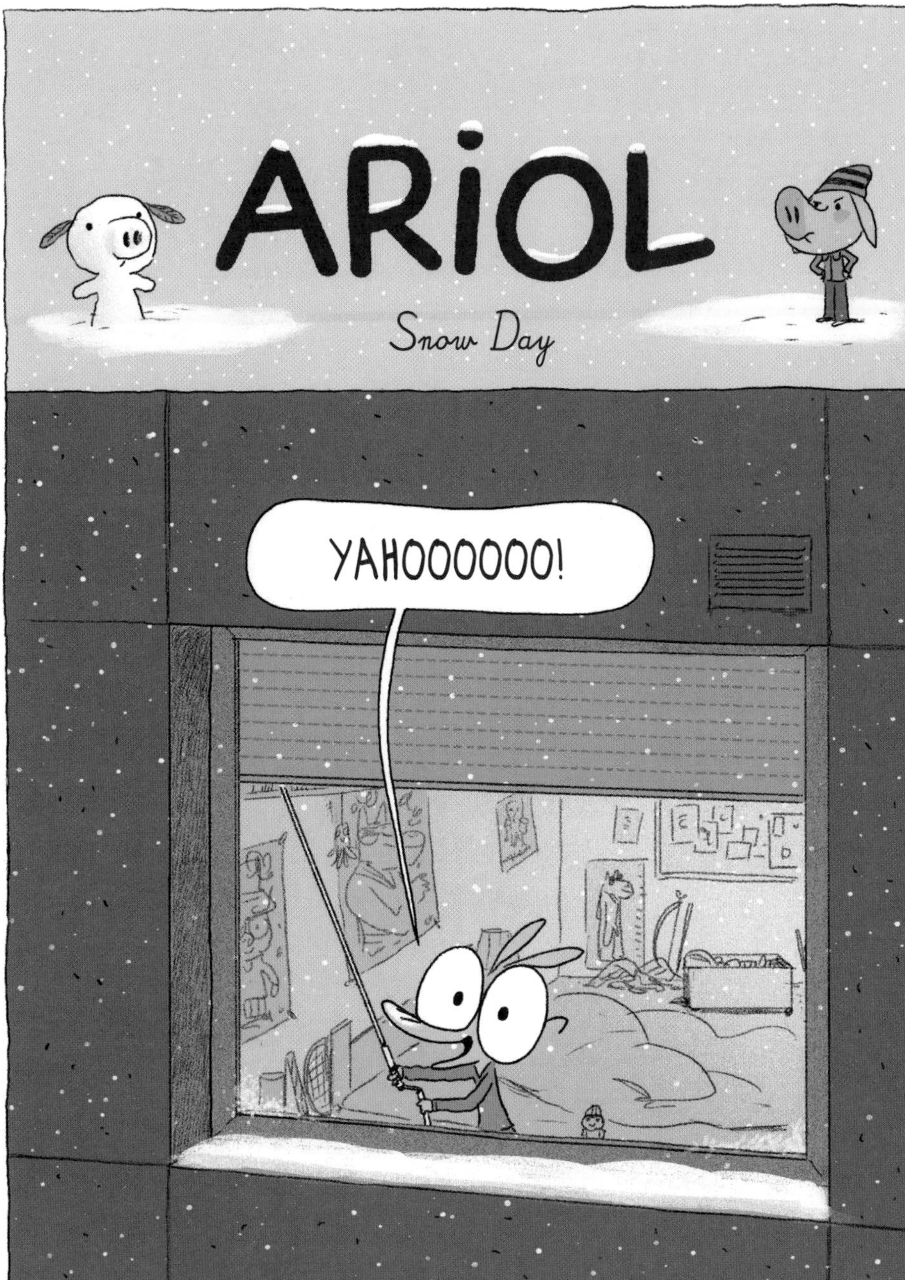
ARIOL
Snow Day
YAHOOOOOO!

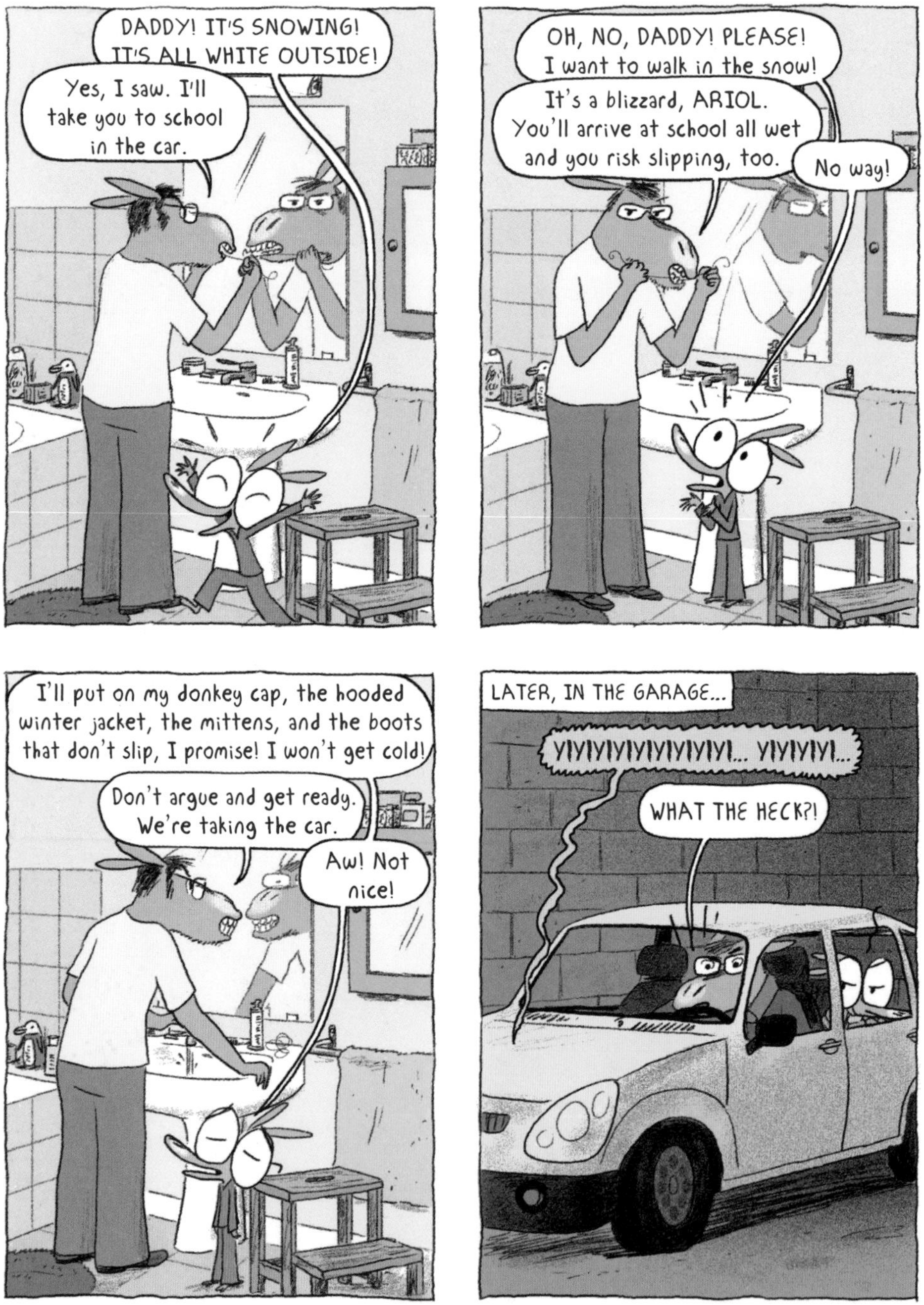
DADDY! IT'S SNOWING! IT'S ALL WHITE OUTSIDE!
Yes, I saw. I'll take you to school in the car.
OH, NO, DADDY! PLEASE! I want to walk in the snow!
It's a blizzard, ARIOL. You'll arrive at school all wet and you risk slipping, too.
No way!
I'll put on my donkey cap, the hooded winter jacket, the mittens, and the boots that don't slip, I promise! I won't get cold!
Don't argue and get ready. We're taking the car.
Aw! Not nice!
LATER, IN THE GARAGE...
YIYIYIYIYIYIYIYIYI... YIYIYIYI...
WHAT THE HECK?!

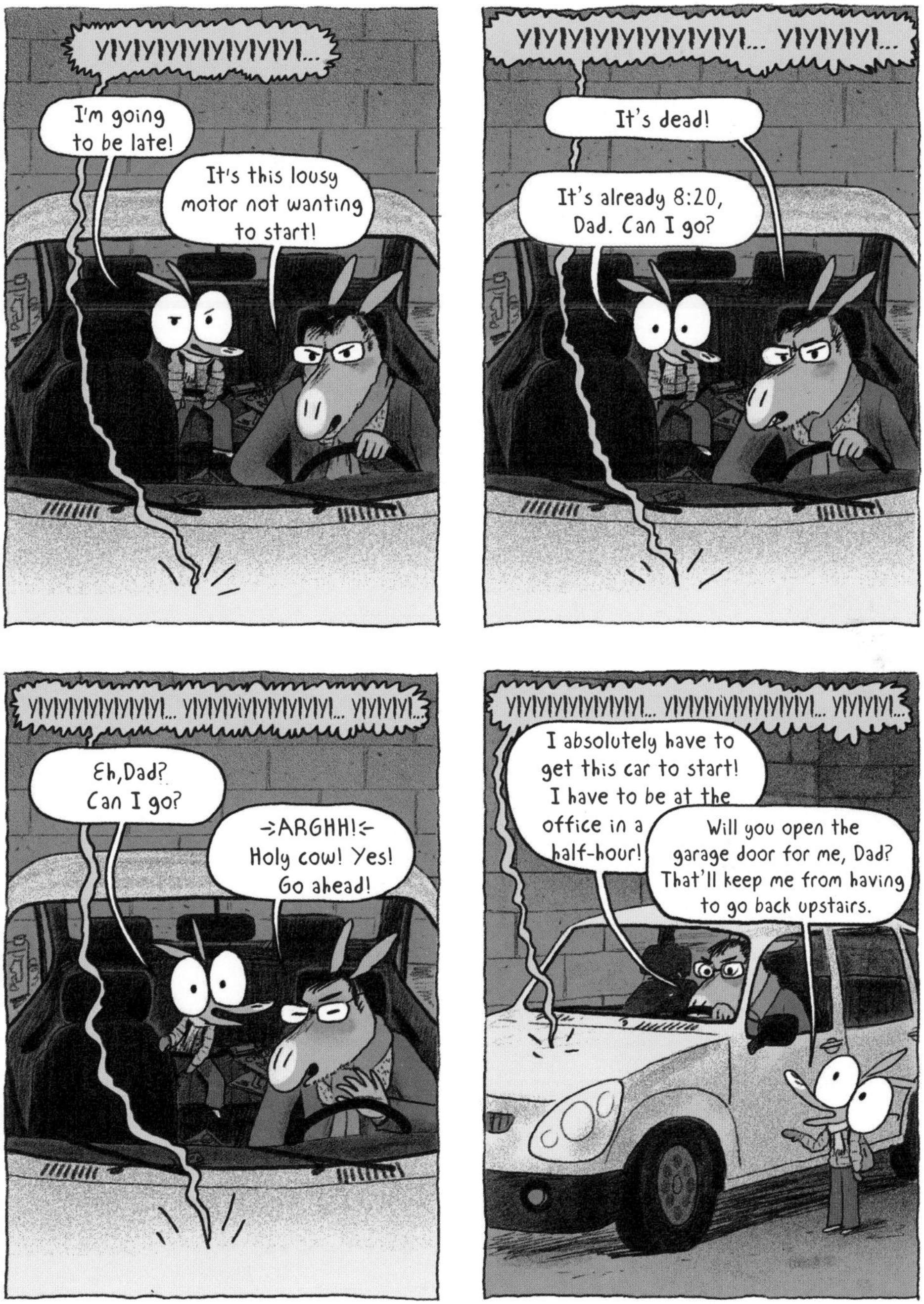

YIYIYIYIYIYIYIYIYI...
I'm going to be late!
It's this lousy motor not wanting to start!
YIYIYIYIYIYIYIYIYI... YIYIYIYI...
It's dead!
It's already 8:20, Dad. Can I go?
YIYIYIYIYIYIYIYIYI... YIYIYIYIYIYIYIYIYI... YIYIYIYI...
Eh, Dad? Can I go?
ARGHH! Holy cow! Yes! Go ahead!
YIYIYIYIYIYIYIYIYI... YIYIYIYIYIYIYIYIYI... YIYIYIYI...
I absolutely have to get this car to start! I have to be at the office in a half-hour!
Will you open the garage door for me, Dad? That'll keep me from having to go back upstairs.

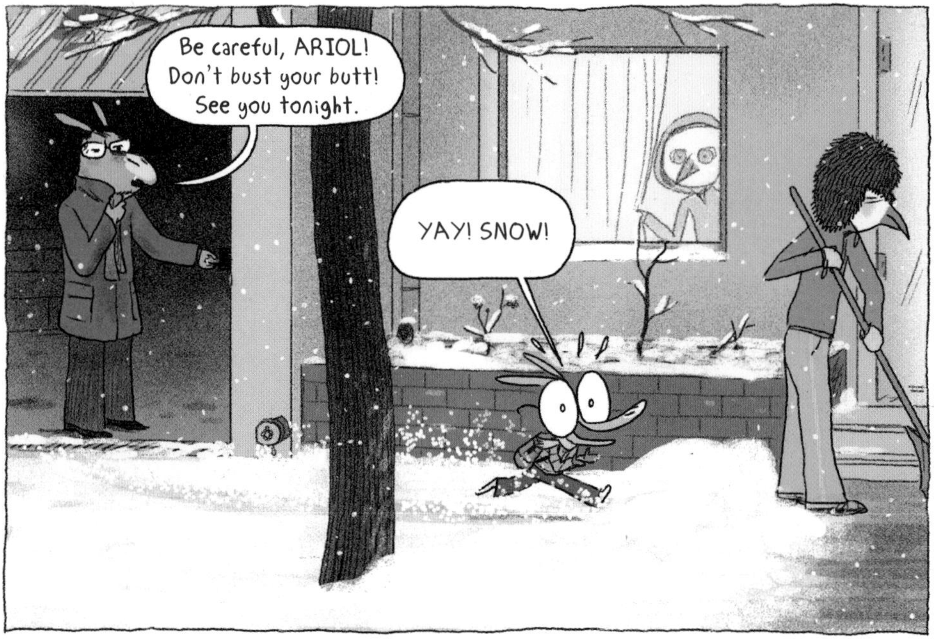
Be careful, ARIOL! Don't bust your butt! See you tonight.
YAY! SNOW!

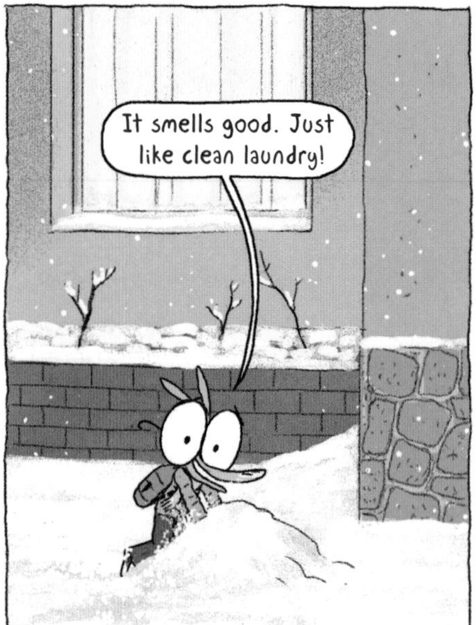
It smells good. Just like clean laundry!

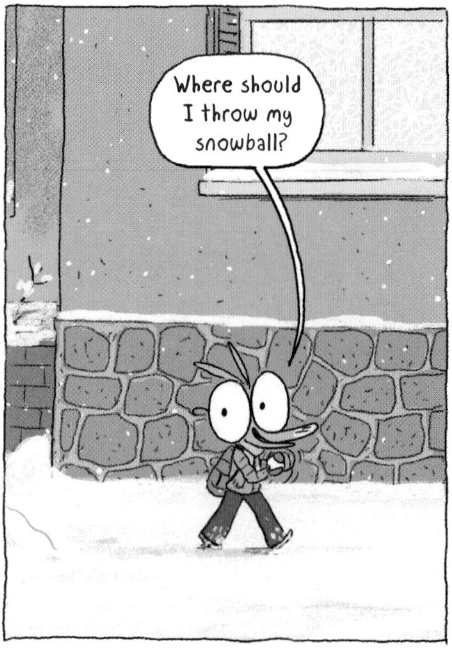
Where should I throw my snowball?

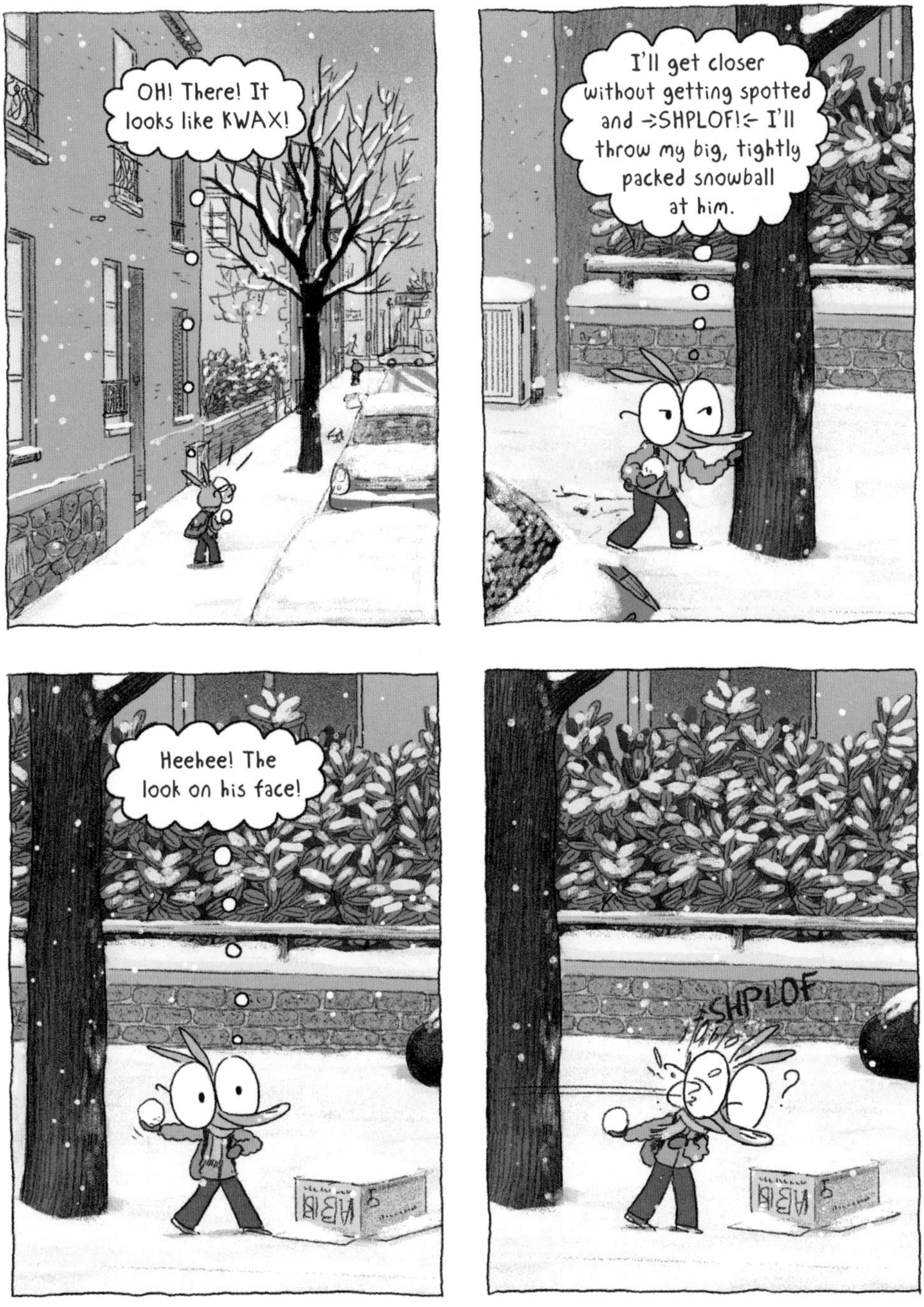
OH! There! It looks like KWAX!
I'll get closer without getting spotted and ->SHPLOF!<- I'll throw my big, tightly packed snowball at him.
Heehee! The look on his face!
SHPLOF
?

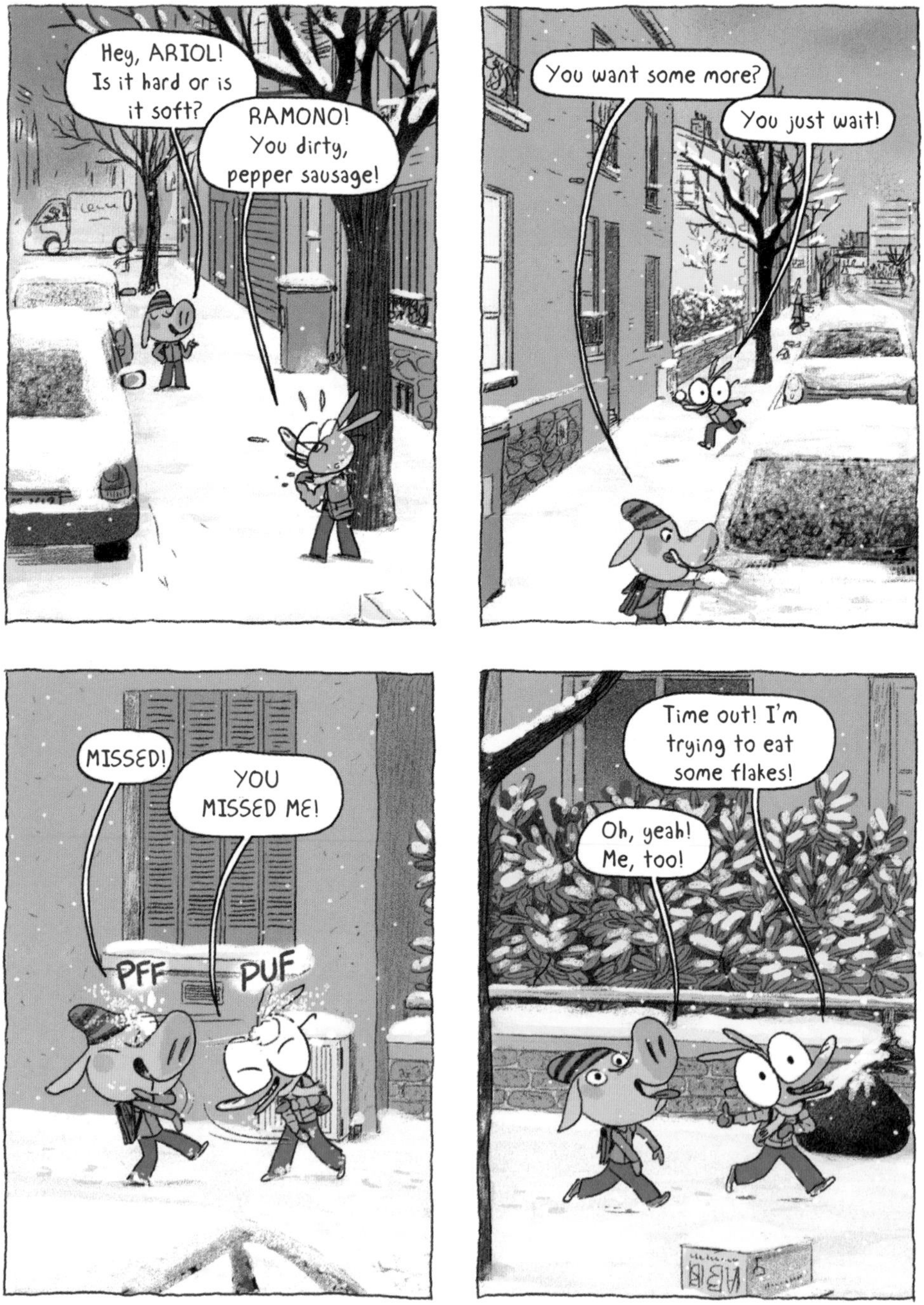

Hey, ARIOL! Is it hard or is it soft?
RAMONO! You dirty, pepper sausage!
You want some more?
You just wait!
MISSED!
YOU MISSED ME!
PFF
PUF
Time out! I'm trying to eat some flakes!
Oh, yeah! Me, too!

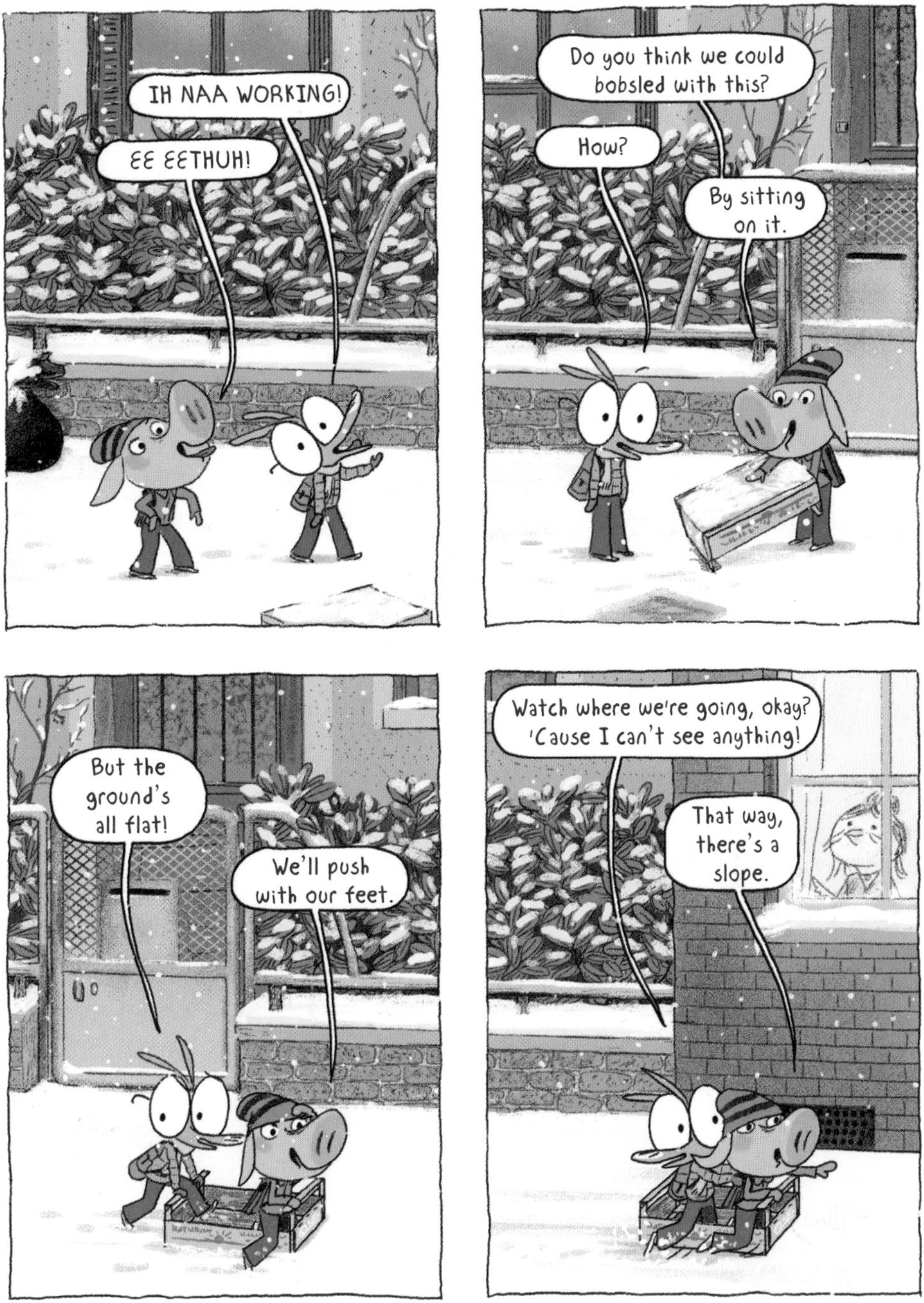
IH NAA WORKING!
EE EETHUH!
Do you think we could bobsled with this?
How?
By sitting on it.
But the ground's all flat!
We'll push with our feet.
Watch where we're going, okay? 'Cause I can't see anything!
That way, there's a slope.

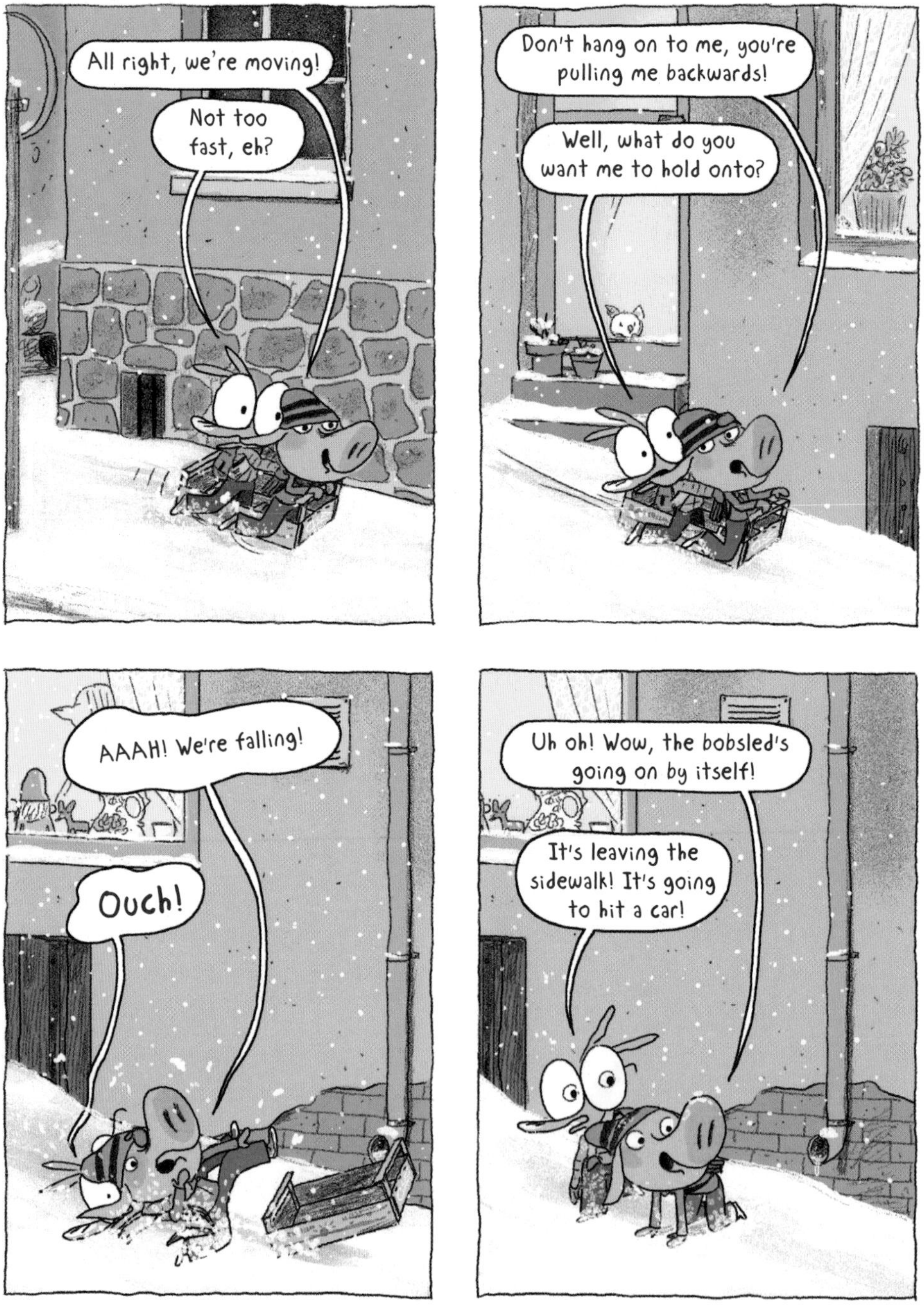
All right, we're moving!
Not too fast, eh?
Don't hang on to me, you're pulling me backwards!
Well, what do you want me to hold onto?
AAAH! We're falling!
Ouch!
Uh oh! Wow, the bobsled's going on by itself!
It's leaving the sidewalk! It's going to hit a car!

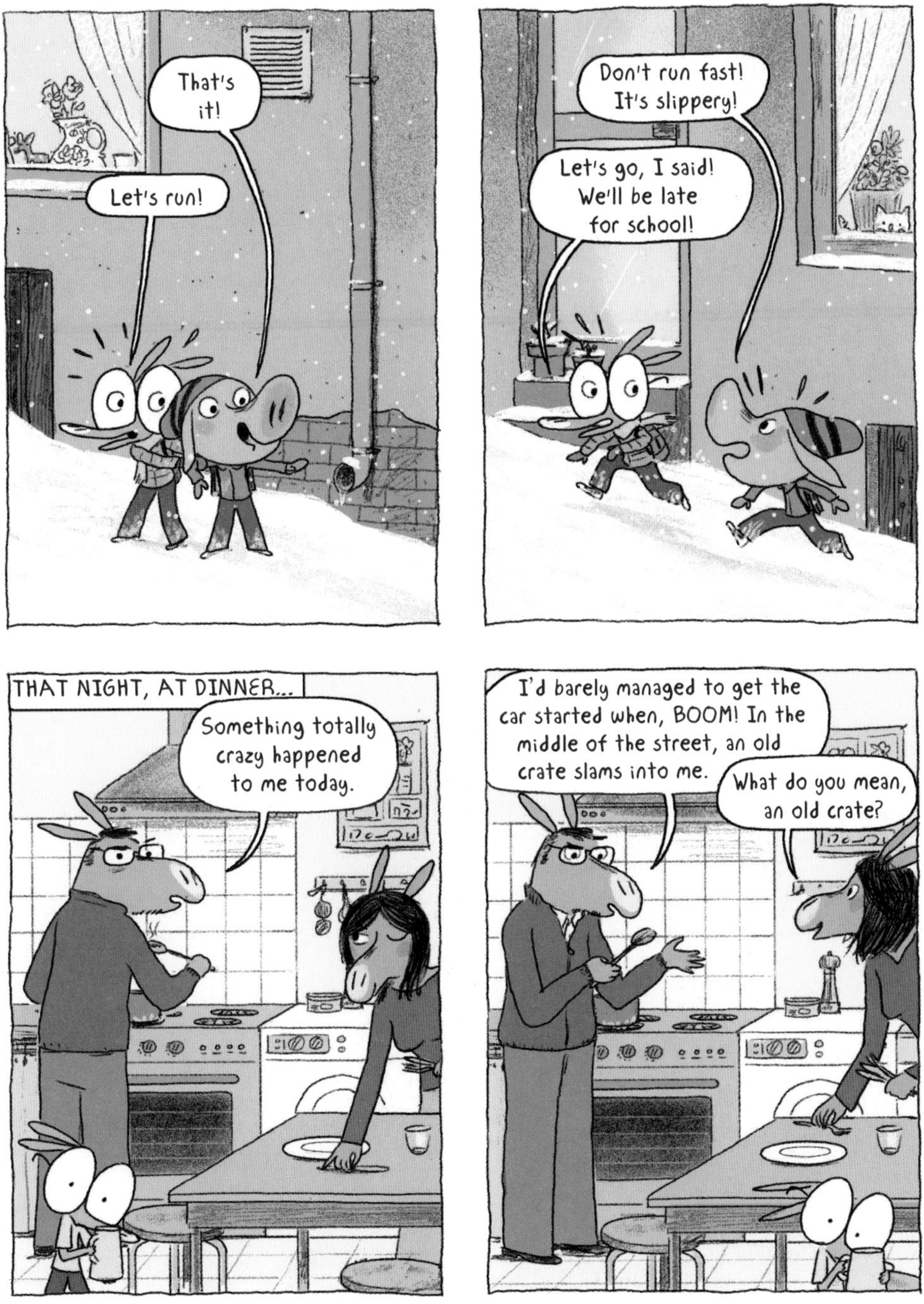
That's it!
Let's run!
Don't run fast! It's slippery!
Let's go, I said! We'll be late for school!
THAT NIGHT, AT DINNER...
Something totally crazy happened to me today.
I'd barely managed to get the car started when, BOOM! In the middle of the street, an old crate slams into me.
What do you mean, an old crate?

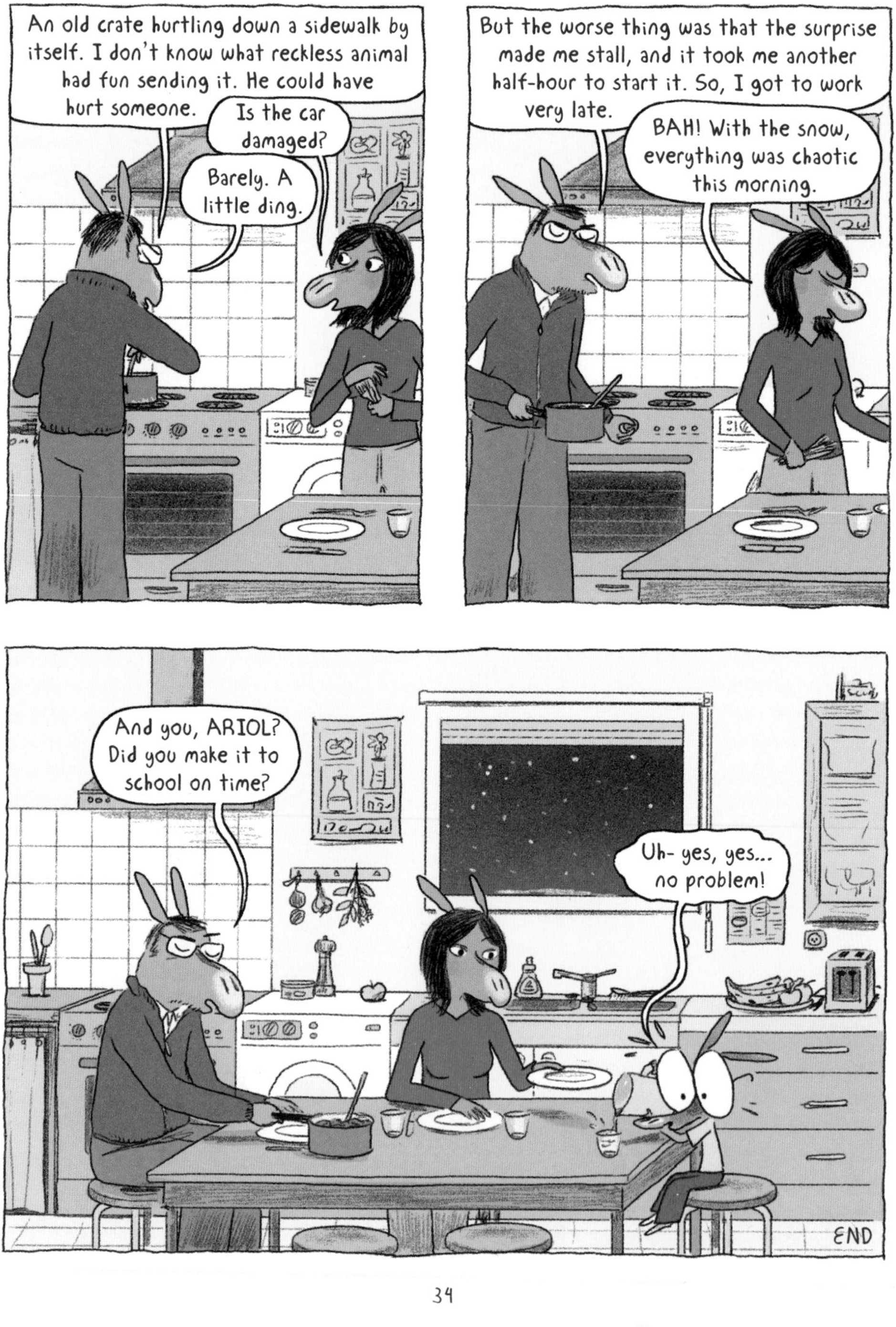
An old crate hurtling down a sidewalk by itself. I don't know what reckless animal had fun sending it. He could have hurt someone.
Is the car damaged?
Barely. A little ding.
But the worse thing was that the surprise made me stall, and it took me another half-hour to start it. So, I got to work very late.
BAH! With the snow, everything was chaotic this morning.
And you, ARIOL? Did you make it to school on time?
Uh- yes, yes... no problem!
END

ARiOL

PETULA! PETULA!

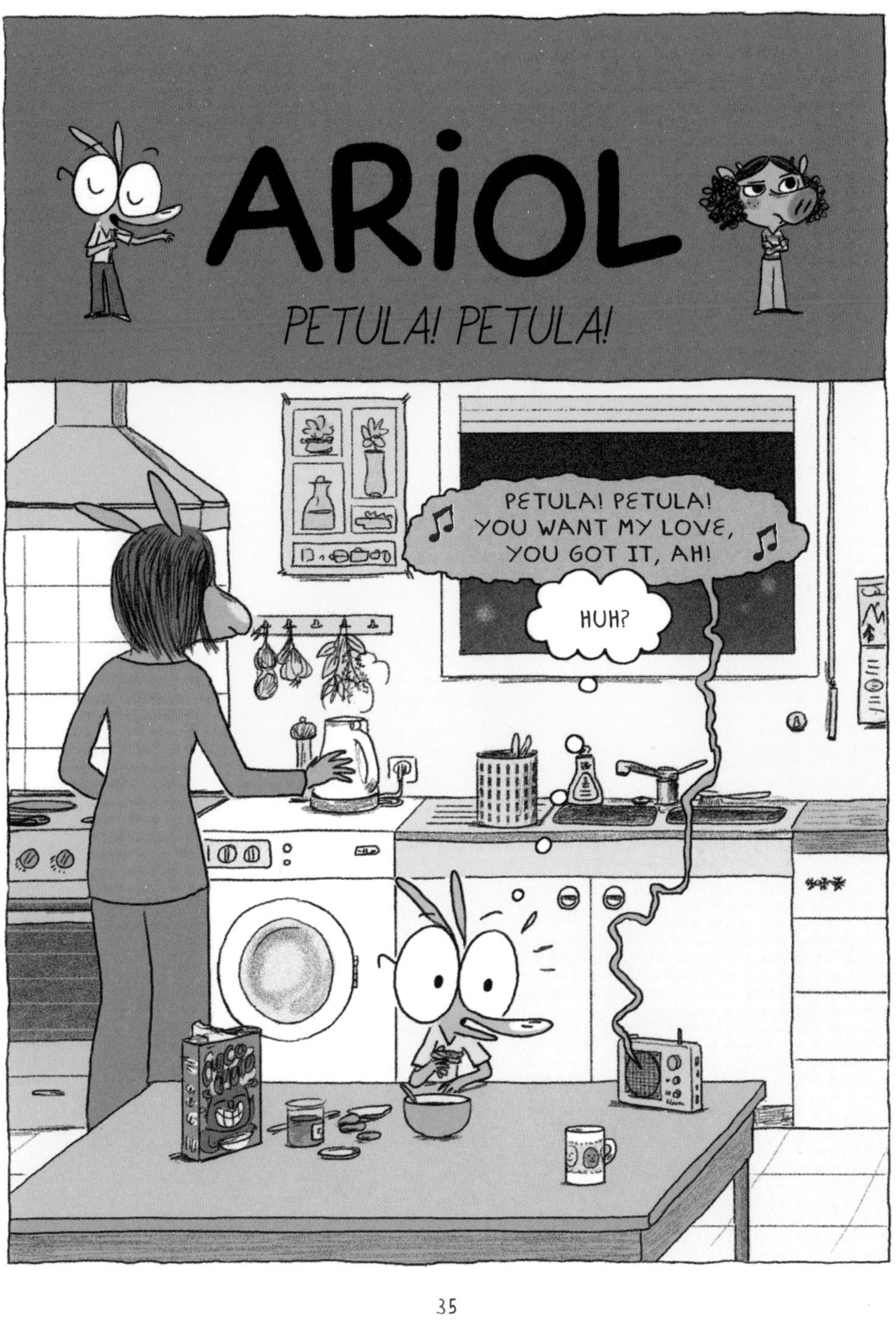

PETULA! PETULA!
YOU WANT MY LOVE,
YOU GOT IT, AH!
HUH?

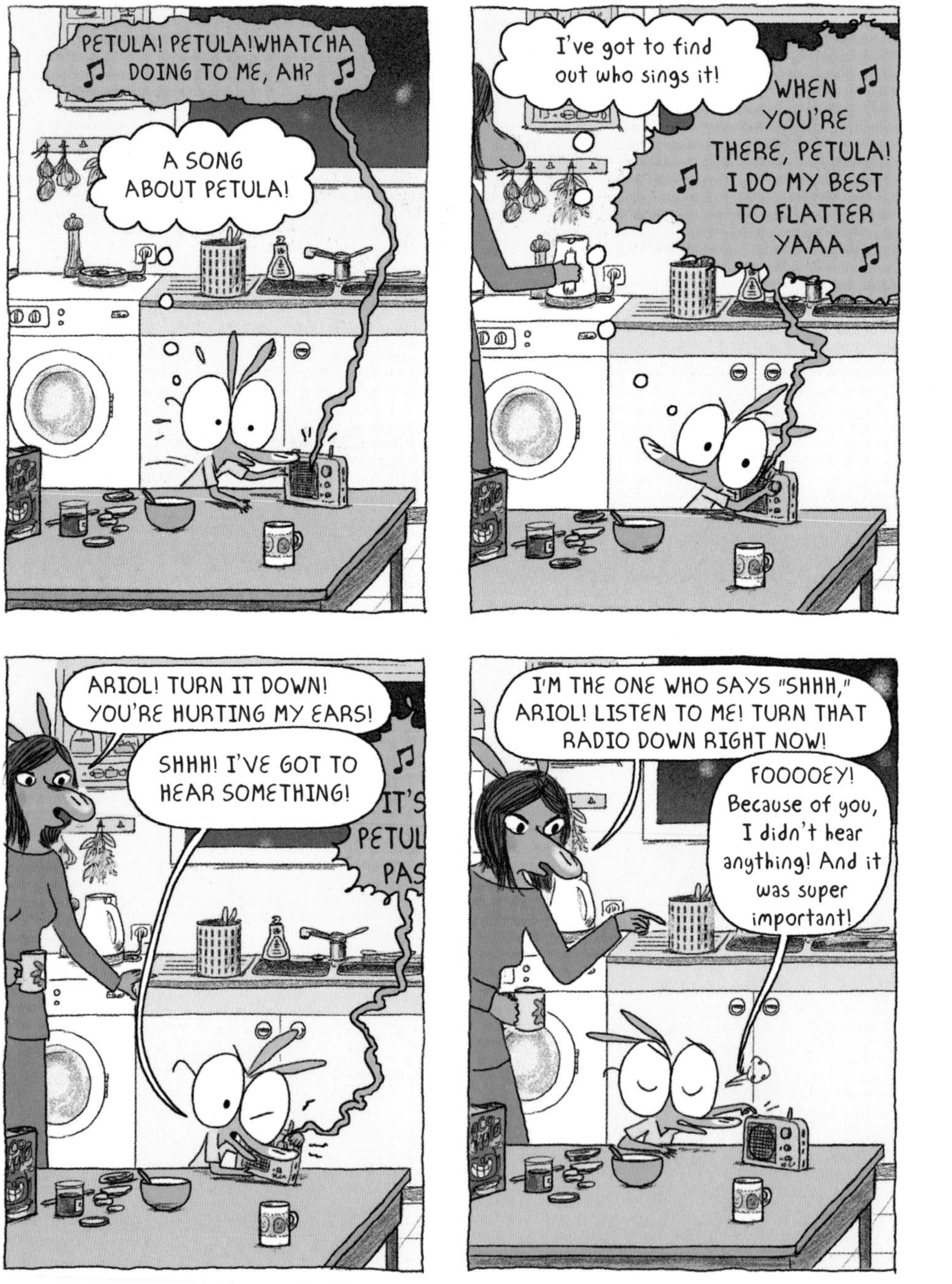

PETULA! PETULA!WHATCHA ♫ DOING TO ME, AH? ♫
A SONG ABOUT PETULA!
I've got to find out who sings it!
WHEN ♫ YOU'RE THERE, PETULA! ♫ I DO MY BEST TO FLATTER YAAA ♫
ARIOL! TURN IT DOWN! YOU'RE HURTING MY EARS!
SHHH! I'VE GOT TO HEAR SOMETHING!
I'M THE ONE WHO SAYS "SHHH," ARIOL! LISTEN TO ME! TURN THAT RADIO DOWN RIGHT NOW!
FOOOOEY! Because of you, I didn't hear anything! And it was super important!

A BIT LATER...
♫ PETULAAA PETULAAA NANANANANANANAAA ♫
So cool.
I've got to find that CD and give it to PETULA.
The problem, because of Mom, is that I didn't hear the title or the name of the singer. What'll I do to find the CD?
BAH! A song that repeats PETULA a thousand times has got to be called "PETULA." I'll go to the music store and ask for "PETULA."
Excuse me, sir, do you have the song "PETULA"?

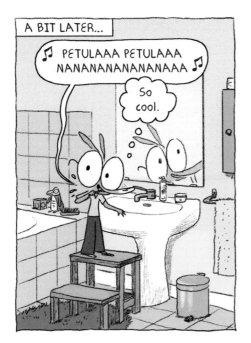

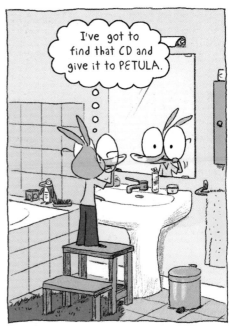

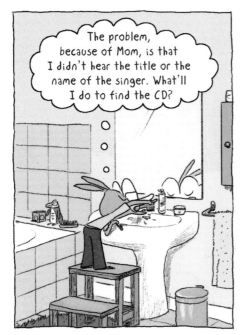

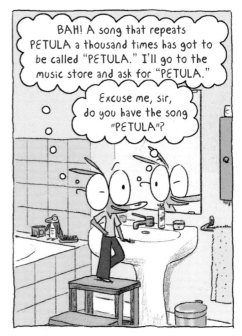

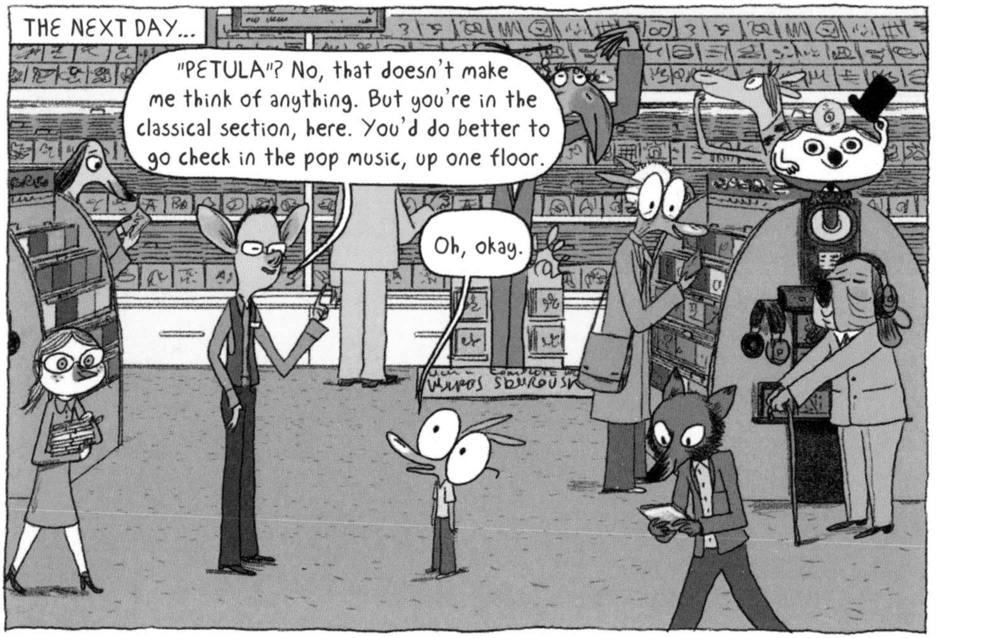
THE NEXT DAY...
"PETULA"? No, that doesn't make me think of anything. But you're in the classical section, here. You'd do better to go check in the pop music, up one floor.
Oh, okay.

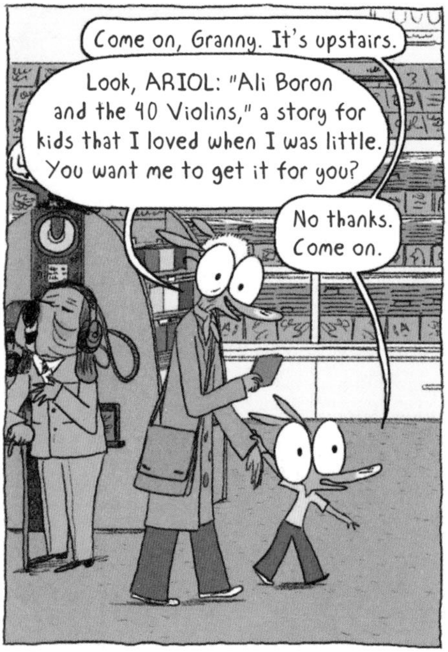
Come on, Granny. It's upstairs.
Look, ARIOL: "Ali Boron and the 40 Violins," a story for kids that I loved when I was little. You want me to get it for you?
No thanks. Come on.

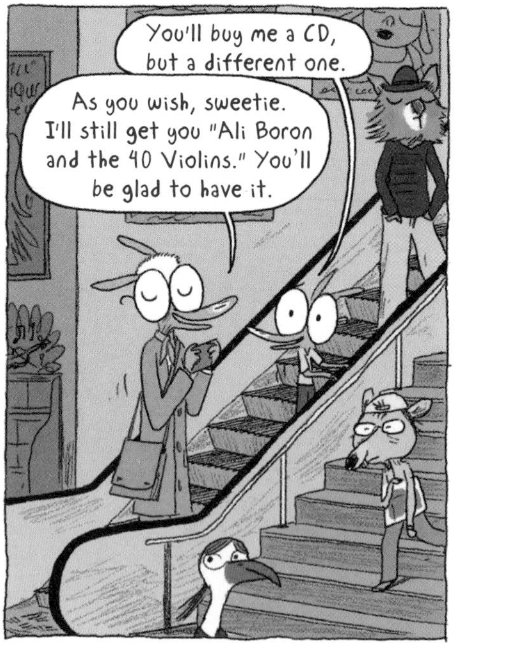
You'll buy me a CD, but a different one.
As you wish, sweetie. I'll still get you "Ali Boron and the 40 Violins." You'll be glad to have it.

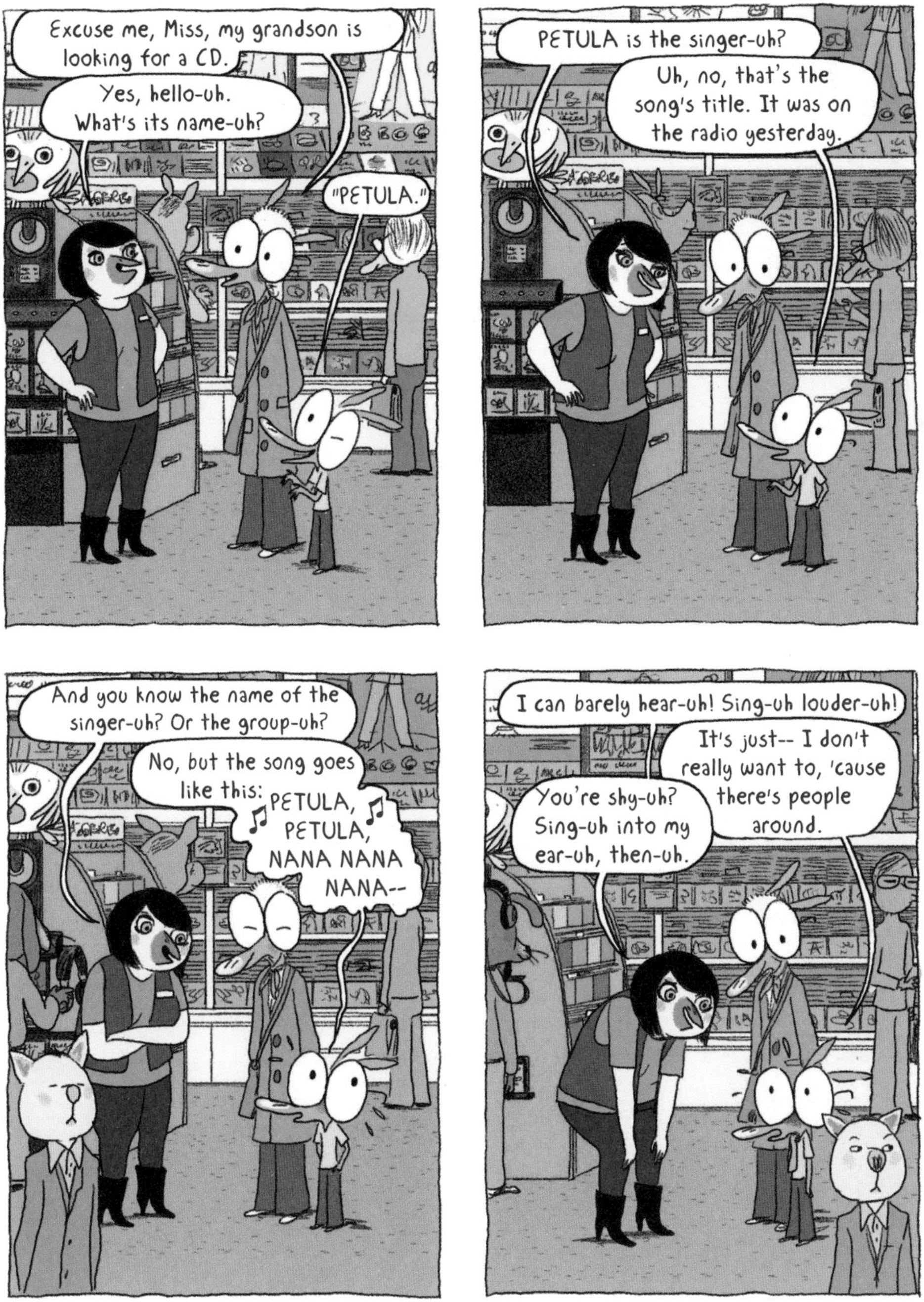
Excuse me, Miss, my grandson is looking for a CD.
Yes, hello-uh. What's its name-uh?
"PETULA."
PETULA is the singer-uh?
Uh, no, that's the song's title. It was on the radio yesterday.
And you know the name of the singer-uh? Or the group-uh?
No, but the song goes like this: ♫ PETULA, PETULA, ♫ NANA NANA NANA--
I can barely hear-uh! Sing-uh louder-uh!
It's just-- I don't really want to, 'cause there's people around.
You're shy-uh? Sing-uh into my ear-uh, then-uh.

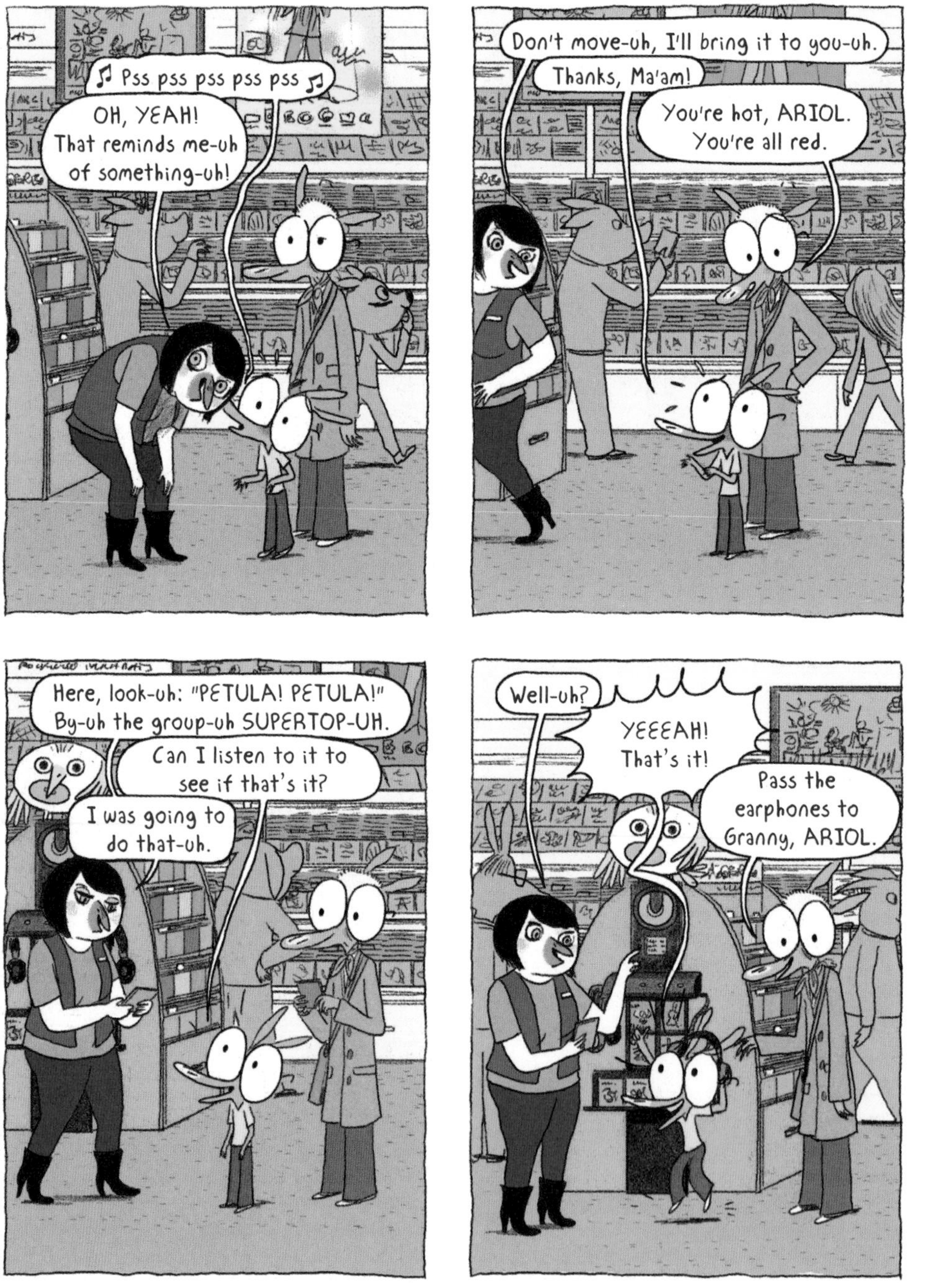

♫ Pss pss pss pss pss ♫
OH, YEAH! That reminds me-uh of something-uh!
Don't move-uh, I'll bring it to you-uh.
Thanks, Ma'am!
You're hot, ARIOL. You're all red.
Here, look-uh: "PETULA! PETULA!" By-uh the group-uh SUPERTOP-UH.
Can I listen to it to see if that's it?
I was going to do that-uh.
Well-uh?
YEEEAH! That's it!
Pass the earphones to Granny, ARIOL.

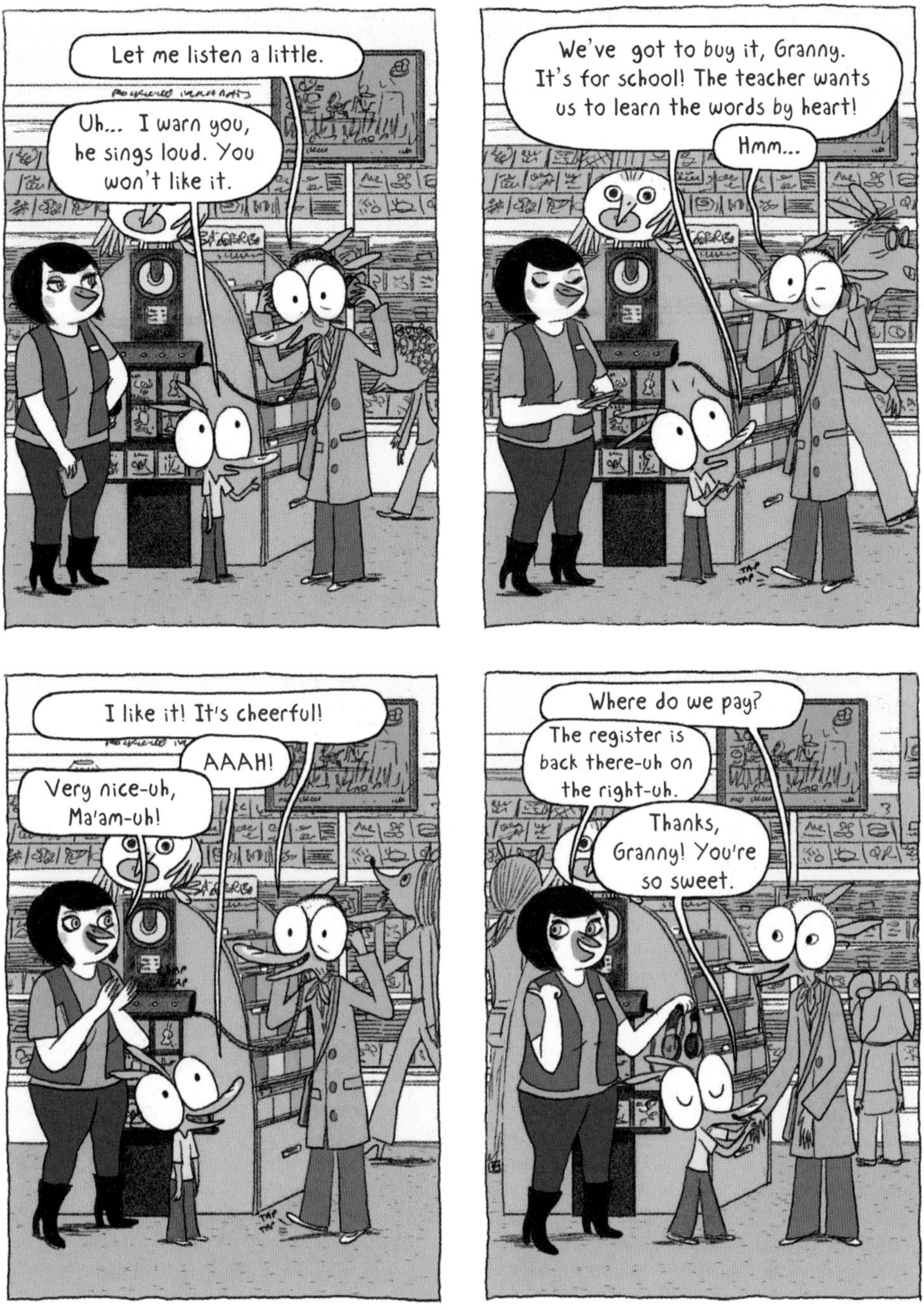
Let me listen a little.
Uh... I warn you, he sings loud. You won't like it.
We've got to buy it, Granny. It's for school! The teacher wants us to learn the words by heart!
Hmm...
I like it! It's cheerful!
AAAH!
Very nice-uh, Ma'am-uh!
Where do we pay?
The register is back there-uh on the right-uh.
Thanks, Granny! You're so sweet.

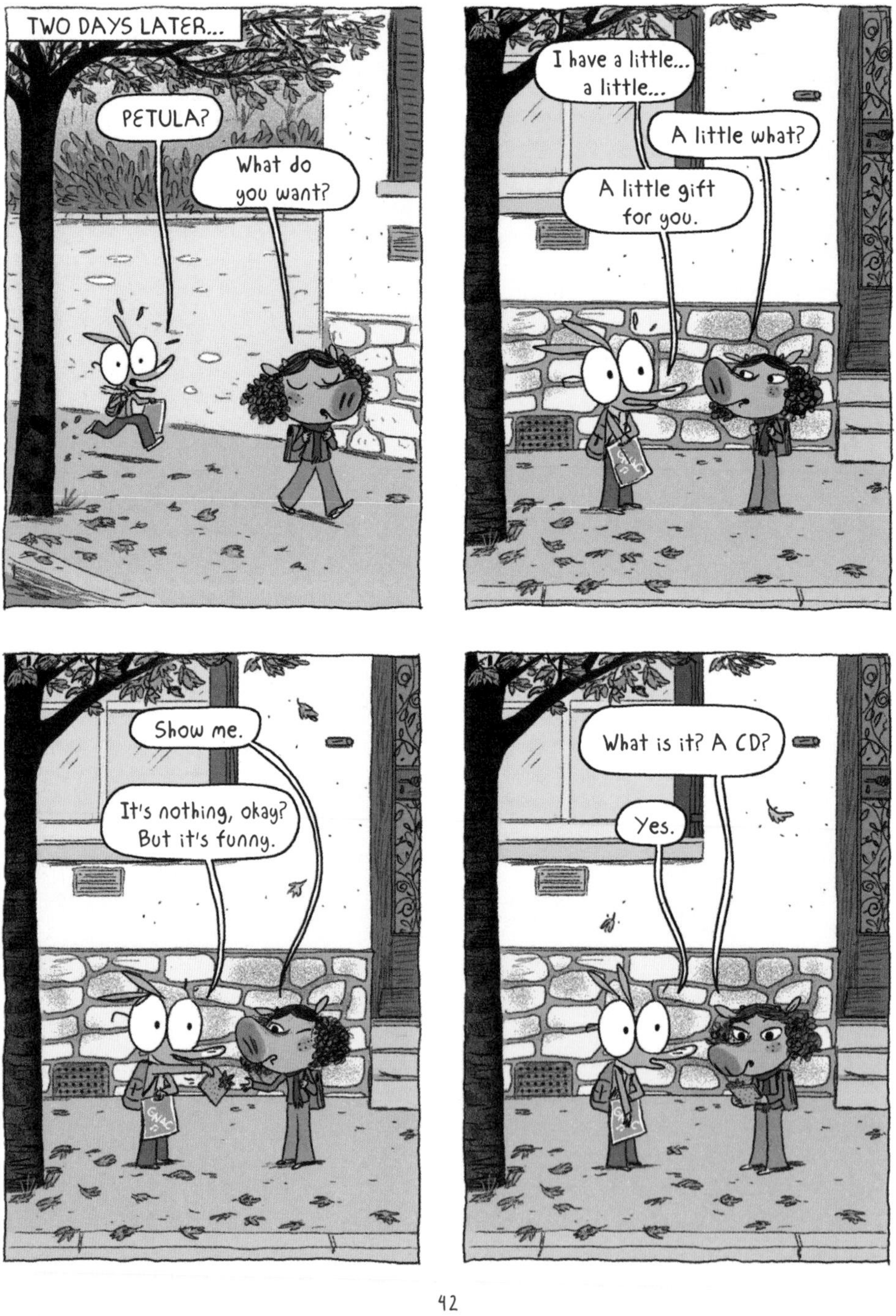
TWO DAYS LATER...
PETULA?
What do you want?
I have a little... a little...
A little what?
A little gift for you.
Show me.
It's nothing, okay? But it's funny.
What is it? A CD?
Yes.

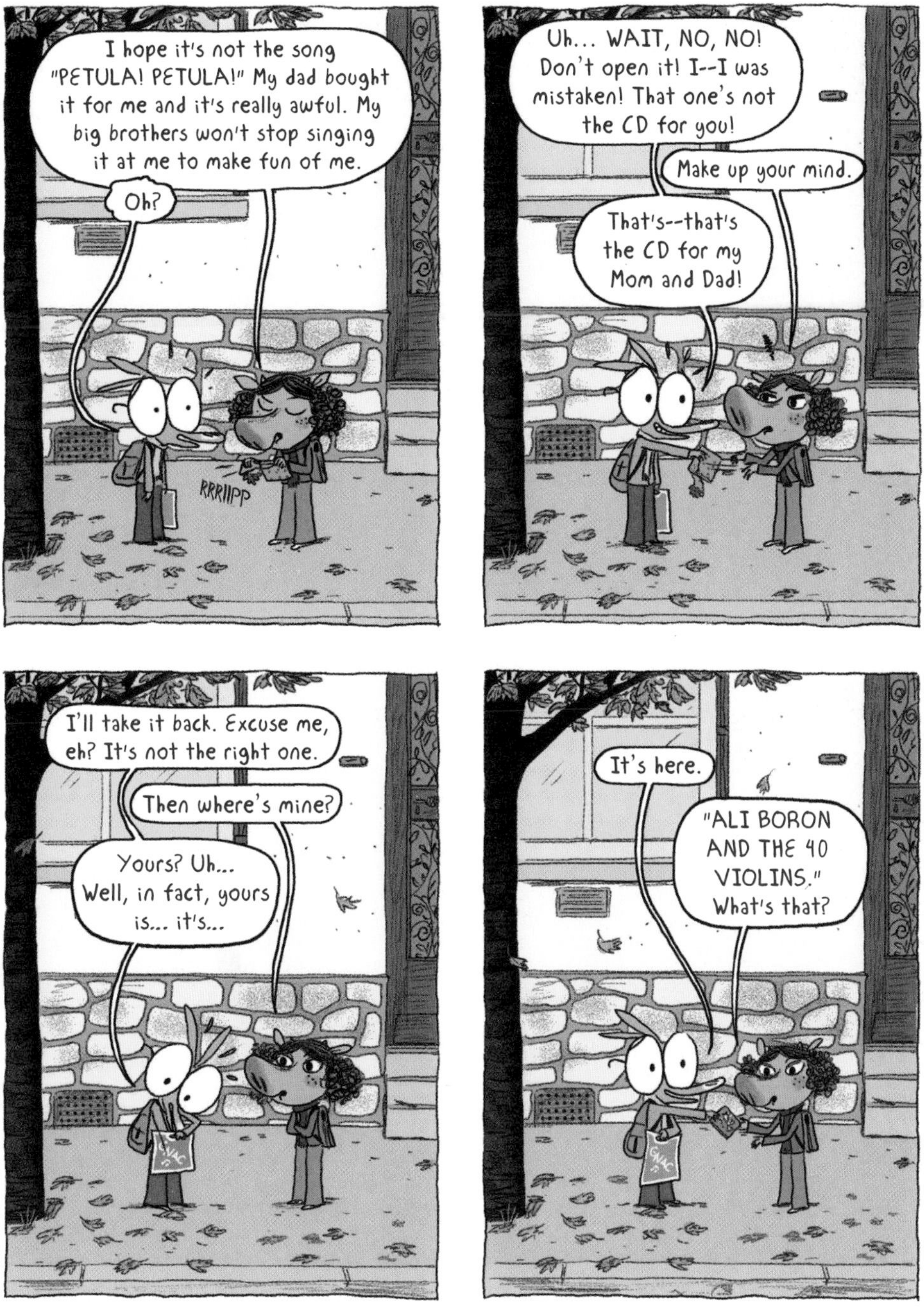
I hope it's not the song "PETULA! PETULA!" My dad bought it for me and it's really awful. My big brothers won't stop singing it at me to make fun of me.
Oh?
RRRIIPP
Uh... WAIT, NO, NO! Don't open it! I--I was mistaken! That one's not the CD for you!
Make up your mind.
That's--that's the CD for my Mom and Dad!
I'll take it back. Excuse me, eh? It's not the right one.
Then where's mine?
Yours? Uh... Well, in fact, yours is... it's...
It's here.
"ALI BORON AND THE 40 VIOLINS." What's that?

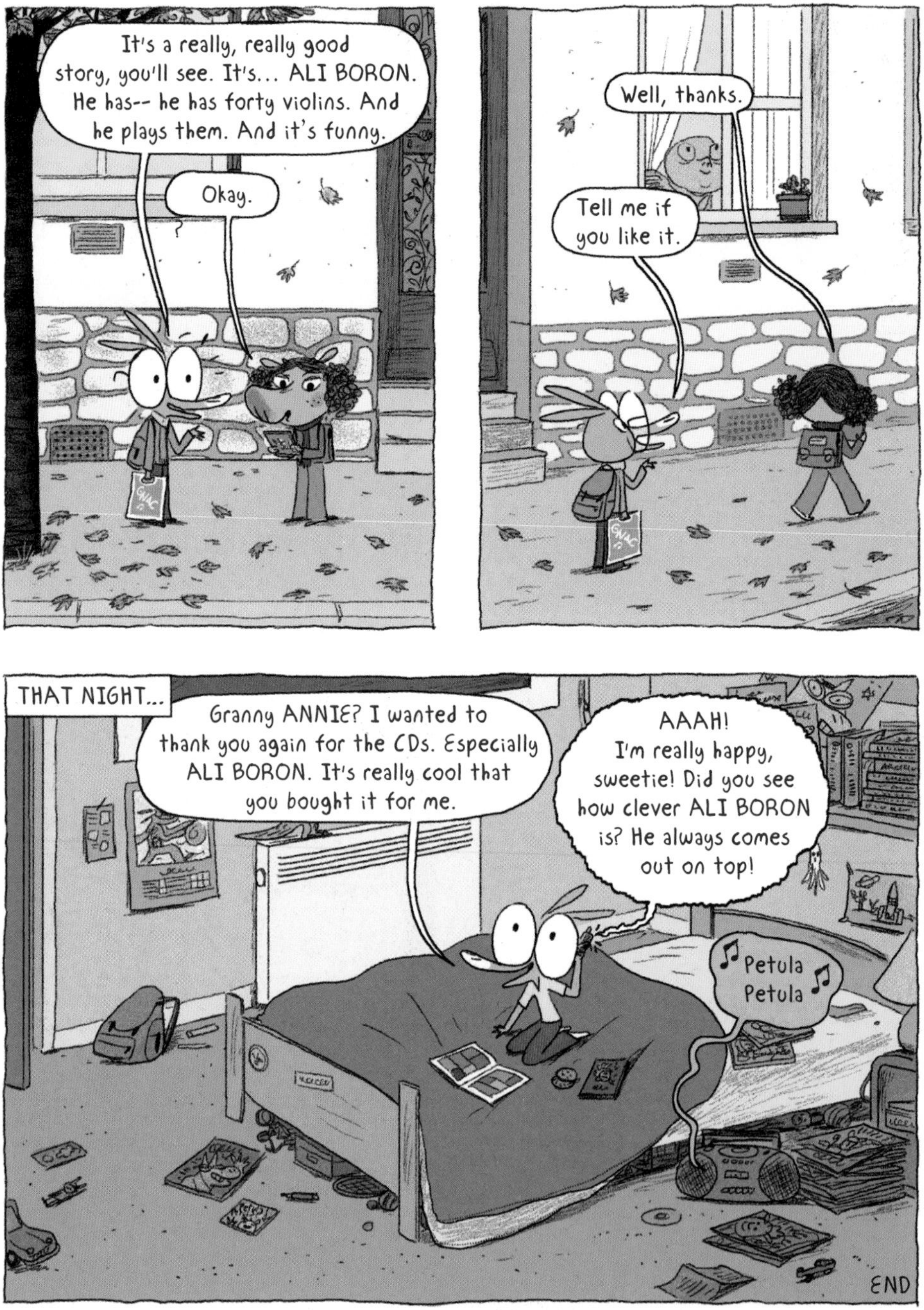
It's a really, really good story, you'll see. It's... ALI BORON. He has-- he has forty violins. And he plays them. And it's funny.
Okay.
?
GNAC
Well, thanks.
Tell me if you like it.
GNAC
THAT NIGHT...
Granny ANNIE? I wanted to thank you again for the CDs. Especially ALI BORON. It's really cool that you bought it for me.
AAAH! I'm really happy, sweetie! Did you see how clever ALI BORON is? He always comes out on top!
Petula Petula
END

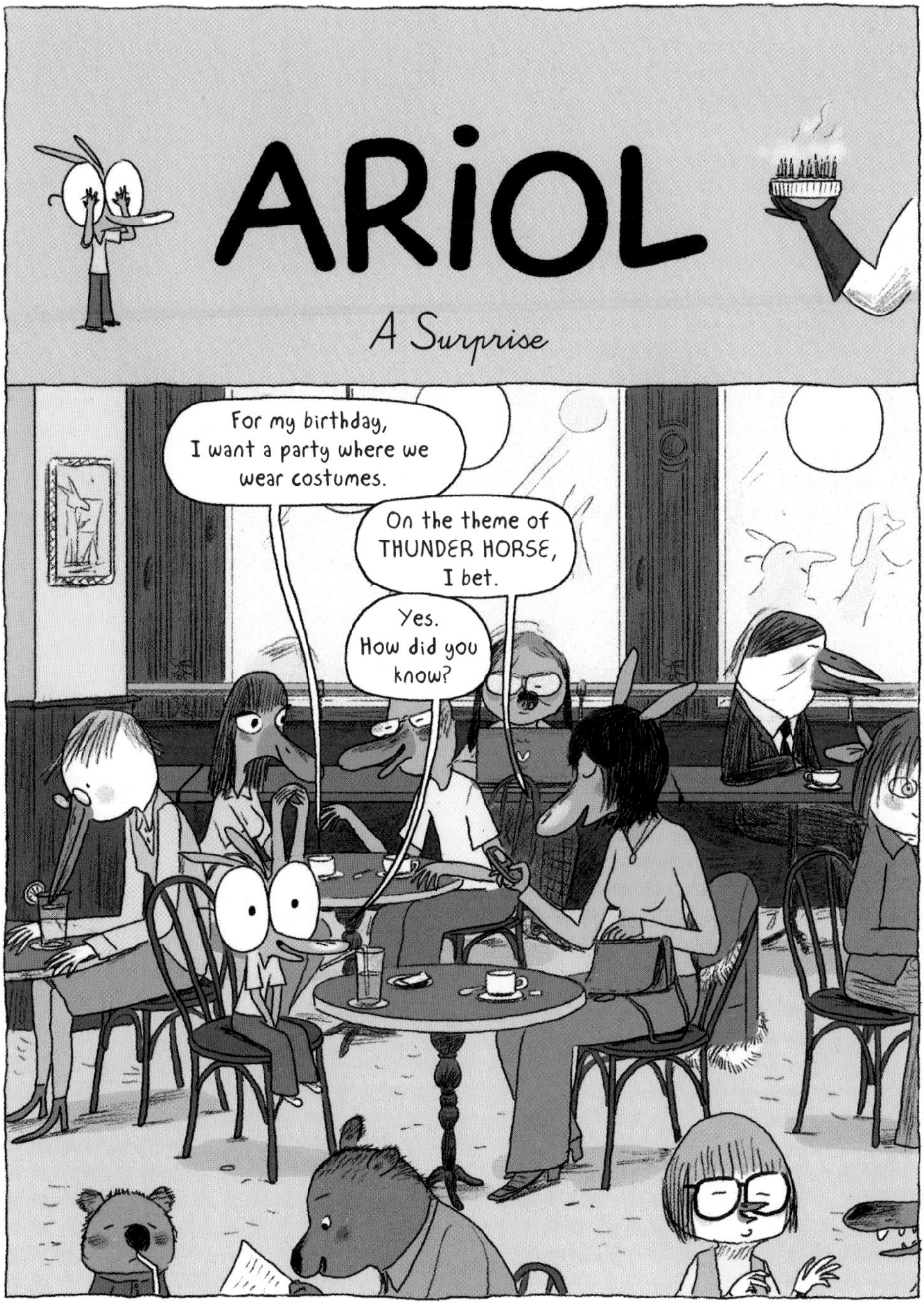
ARIOL
A Surprise
For my birthday, I want a party where we wear costumes.
On the theme of THUNDER HORSE, I bet.
Yes. How did you know?

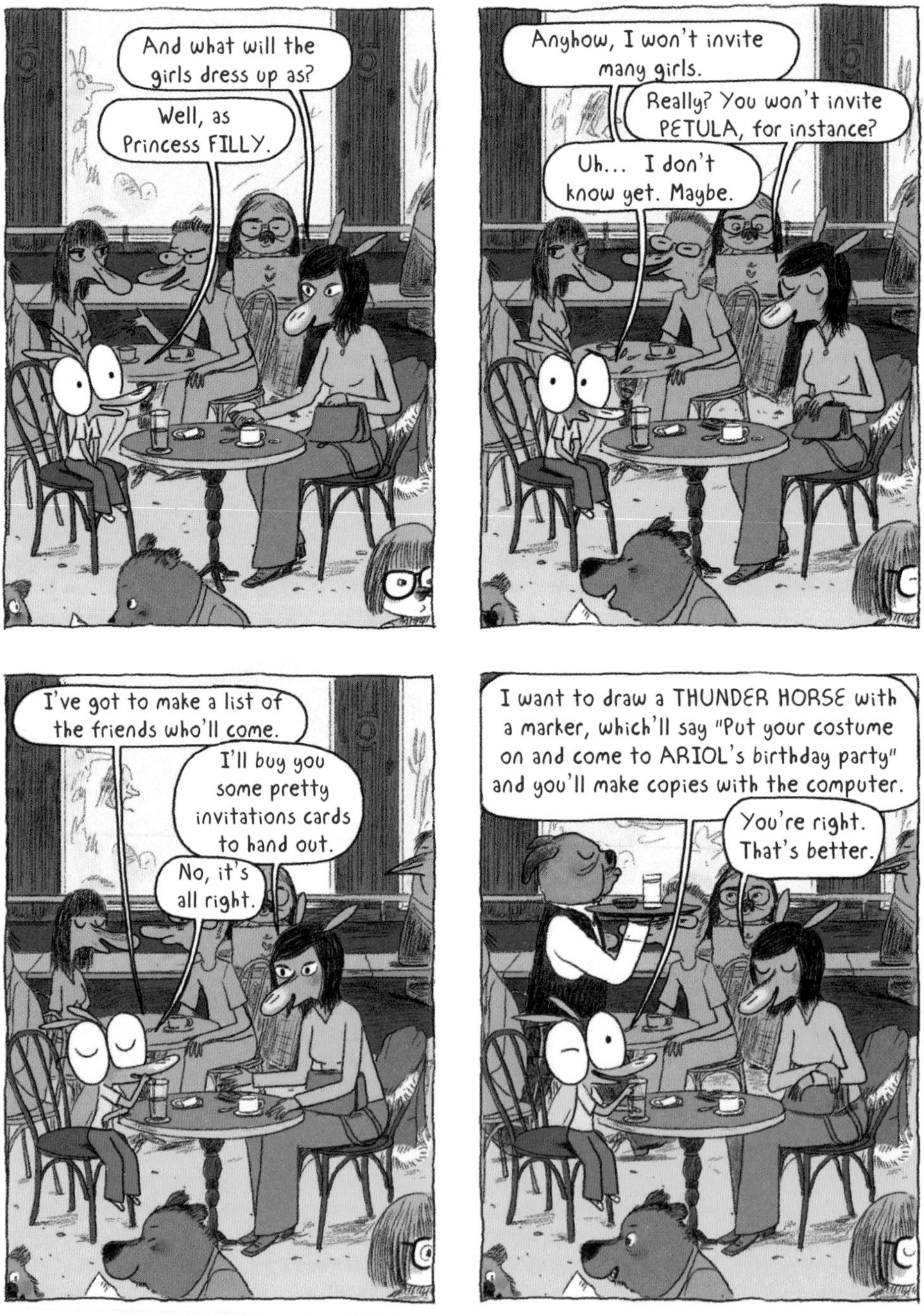
And what will the girls dress up as?
Well, as Princess FILLY.
Anyhow, I won't invite many girls.
Really? You won't invite PETULA, for instance?
Uh... I don't know yet. Maybe.
I've got to make a list of the friends who'll come.
I'll buy you some pretty invitations cards to hand out.
No, it's all right.
I want to draw a THUNDER HORSE with a marker, which'll say "Put your costume on and come to ARIOL's birthday party" and you'll make copies with the computer.
You're right. That's better.

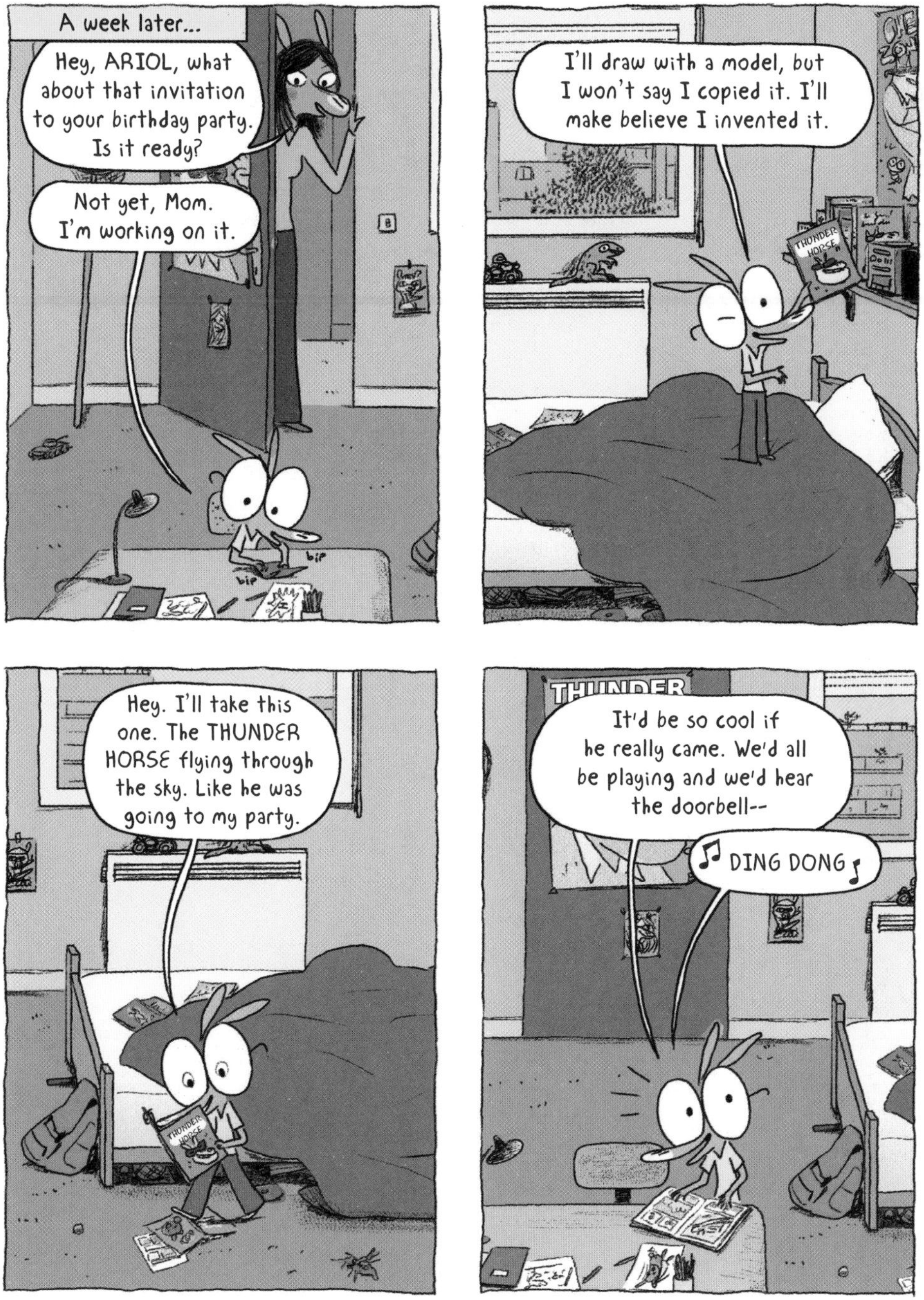
A week later...
Hey, ARIOL, what about that invitation to your birthday party. Is it ready?
Not yet, Mom. I'm working on it.
bip
bip
I'll draw with a model, but I won't say I copied it. I'll make believe I invented it.
THUNDER HORSE
Hey. I'll take this one. The THUNDER HORSE flying through the sky. Like he was going to my party.
THUNDER HORSE
THUNDER
It'd be so cool if he really came. We'd all be playing and we'd hear the doorbell--
DING DONG

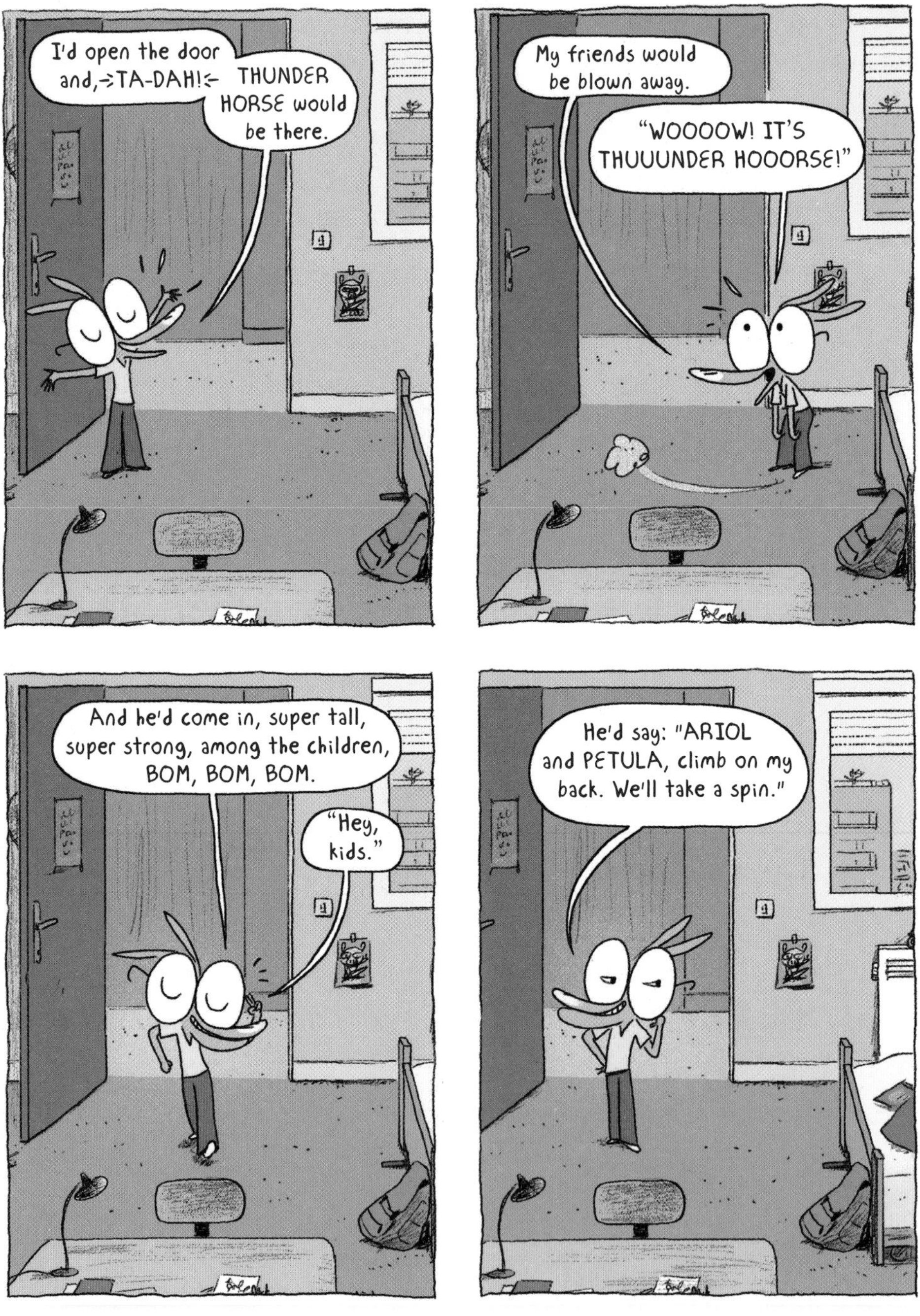
I'd open the door and, ⇒TA-DAH!⇐
THUNDER HORSE would be there.
My friends would be blown away.
"WOOOOW! IT'S THUUUNDER HOOORSE!"
And he'd come in, super tall, super strong, among the children, BOM, BOM, BOM.
"Hey, kids."
He'd say: "ARIOL and PETULA, climb on my back. We'll take a spin."

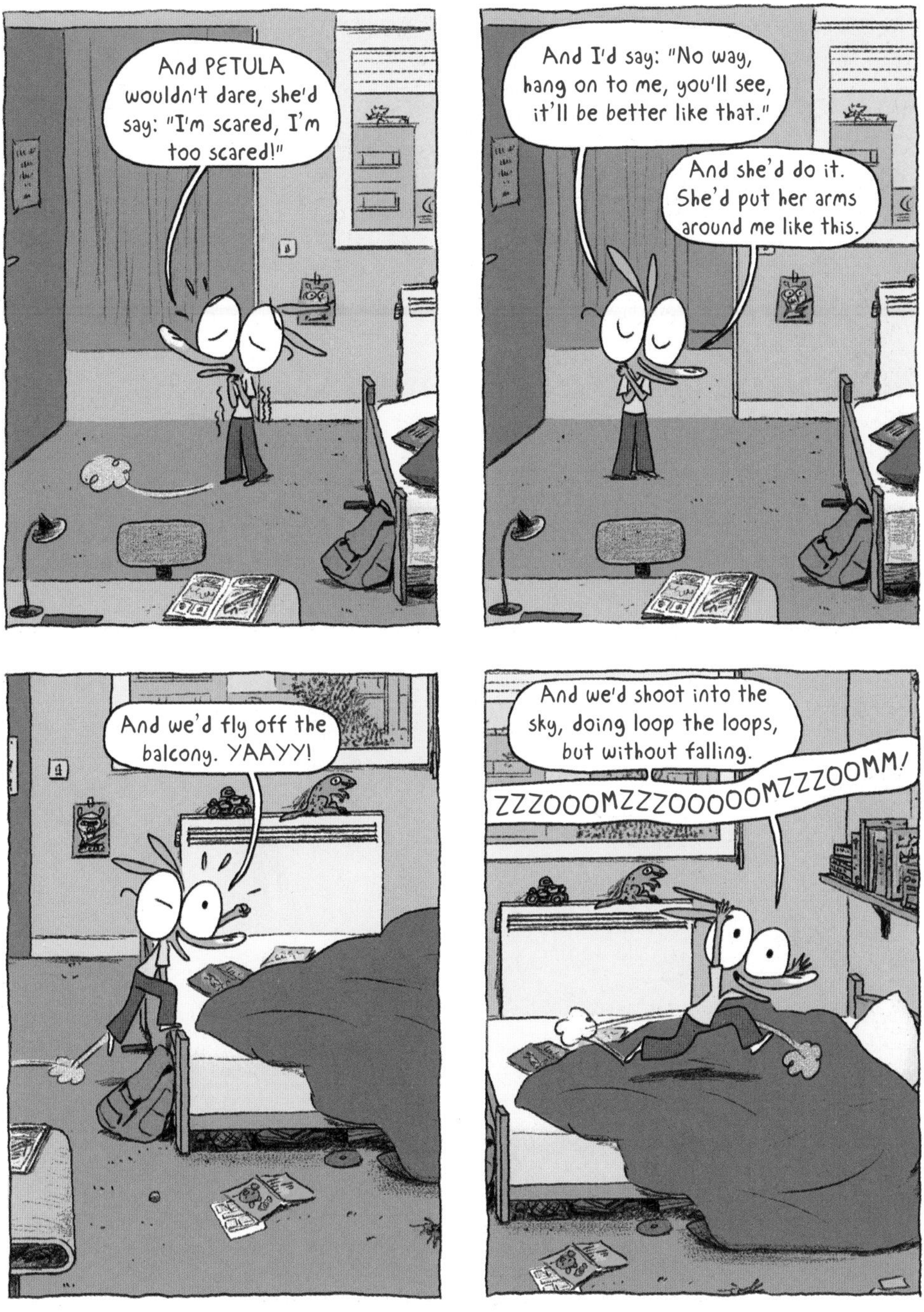
And PETULA wouldn't dare, she'd say: "I'm scared, I'm too scared!"
And I'd say: "No way, hang on to me, you'll see, it'll be better like that."
And she'd do it. She'd put her arms around me like this.
And we'd fly off the balcony. YAAYY!
And we'd shoot into the sky, doing loop the loops, but without falling.
ZZZOOOMZZZOOOOOMZZZOOMM!

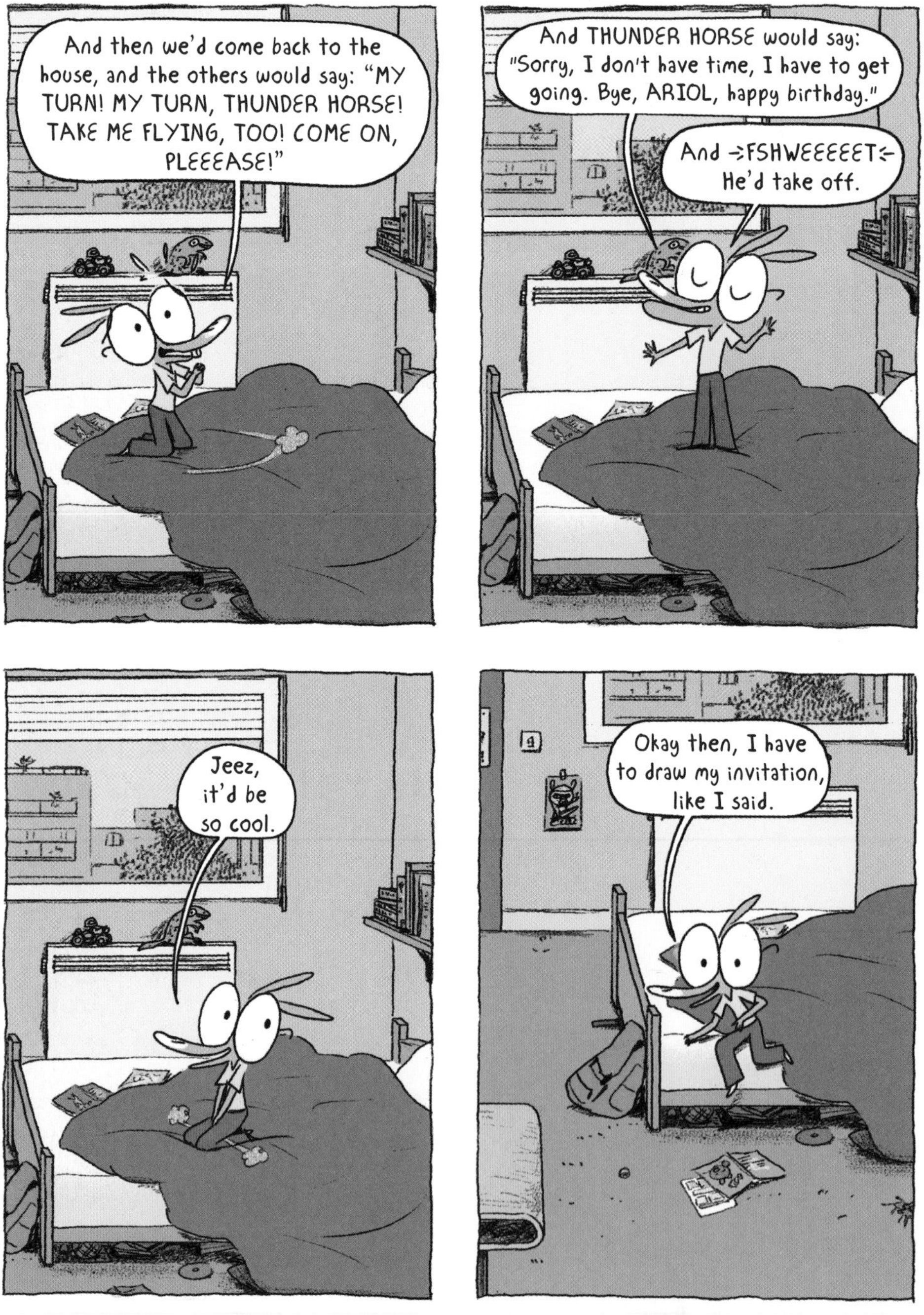
And then we'd come back to the house, and the others would say: "MY TURN! MY TURN, THUNDER HORSE! TAKE ME FLYING, TOO! COME ON, PLEEEASE!"
And THUNDER HORSE would say: "Sorry, I don't have time, I have to get going. Bye, ARIOL, happy birthday."
And ⇒FSHWEEEEET⇐ He'd take off.
Jeez, it'd be so cool.
Okay then, I have to draw my invitation, like I said.

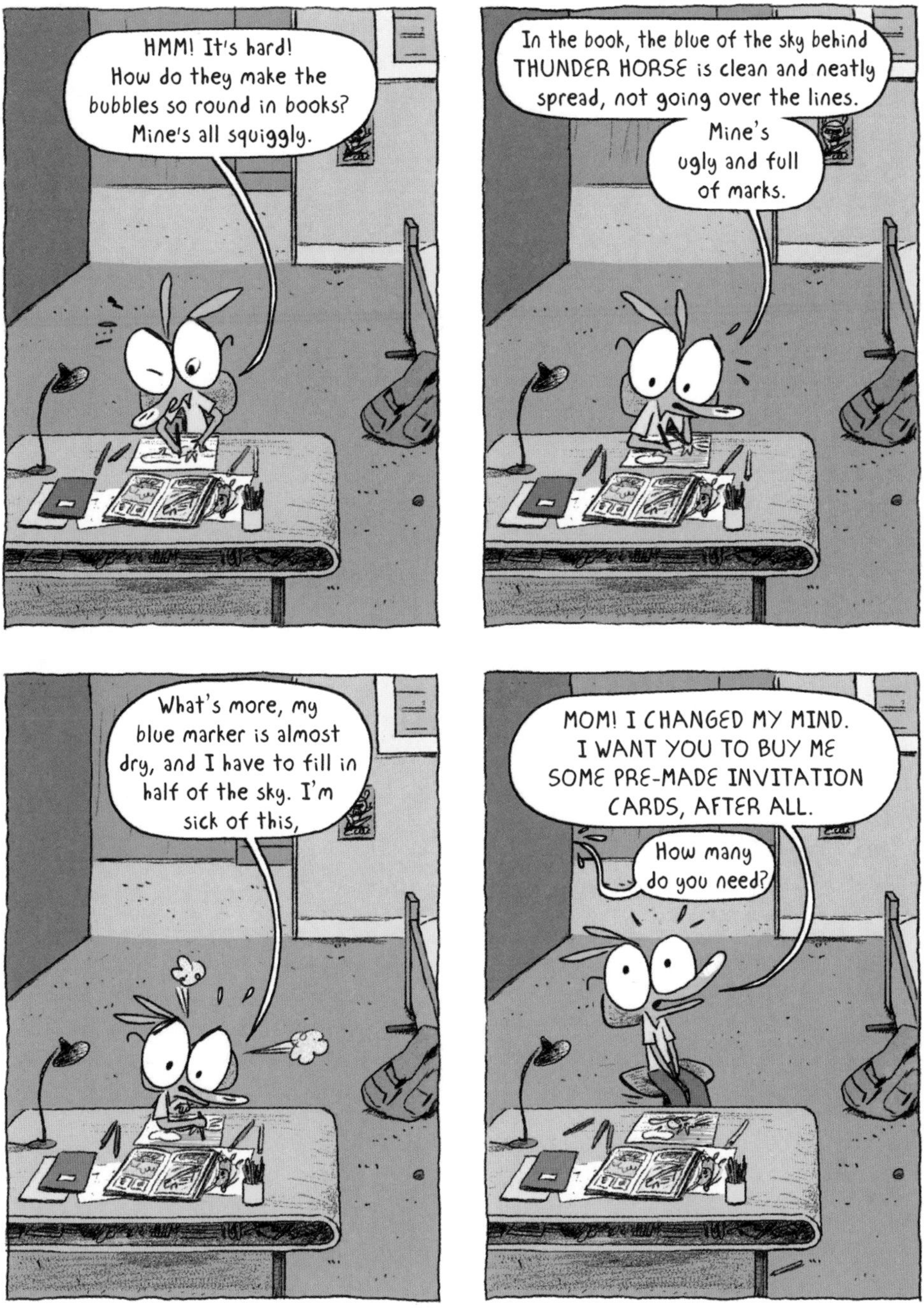

HMM! It's hard! How do they make the bubbles so round in books? Mine's all squiggly.
In the book, the blue of the sky behind THUNDER HORSE is clean and neatly spread, not going over the lines.
Mine's ugly and full of marks.
What's more, my blue marker is almost dry, and I have to fill in half of the sky. I'm sick of this,
MOM! I CHANGED MY MIND. I WANT YOU TO BUY ME SOME PRE-MADE INVITATION CARDS, AFTER ALL.
How many do you need?

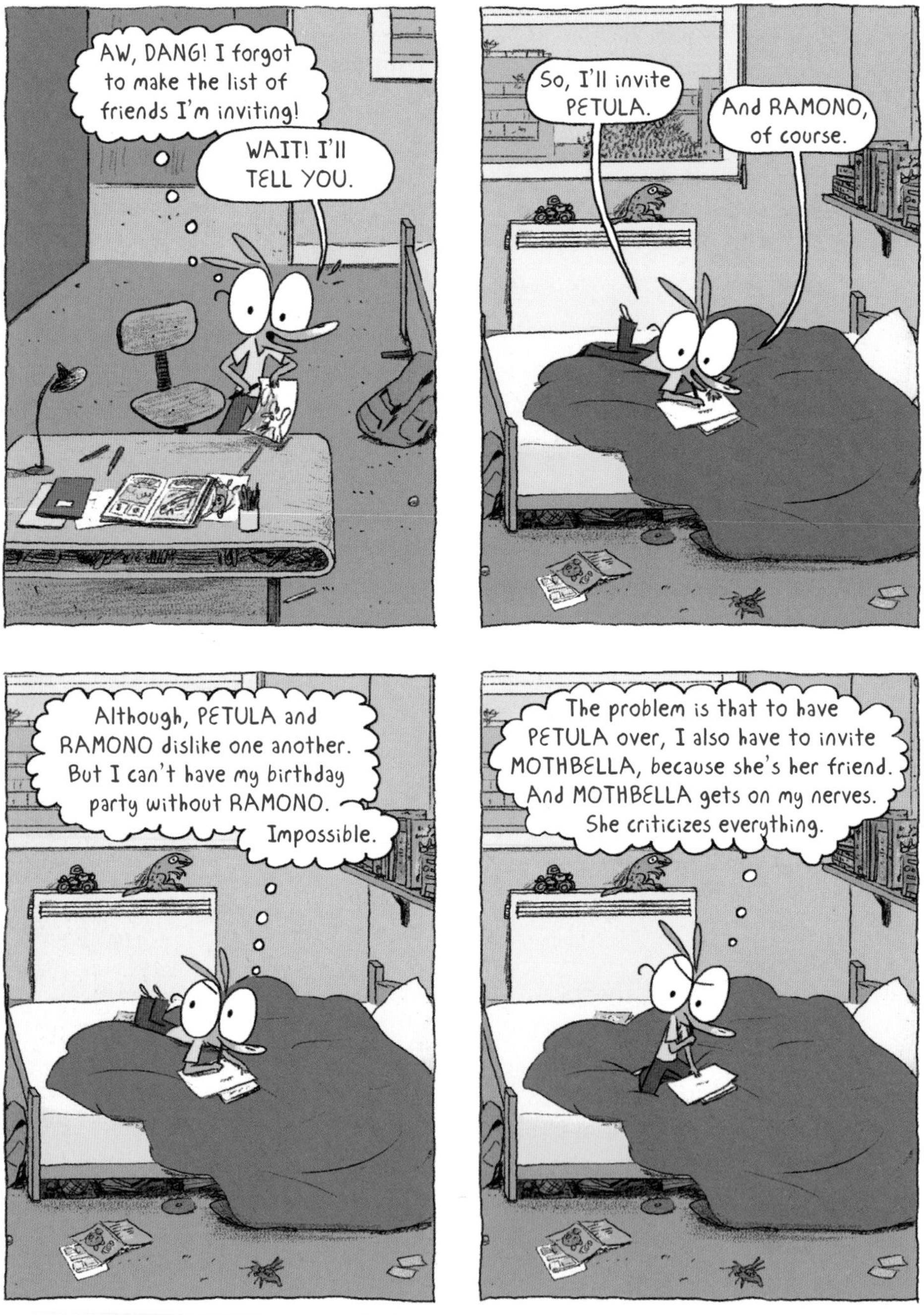
AW, DANG! I forgot to make the list of friends I'm inviting!
WAIT! I'll TELL YOU.
So, I'll invite PETULA.
And RAMONO, of course.
Although, PETULA and RAMONO dislike one another. But I can't have my birthday party without RAMONO.
Impossible.
The problem is that to have PETULA over, I also have to invite MOTHBELLA, because she's her friend. And MOTHBELLA gets on my nerves. She criticizes everything.

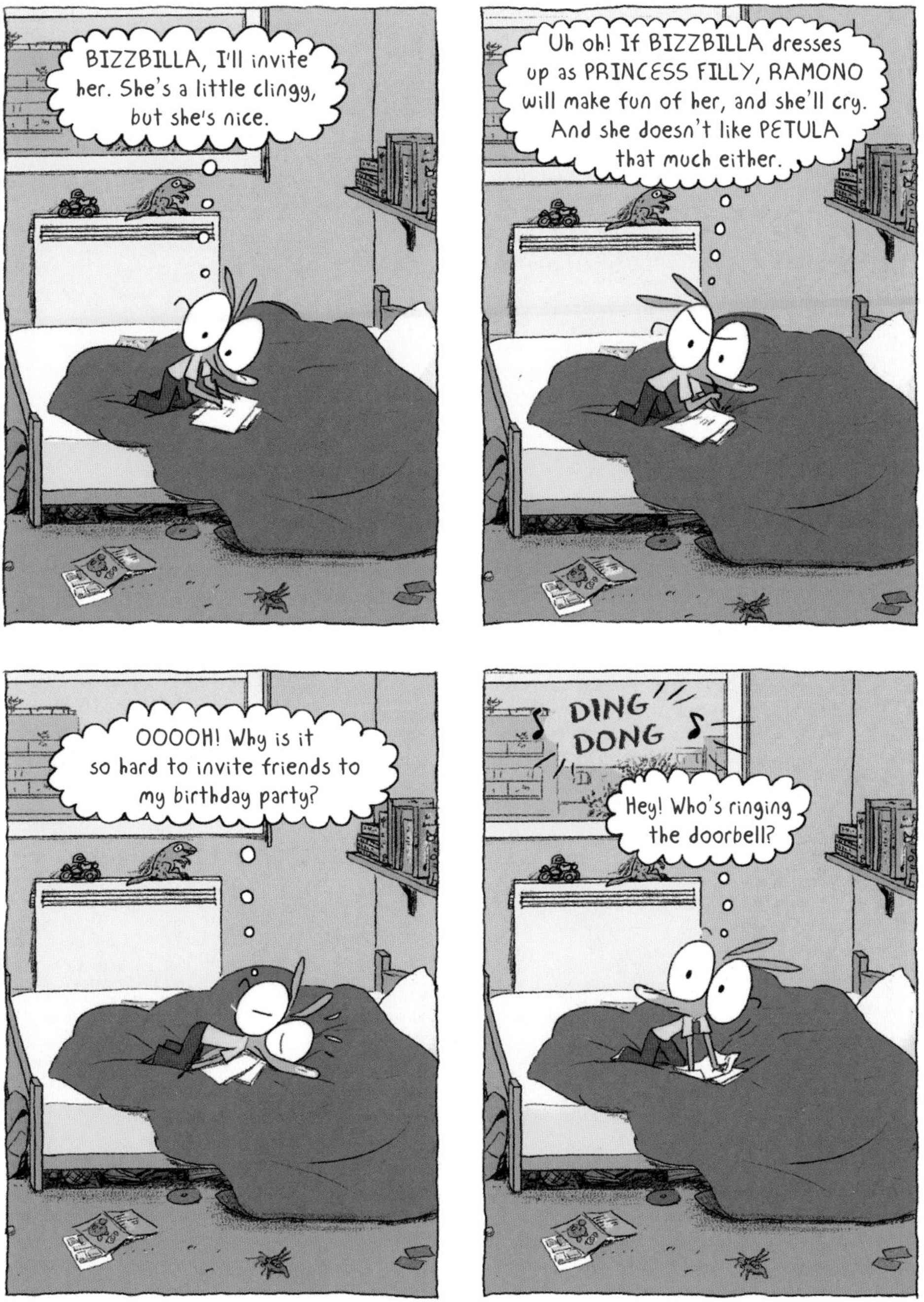
BIZZBILLA, I'll invite her. She's a little clingy, but she's nice.
Uh oh! If BIZZBILLA dresses up as PRINCESS FILLY, RAMONO will make fun of her, and she'll cry. And she doesn't like PETULA that much either.
OOOOH! Why is it so hard to invite friends to my birthday party?
DING DONG
Hey! Who's ringing the doorbell?

ARIOL? Come see, it's for you.
Who is it?
A surprise.
It isn't THUNDER HORSE, is it?
Almost.
HAPPY BIRTHDAY!
END

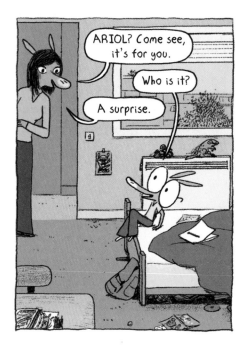

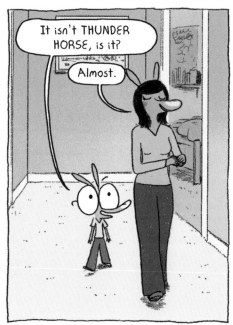

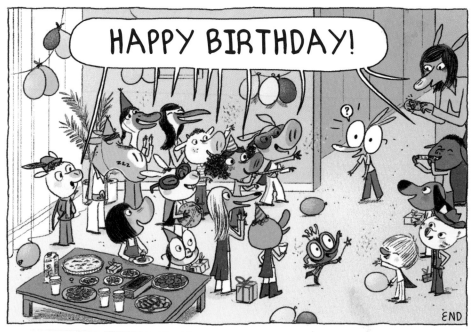

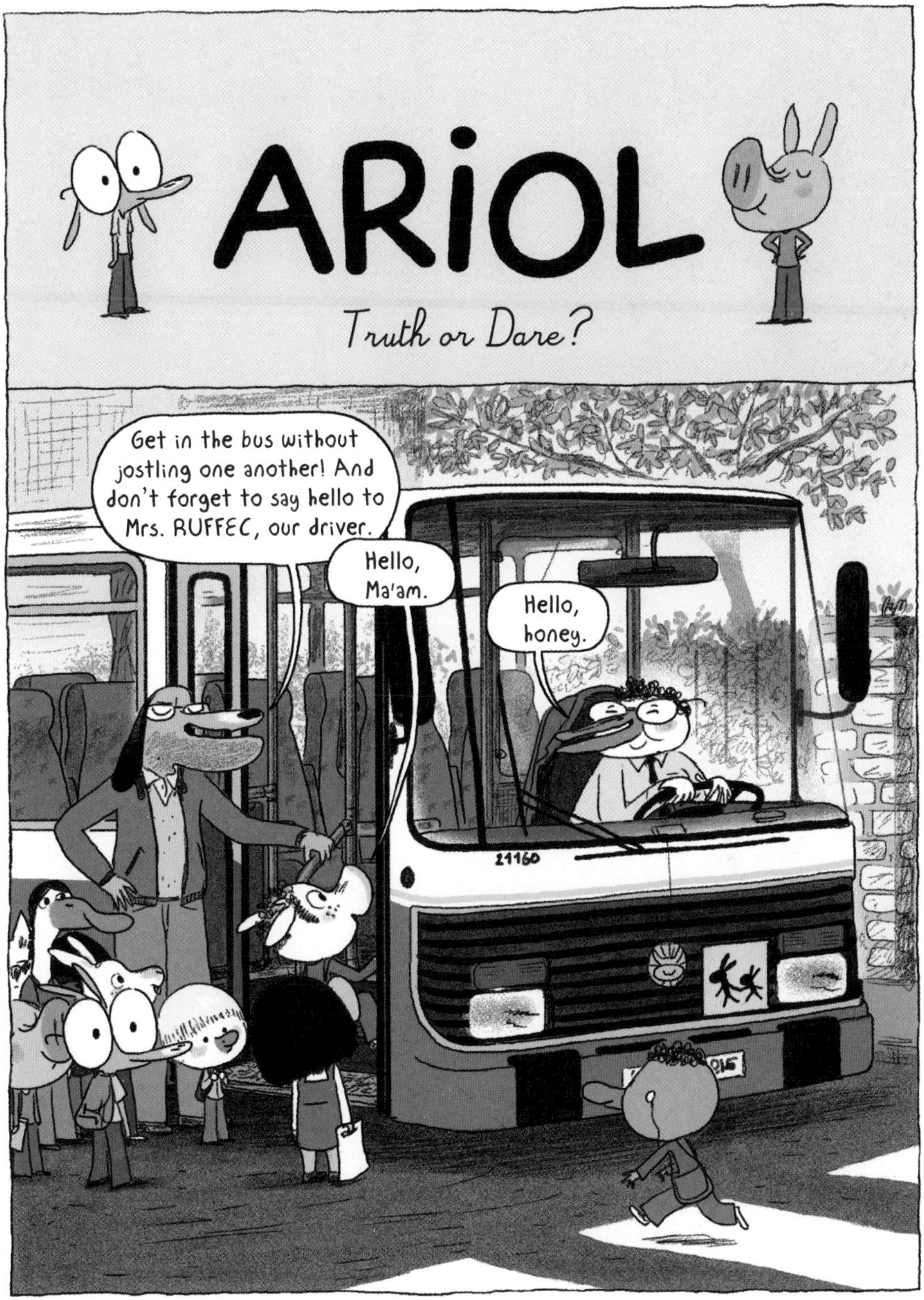
ARiOL
Truth or Dare?
Get in the bus without jostling one another! And don't forget to say hello to Mrs. RUFFEC, our driver.
Hello, Ma'am.
Hello, honey.
21160

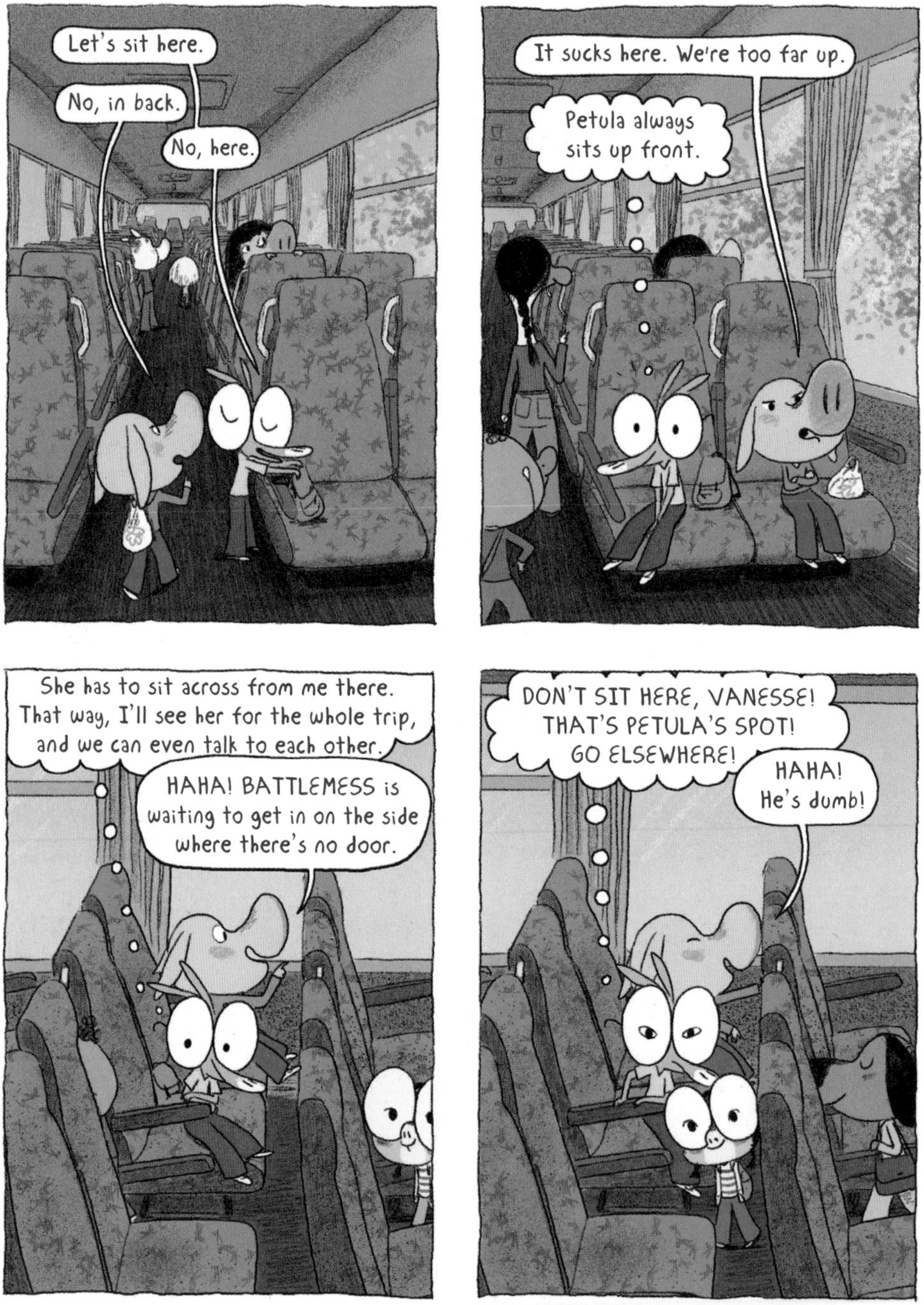
Let's sit here.
No, in back.
No, here.
It sucks here. We're too far up.
Petula always sits up front.
She has to sit across from me there. That way, I'll see her for the whole trip, and we can even talk to each other.
HAHA! BATTLEMESS is waiting to get in on the side where there's no door.
DON'T SIT HERE, VANESSE! THAT'S PETULA'S SPOT! GO ELSEWHERE!
HAHA! He's dumb!

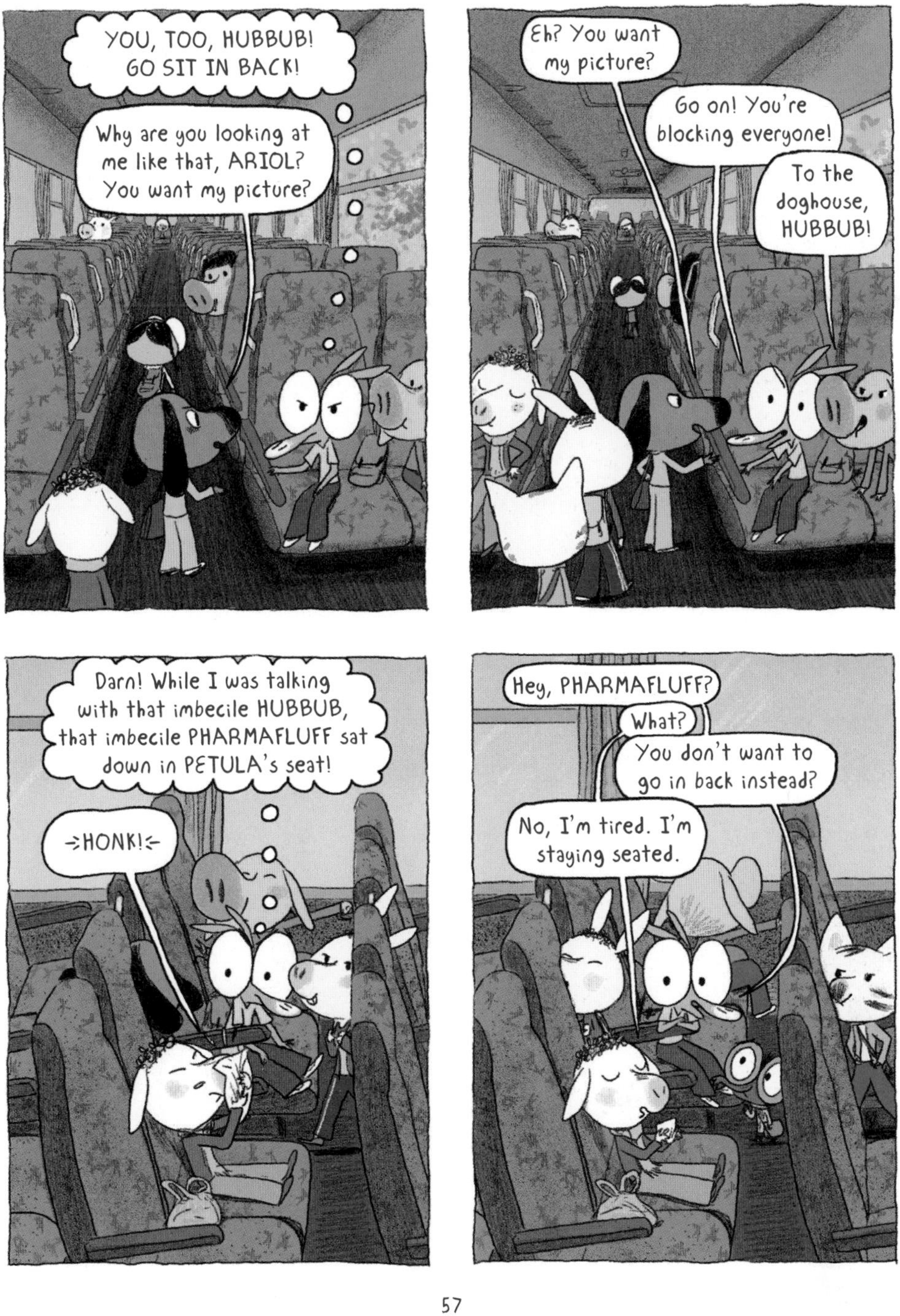
YOU, TOO, HUBBUB! GO SIT IN BACK!
Why are you looking at me like that, ARIOL? You want my picture?
Eh? You want my picture?
Go on! You're blocking everyone!
To the doghouse, HUBBUB!
Darn! While I was talking with that imbecile HUBBUB, that imbecile PHARMAFLUFF sat down in PETULA's seat!
HONK!
Hey, PHARMAFLUFF?
What?
You don't want to go in back instead?
No, I'm tired. I'm staying seated.

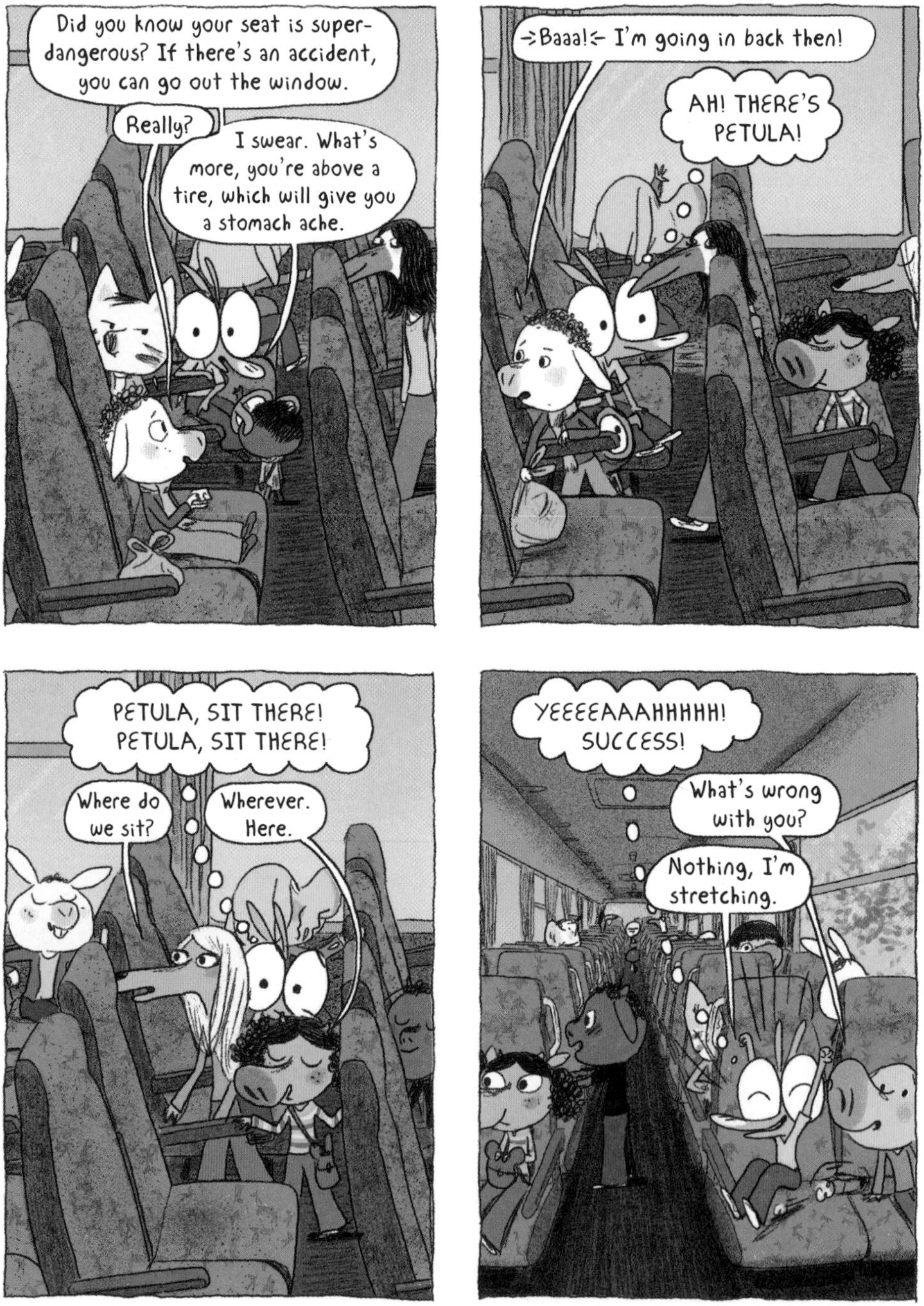
Did you know your seat is super-dangerous? If there's an accident, you can go out the window.
Really?
I swear. What's more, you're above a tire, which will give you a stomach ache.
⇒Baaa!⇐ I'm going in back then!
AH! THERE'S PETULA!
PETULA, SIT THERE! PETULA, SIT THERE!
Where do we sit?
Wherever. Here.
YEEEEAAAHHHHH! SUCCESS!
What's wrong with you?
Nothing, I'm stretching.

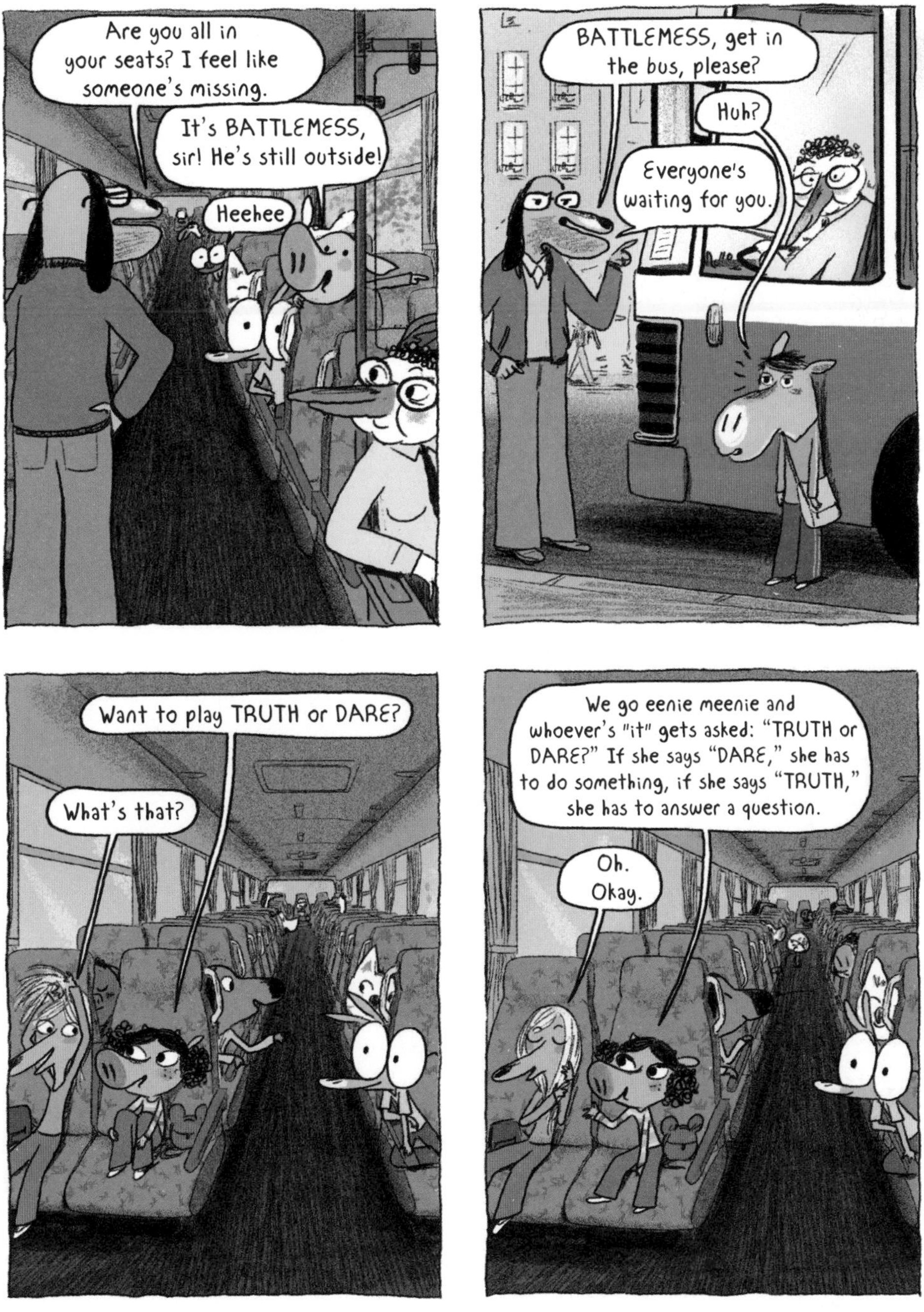
Are you all in your seats? I feel like someone's missing.
It's BATTLEMESS, sir! He's still outside!
Heehee
BATTLEMESS, get in the bus, please?
Huh?
Everyone's waiting for you.
Want to play TRUTH or DARE?
What's that?
We go eenie meenie and whoever's "it" gets asked: "TRUTH or DARE?" If she says "DARE," she has to do something, if she says "TRUTH," she has to answer a question.
Oh. Okay.

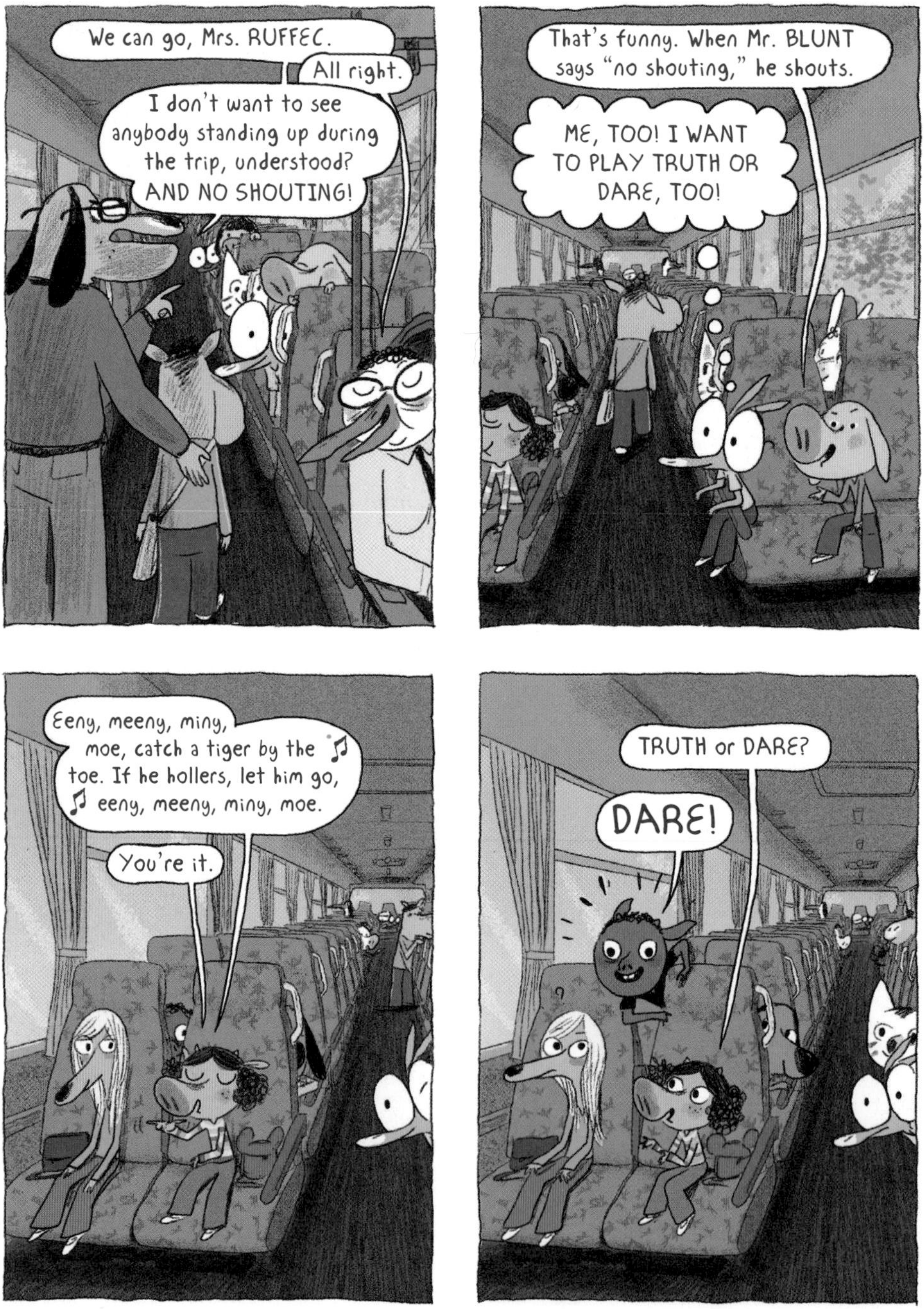
We can go, Mrs. RUFFEC.
All right.
I don't want to see anybody standing up during the trip, understood? AND NO SHOUTING!
That's funny. When Mr. BLUNT says "no shouting," he shouts.
ME, TOO! I WANT TO PLAY TRUTH OR DARE, TOO!
Eeny, meeny, miny, moe, catch a tiger by the toe. If he hollers, let him go, eeny, meeny, miny, moe.
You're it.
TRUTH or DARE?
DARE!

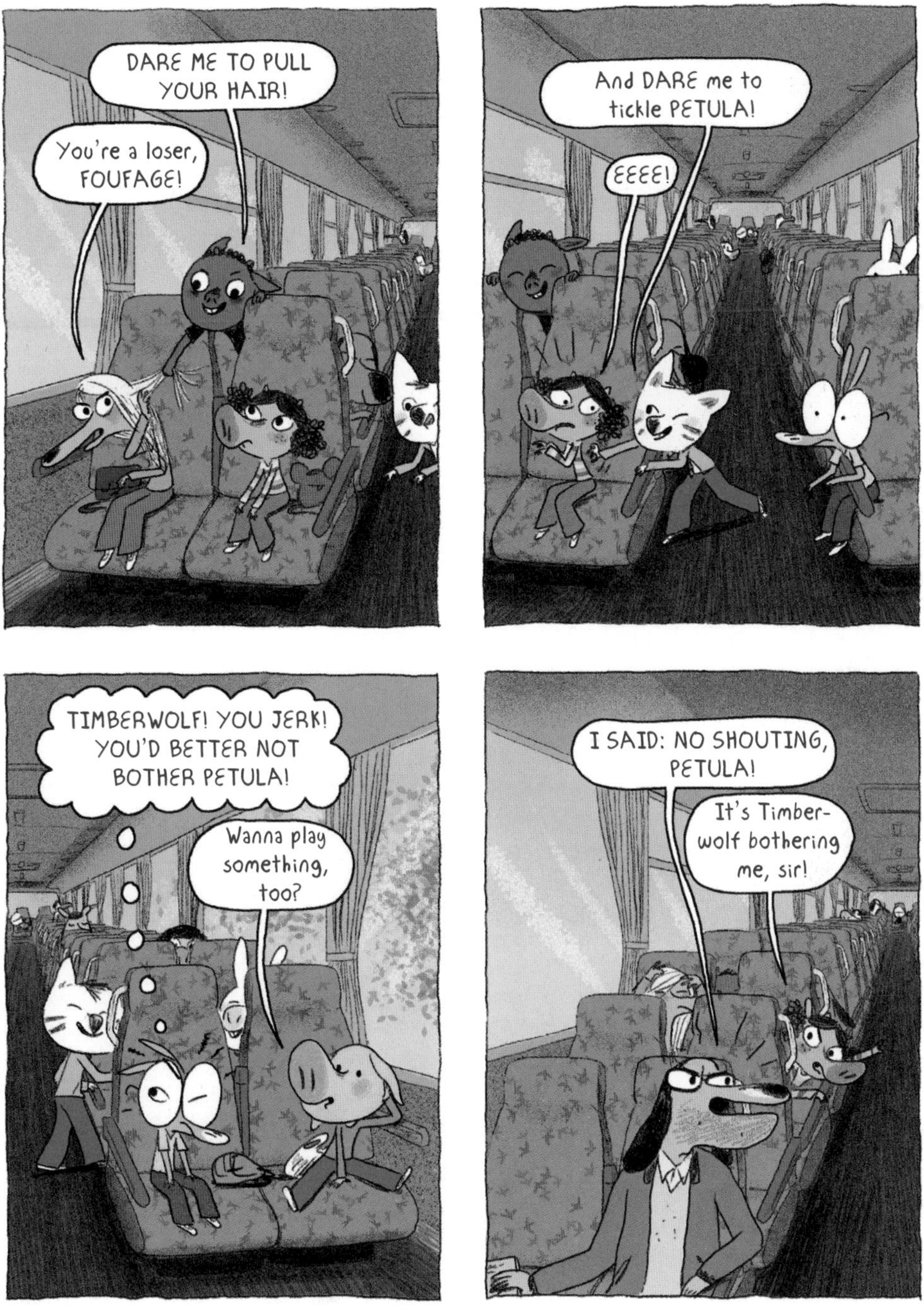
DARE ME TO PULL YOUR HAIR!
You're a loser, FOUFAGE!
And DARE me to tickle PETULA!
EEEE!
TIMBERWOLF! YOU JERK! YOU'D BETTER NOT BOTHER PETULA!
Wanna play something, too?
I SAID: NO SHOUTING, PETULA!
It's Timber-wolf bothering me, sir!

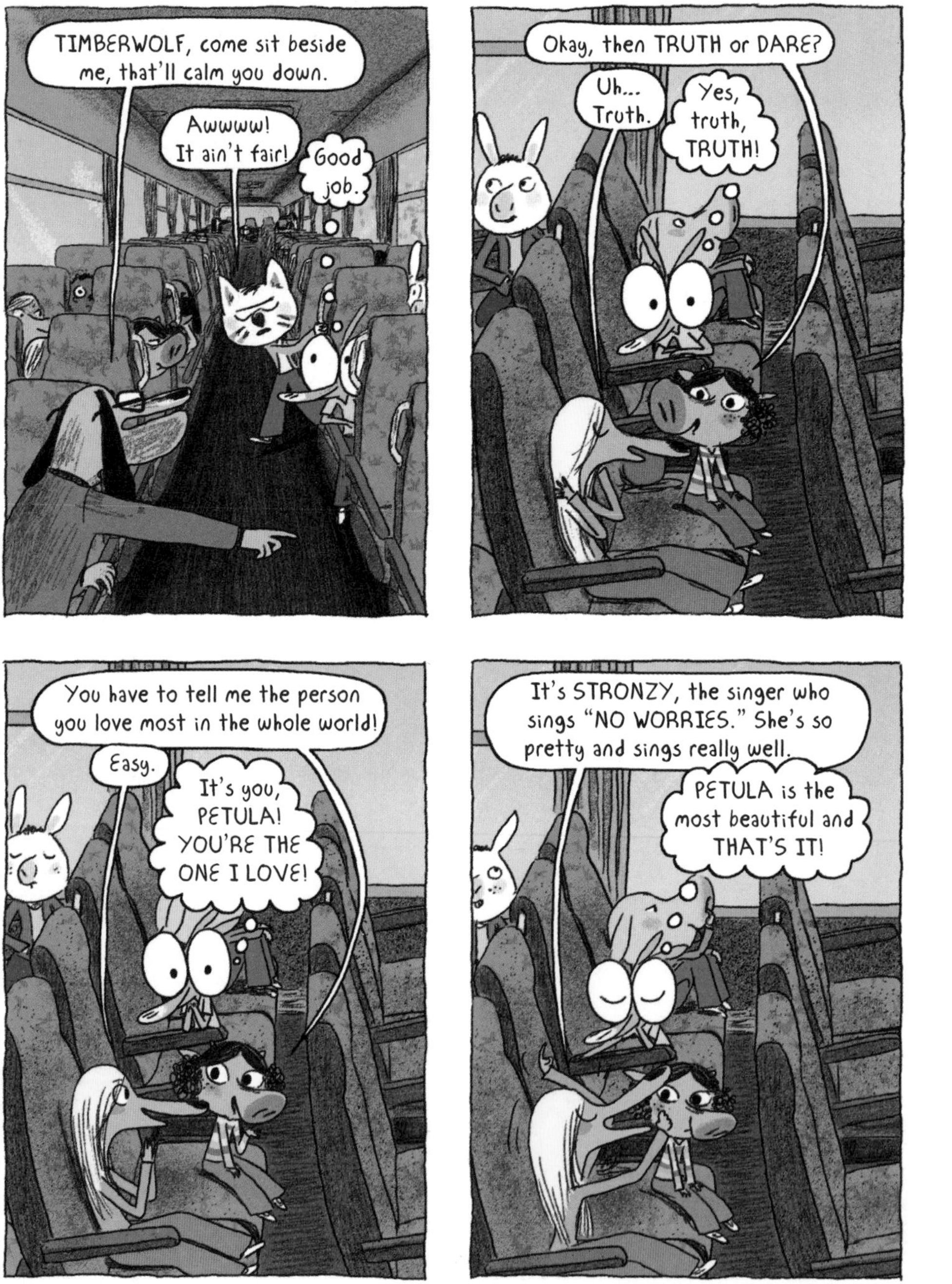
TIMBERWOLF, come sit beside me, that'll calm you down.
Awwww! It ain't fair!
Good job.
Okay, then TRUTH or DARE?
Uh... Truth.
Yes, truth, TRUTH!
You have to tell me the person you love most in the whole world!
Easy.
It's you, PETULA! YOU'RE THE ONE I LOVE!
It's STRONZY, the singer who sings "NO WORRIES." She's so pretty and sings really well.
PETULA is the most beautiful and THAT'S IT!

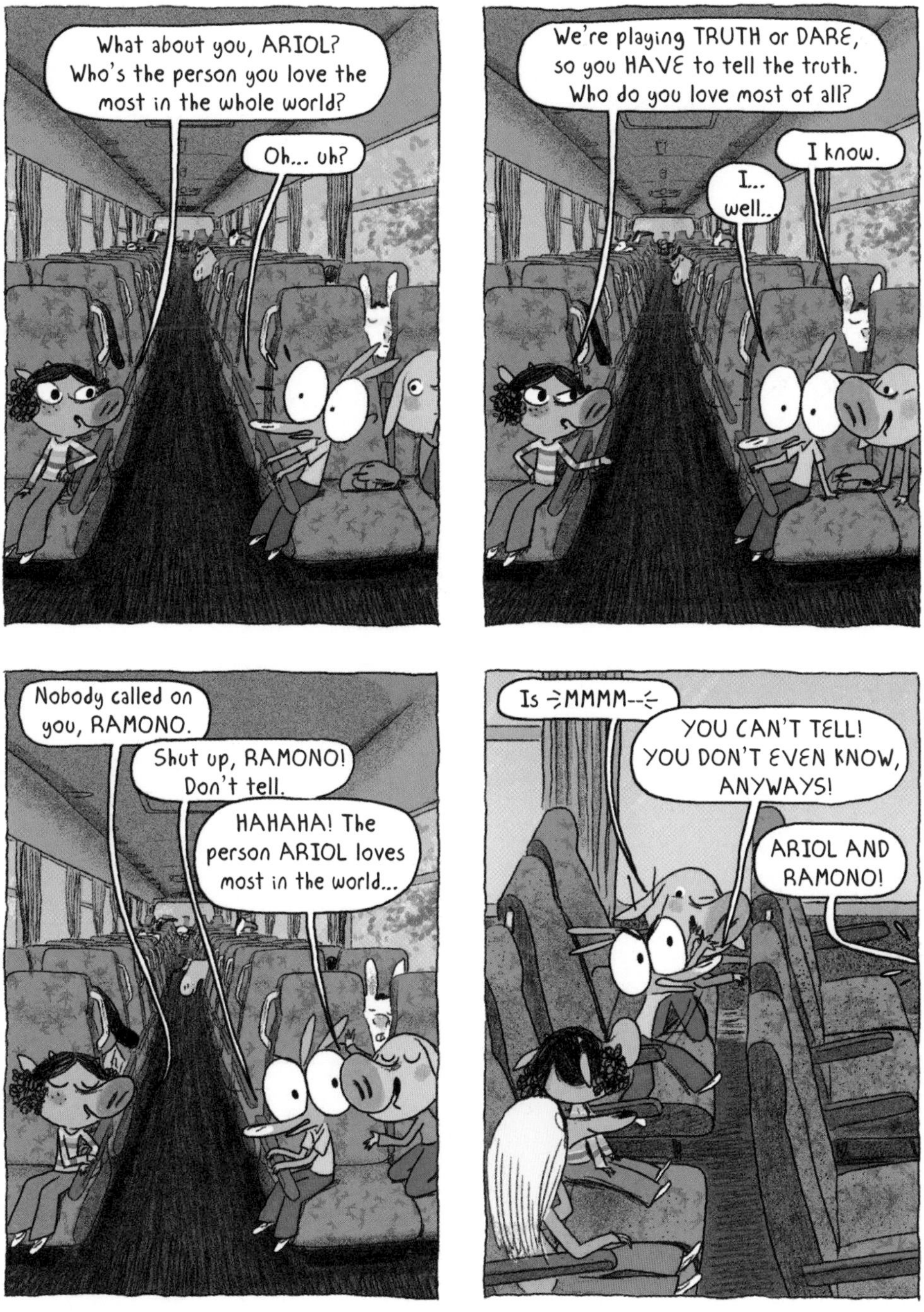
What about you, ARIOL? Who's the person you love the most in the whole world?
Oh... uh?
We're playing TRUTH or DARE, so you HAVE to tell the truth. Who do you love most of all?
I... well...
I know.
Nobody called on you, RAMONO.
Shut up, RAMONO! Don't tell.
HAHAHA! The person ARIOL loves most in the world...
Is MMMM--
YOU CAN'T TELL! YOU DON'T EVEN KNOW, ANYWAYS!
ARIOL AND RAMONO!

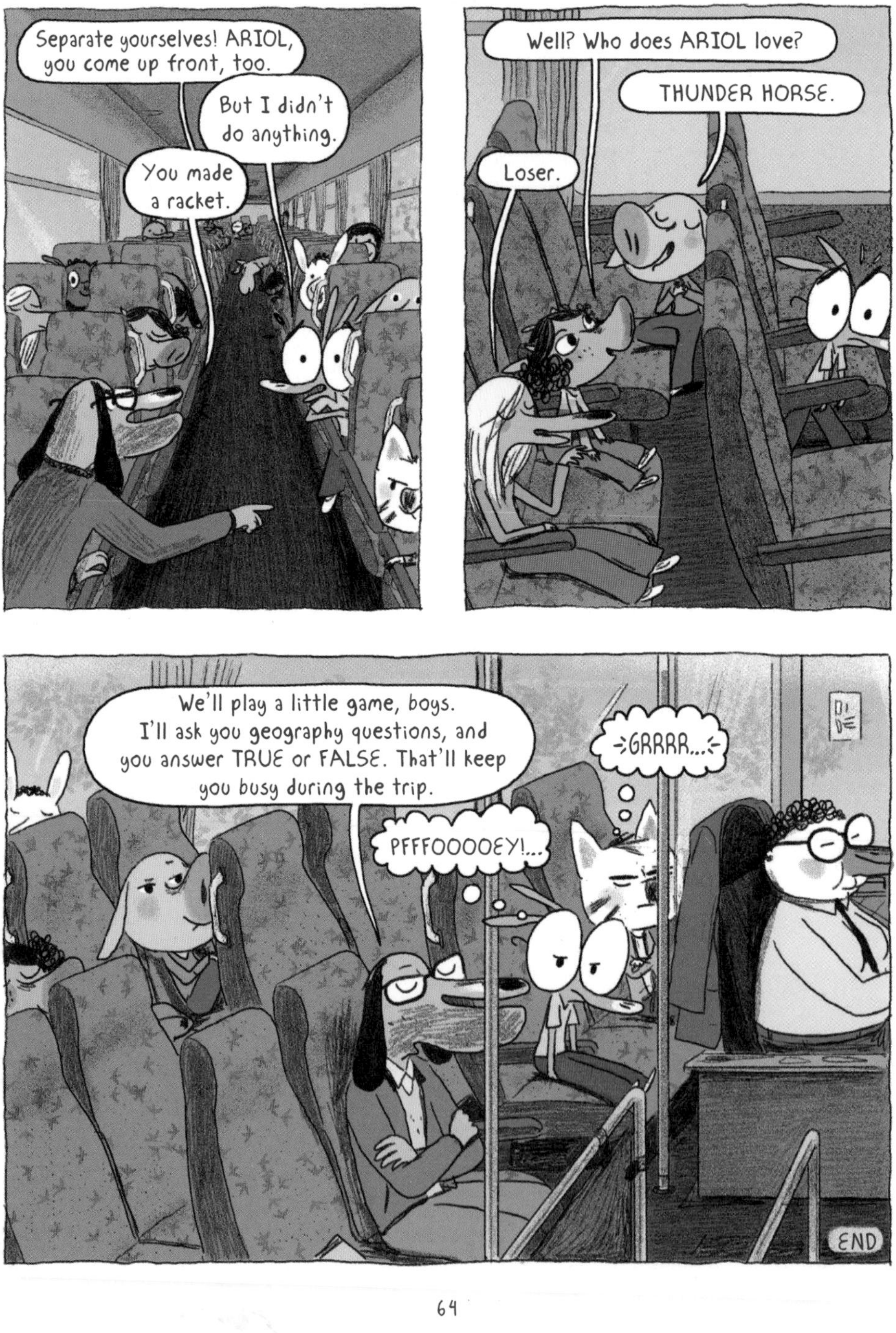
Separate yourselves! ARIOL, you come up front, too.
But I didn't do anything.
You made a racket.
Well? Who does ARIOL love?
THUNDER HORSE.
Loser.
We'll play a little game, boys. I'll ask you geography questions, and you answer TRUE or FALSE. That'll keep you busy during the trip.
GRRRR...
PFFFOOOOEY!...
END

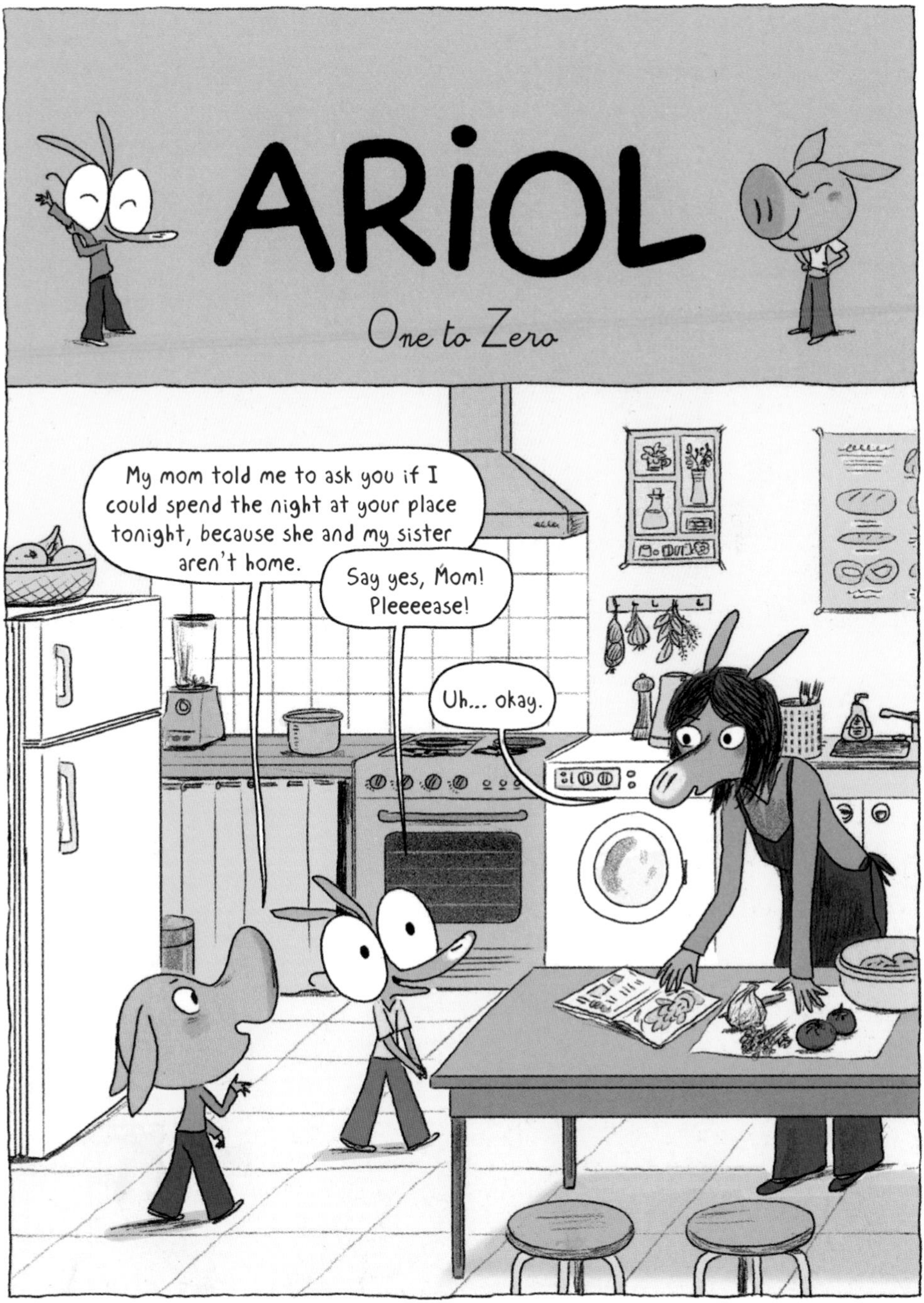
ARIOL
One to Zero
My mom told me to ask you if I could spend the night at your place tonight, because she and my sister aren't home.
Say yes, Mom! Pleeeease!
Uh... okay.

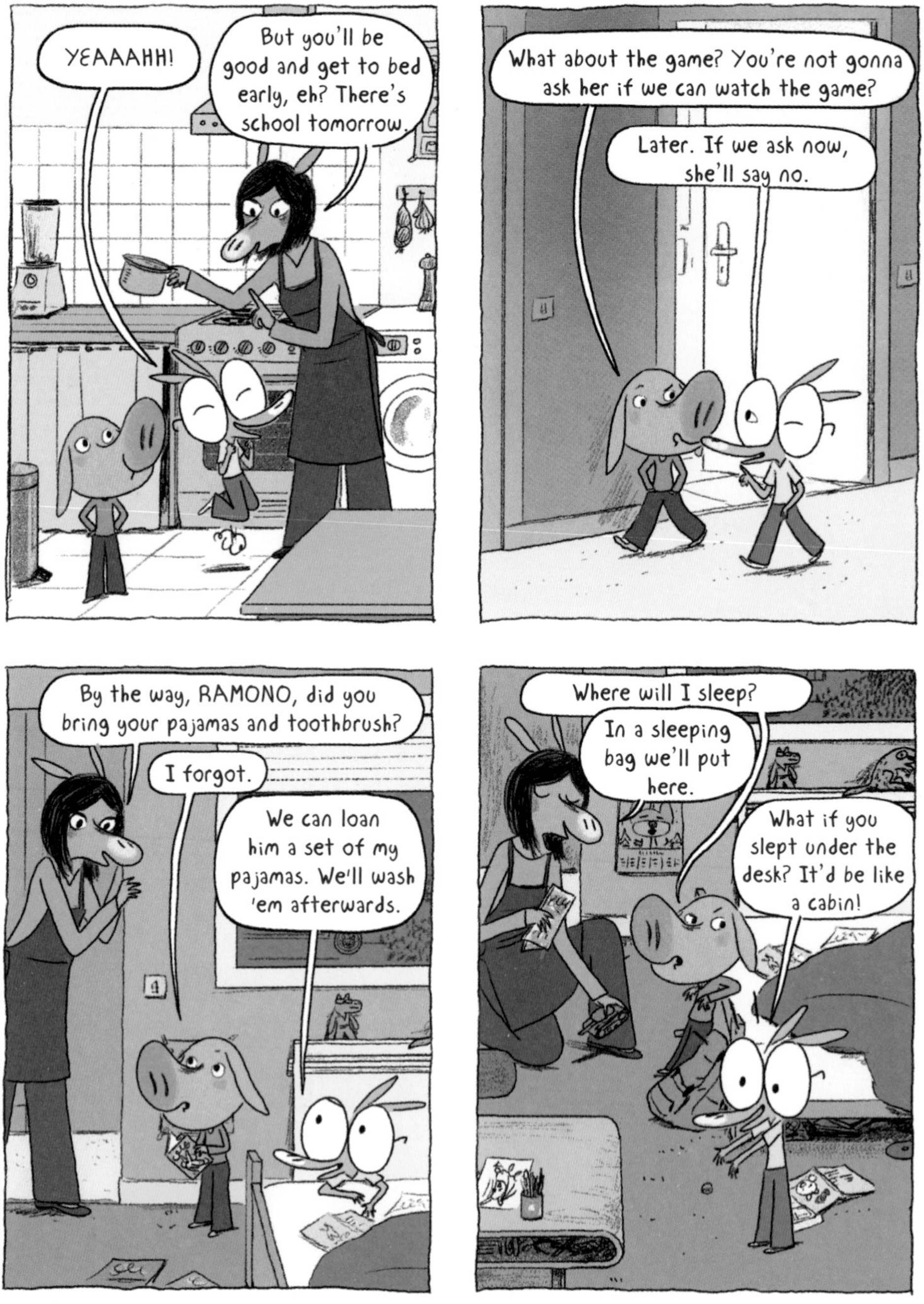
YEAAAHH!
But you'll be good and get to bed early, eh? There's school tomorrow.
What about the game? You're not gonna ask her if we can watch the game?
Later. If we ask now, she'll say no.
By the way, RAMONO, did you bring your pajamas and toothbrush?
I forgot.
We can loan him a set of my pajamas. We'll wash 'em afterwards.
Where will I sleep?
In a sleeping bag we'll put here.
What if you slept under the desk? It'd be like a cabin!

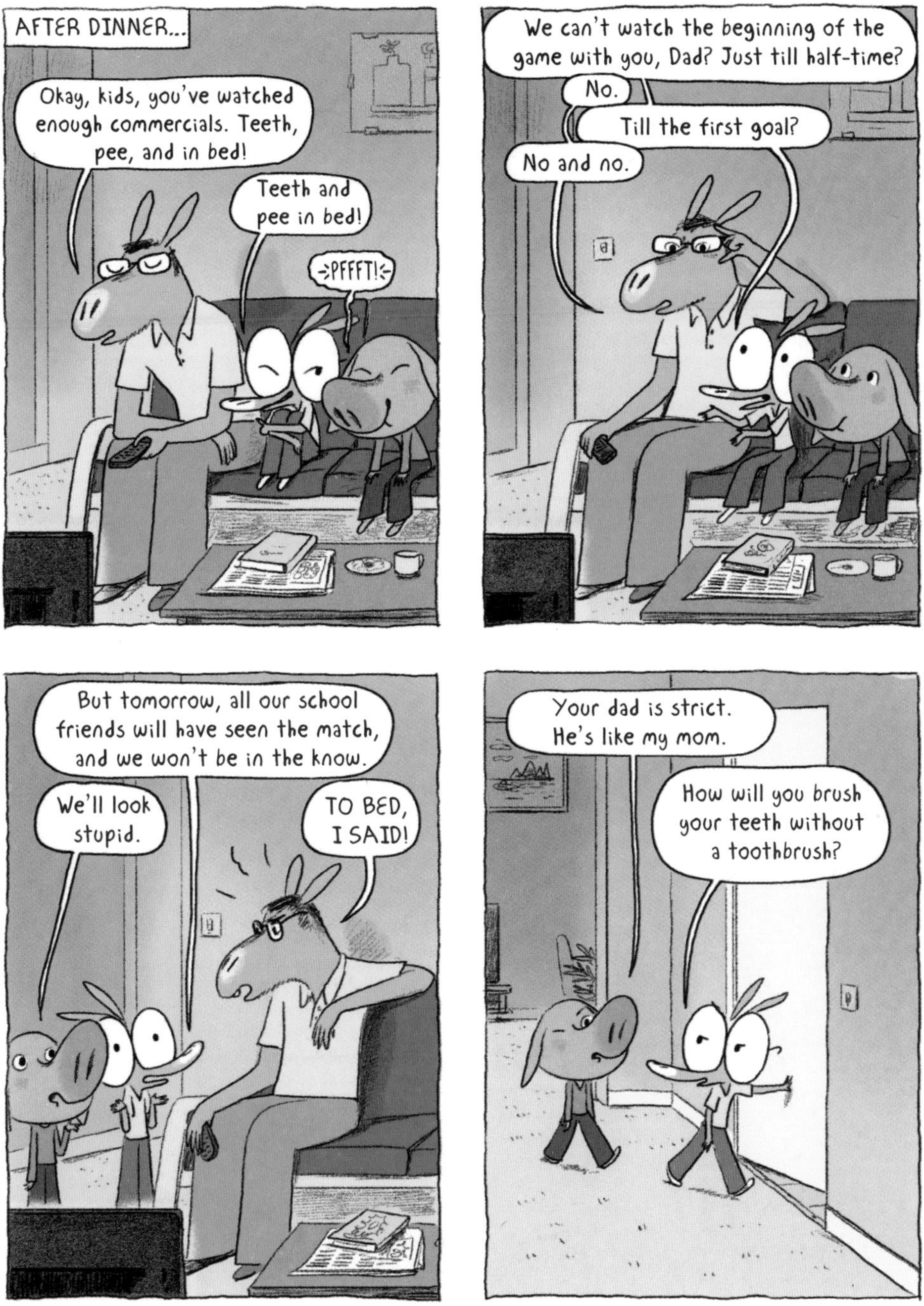
AFTER DINNER...
Okay, kids, you've watched enough commercials. Teeth, pee, and in bed!
Teeth and pee in bed!
PFFFT!
We can't watch the beginning of the game with you, Dad? Just till half-time?
No.
Till the first goal?
No and no.
But tomorrow, all our school friends will have seen the match, and we won't be in the know.
We'll look stupid.
TO BED, I SAID!
Your dad is strict. He's like my mom.
How will you brush your teeth without a toothbrush?

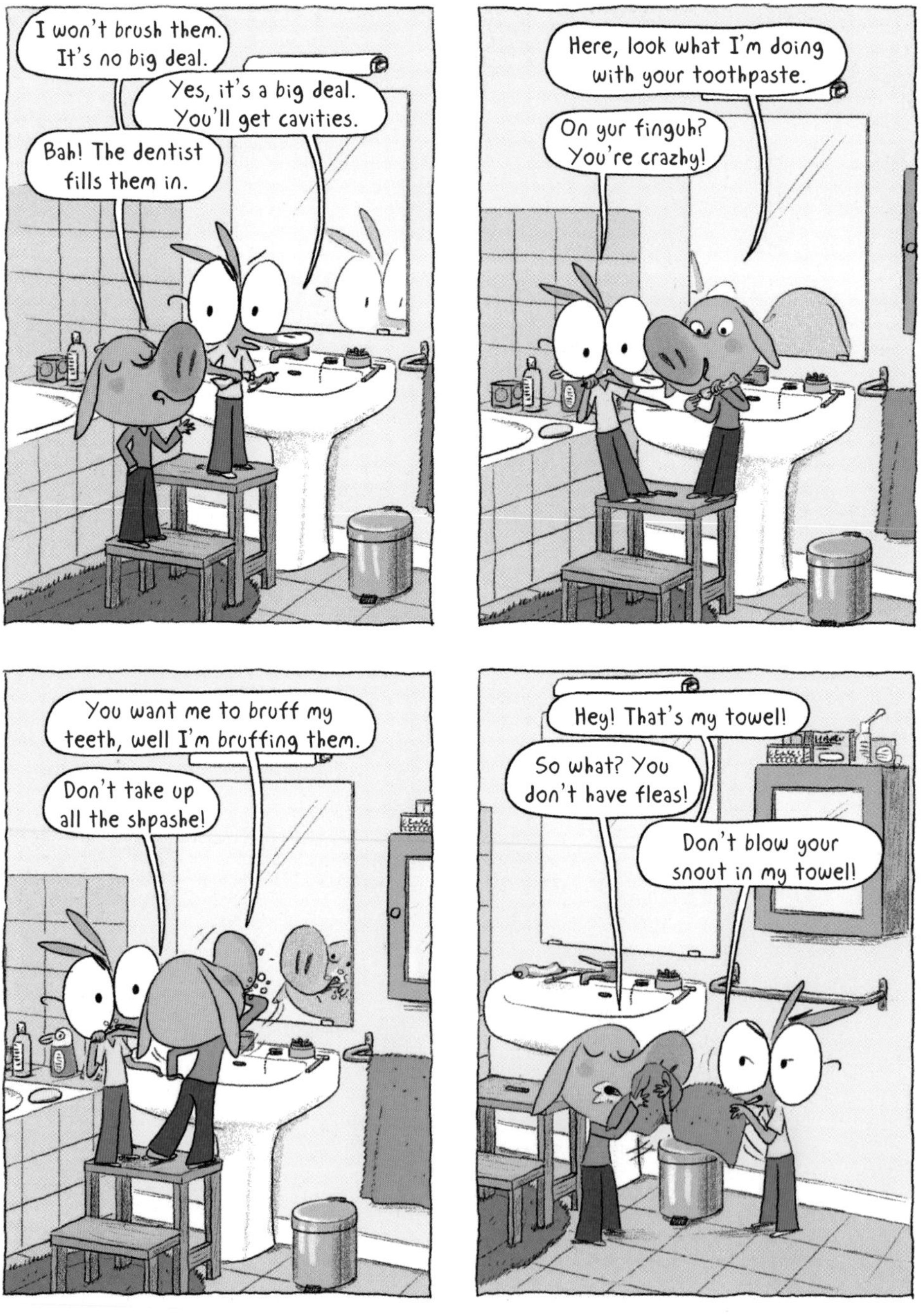
I won't brush them. It's no big deal.
Yes, it's a big deal. You'll get cavities.
Bah! The dentist fills them in.
Here, look what I'm doing with your toothpaste.
On yur finguh? You're crazhy!
You want me to bruff my teeth, well I'm bruffing them.
Don't take up all the shpashe!
Hey! That's my towel!
So what? You don't have fleas!
Don't blow your snout in my towel!

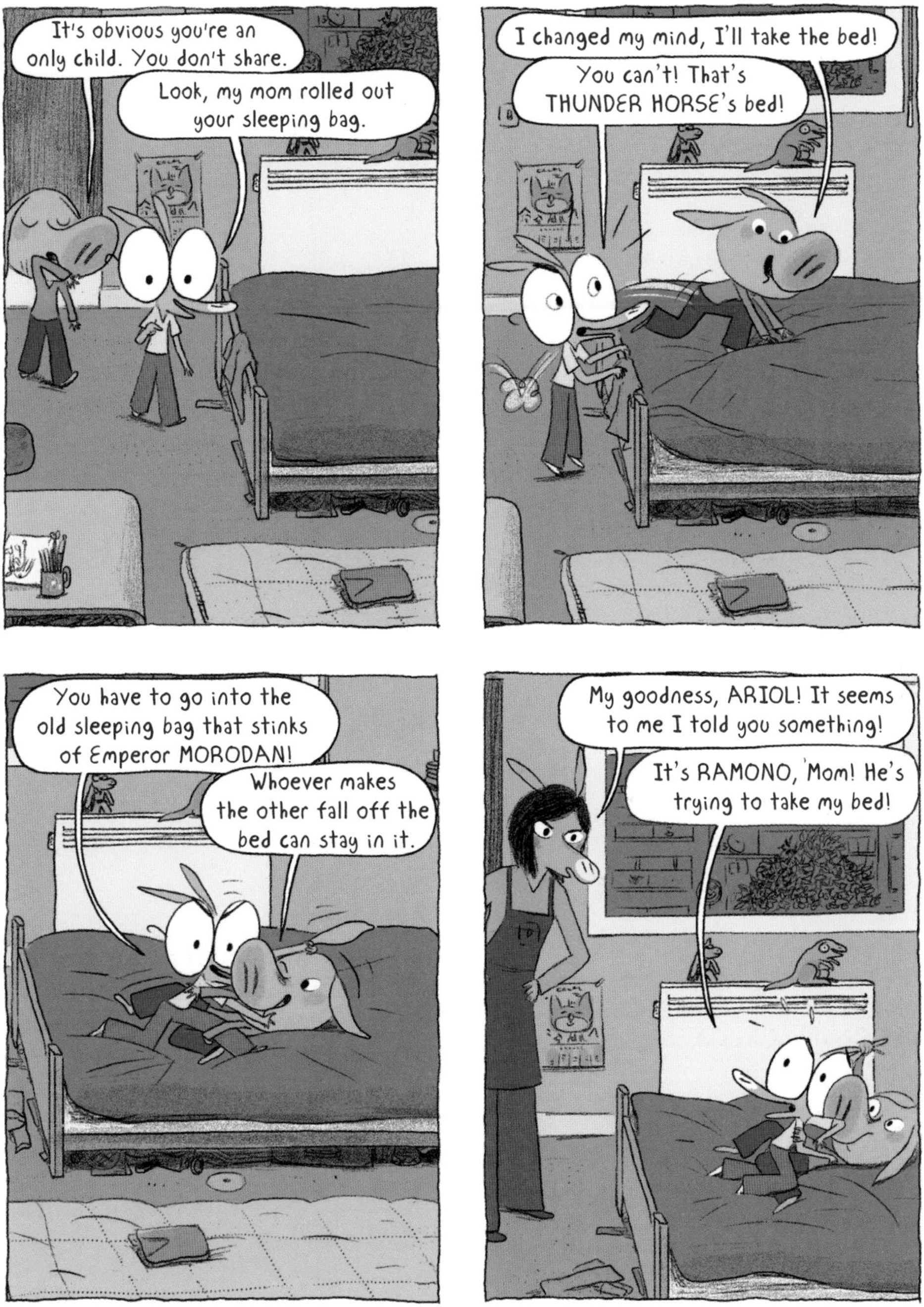
It's obvious you're an only child. You don't share.
Look, my mom rolled out your sleeping bag.
I changed my mind, I'll take the bed!
You can't! That's THUNDER HORSE's bed!
You have to go into the old sleeping bag that stinks of Emperor MORODAN!
Whoever makes the other fall off the bed can stay in it.
My goodness, ARIOL! It seems to me I told you something!
It's RAMONO, Mom! He's trying to take my bed!

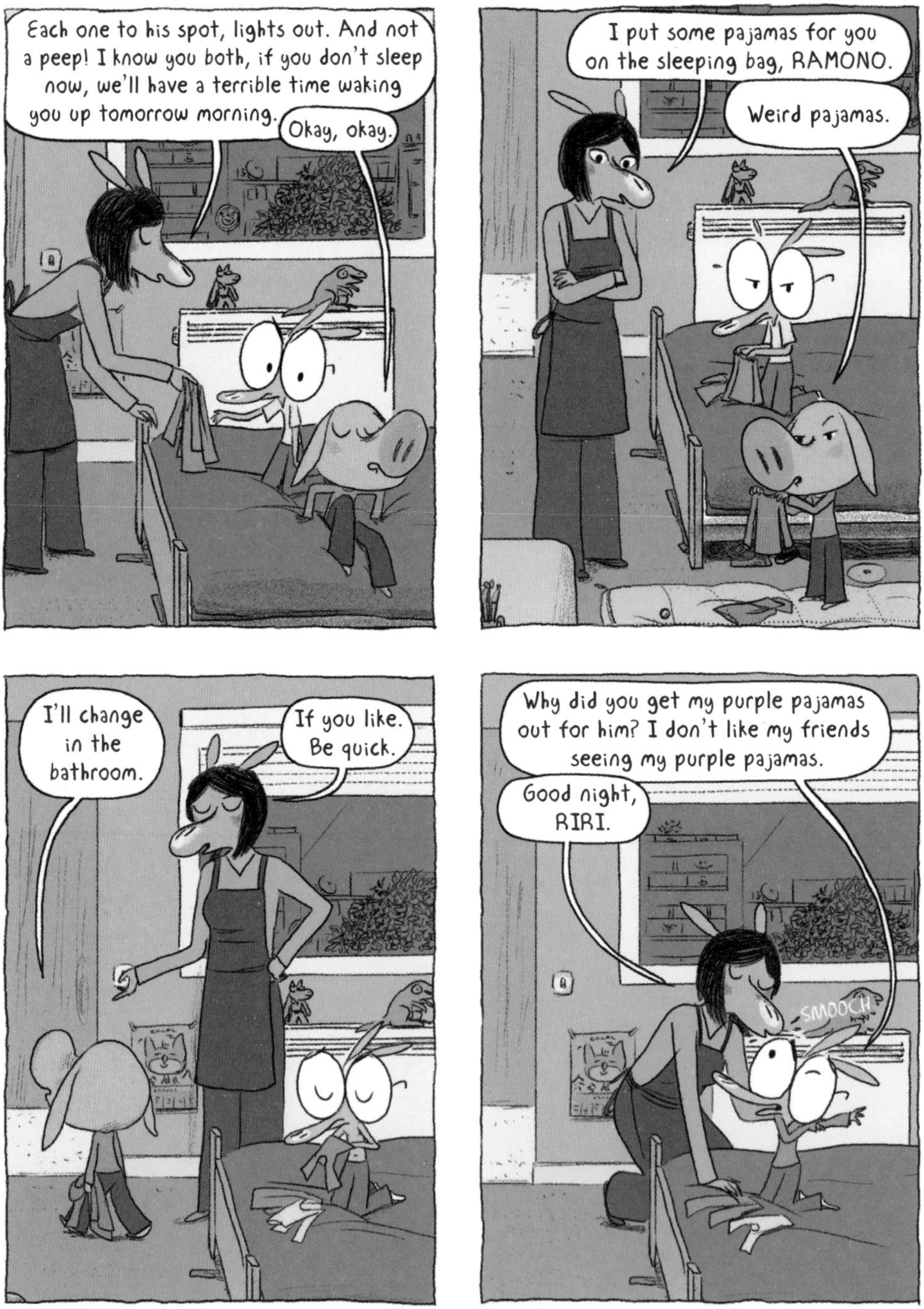
Each one to his spot, lights out. And not a peep! I know you both, if you don't sleep now, we'll have a terrible time waking you up tomorrow morning.
Okay, okay.
I put some pajamas for you on the sleeping bag, RAMONO.
Weird pajamas.
I'll change in the bathroom.
If you like. Be quick.
Why did you get my purple pajamas out for him? I don't like my friends seeing my purple pajamas.
Good night, RIRI.
SMOOCH

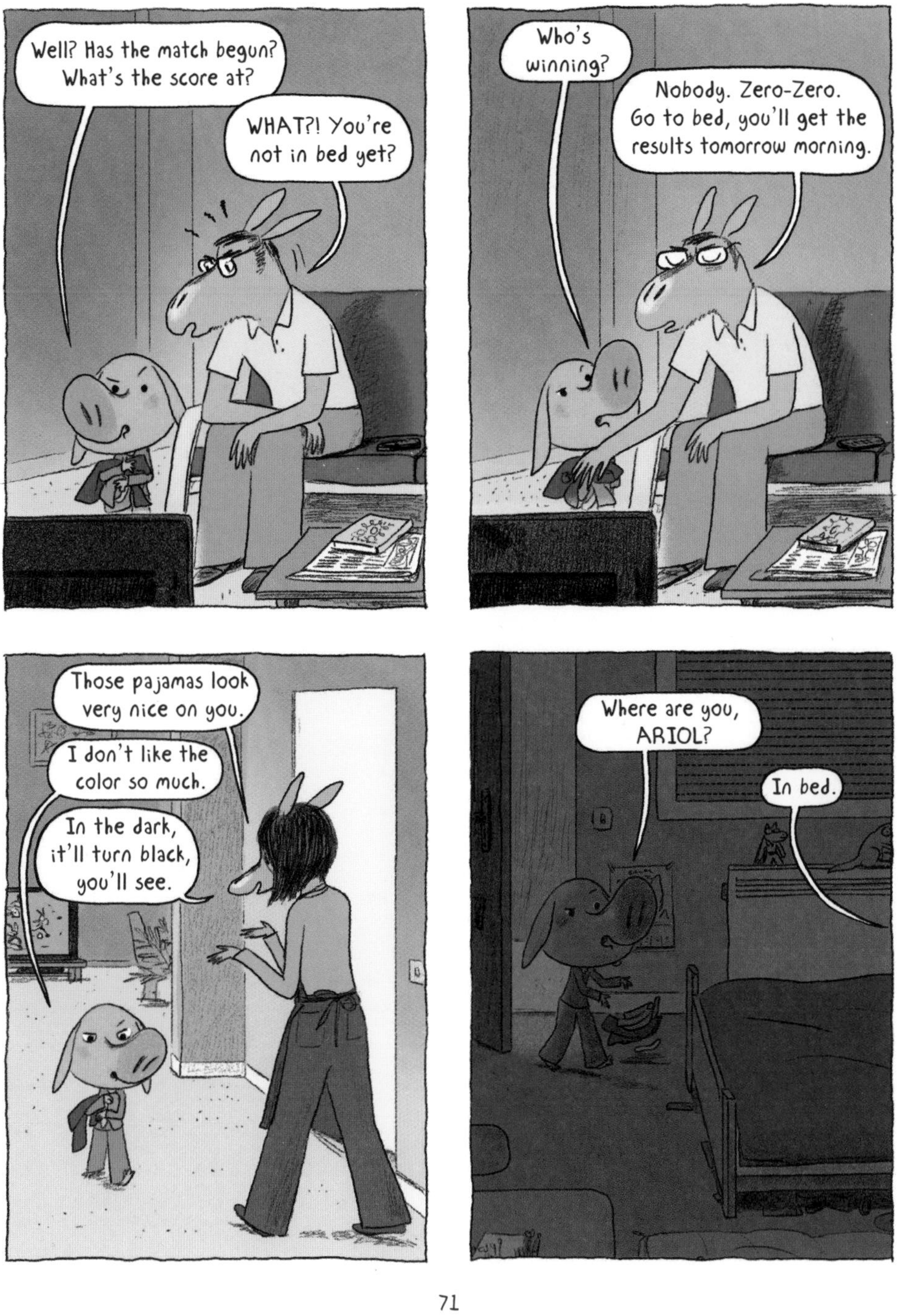
Well? Has the match begun? What's the score at?
WHAT?! You're not in bed yet?
Who's winning?
Nobody. Zero-Zero. Go to bed, you'll get the results tomorrow morning.
Those pajamas look very nice on you.
I don't like the color so much.
In the dark, it'll turn black, you'll see.
Where are you, ARIOL?
In bed.

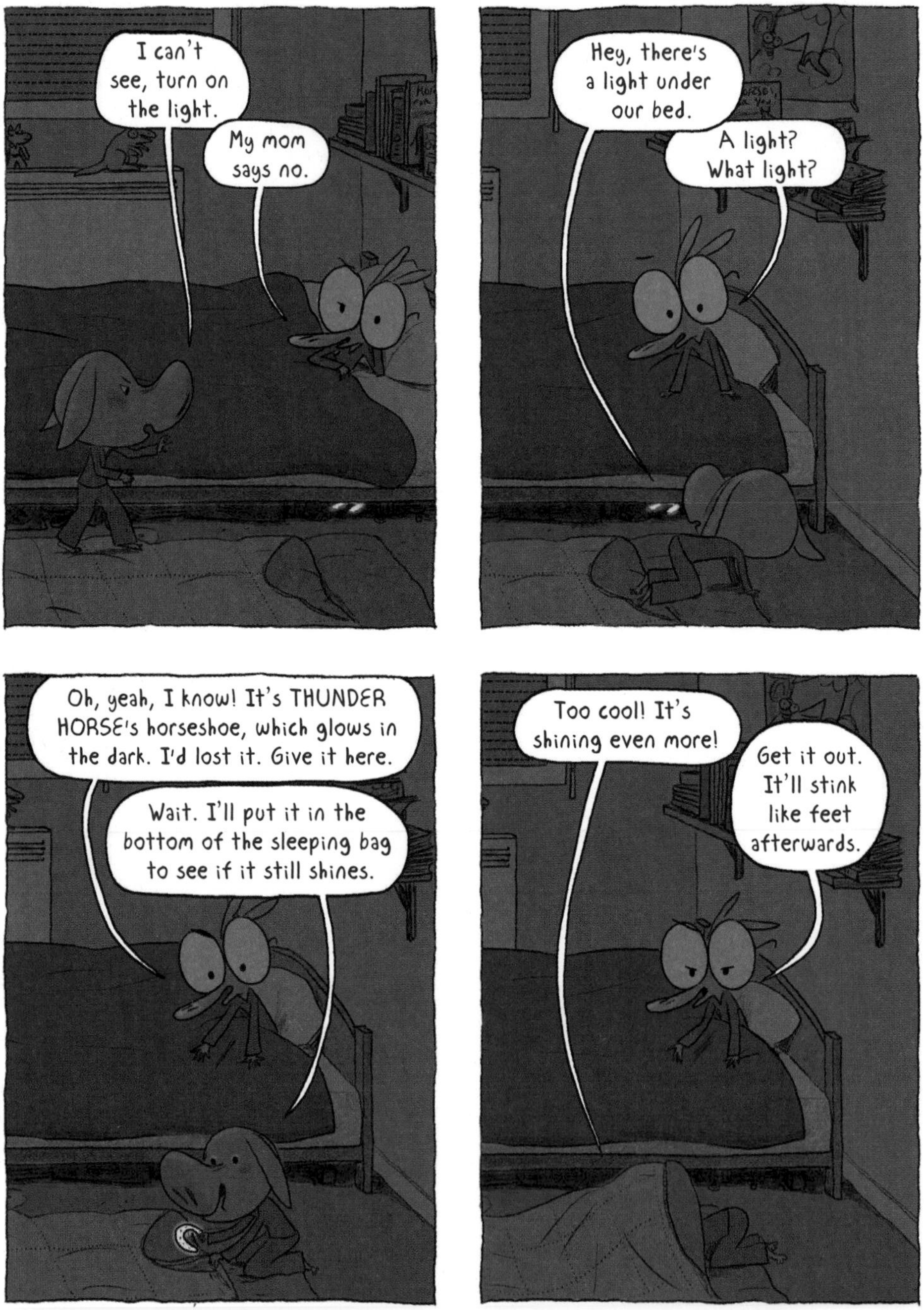
I can't see, turn on the light.
My mom says no.
Hey, there's a light under our bed.
A light? What light?
Oh, yeah, I know! It's THUNDER HORSE's horseshoe, which glows in the dark. I'd lost it. Give it here.
Wait. I'll put it in the bottom of the sleeping bag to see if it still shines.
Too cool! It's shining even more!
Get it out. It'll stink like feet afterwards.

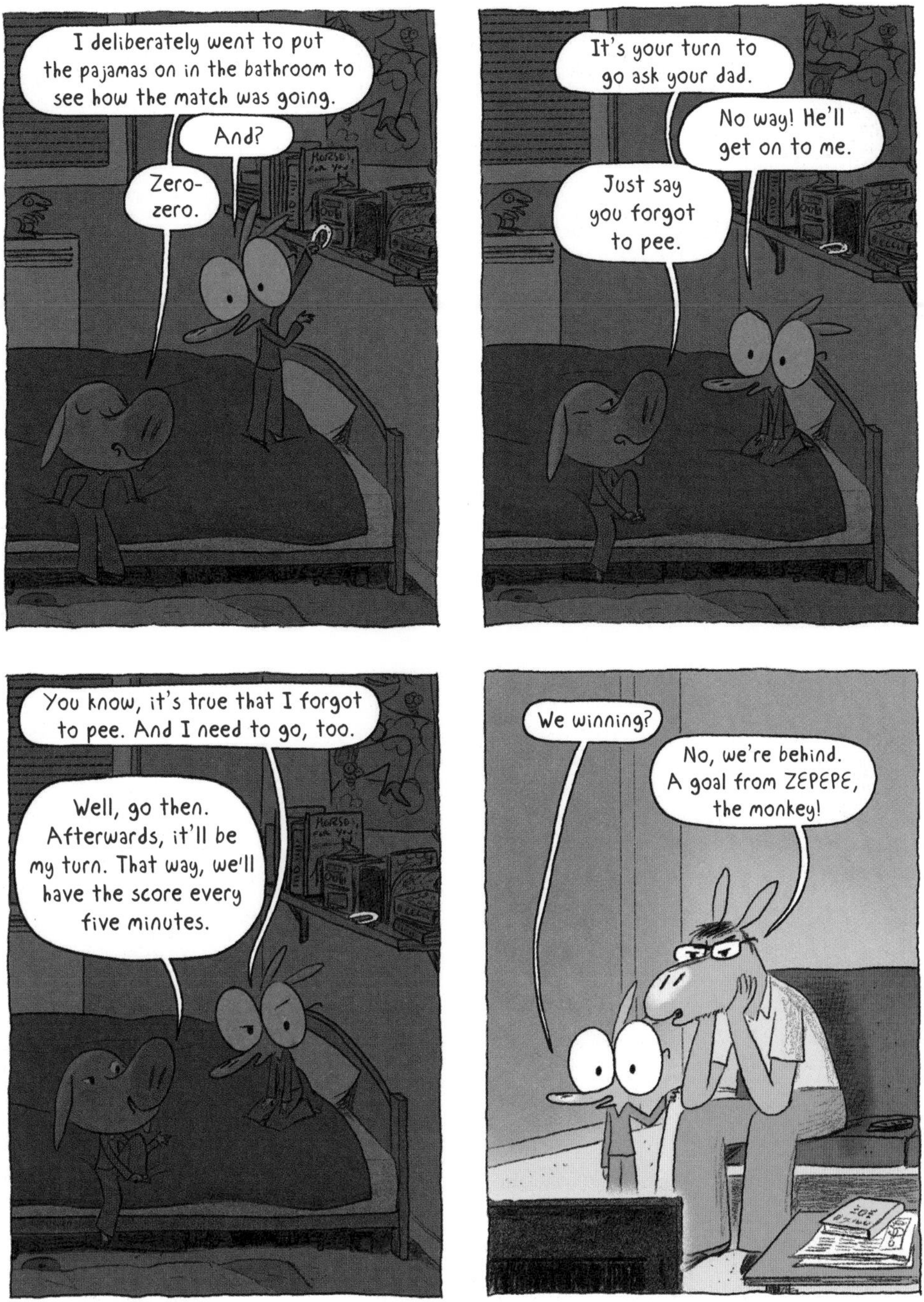
I deliberately went to put the pajamas on in the bathroom to see how the match was going.
And?
Zero-zero.
It's your turn to go ask your dad.
No way! He'll get on to me.
Just say you forgot to pee.
You know, it's true that I forgot to pee. And I need to go, too.
Well, go then. Afterwards, it'll be my turn. That way, we'll have the score every five minutes.
We winning?
No, we're behind. A goal from ZEPEPE, the monkey!

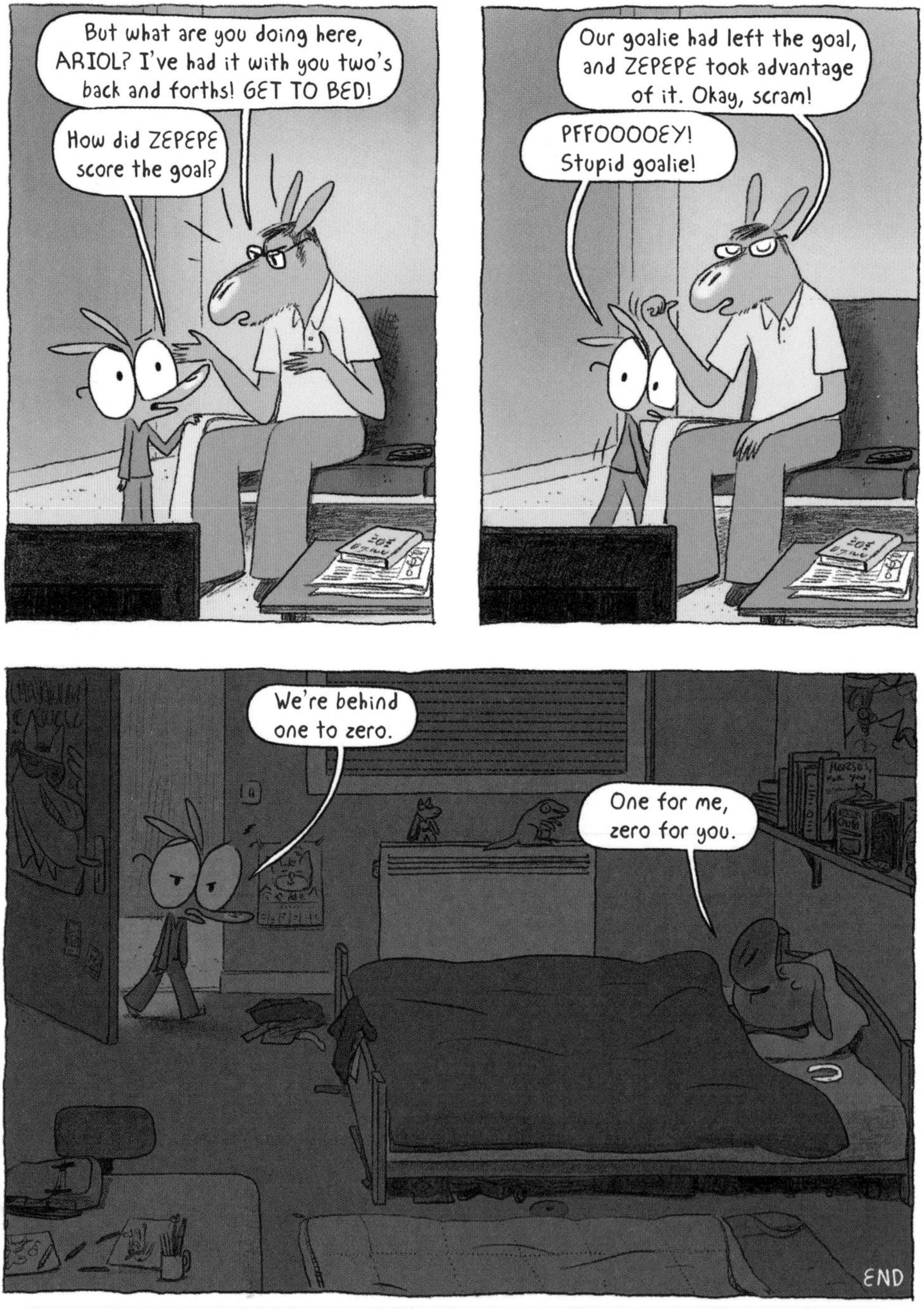
How did ZEPEPE score the goal?
But what are you doing here, ARIOL? I've had it with you two's back and forths! GET TO BED!
PFFOOOOEY! Stupid goalie!
Our goalie had left the goal, and ZEPEPE took advantage of it. Okay, scram!
We're behind one to zero.
One for me, zero for you.
END

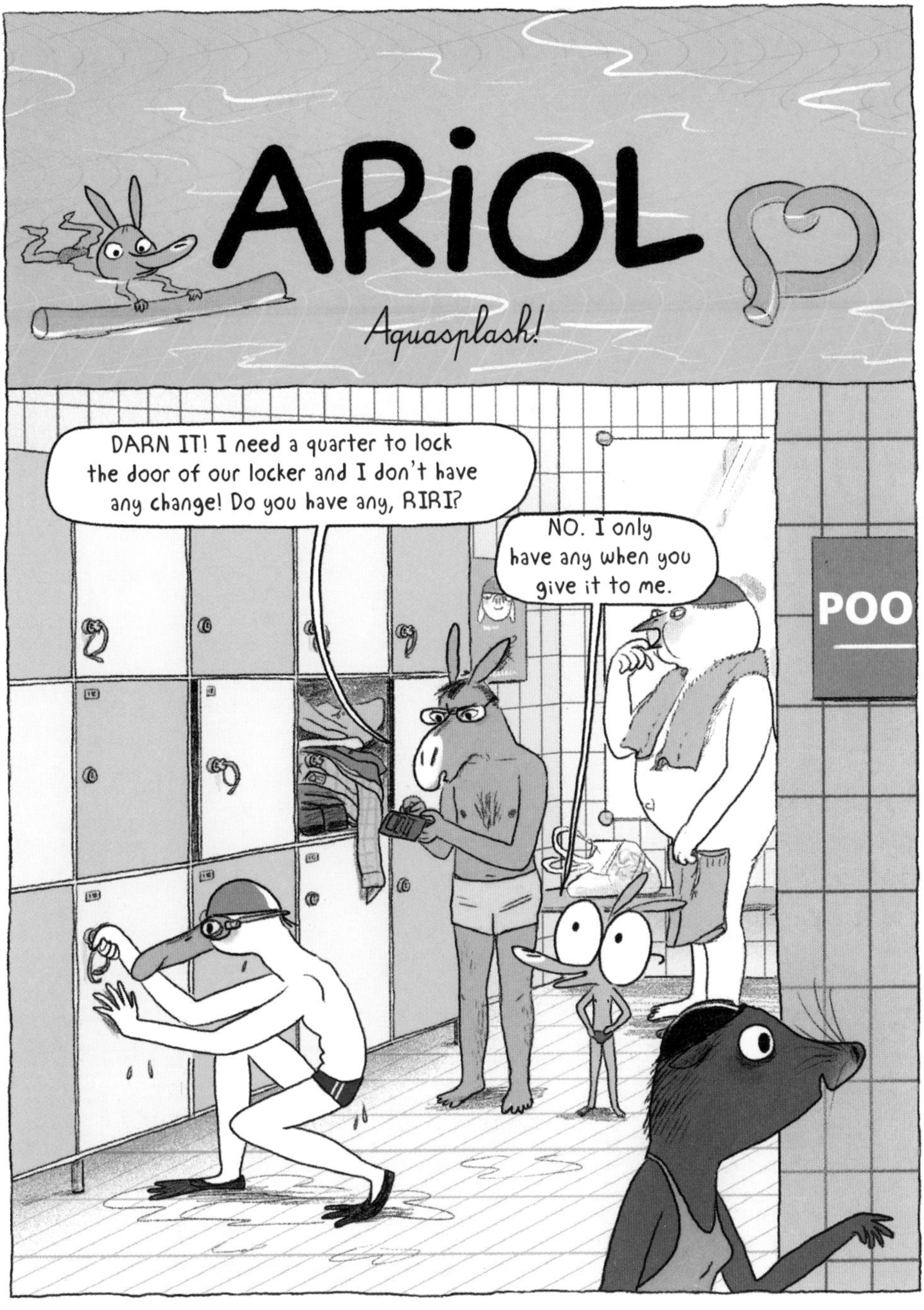
ARiOL
Aquasplash!
DARN IT! I need a quarter to lock the door of our locker and I don't have any change! Do you have any, RIRI?
NO. I only have any when you give it to me.
POO

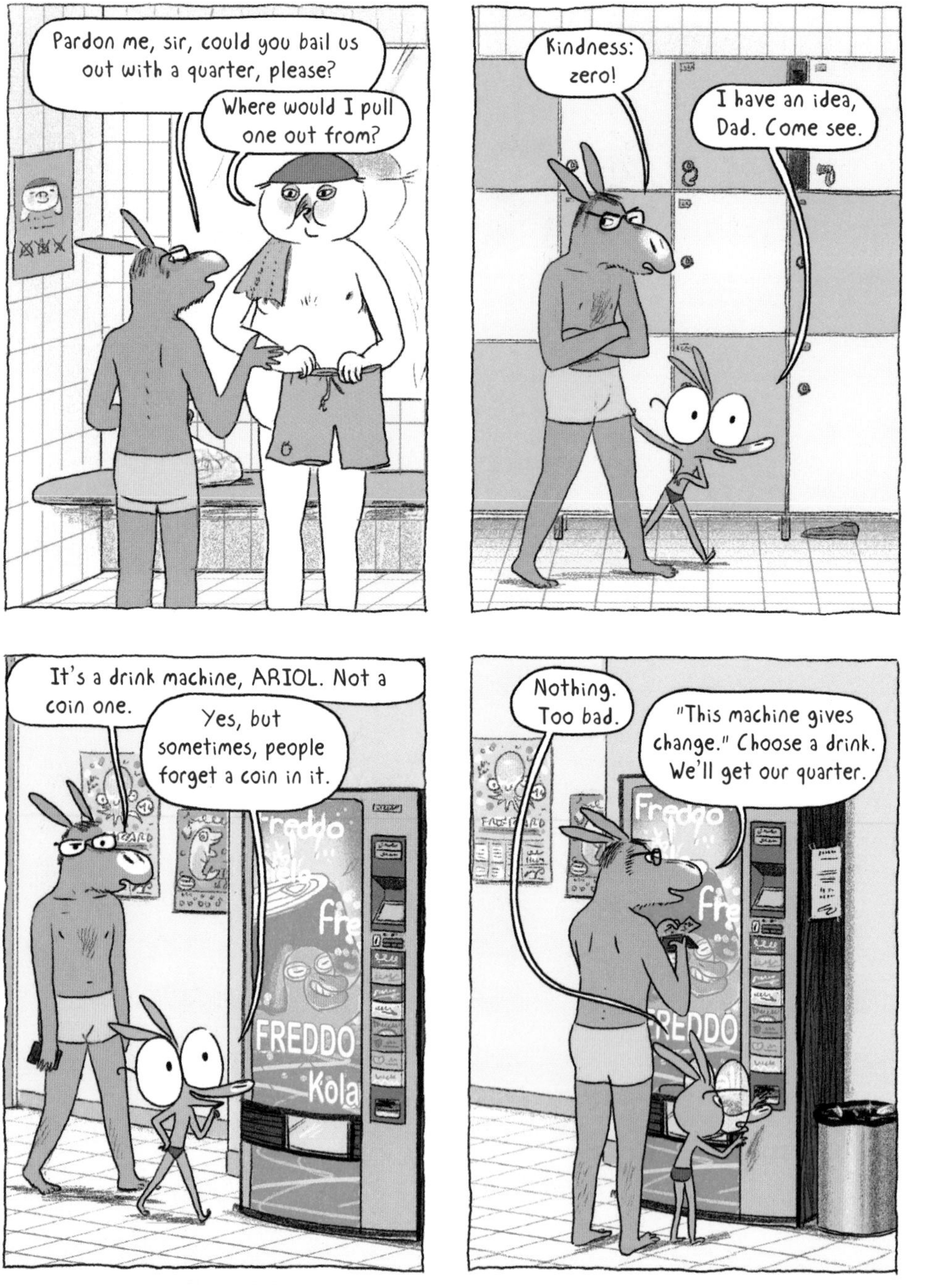
Pardon me, sir, could you bail us out with a quarter, please?
Where would I pull one out from?
Kindness: zero!
I have an idea, Dad. Come see.
It's a drink machine, ARIOL. Not a coin one.
Yes, but sometimes, people forget a coin in it.
FREDDO
Kola
Nothing. Too bad.
"This machine gives change." Choose a drink. We'll get our quarter.
FREDDO

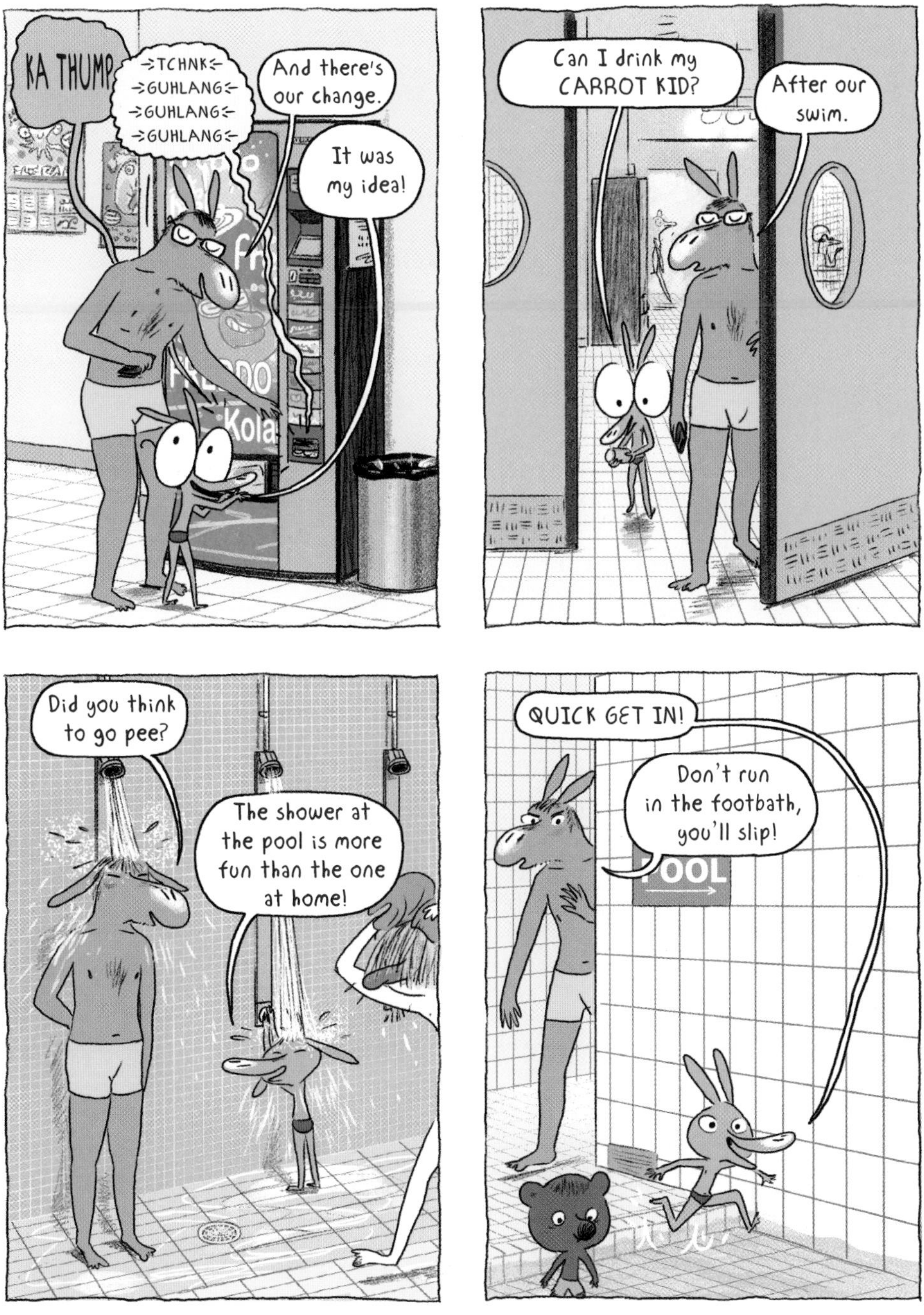
KA THUMP
TCHNK GUHLANG GUHLANG GUHLANG
And there's our change.
It was my idea!
Can I drink my CARROT KID?
After our swim.
Did you think to go pee?
The shower at the pool is more fun than the one at home!
QUICK GET IN!
Don't run in the footbath, you'll slip!
POOL

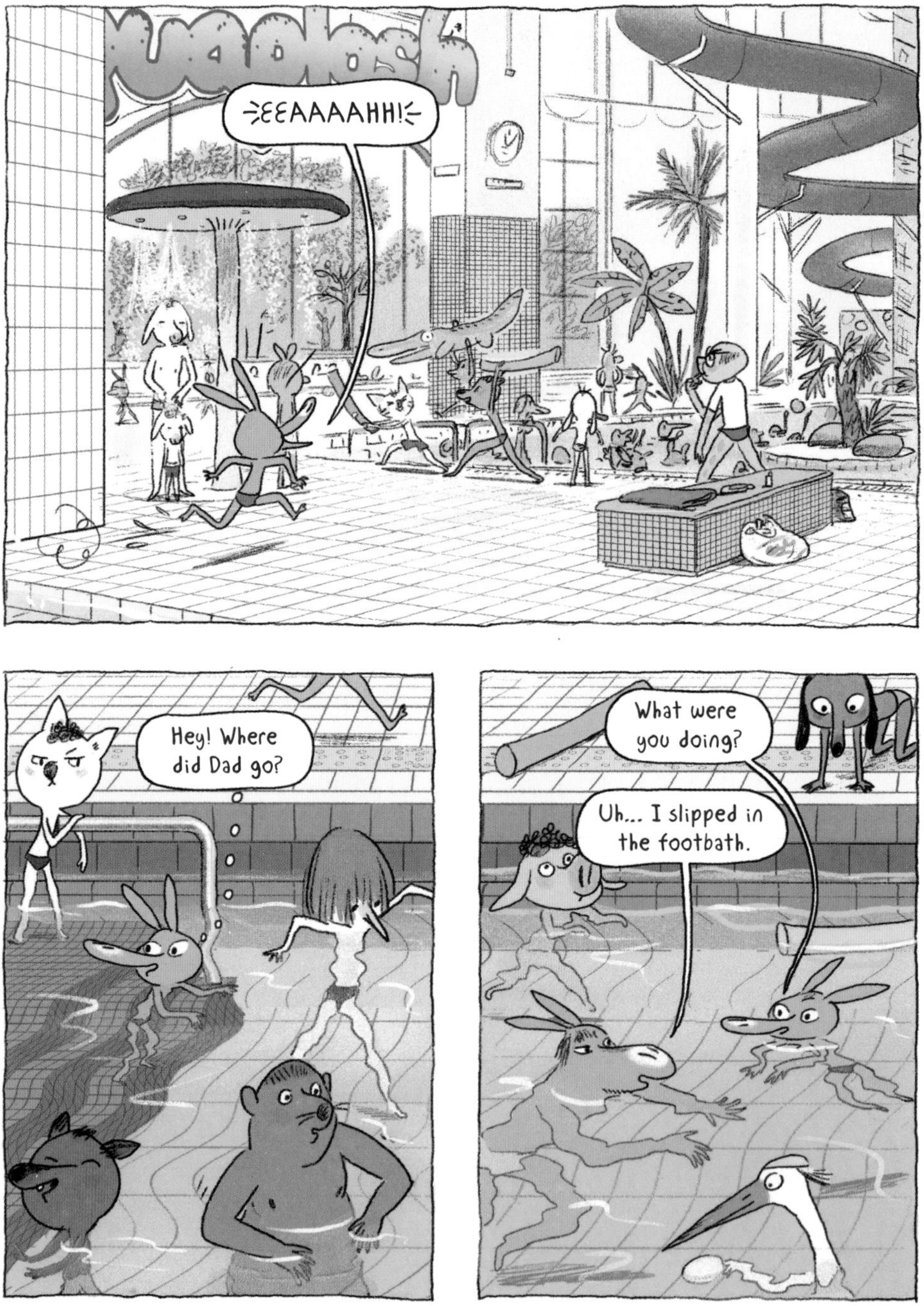

EEAAAAAHH!
Hey! Where did Dad go?
What were you doing?
Uh... I slipped in the footbath.

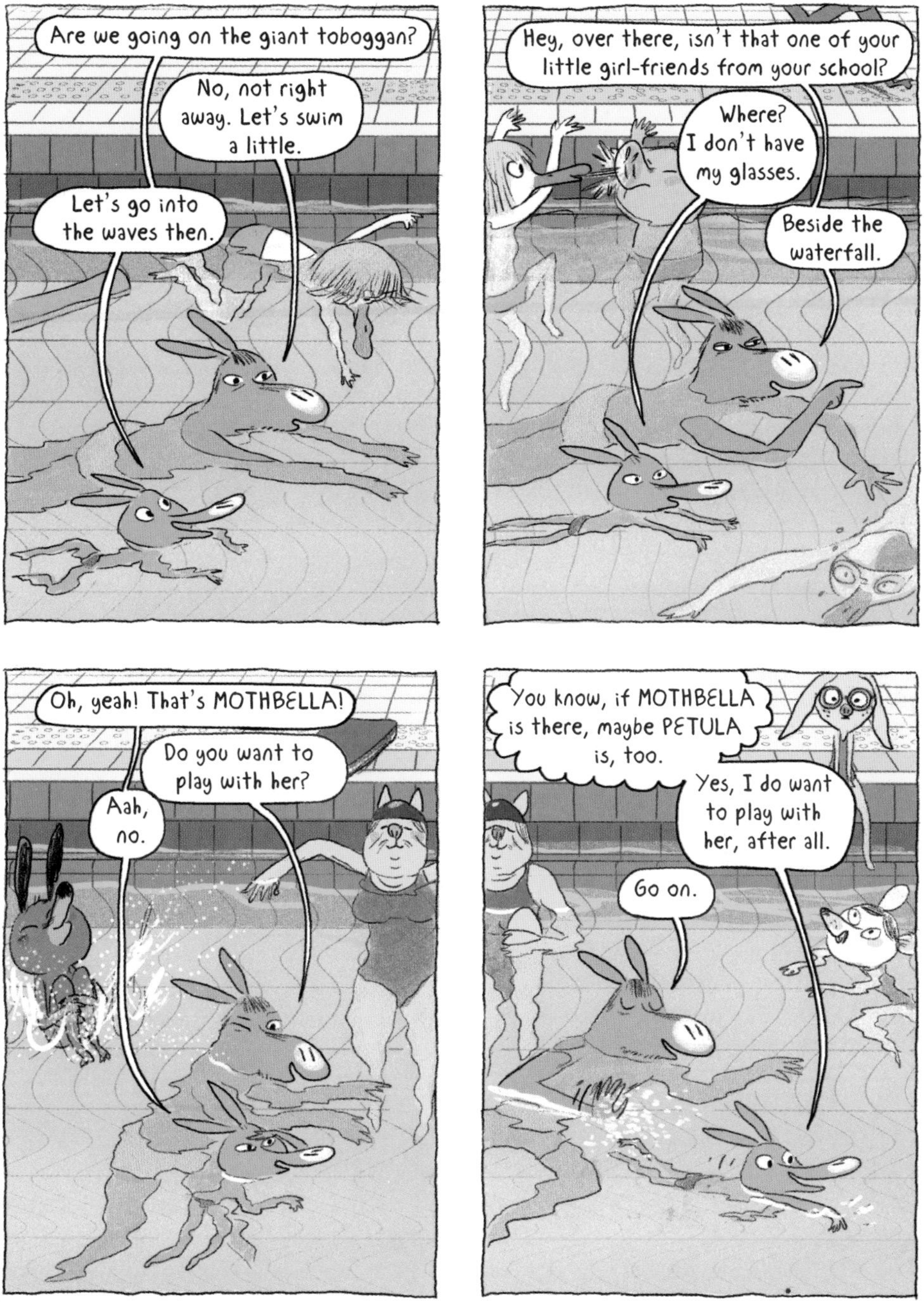
Are we going on the giant toboggan?
No, not right away. Let's swim a little.
Let's go into the waves then.
Hey, over there, isn't that one of your little girl-friends from your school?
Where? I don't have my glasses.
Beside the waterfall.
Oh, yeah! That's MOTHBELLA!
Do you want to play with her?
Aah, no.
You know, if MOTHBELLA is there, maybe PETULA is, too.
Yes, I do want to play with her, after all.
Go on.

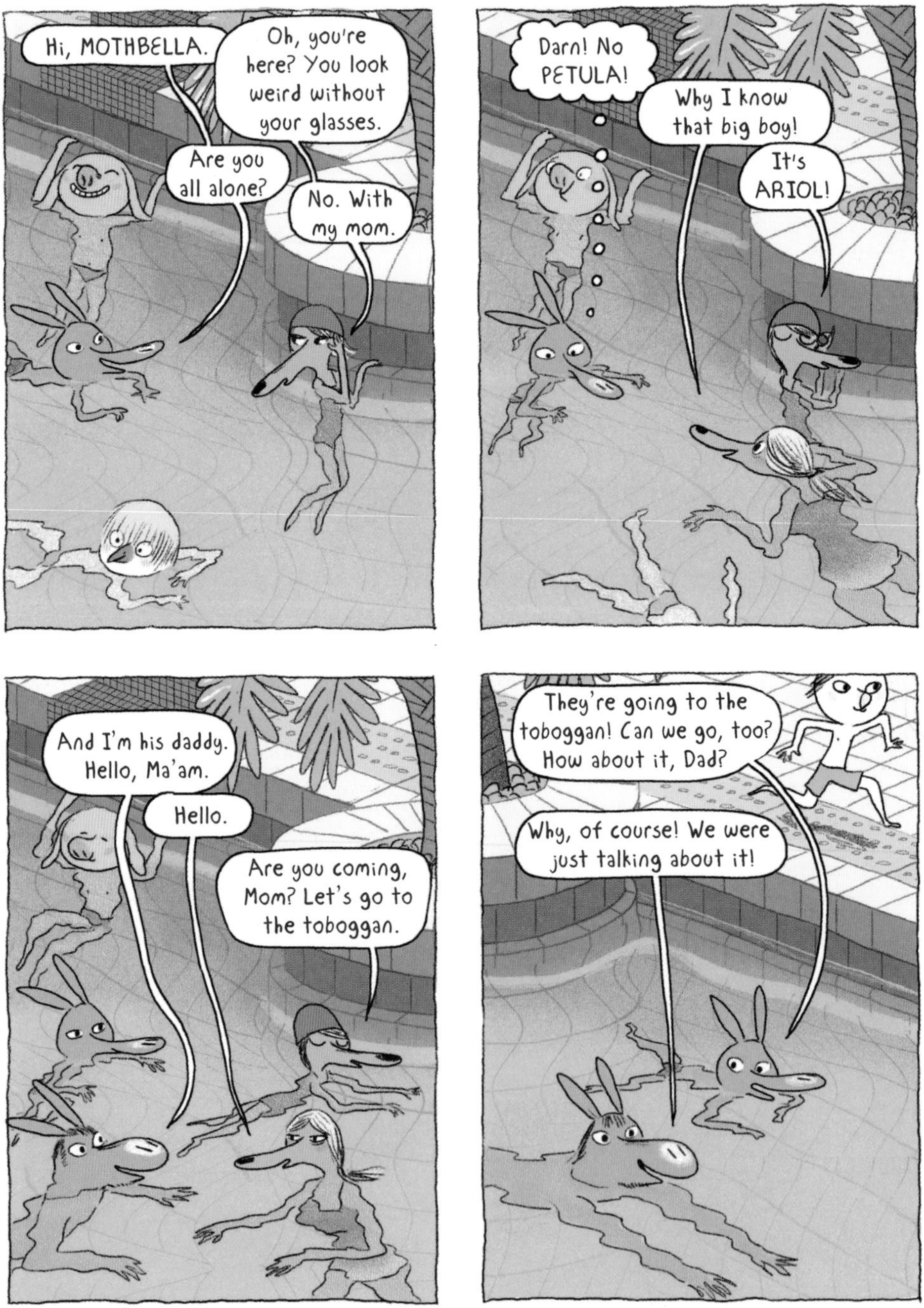
Hi, MOTHBELLA.
Oh, you're here? You look weird without your glasses.
Are you all alone?
No. With my mom.
Darn! No PETULA!
Why I know that big boy!
It's ARIOL!
And I'm his daddy. Hello, Ma'am.
Hello.
Are you coming, Mom? Let's go to the toboggan.
They're going to the toboggan! Can we go, too? How about it, Dad?
Why, of course! We were just talking about it!

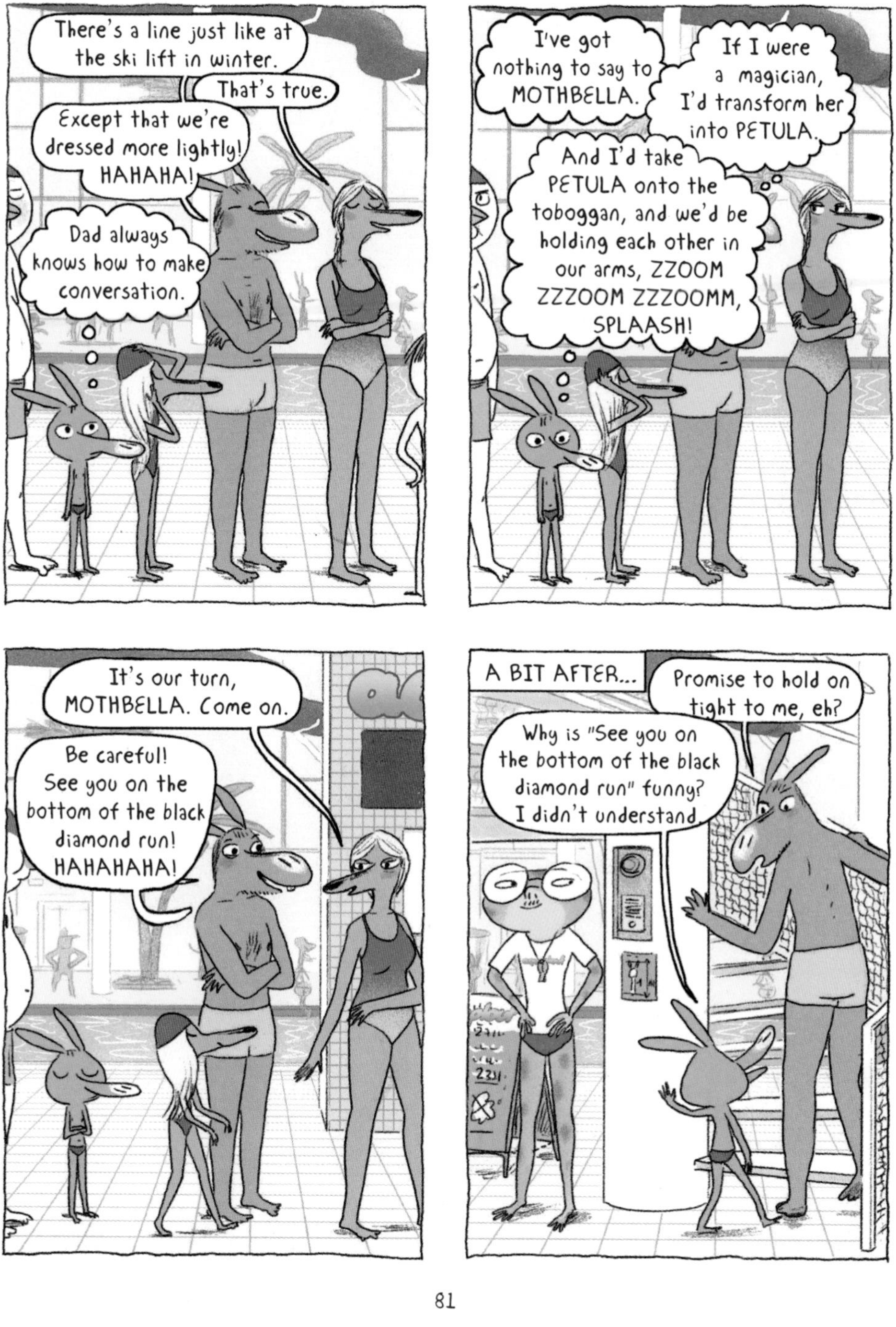
There's a line just like at the ski lift in winter.
That's true.
Except that we're dressed more lightly! HAHAHA!
Dad always knows how to make conversation.
I've got nothing to say to MOTHBELLA.
If I were a magician, I'd transform her into PETULA.
And I'd take PETULA onto the toboggan, and we'd be holding each other in our arms, ZZOOM ZZZOOM ZZZOOMM, SPLAASH!
It's our turn, MOTHBELLA. Come on.
Be careful! See you on the bottom of the black diamond run! HAHAHAHA!
A BIT AFTER...
Promise to hold on tight to me, eh?
Why is "See you on the bottom of the black diamond run" funny? I didn't understand.

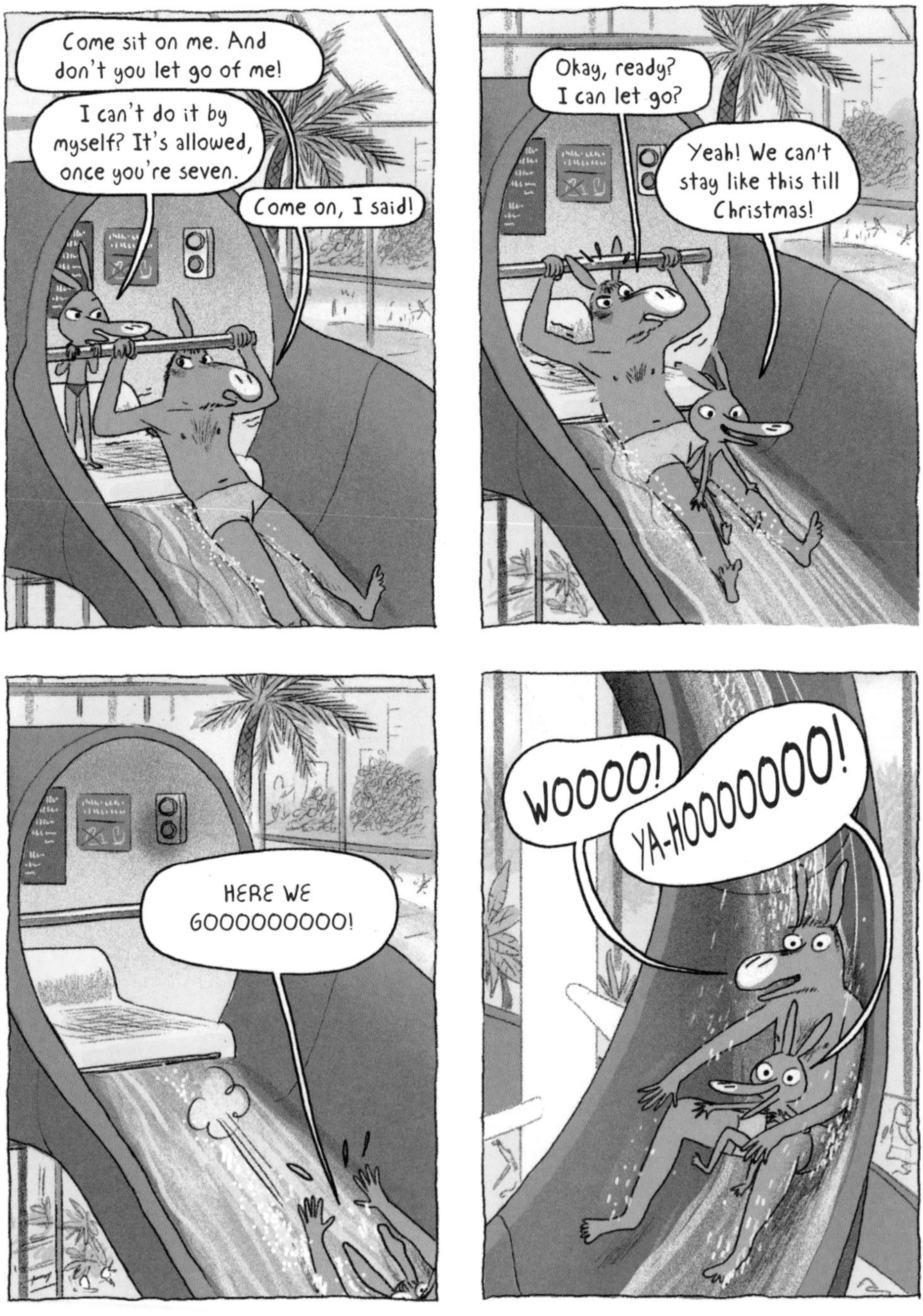
Come sit on me. And don't you let go of me!
I can't do it by myself? It's allowed, once you're seven.
Come on, I said!
Okay, ready? I can let go?
Yeah! We can't stay like this till Christmas!
HERE WE GOOOOOOOOO!
WOOOO!
YA-HOOOOOOO!

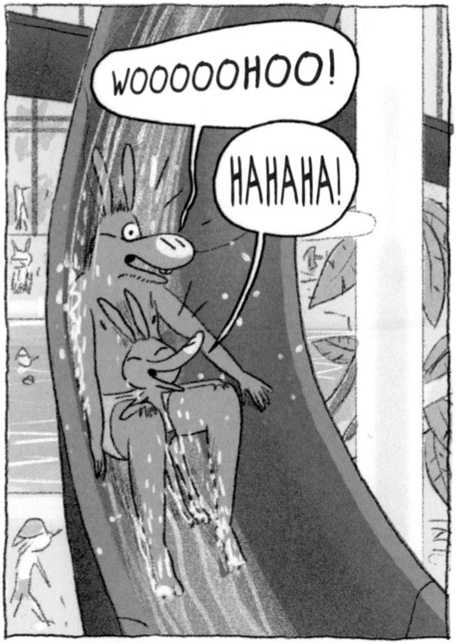
WOOOOOHOO!
HAHAHA!

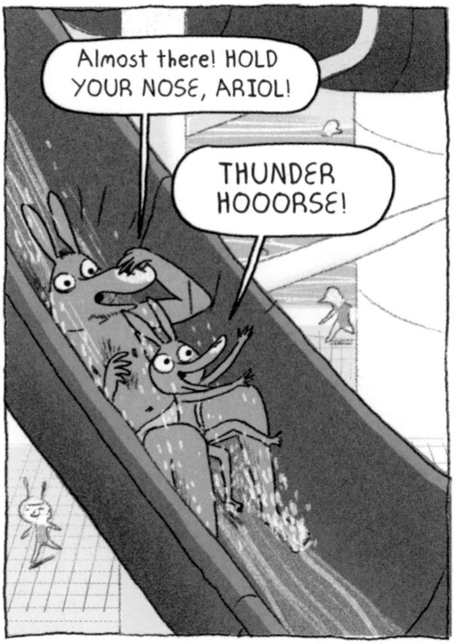
Almost there! HOLD YOUR NOSE, ARIOL!
THUNDER HOOORSE!

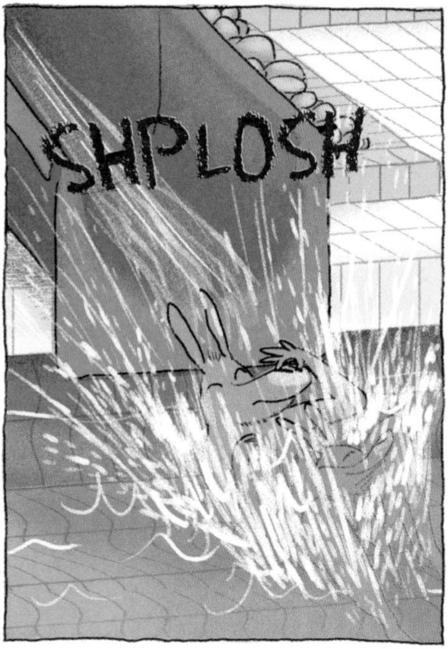
SHPLOSH

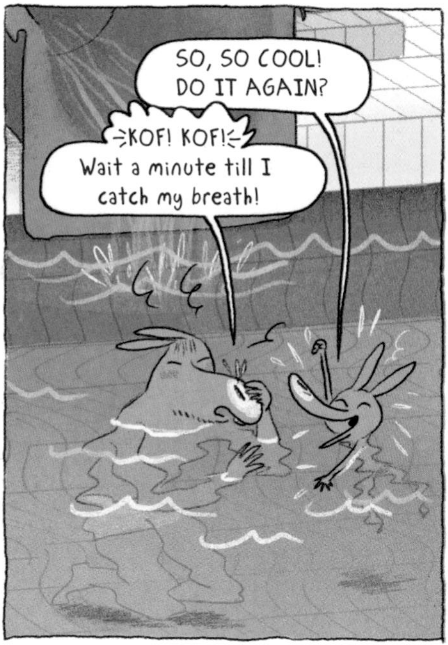
SO, SO COOL! DO IT AGAIN?
KOF! KOF!
Wait a minute till I catch my breath!

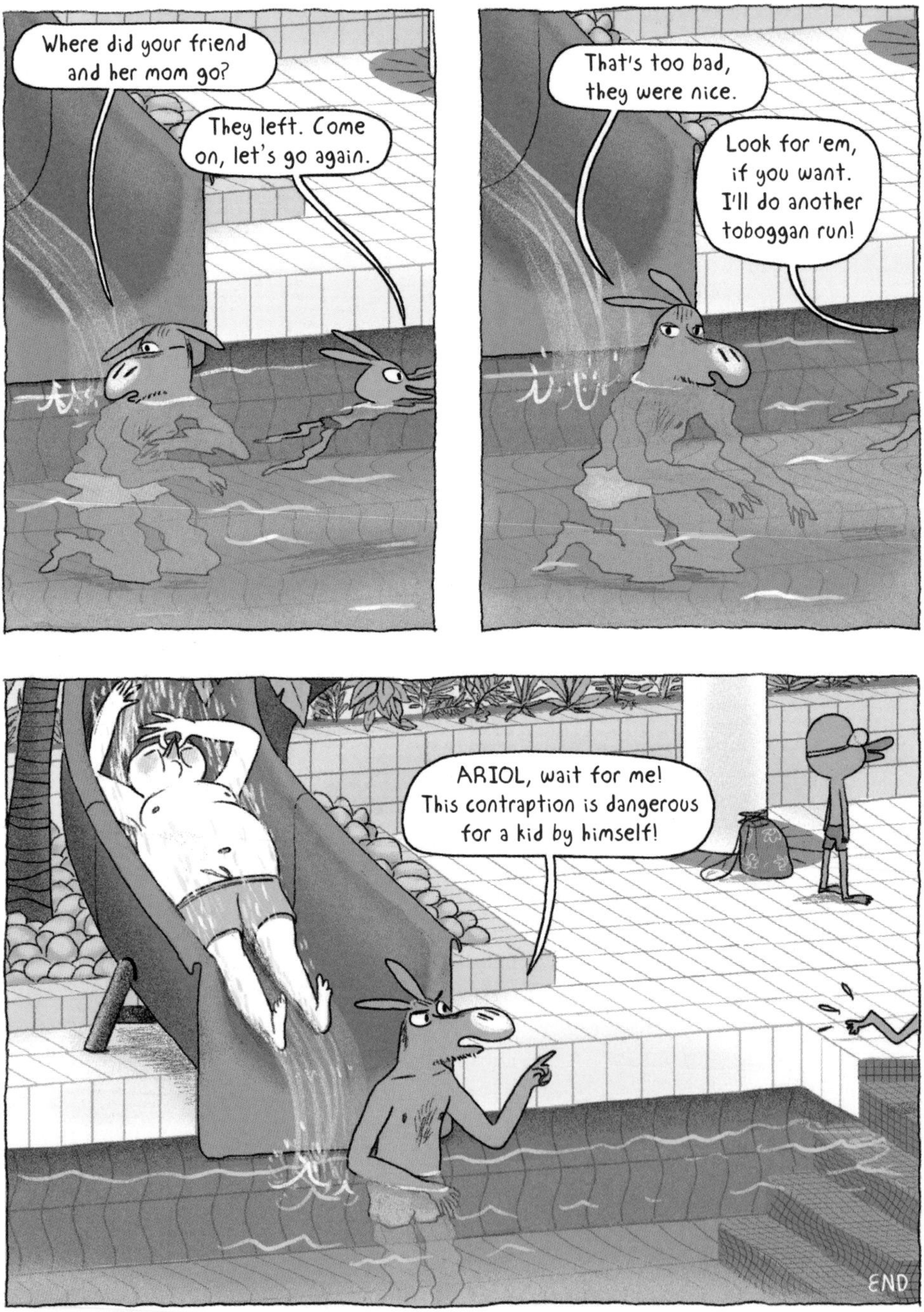
Where did your friend and her mom go?
They left. Come on, let's go again.
That's too bad, they were nice.
Look for 'em, if you want. I'll do another toboggan run!
ARIOL, wait for me! This contraption is dangerous for a kid by himself!
END

ARiOL

Mrs. SAPOLIN's Pies

How many days till the bazaar, Granny?
It's tomorrow.
I don't wanna go.

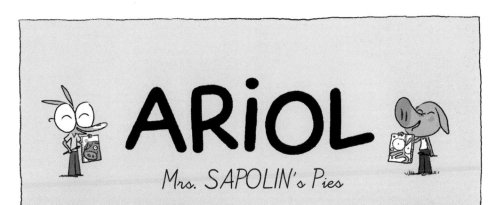

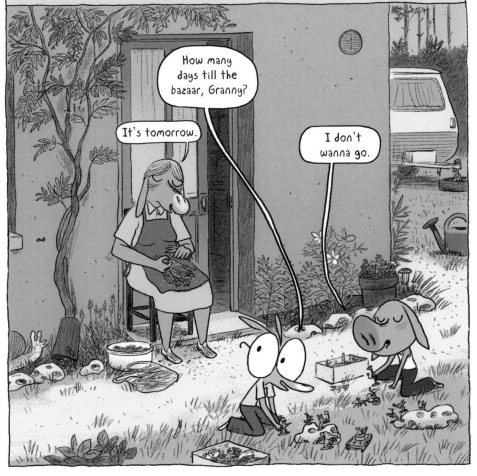

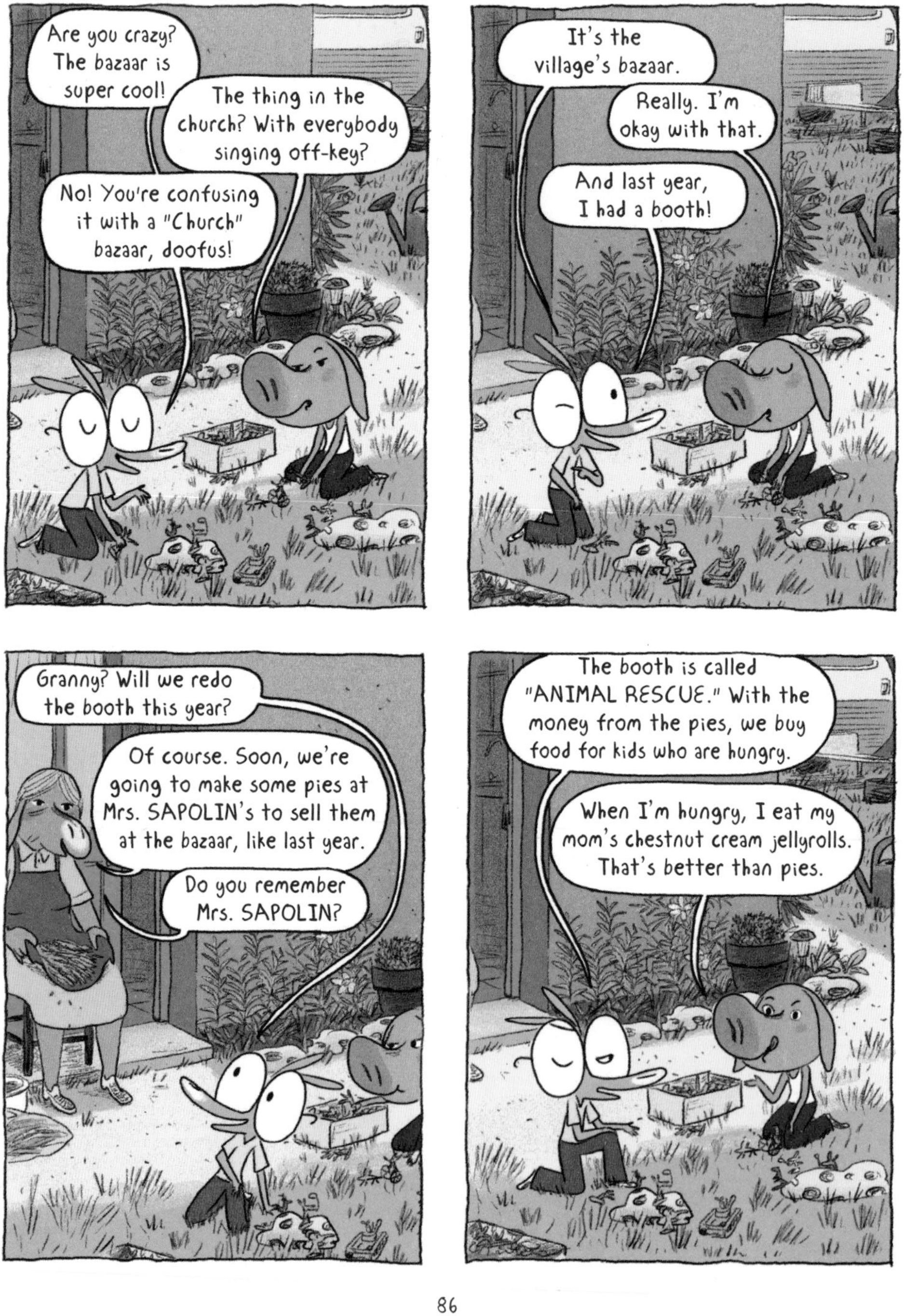
Are you crazy? The bazaar is super cool!
The thing in the church? With everybody singing off-key?
No! You're confusing it with a "Church" bazaar, doofus!
It's the village's bazaar.
Really. I'm okay with that.
And last year, I had a booth!
Granny? Will we redo the booth this year?
Of course. Soon, we're going to make some pies at Mrs. SAPOLIN's to sell them at the bazaar, like last year.
Do you remember Mrs. SAPOLIN?
The booth is called "ANIMAL RESCUE." With the money from the pies, we buy food for kids who are hungry.
When I'm hungry, I eat my mom's chestnut cream jellyrolls. That's better than pies.

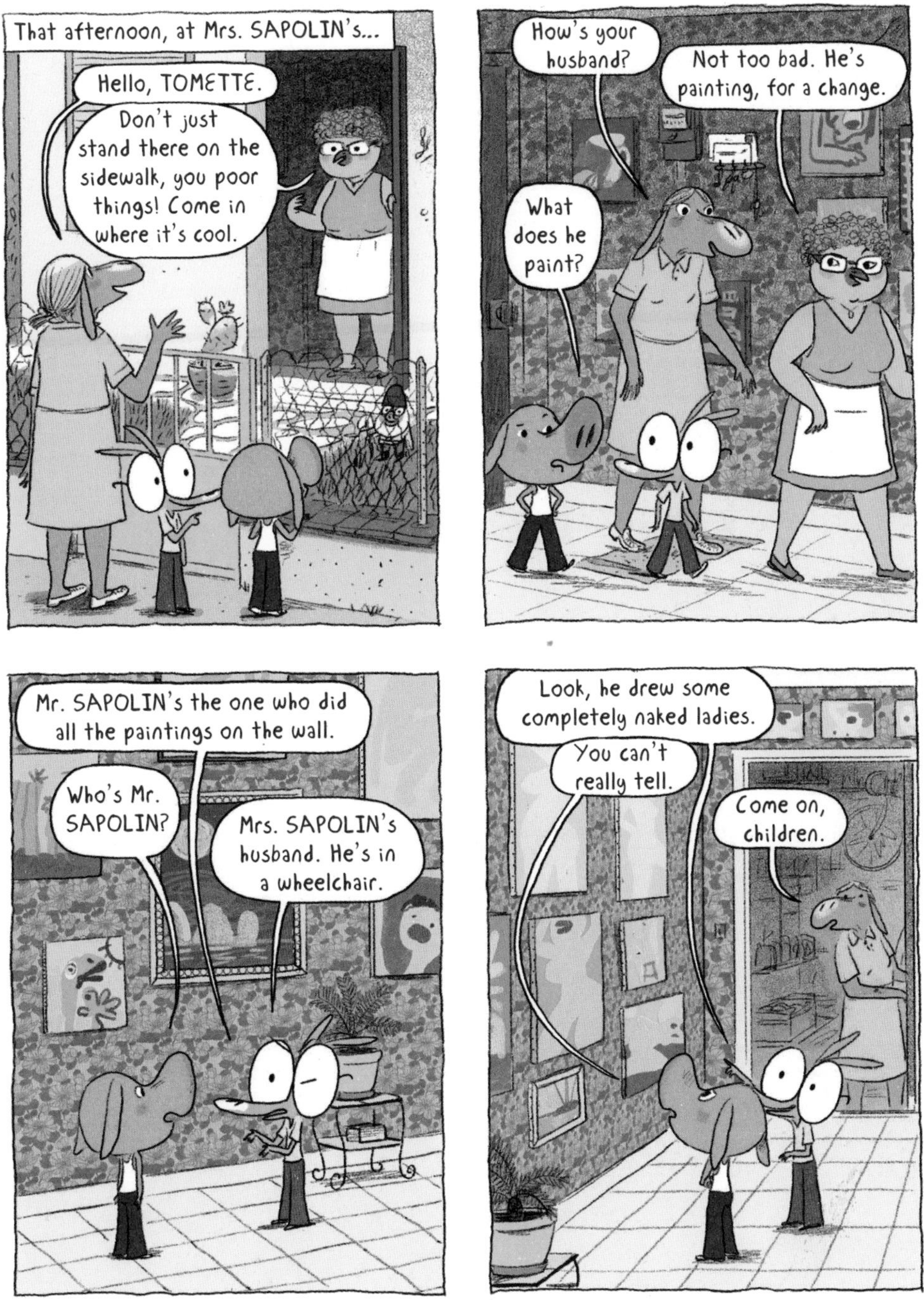
That afternoon, at Mrs. SAPOLIN's...
Hello, TOMETTE.
Don't just stand there on the sidewalk, you poor things! Come in where it's cool.
How's your husband?
Not too bad. He's painting, for a change.
What does he paint?
Mr. SAPOLIN's the one who did all the paintings on the wall.
Who's Mr. SAPOLIN?
Mrs. SAPOLIN's husband. He's in a wheelchair.
Look, he drew some completely naked ladies.
You can't really tell.
Come on, children.

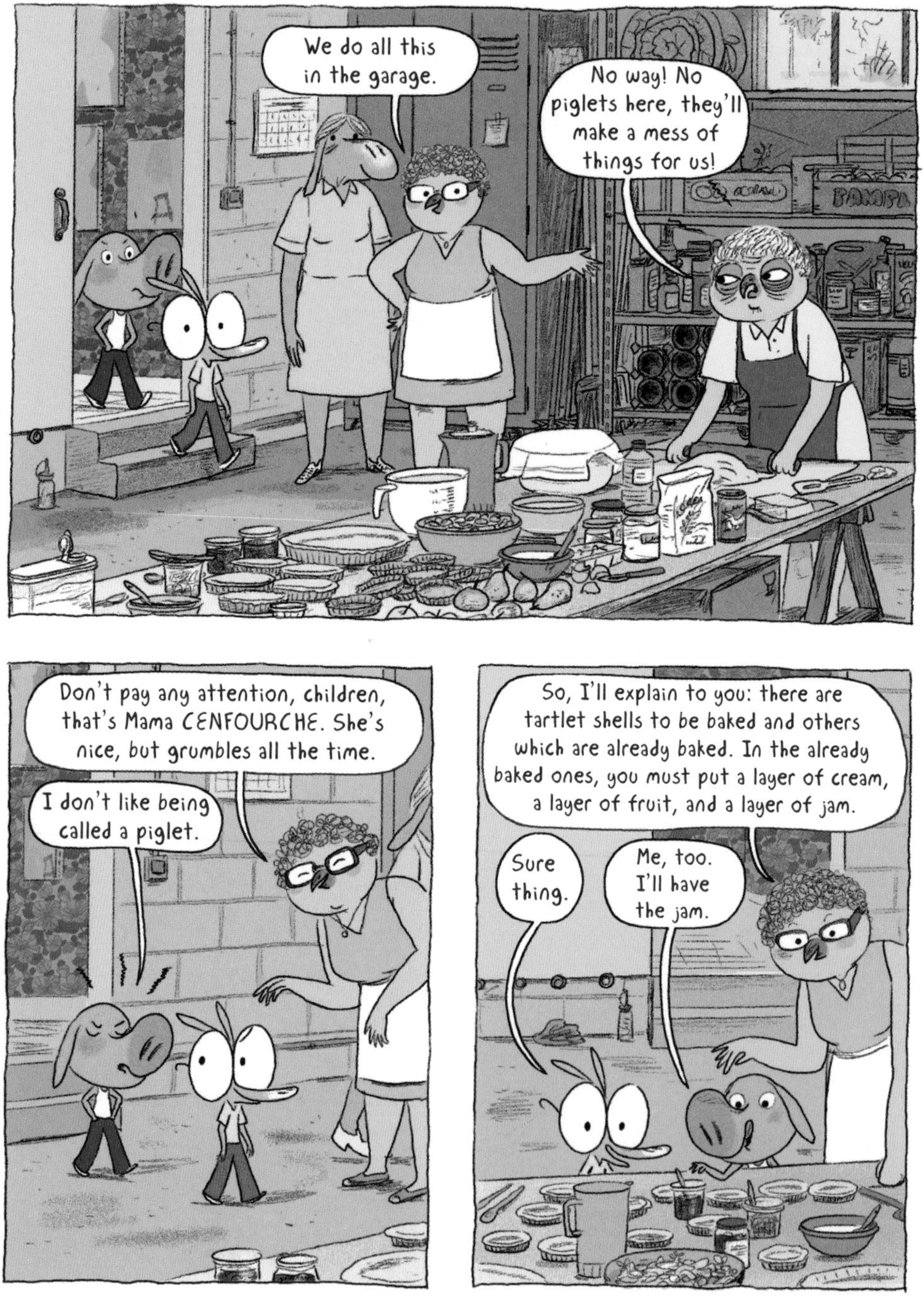
We do all this in the garage.
No way! No piglets here, they'll make a mess of things for us!
Don't pay any attention, children, that's Mama CENFOURCHE. She's nice, but grumbles all the time.
I don't like being called a piglet.
So, I'll explain to you: there are tartlet shells to be baked and others which are already baked. In the already baked ones, you must put a layer of cream, a layer of fruit, and a layer of jam.
Sure thing.
Me, too. I'll have the jam.

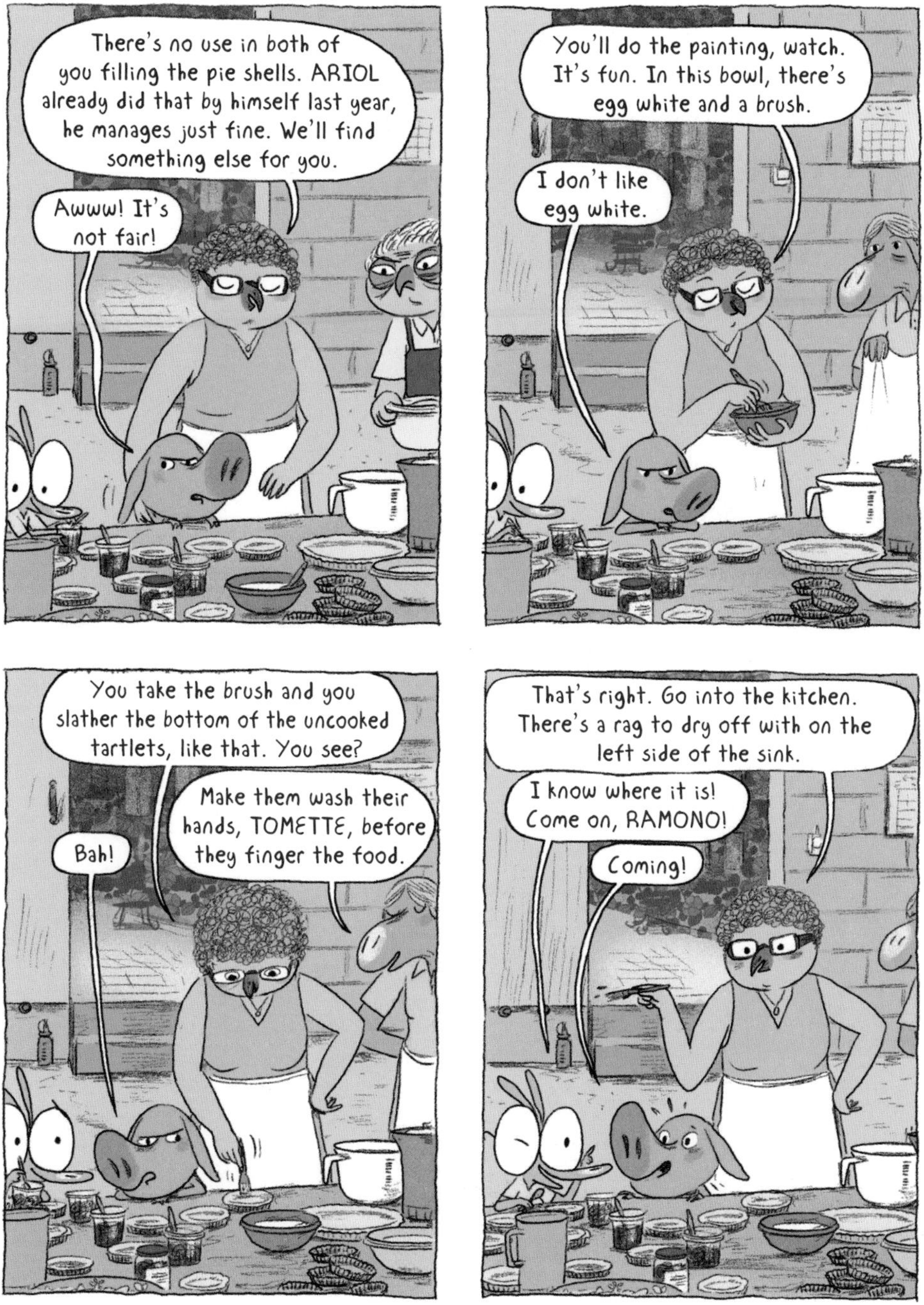
There's no use in both of you filling the pie shells. ARIOL already did that by himself last year, he manages just fine. We'll find something else for you.
Awww! It's not fair!
You'll do the painting, watch. It's fun. In this bowl, there's egg white and a brush.
I don't like egg white.
You take the brush and you slather the bottom of the uncooked tartlets, like that. You see?
Bah!
Make them wash their hands, TOMETTE, before they finger the food.
That's right. Go into the kitchen. There's a rag to dry off with on the left side of the sink.
I know where it is! Come on, RAMONO!
Coming!

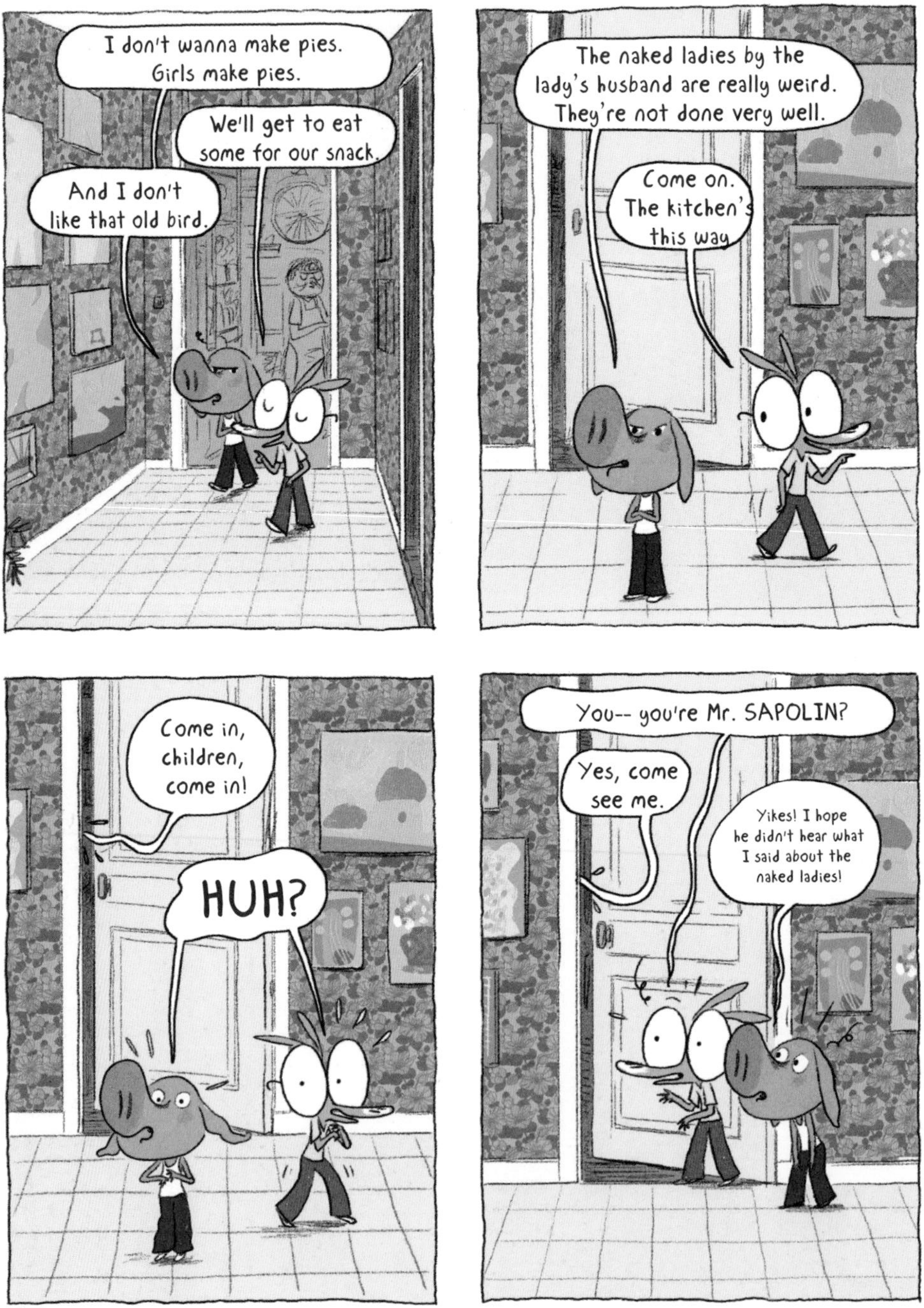
I don't wanna make pies. Girls make pies.
We'll get to eat some for our snack.
And I don't like that old bird.
The naked ladies by the lady's husband are really weird. They're not done very well.
Come on. The kitchen's this way
Come in, children, come in!
HUH?
You-- you're Mr. SAPOLIN?
Yes, come see me.
Yikes! I hope he didn't hear what I said about the naked ladies!

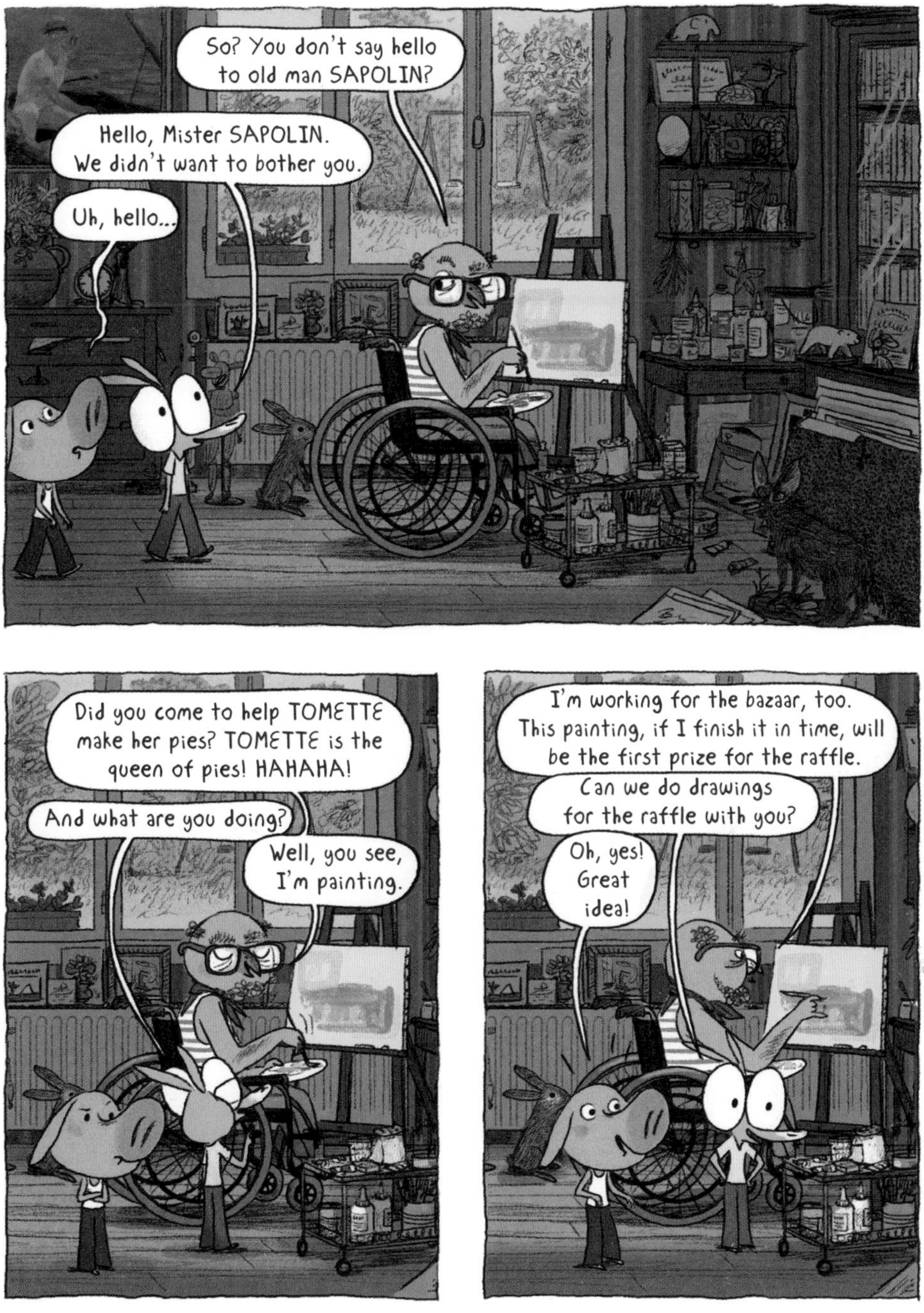
So? You don't say hello to old man SAPOLIN?
Hello, Mister SAPOLIN. We didn't want to bother you.
Uh, hello...
Did you come to help TOMETTE make her pies? TOMETTE is the queen of pies! HAHAHA!
And what are you doing?
Well, you see, I'm painting.
I'm working for the bazaar, too. This painting, if I finish it in time, will be the first prize for the raffle.
Can we do drawings for the raffle with you?
Oh, yes! Great idea!

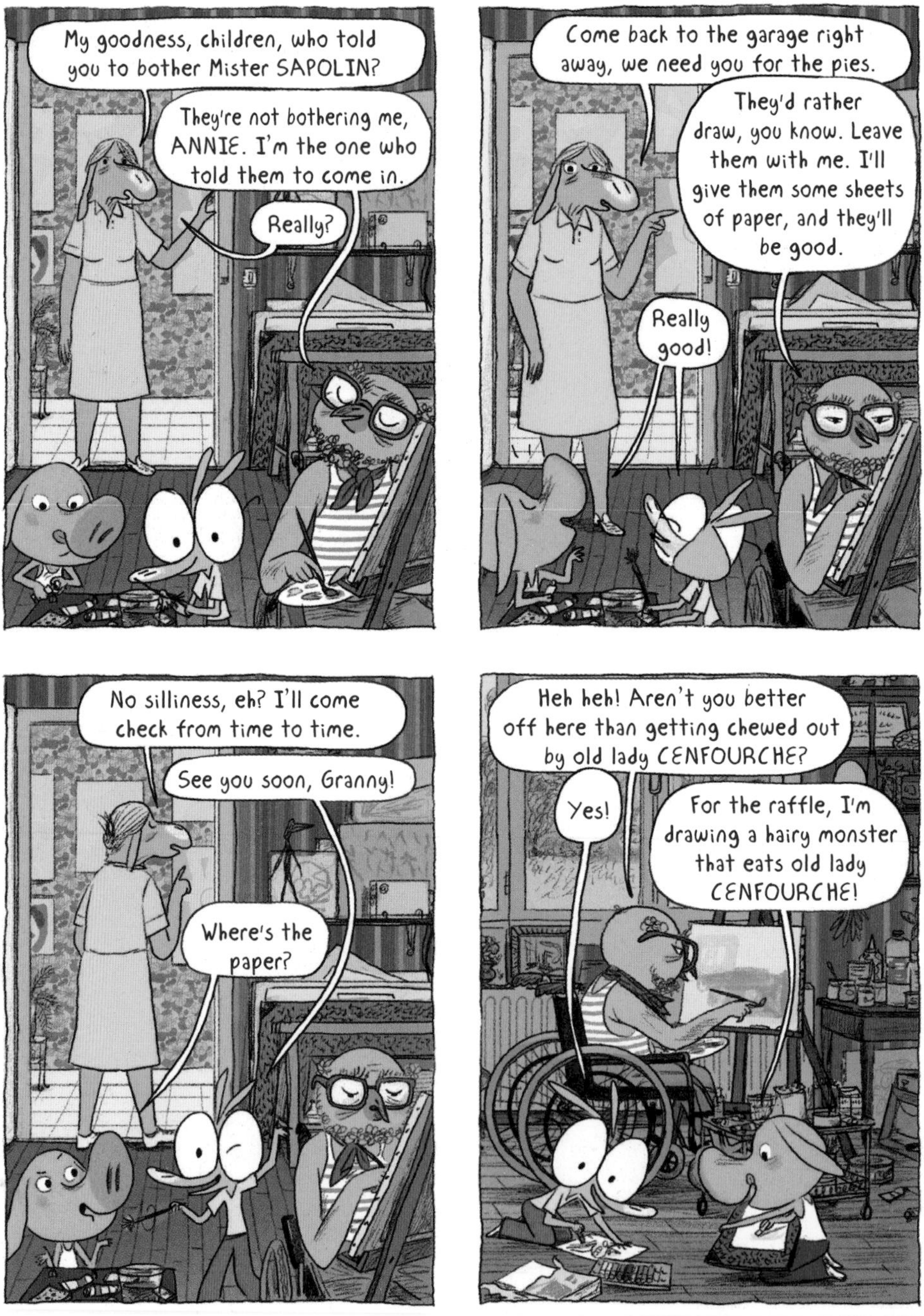
My goodness, children, who told you to bother Mister SAPOLIN?
They're not bothering me, ANNIE. I'm the one who told them to come in.
Really?
Come back to the garage right away, we need you for the pies.
They'd rather draw, you know. Leave them with me. I'll give them some sheets of paper, and they'll be good.
Really good!
No silliness, eh? I'll come check from time to time.
See you soon, Granny!
Where's the paper?
Heh heh! Aren't you better off here than getting chewed out by old lady CENFOURCHE?
Yes!
For the raffle, I'm drawing a hairy monster that eats old lady CENFOURCHE!

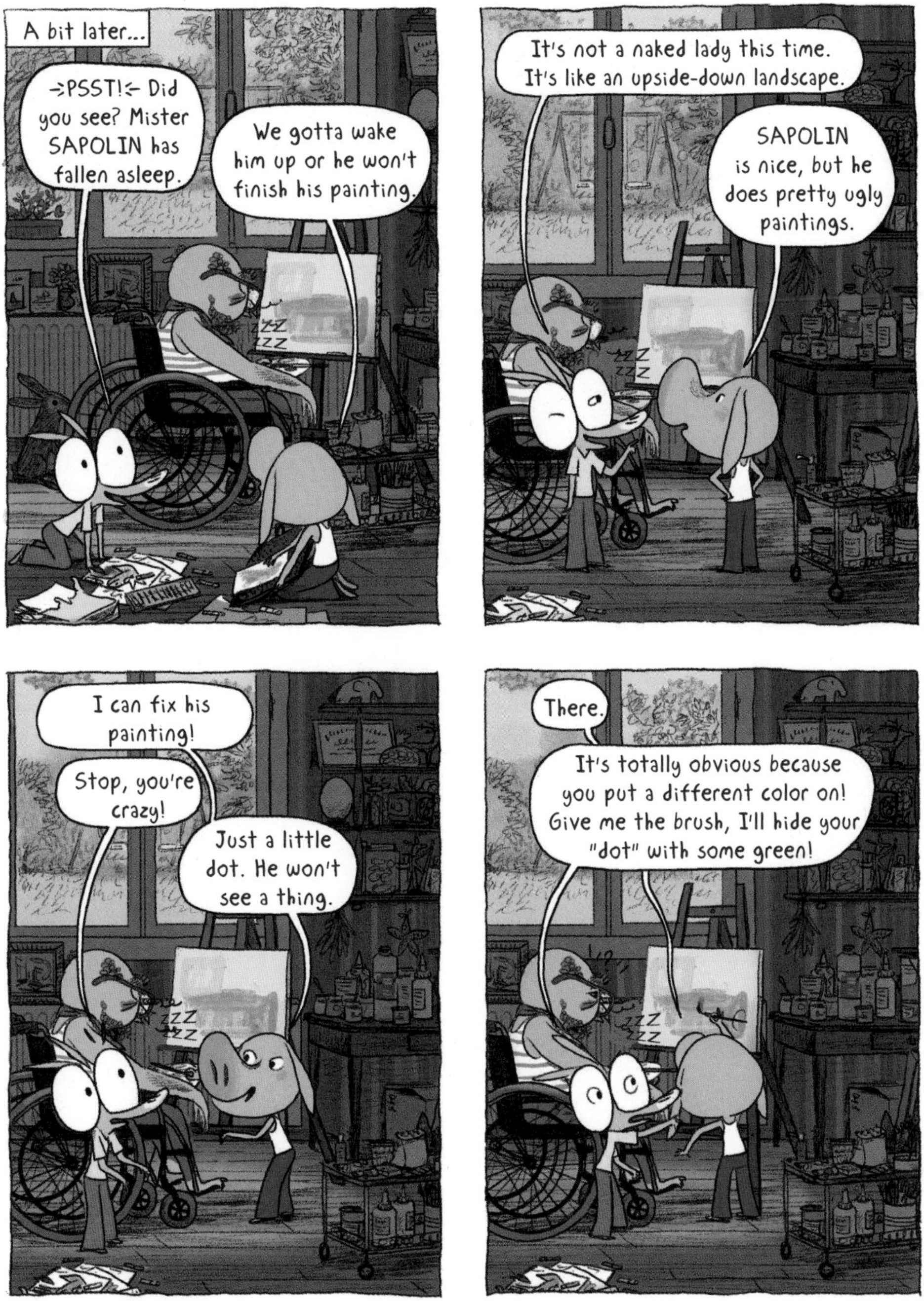
A bit later...
⇒PSST!⇐ Did you see? Mister SAPOLIN has fallen asleep.
We gotta wake him up or he won't finish his painting.
It's not a naked lady this time. It's like an upside-down landscape.
SAPOLIN is nice, but he does pretty ugly paintings.
ZZZ
I can fix his painting!
Stop, you're crazy!
Just a little dot. He won't see a thing.
ZZZ
There.
It's totally obvious because you put a different color on! Give me the brush, I'll hide your "dot" with some green!

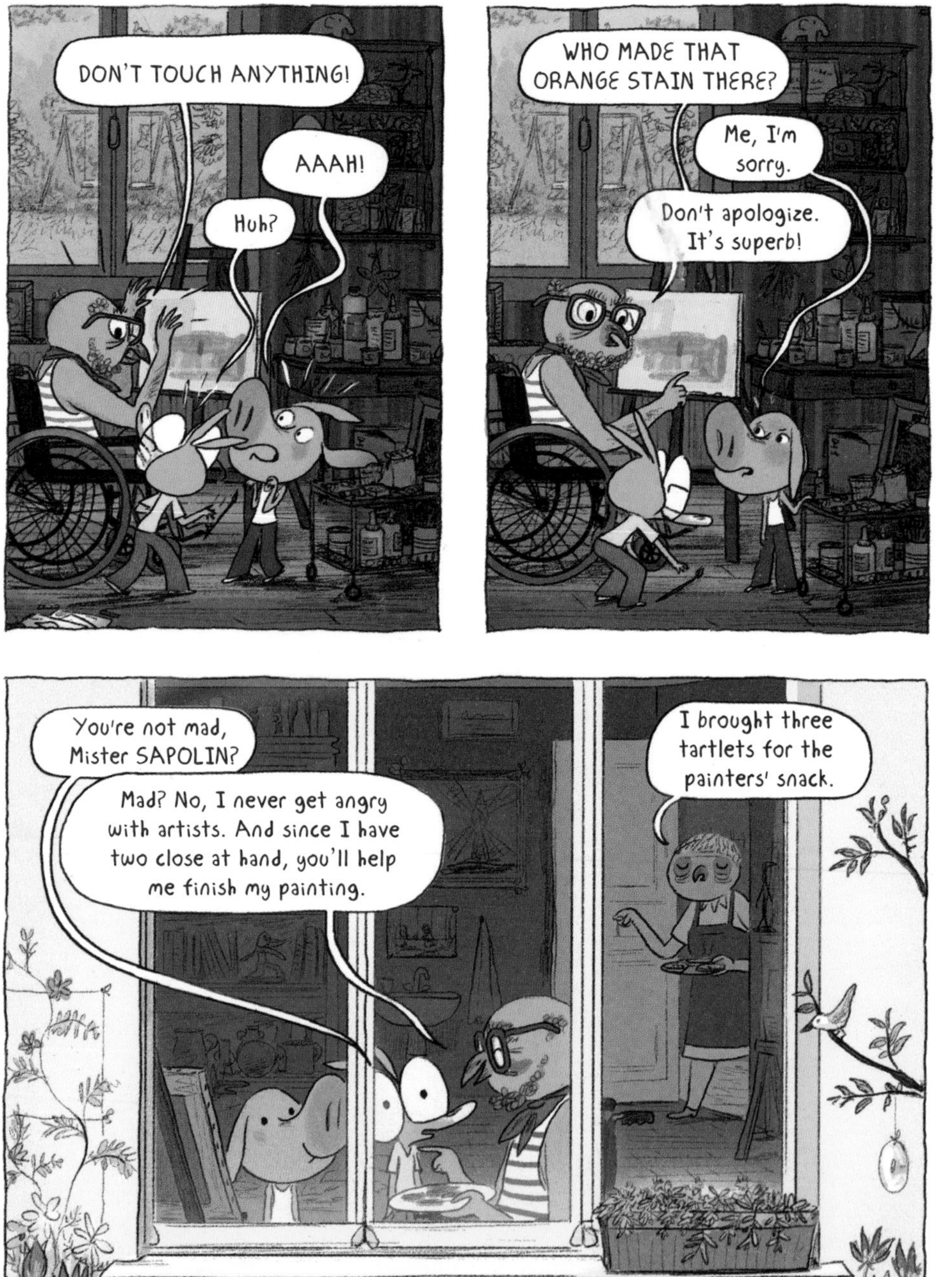
DON'T TOUCH ANYTHING!
AAAH!
Huh?
WHO MADE THAT ORANGE STAIN THERE?
Me, I'm sorry.
Don't apologize. It's superb!
You're not mad, Mister SAPOLIN?
Mad? No, I never get angry with artists. And since I have two close at hand, you'll help me finish my painting.
I brought three tartlets for the painters' snack.
END

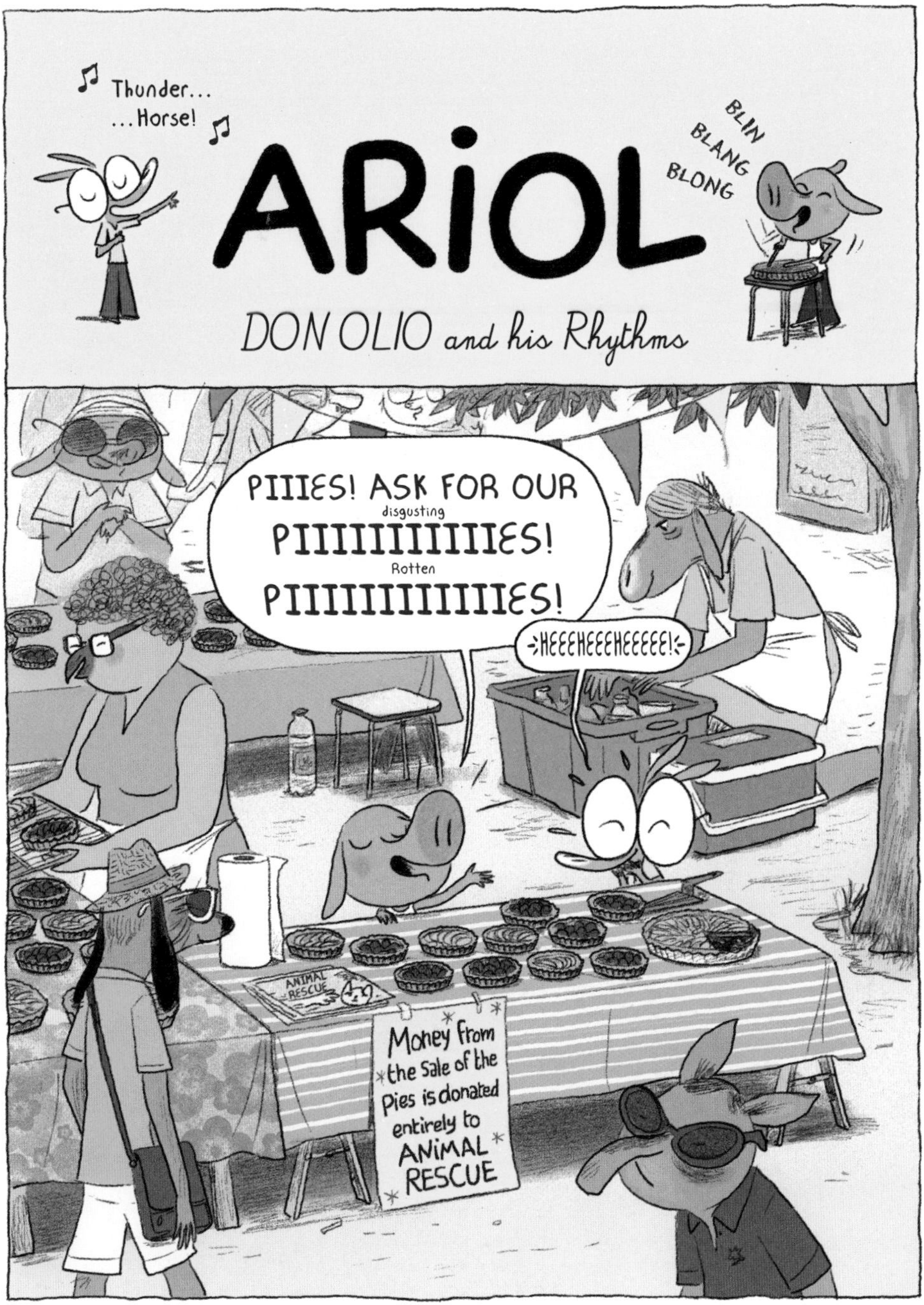
Thunder...
...Horse!
BLIN
BLANG
BLONG
ARiOL
DON OLIO and his Rhythms
PIIIES! ASK FOR OUR disgusting PIIIIIIIIIIIES! Rotten PIIIIIIIIIIIIES!
HEEEHEEEHEEEEE!
ANIMAL RESCUE
Money from the sale of the pies is donated entirely to ANIMAL RESCUE

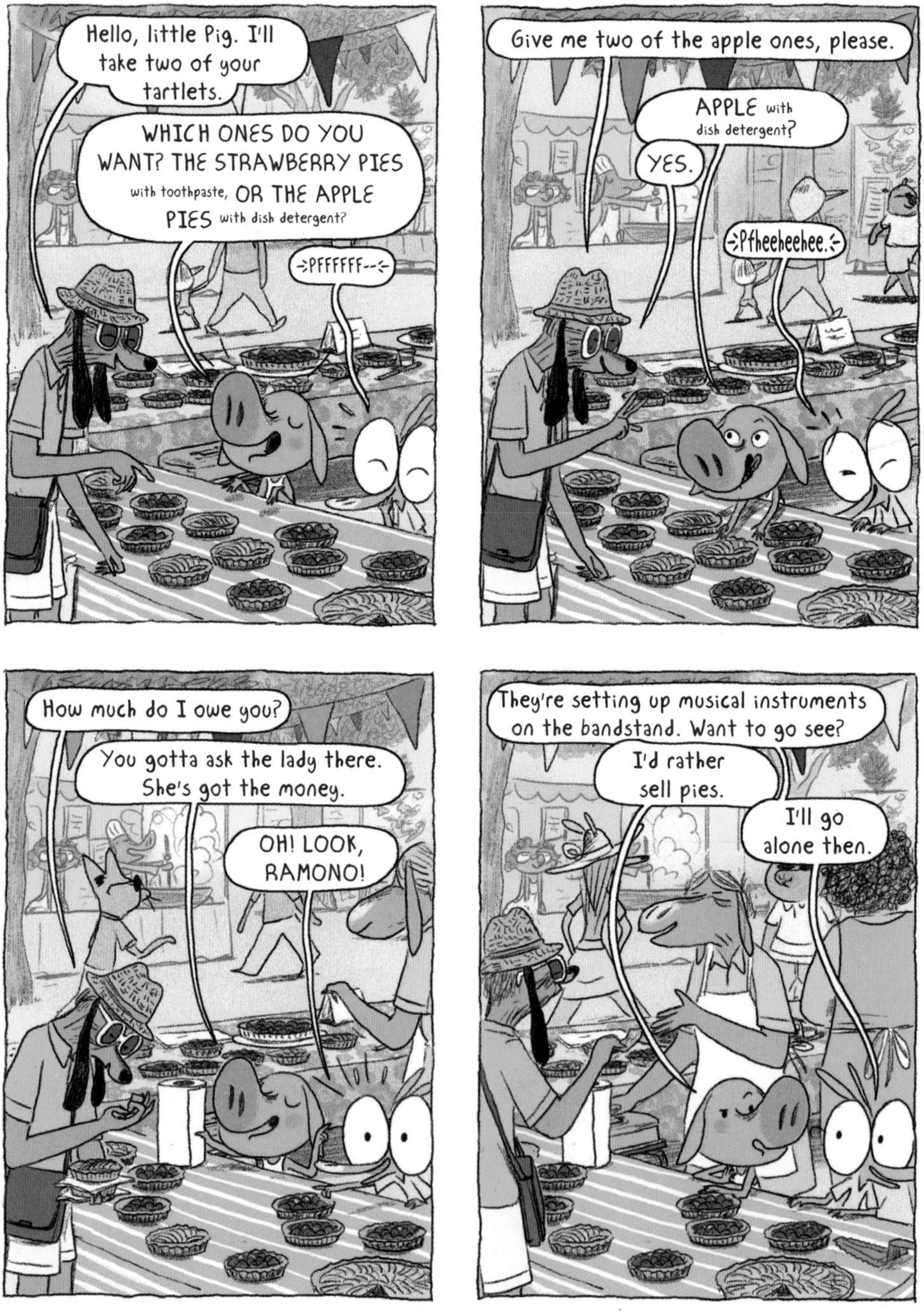
Hello, little Pig. I'll take two of your tartlets.
WHICH ONES DO YOU WANT? THE STRAWBERRY PIES with toothpaste, OR THE APPLE PIES with dish detergent?
PFFFFFF--
Give me two of the apple ones, please.
APPLE with dish detergent?
YES.
Pfheeheehee.
How much do I owe you?
You gotta ask the lady there. She's got the money.
OH! LOOK, RAMONO!
They're setting up musical instruments on the bandstand. Want to go see?
I'd rather sell pies.
I'll go alone then.

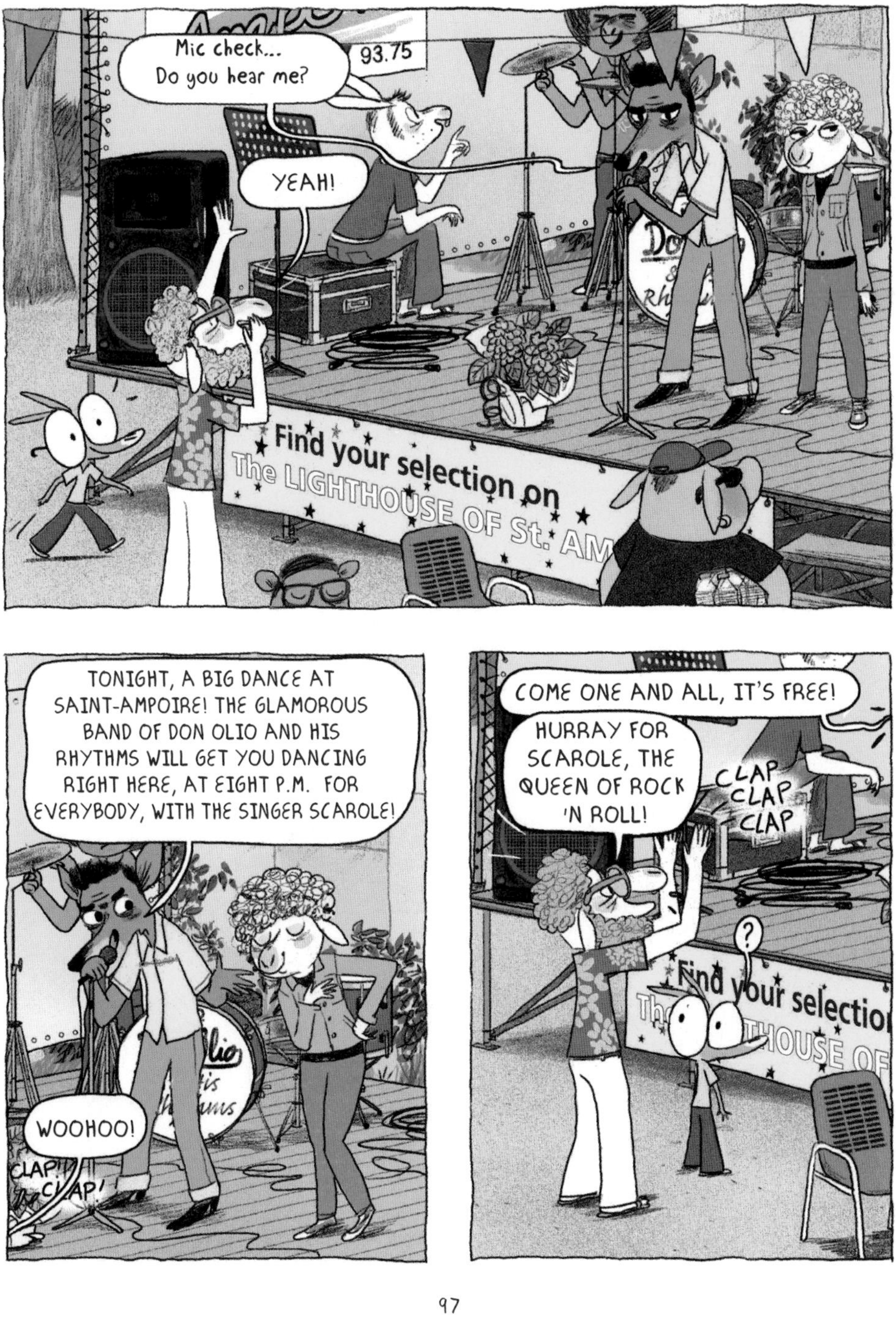

Mic check...
Do you hear me?
93.75
YEAH!
Find your selection on
The LIGHTHOUSE OF St. AM
TONIGHT, A BIG DANCE AT SAINT-AMPOIRE! THE GLAMOROUS BAND OF DON OLIO AND HIS RHYTHMS WILL GET YOU DANCING RIGHT HERE, AT EIGHT P.M. FOR EVERYBODY, WITH THE SINGER SCAROLE!
WOOHOO!
CLAP! CLAP!
COME ONE AND ALL, IT'S FREE!
HURRAY FOR SCAROLE, THE QUEEN OF ROCK 'N ROLL!
CLAP CLAP CLAP
?
Find your selection

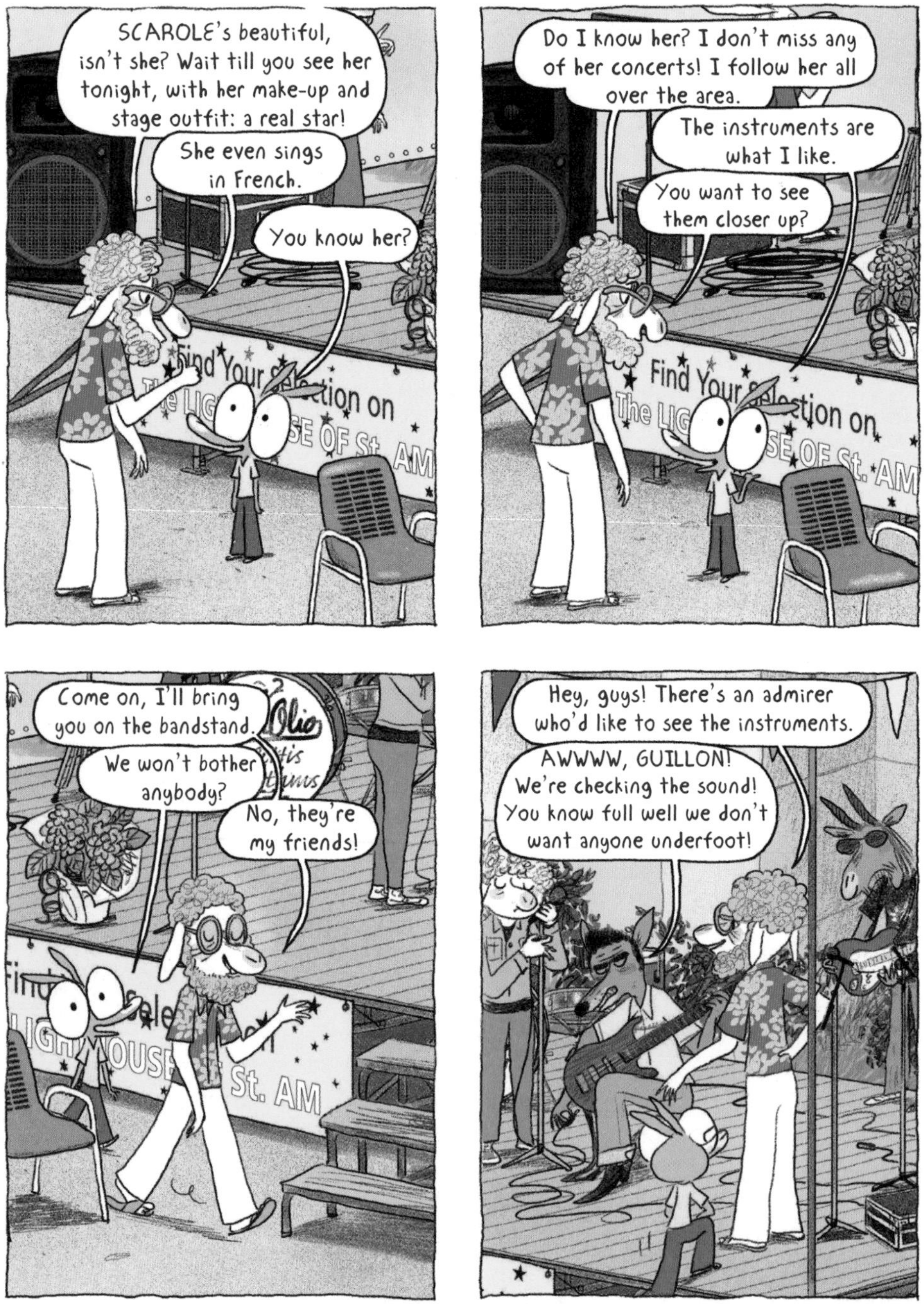
SCAROLE's beautiful, isn't she? Wait till you see her tonight, with her make-up and stage outfit: a real star!
She even sings in French.
You know her?
Find Your Selection on
The LIGHTHOUSE OF St. AM
Do I know her? I don't miss any of her concerts! I follow her all over the area.
The instruments are what I like.
You want to see them closer up?
Come on, I'll bring you on the bandstand.
We won't bother anybody?
No, they're my friends!
Hey, guys! There's an admirer who'd like to see the instruments.
AWWWW, GUILLON! We're checking the sound! You know full well we don't want anyone underfoot!

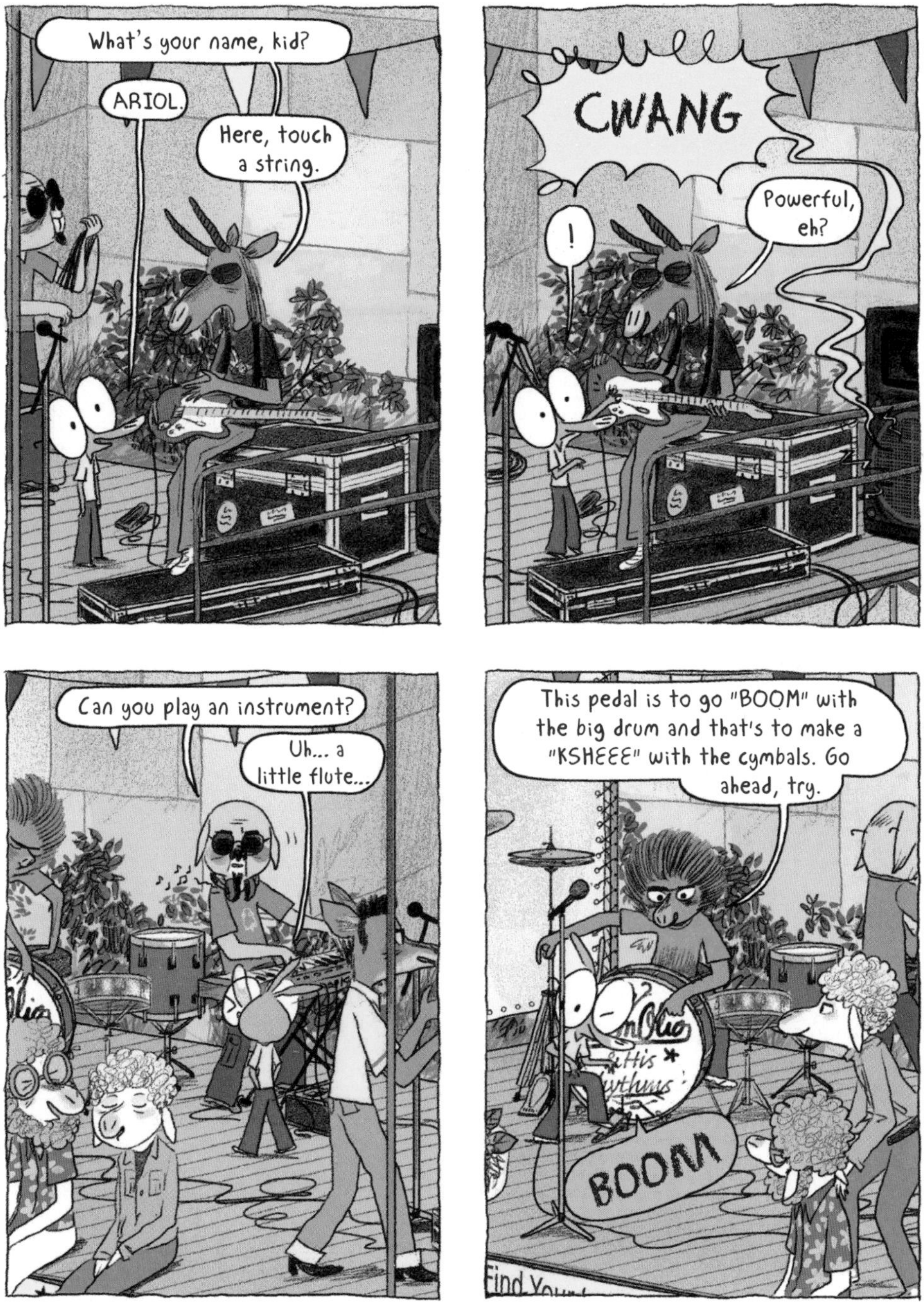
What's your name, kid?
ARIOL.
Here, touch a string.
CWANG
!
Powerful, eh?
Can you play an instrument?
Uh... a little flute...
This pedal is to go "BOOM" with the big drum and that's to make a "KSHEEE" with the cymbals. Go ahead, try.
BOOM

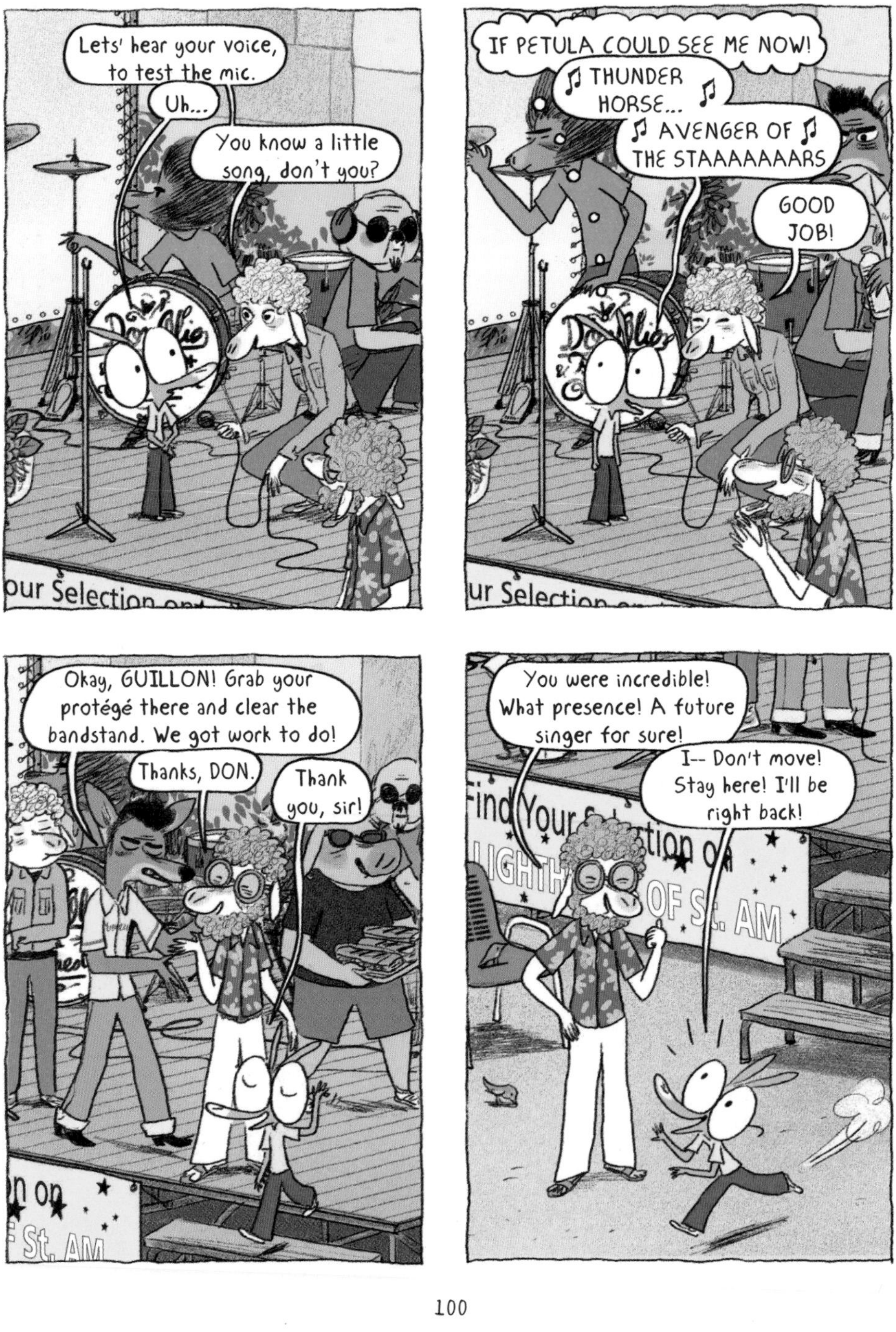
Lets' hear your voice, to test the mic.
Uh...
You know a little song, don't you?
IF PETULA COULD SEE ME NOW!
♫ THUNDER HORSE... ♫
♫ AVENGER OF ♫ THE STAAAAAAARS
GOOD JOB!
Okay, GUILLON! Grab your protégé there and clear the bandstand. We got work to do!
Thanks, DON.
Thank you, sir!
You were incredible! What presence! A future singer for sure!
I-- Don't move! Stay here! I'll be right back!

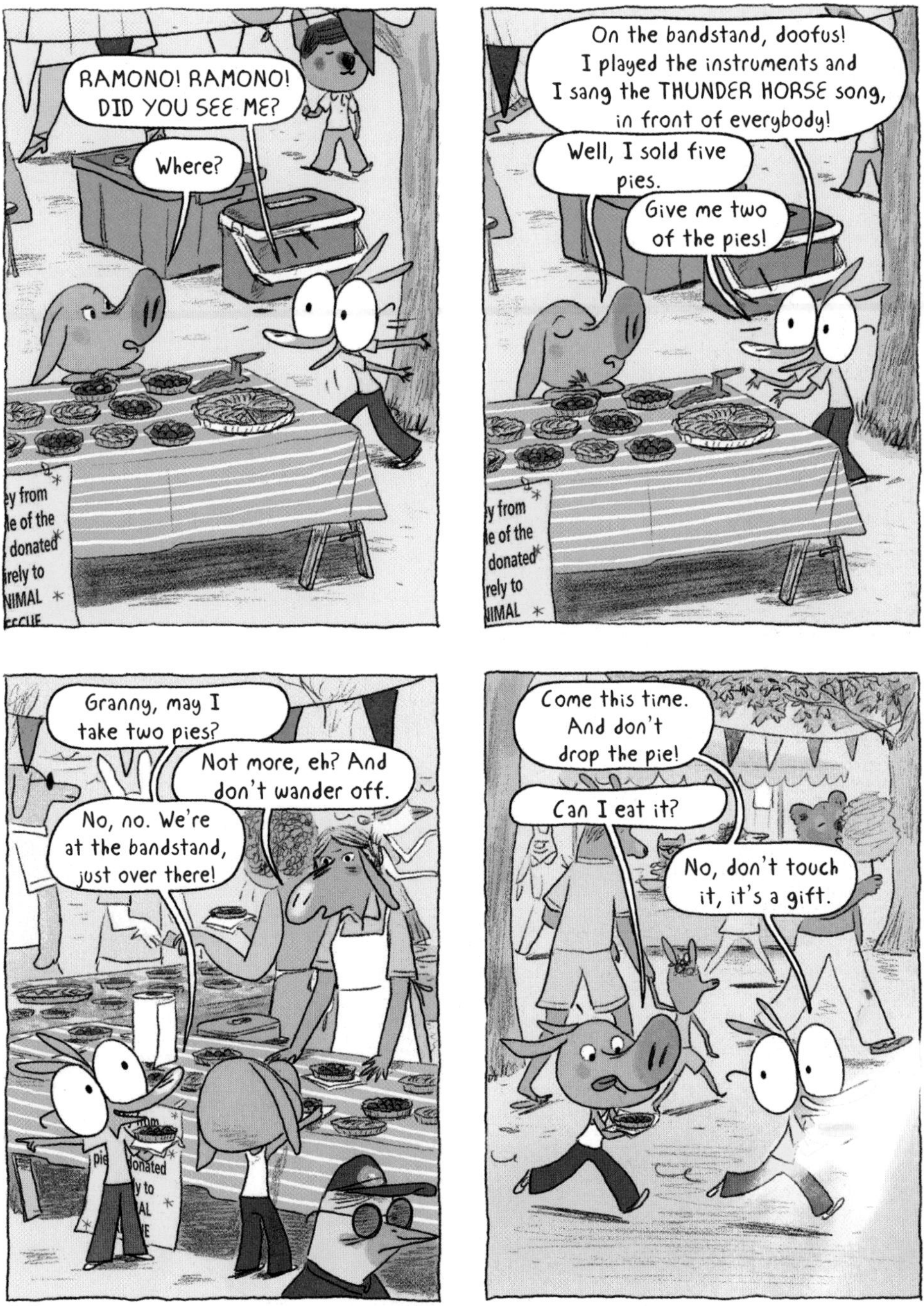
RAMONO! RAMONO! DID YOU SEE ME?
Where?
On the bandstand, doofus! I played the instruments and I sang the THUNDER HORSE song, in front of everybody!
Well, I sold five pies.
Give me two of the pies!
Granny, may I take two pies?
Not more, eh? And don't wander off.
No, no. We're at the bandstand, just over there!
Come this time. And don't drop the pie!
Can I eat it?
No, don't touch it, it's a gift.

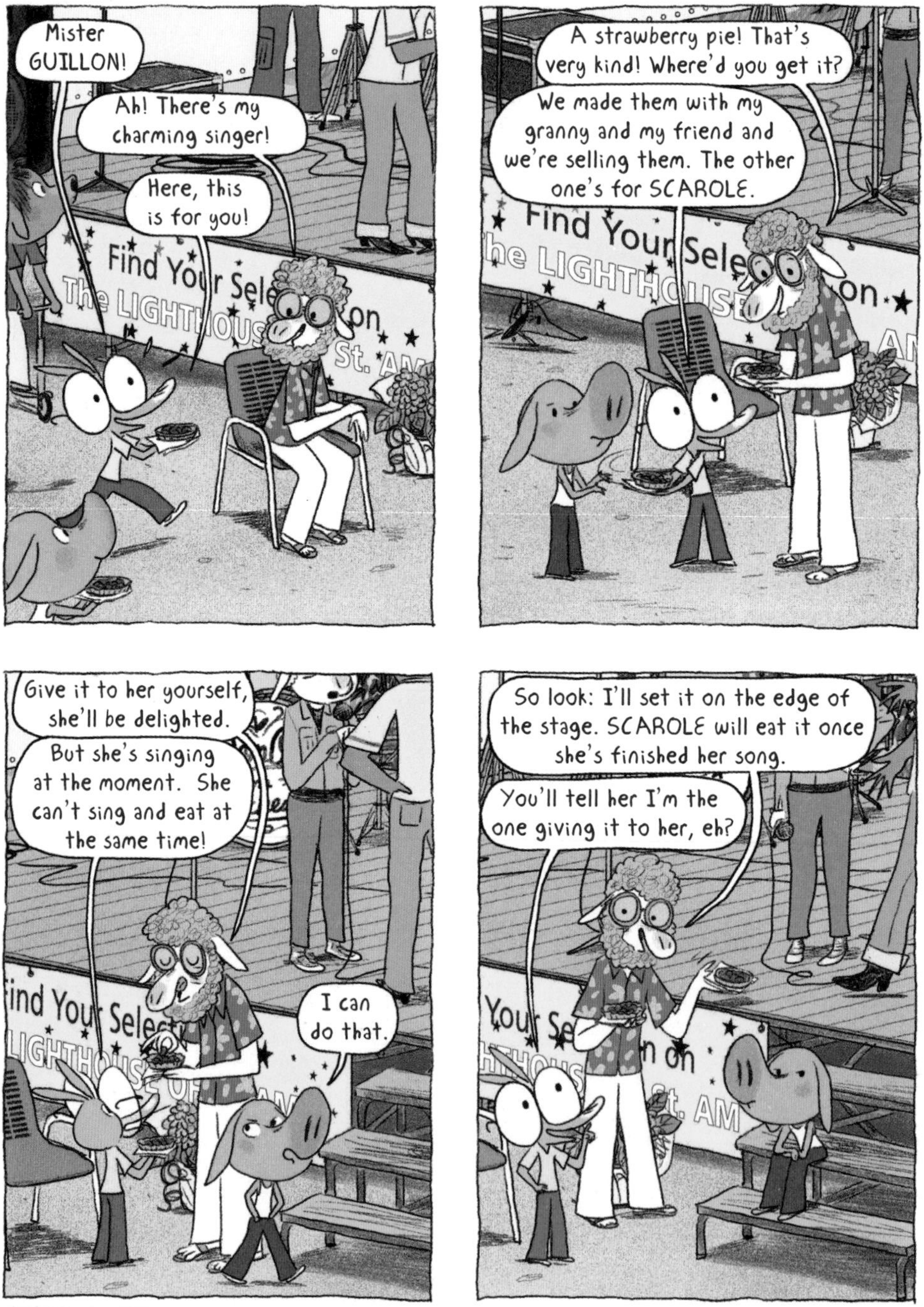
Mister GUILLON!
Ah! There's my charming singer!
Here, this is for you!
A strawberry pie! That's very kind! Where'd you get it?
We made them with my granny and my friend and we're selling them. The other one's for SCAROLE.
Give it to her yourself, she'll be delighted.
But she's singing at the moment. She can't sing and eat at the same time!
I can do that.
So look: I'll set it on the edge of the stage. SCAROLE will eat it once she's finished her song.
You'll tell her I'm the one giving it to her, eh?

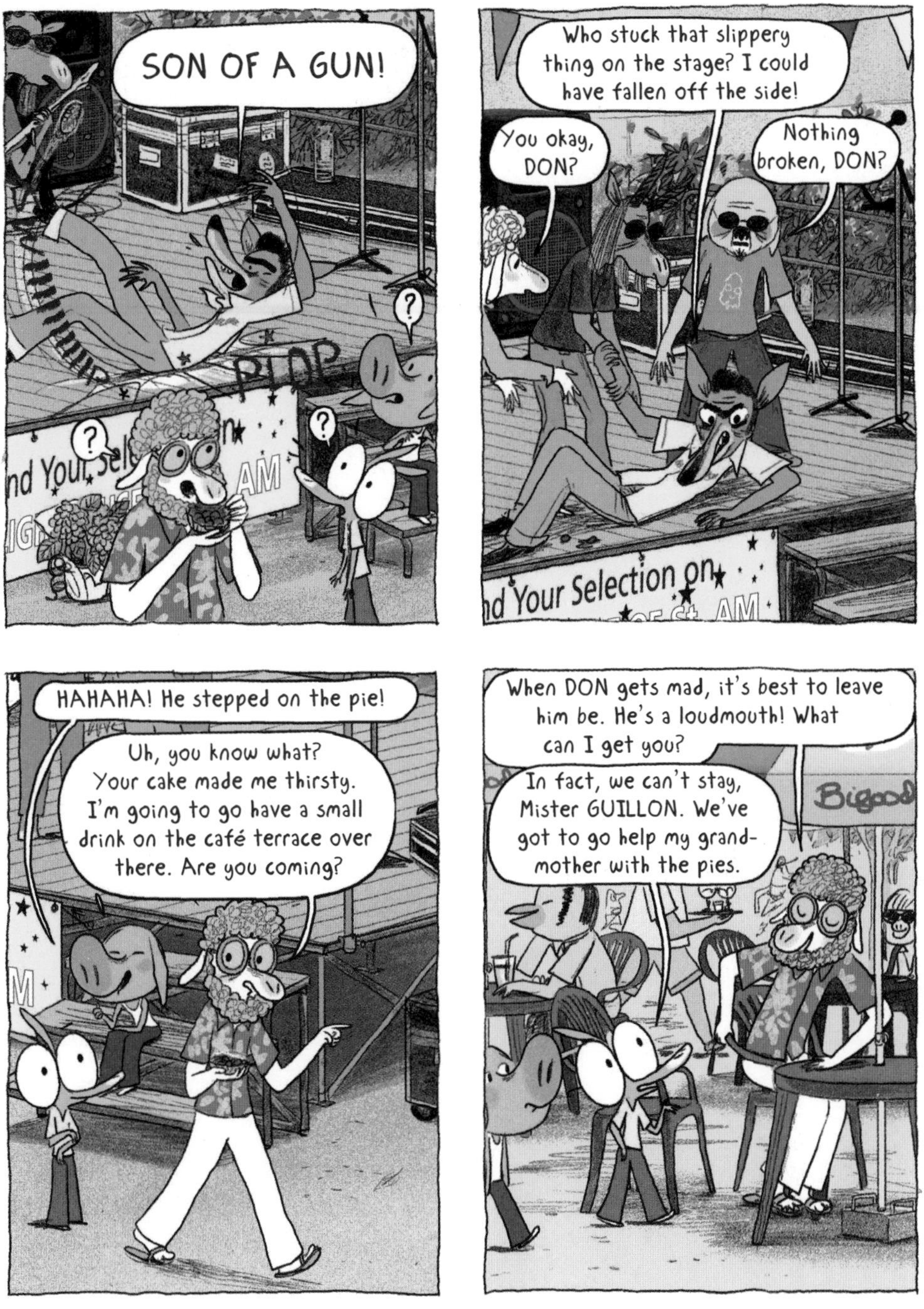
SON OF A GUN!
PLOP
?
?
?
Who stuck that slippery thing on the stage? I could have fallen off the side!
You okay, DON?
Nothing broken, DON?
nd Your Selection on
AM
HAHAHA! He stepped on the pie!
Uh, you know what? Your cake made me thirsty. I'm going to go have a small drink on the café terrace over there. Are you coming?
When DON gets mad, it's best to leave him be. He's a loudmouth! What can I get you?
In fact, we can't stay, Mister GUILLON. We've got to go help my grand-mother with the pies.

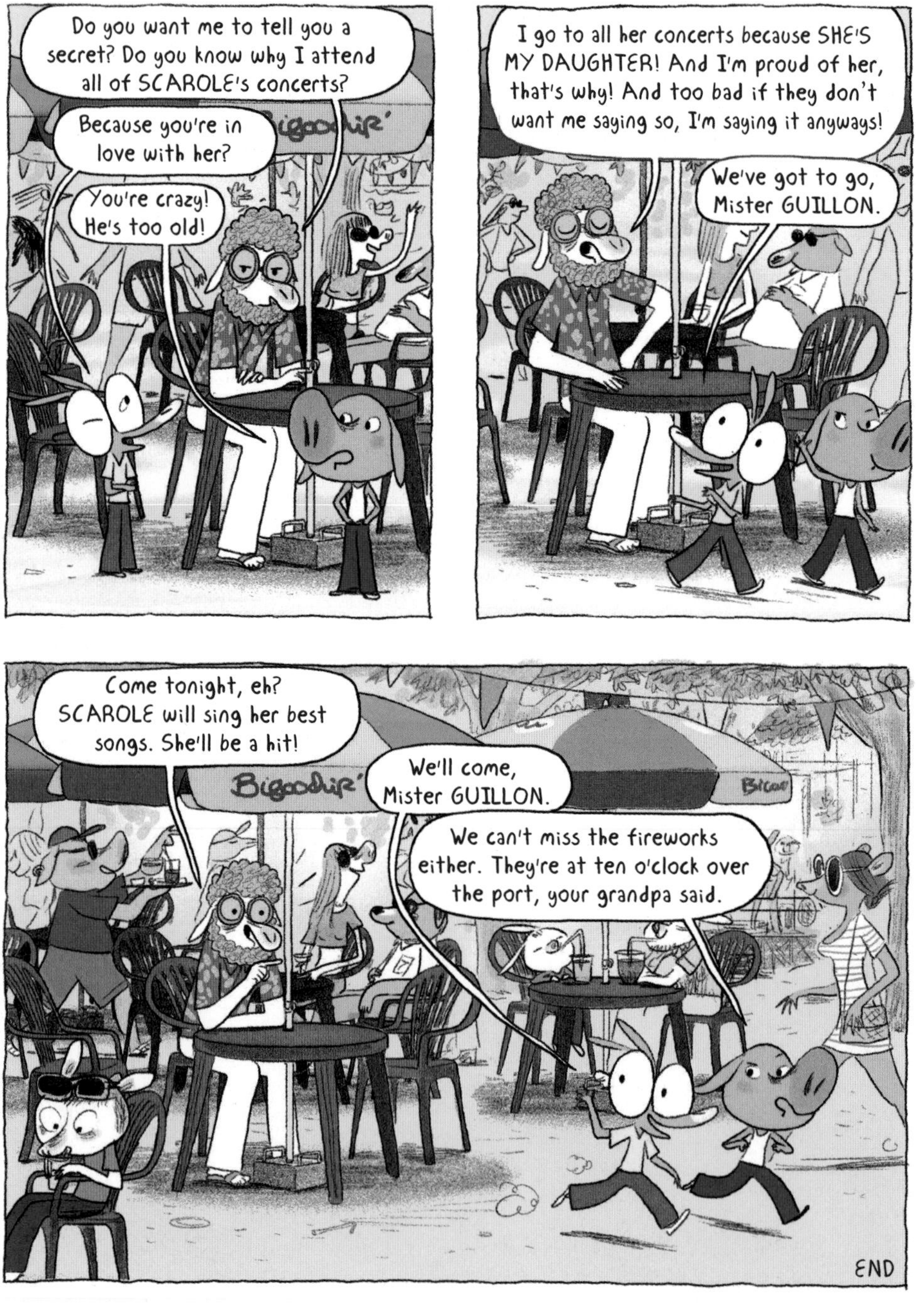
Do you want me to tell you a secret? Do you know why I attend all of SCAROLE's concerts?
Because you're in love with her?
You're crazy! He's too old!
I go to all her concerts because SHE'S MY DAUGHTER! And I'm proud of her, that's why! And too bad if they don't want me saying so, I'm saying it anyways!
We've got to go, Mister GUILLON.
Come tonight, eh? SCAROLE will sing her best songs. She'll be a hit!
We'll come, Mister GUILLON.
We can't miss the fireworks either. They're at ten o'clock over the port, your grandpa said.
END

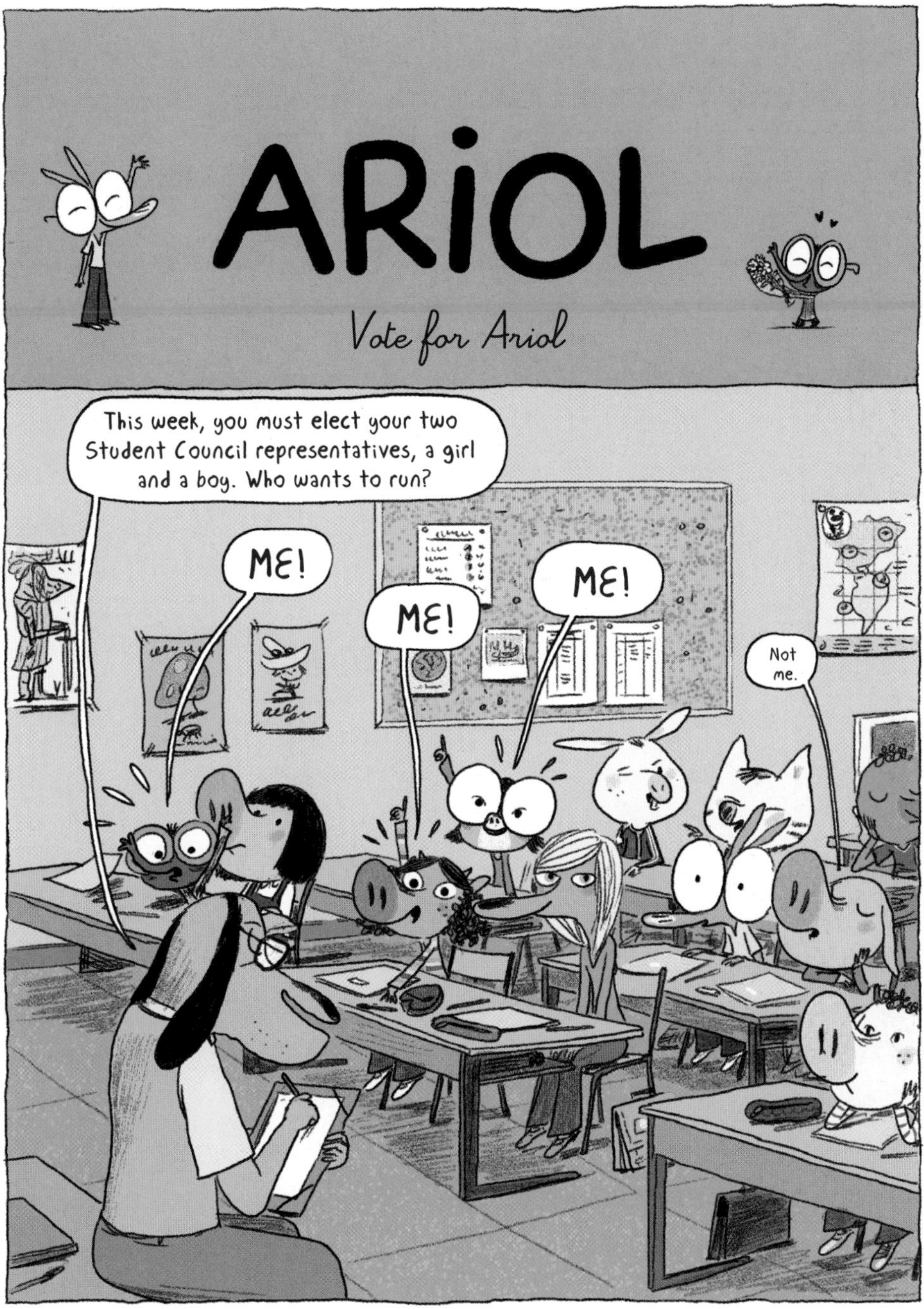
ARiOL
Vote for Ariol
This week, you must elect your two Student Council representatives, a girl and a boy. Who wants to run?
ME!
ME!
ME!
Not me.

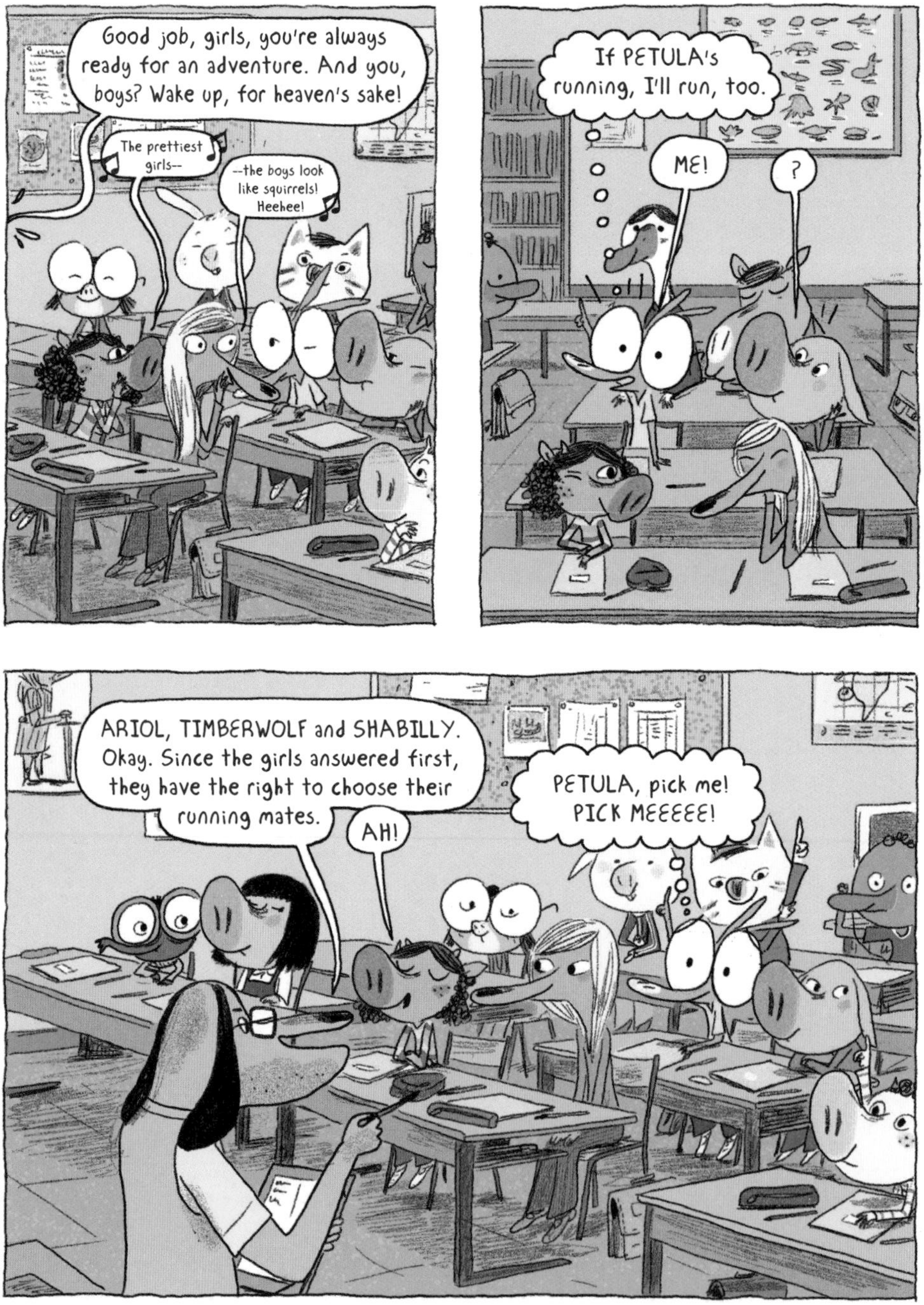

Good job, girls, you're always ready for an adventure. And you, boys? Wake up, for heaven's sake!
The prettiest girls--
--the boys look like squirrels! Heehee!
If PETULA's running, I'll run, too.
ME!
?
ARIOL, TIMBERWOLF and SHABILLY. Okay. Since the girls answered first, they have the right to choose their running mates.
AH!
PETULA, pick me! PICK MEEEEE!

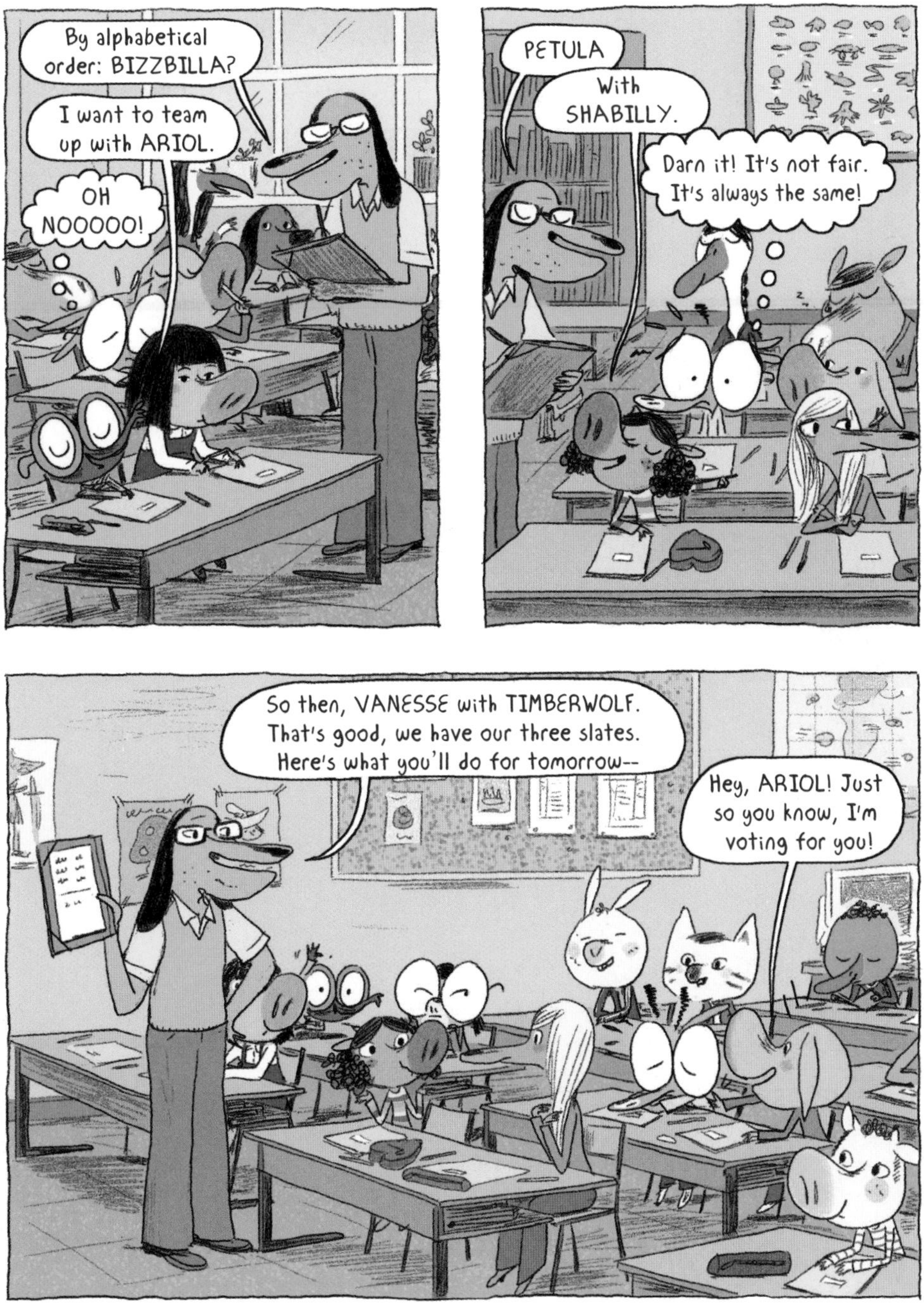
By alphabetical order: BIZZBILLA?
I want to team up with ARIOL.
OH NOOOOO!
PETULA
With SHABILLY.
Darn it! It's not fair. It's always the same!
So then, VANESSE with TIMBERWOLF. That's good, we have our three slates. Here's what you'll do for tomorrow--
Hey, ARIOL! Just so you know, I'm voting for you!

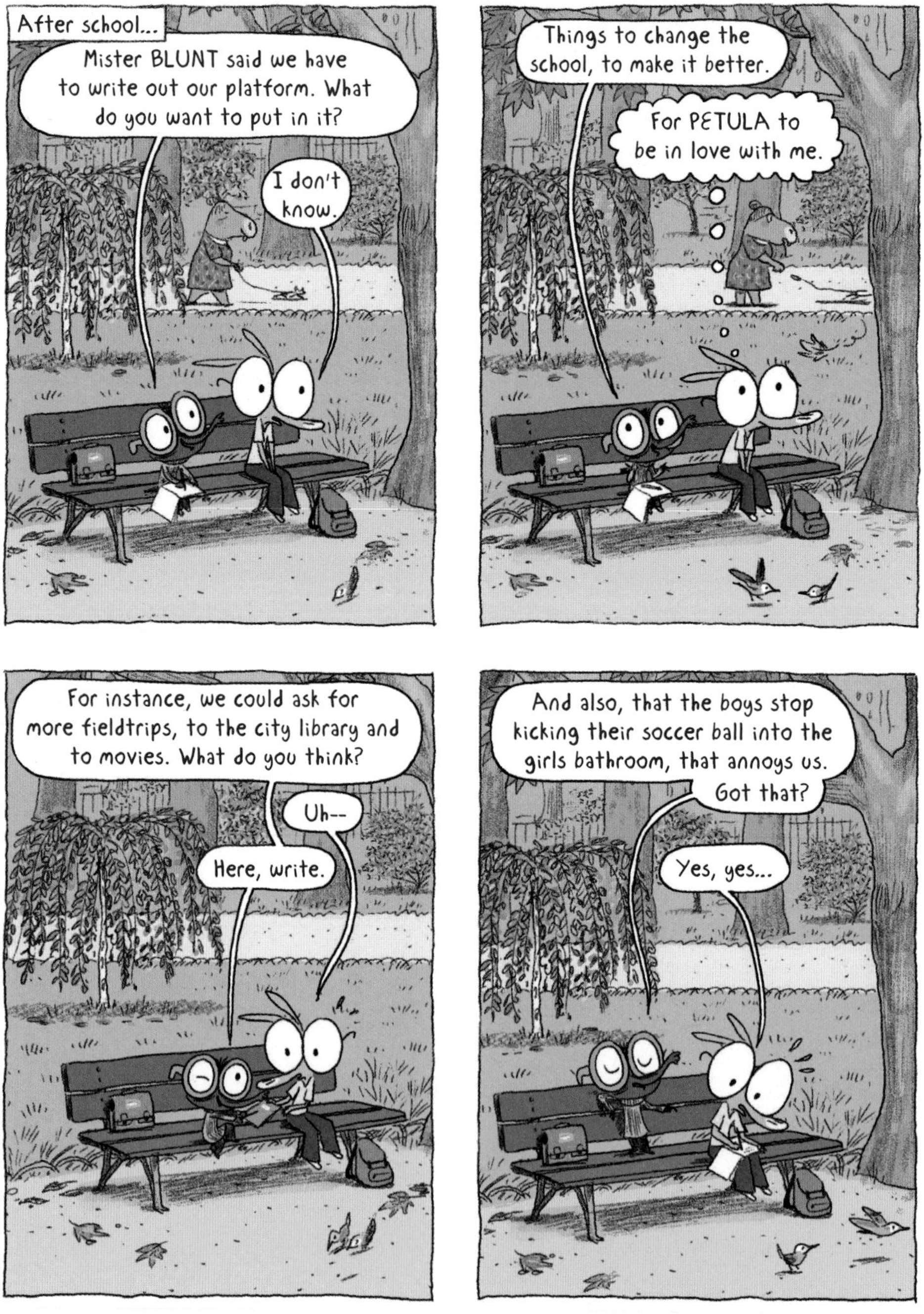
After school...
Mister BLUNT said we have to write out our platform. What do you want to put in it?
I don't know.
Things to change the school, to make it better.
For PETULA to be in love with me.
For instance, we could ask for more fieldtrips, to the city library and to movies. What do you think?
Uh--
Here, write.
And also, that the boys stop kicking their soccer ball into the girls bathroom, that annoys us.
Got that?
Yes, yes...

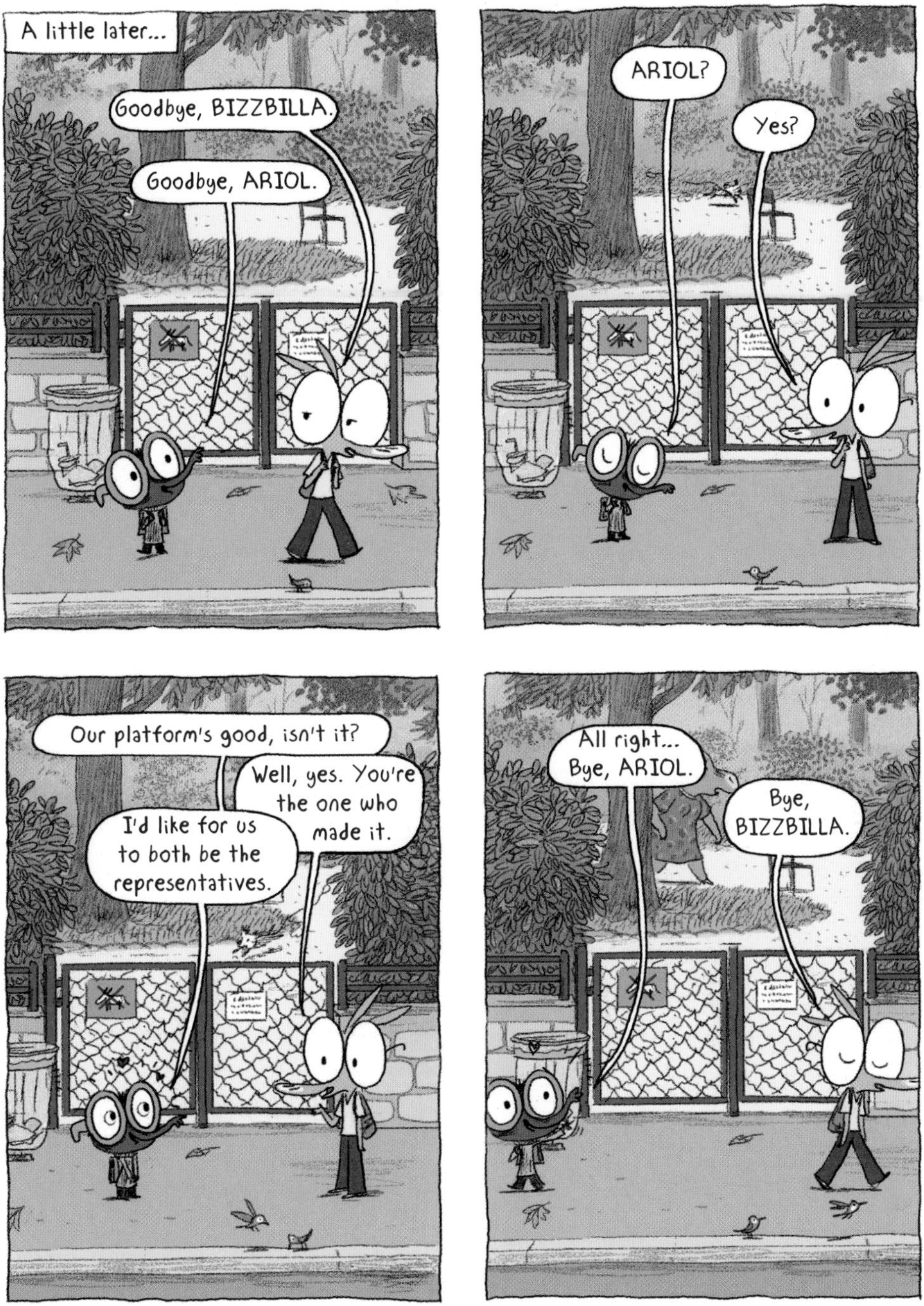
A little later...
Goodbye, BIZZBILLA.
Goodbye, ARIOL.
ARIOL?
Yes?
Our platform's good, isn't it?
Well, yes. You're the one who made it.
I'd like for us to both be the representatives.
All right... Bye, ARIOL.
Bye, BIZZBILLA.

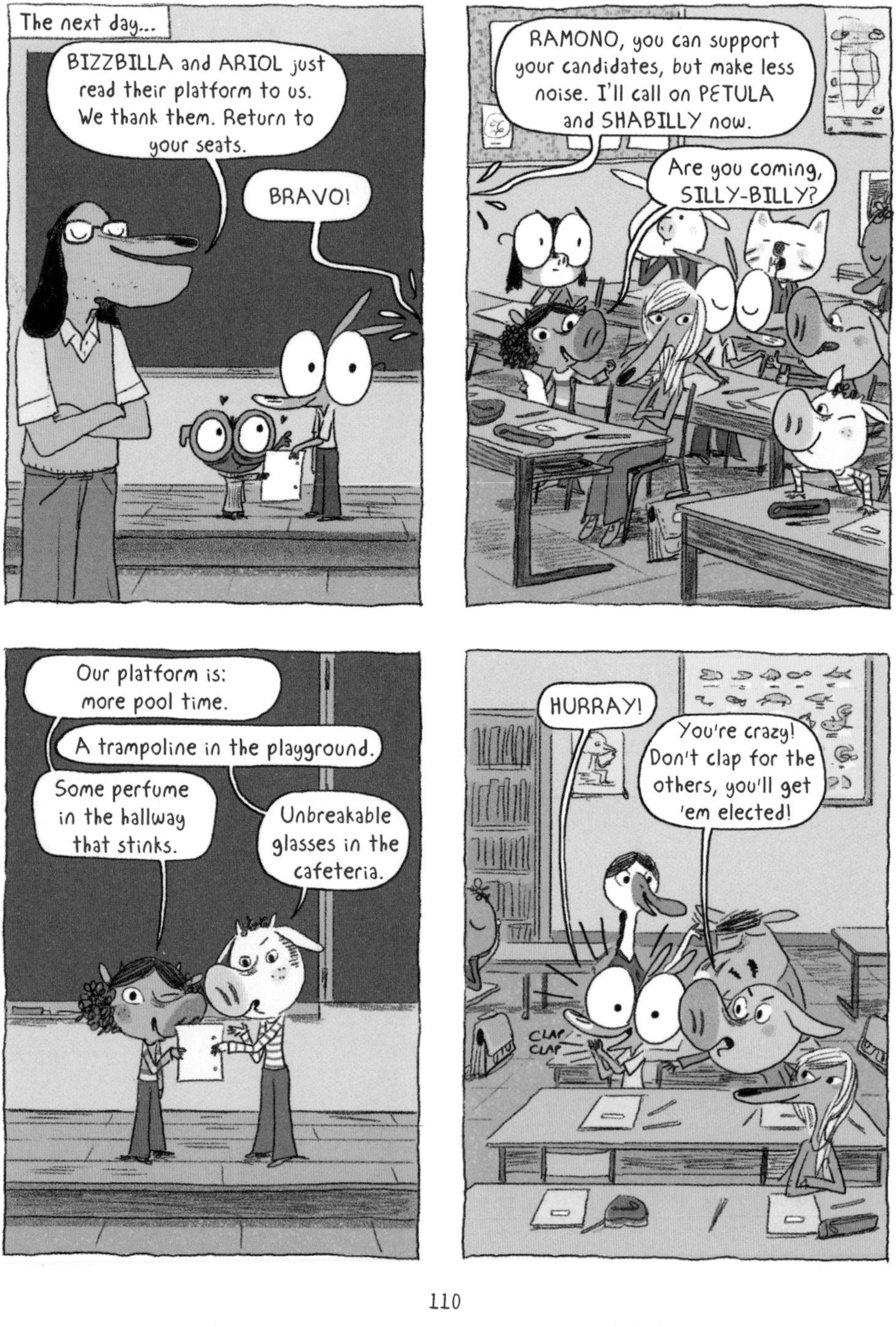
The next day...
BIZZBILLA and ARIOL just read their platform to us. We thank them. Return to your seats.
BRAVO!
RAMONO, you can support your candidates, but make less noise. I'll call on PETULA and SHABILLY now.
Are you coming, SILLY-BILLY?
Our platform is: more pool time.
A trampoline in the playground.
Some perfume in the hallway that stinks.
Unbreakable glasses in the cafeteria.
HURRAY!
You're crazy! Don't clap for the others, you'll get 'em elected!
CLAP/ CLAP

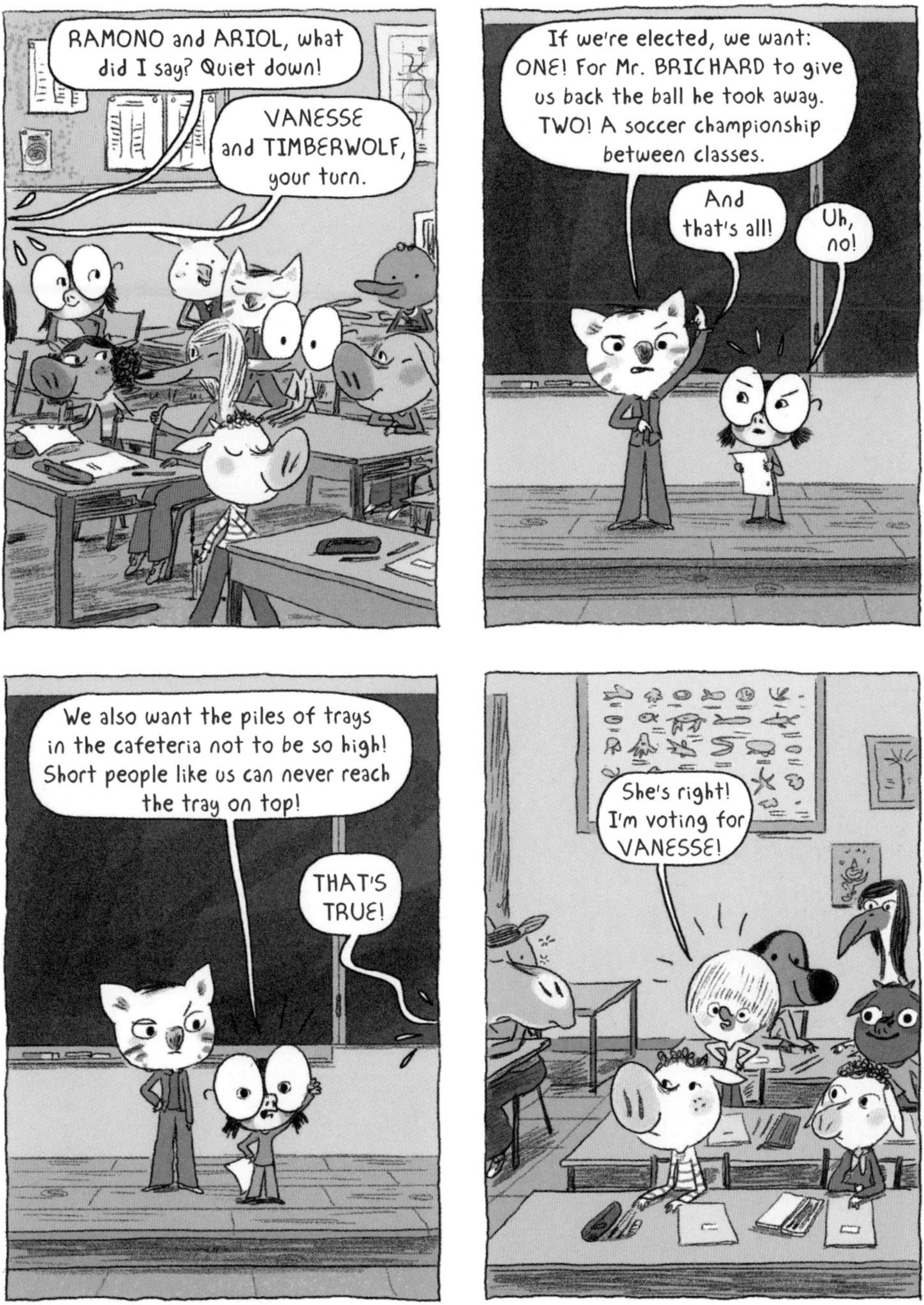
RAMONO and ARIOL, what did I say? Quiet down!
VANESSE and TIMBERWOLF, your turn.
If we're elected, we want: ONE! For Mr. BRICHARD to give us back the ball he took away. TWO! A soccer championship between classes.
And that's all!
Uh, no!
We also want the piles of trays in the cafeteria not to be so high! Short people like us can never reach the tray on top!
THAT'S TRUE!
She's right! I'm voting for VANESSE!

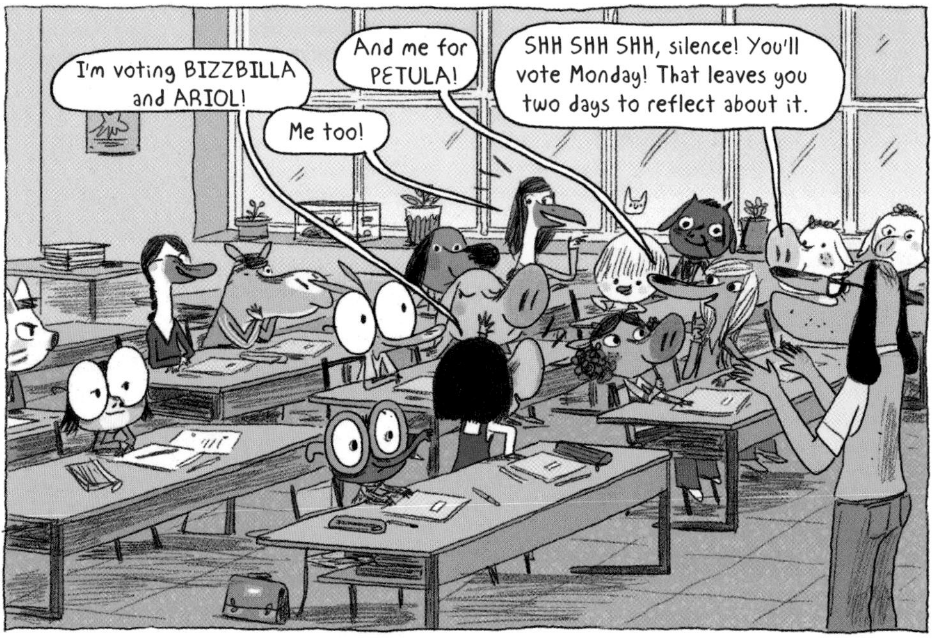
I'm voting BIZZBILLA and ARIOL!
Me too!
And me for PETULA!
SHH SHH SHH, silence! You'll vote Monday! That leaves you two days to reflect about it.

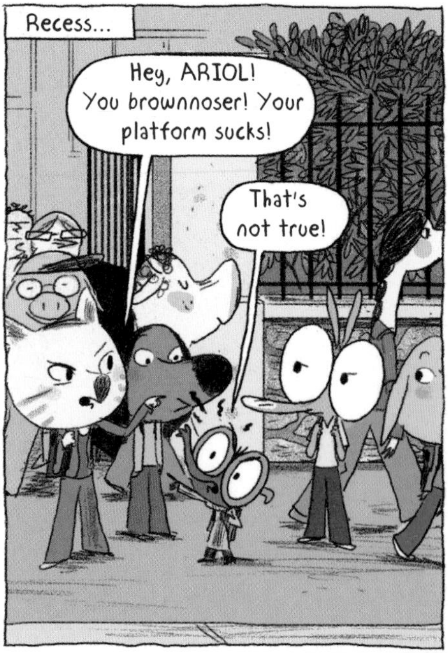
Recess...
Hey, ARIOL! You brownnoser! Your platform sucks!
That's not true!

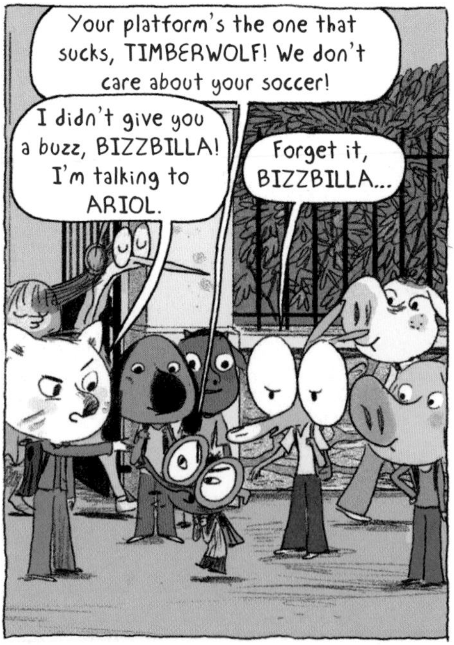
Your platform's the one that sucks, TIMBERWOLF! We don't care about your soccer!
I didn't give you a buzz, BIZZBILLA! I'm talking to ARIOL.
Forget it, BIZZBILLA...

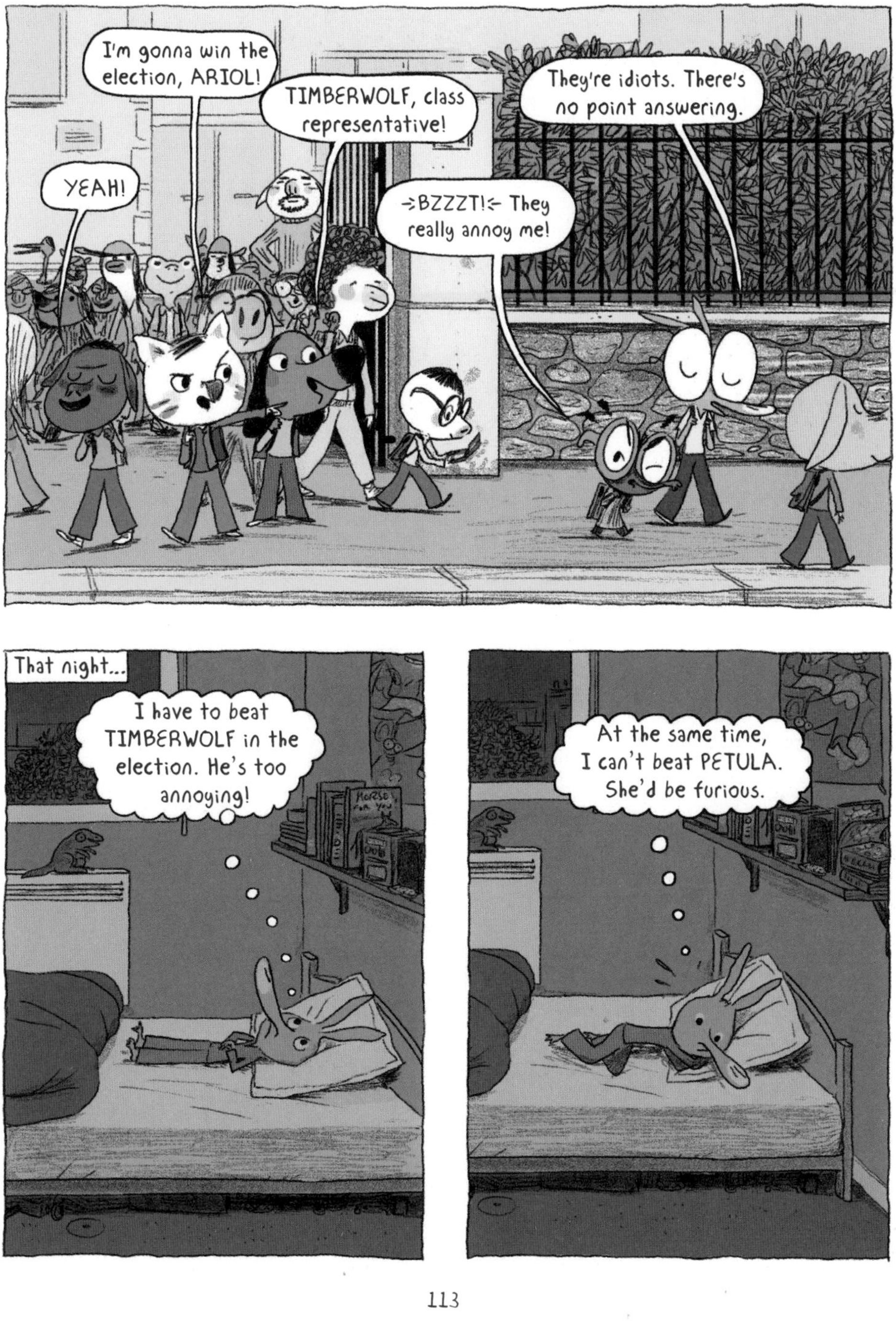
I'm gonna win the election, ARIOL!
YEAH!
TIMBERWOLF, class representative!
⇒BZZZT!⇐ They really annoy me!
They're idiots. There's no point answering.
That night...
I have to beat TIMBERWOLF in the election. He's too annoying!
At the same time, I can't beat PETULA. She'd be furious.

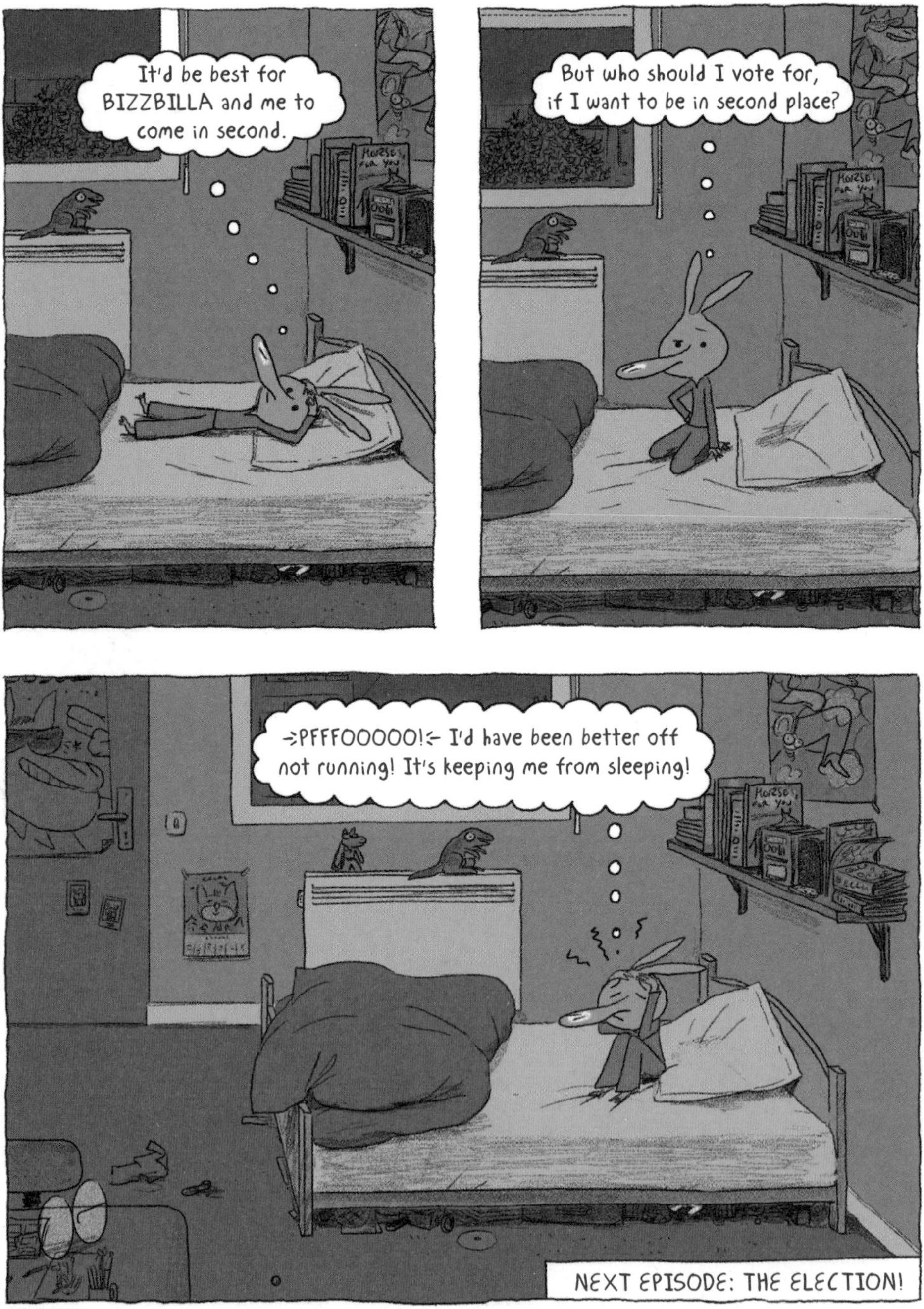
It'd be best for BIZZBILLA and me to come in second.
But who should I vote for, if I want to be in second place?
Horses for you
→PFFFOOOOO!← I'd have been better off not running! It's keeping me from sleeping!
NEXT EPISODE: THE ELECTION!

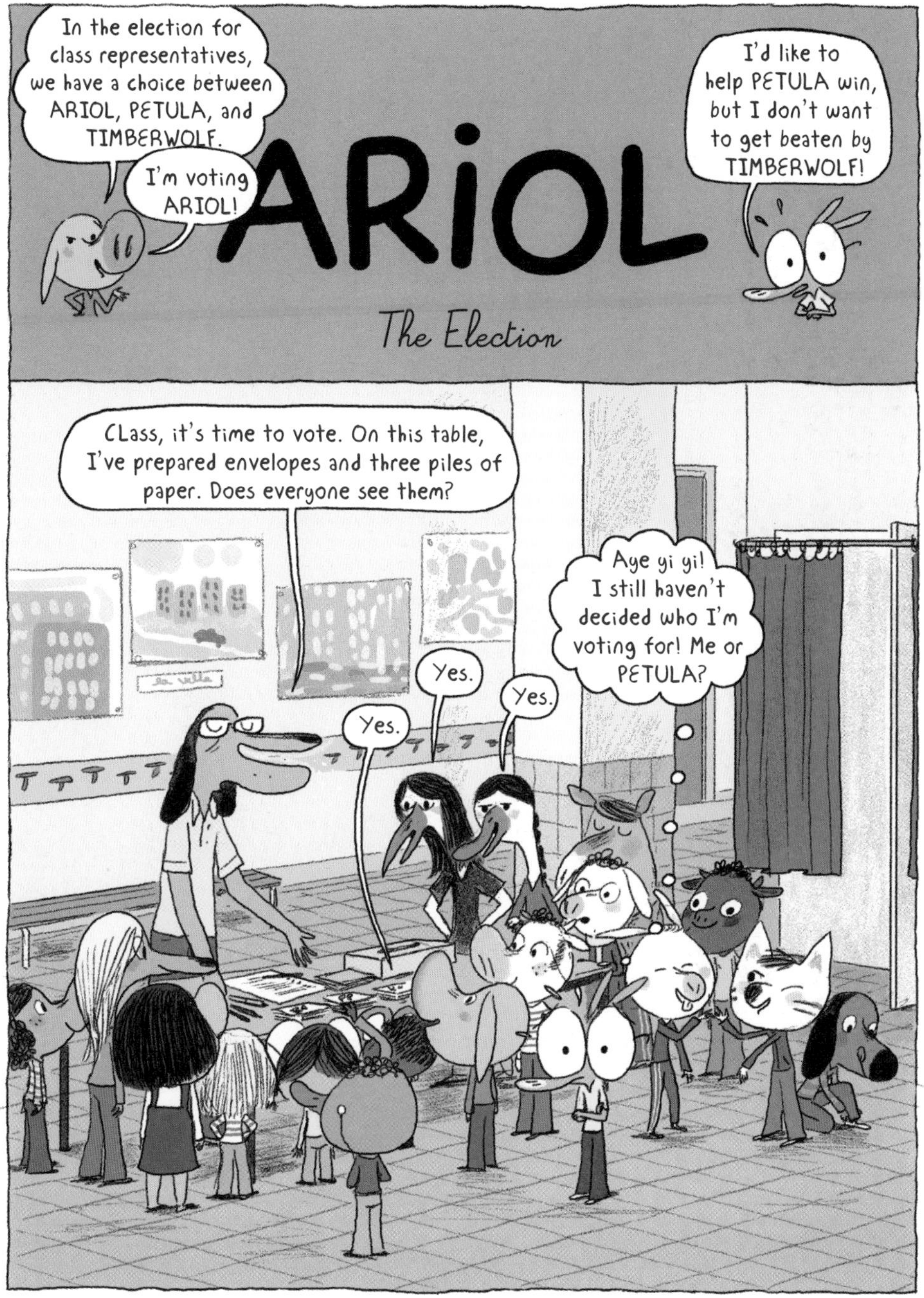
In the election for class representatives, we have a choice between ARIOL, PETULA, and TIMBERWOLF.
I'm voting ARIOL!
ARIOL
I'd like to help PETULA win, but I don't want to get beaten by TIMBERWOLF!
The Election
CLass, it's time to vote. On this table, I've prepared envelopes and three piles of paper. Does everyone see them?
Yes.
Yes.
Yes.
Aye yi yi! I still haven't decided who I'm voting for! Me or PETULA?

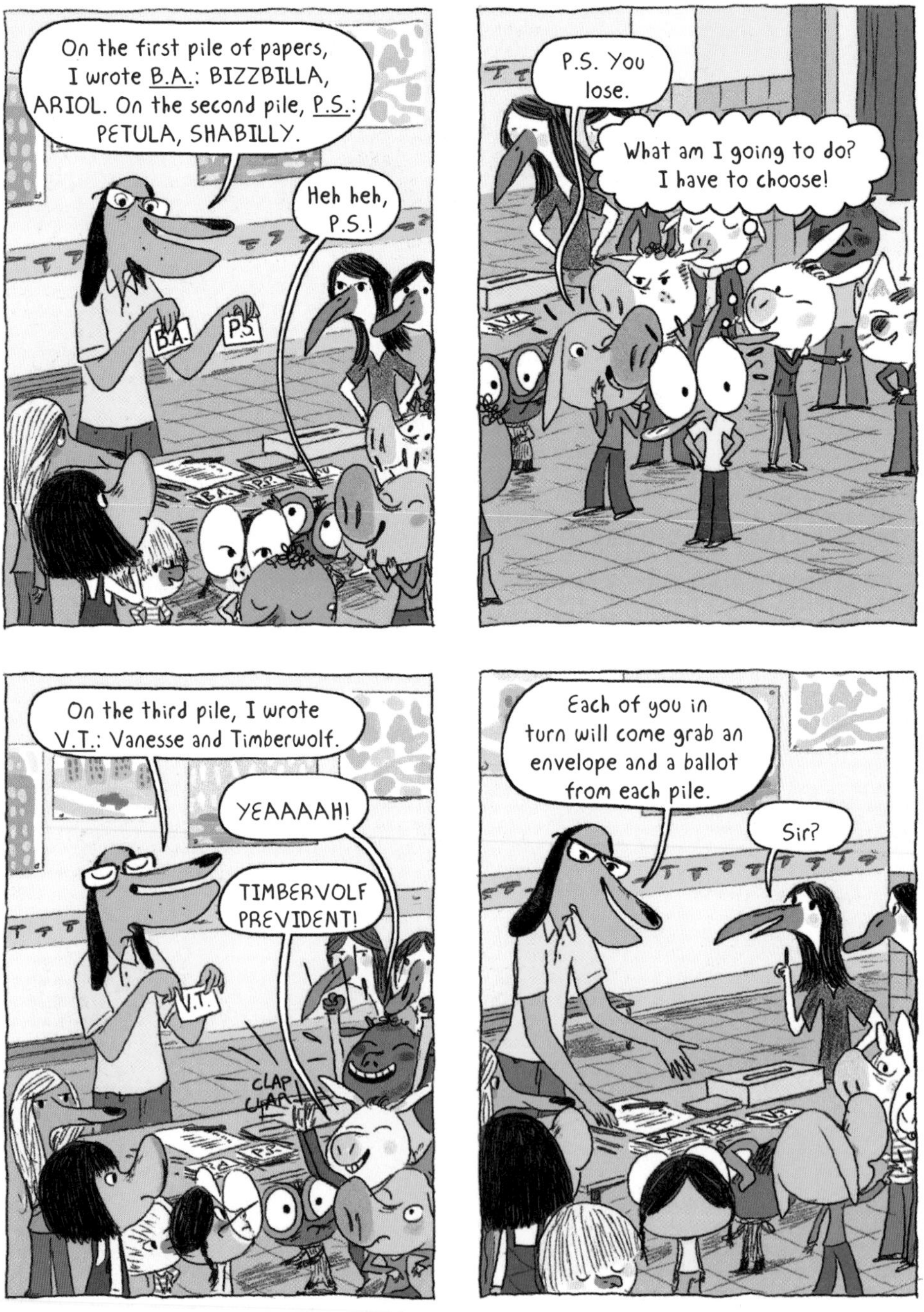
On the first pile of papers, I wrote B.A.: BIZZBILLA, ARIOL. On the second pile, P.S.: PETULA, SHABILLY.
B.A.
P.S.
Heh heh, P.S.!
P.S. You lose.
What am I going to do? I have to choose!
On the third pile, I wrote V.T.: Vanesse and Timberwolf.
V.T.
YEAAAAH!
TIMBERVOLF PREVIDENT!
CLAP CLAP
Each of you in turn will come grab an envelope and a ballot from each pile.
Sir?

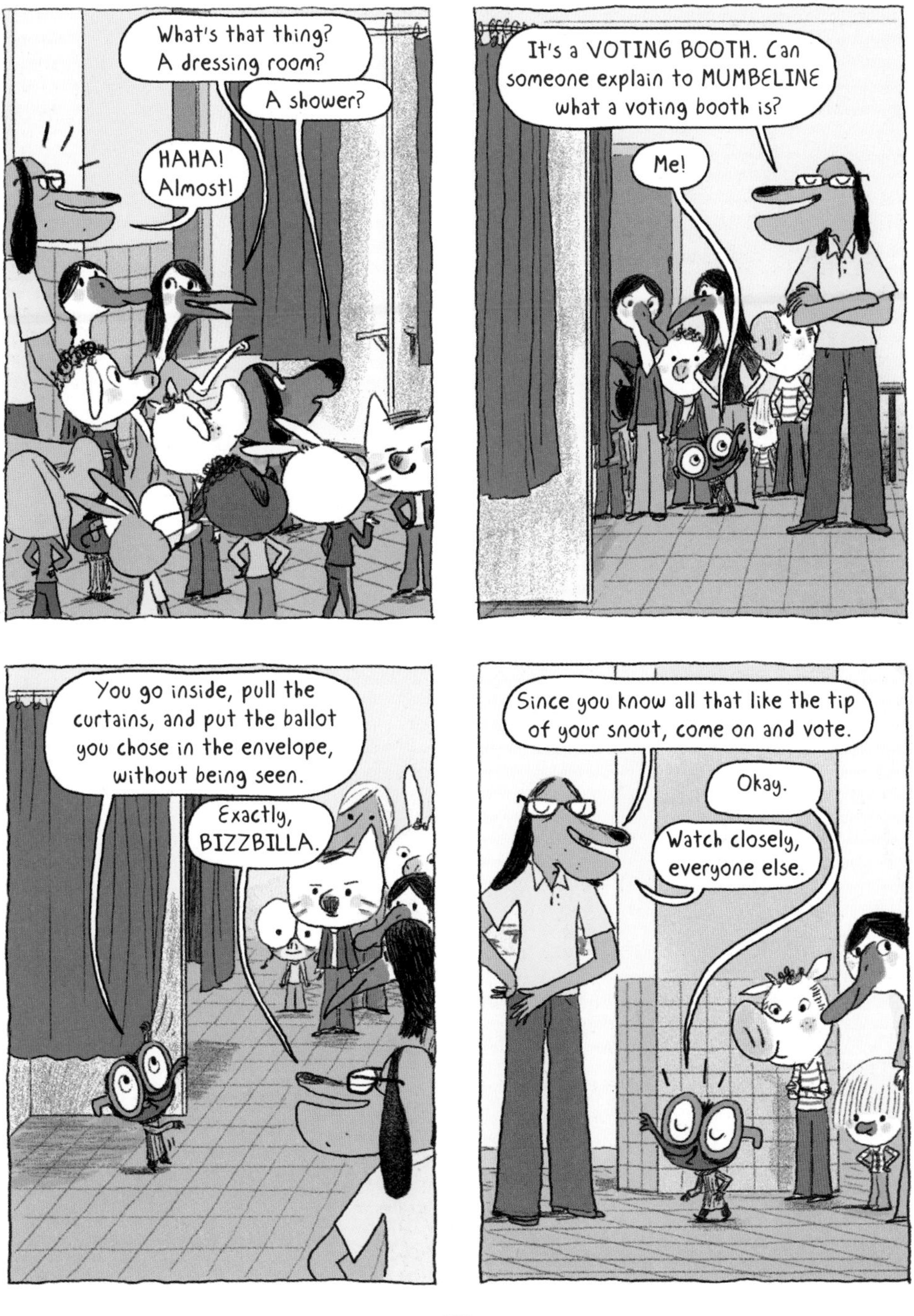
What's that thing? A dressing room?
A shower?
HAHA! Almost!
It's a VOTING BOOTH. Can someone explain to MUMBELINE what a voting booth is?
Me!
You go inside, pull the curtains, and put the ballot you chose in the envelope, without being seen.
Exactly, BIZZBILLA.
Since you know all that like the tip of your snout, come on and vote.
Okay.
Watch closely, everyone else.

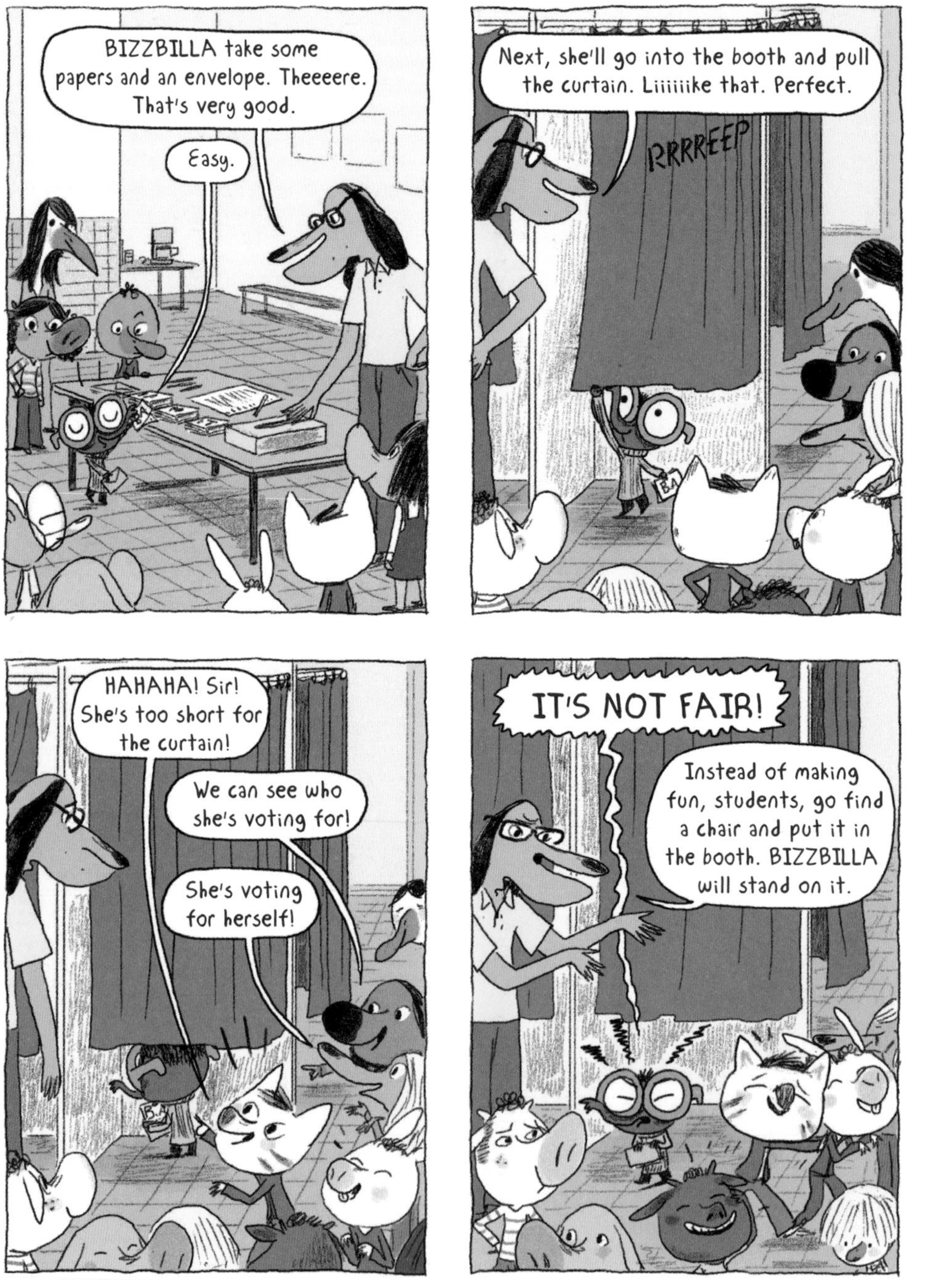
BIZZBILLA take some papers and an envelope. Theeeere. That's very good.
Easy.
Next, she'll go into the booth and pull the curtain. Liiiiiike that. Perfect.
RRRREEP
HAHAHA! Sir! She's too short for the curtain!
We can see who she's voting for!
She's voting for herself!
IT'S NOT FAIR!
Instead of making fun, students, go find a chair and put it in the booth. BIZZBILLA will stand on it.

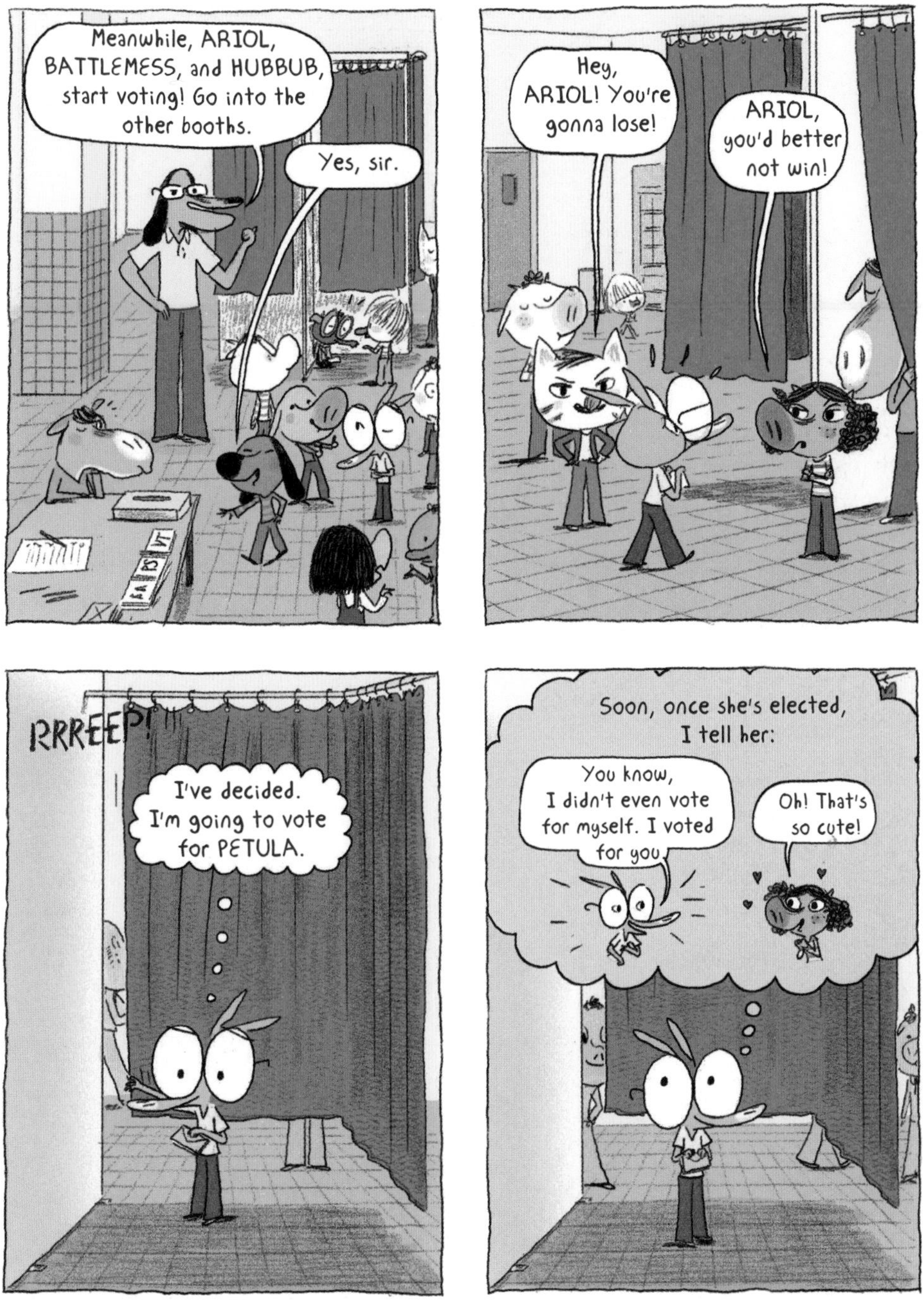

Meanwhile, ARIOL, BATTLEMESS, and HUBBUB, start voting! Go into the other booths.
Yes, sir.
Hey, ARIOL! You're gonna lose!
ARIOL, you'd better not win!
RRREEP!
I've decided. I'm going to vote for PETULA.
Soon, once she's elected, I tell her:
You know, I didn't even vote for myself. I voted for you.
Oh! That's so cute!

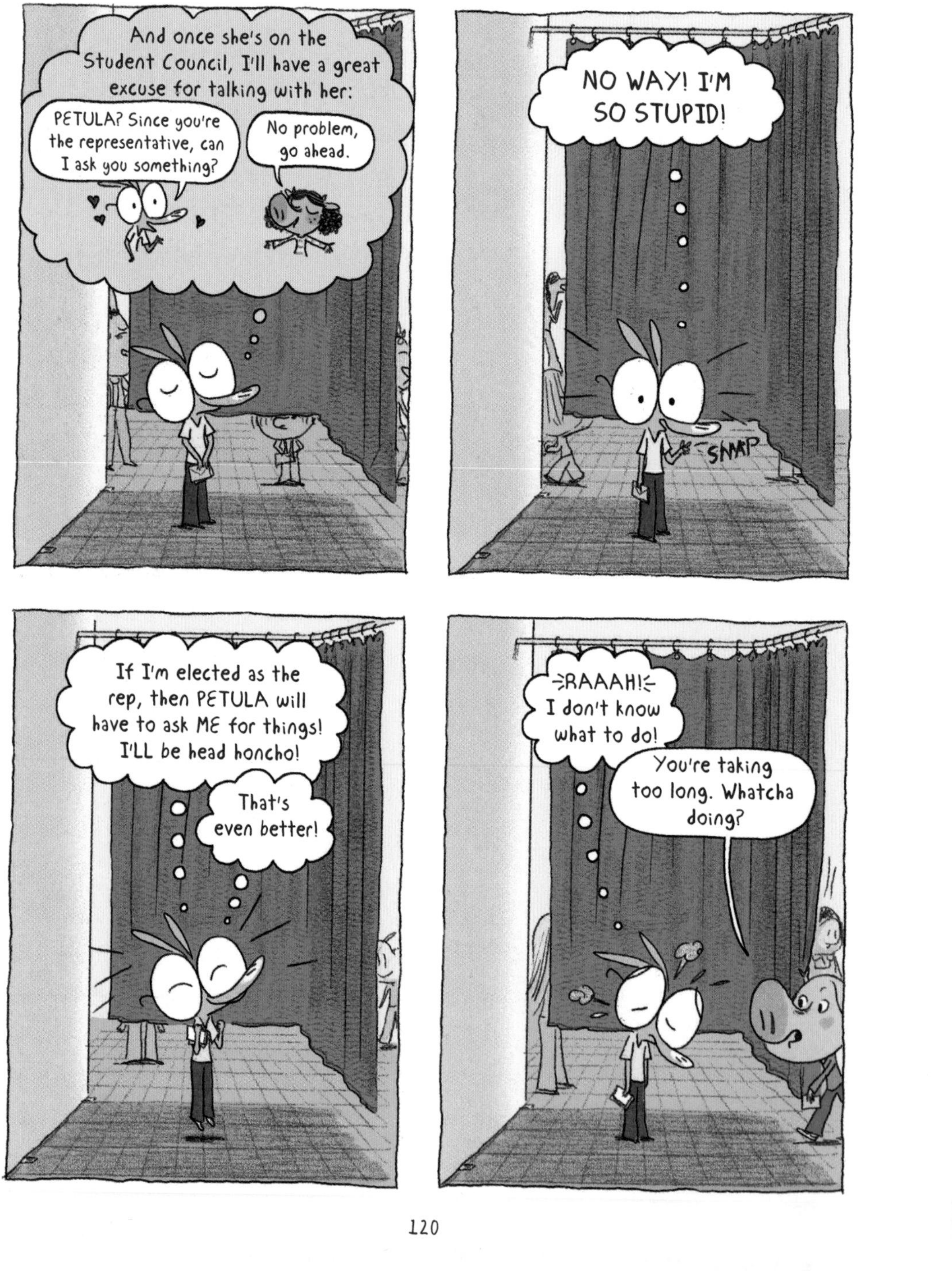
And once she's on the Student Council, I'll have a great excuse for talking with her:
PETULA? Since you're the representative, can I ask you something?
No problem, go ahead.
NO WAY! I'M SO STUPID!
SNAP
If I'm elected as the rep, then PETULA will have to ask ME for things! I'LL be head honcho!
That's even better!
RAAAH! I don't know what to do!
You're taking too long. Whatcha doing?

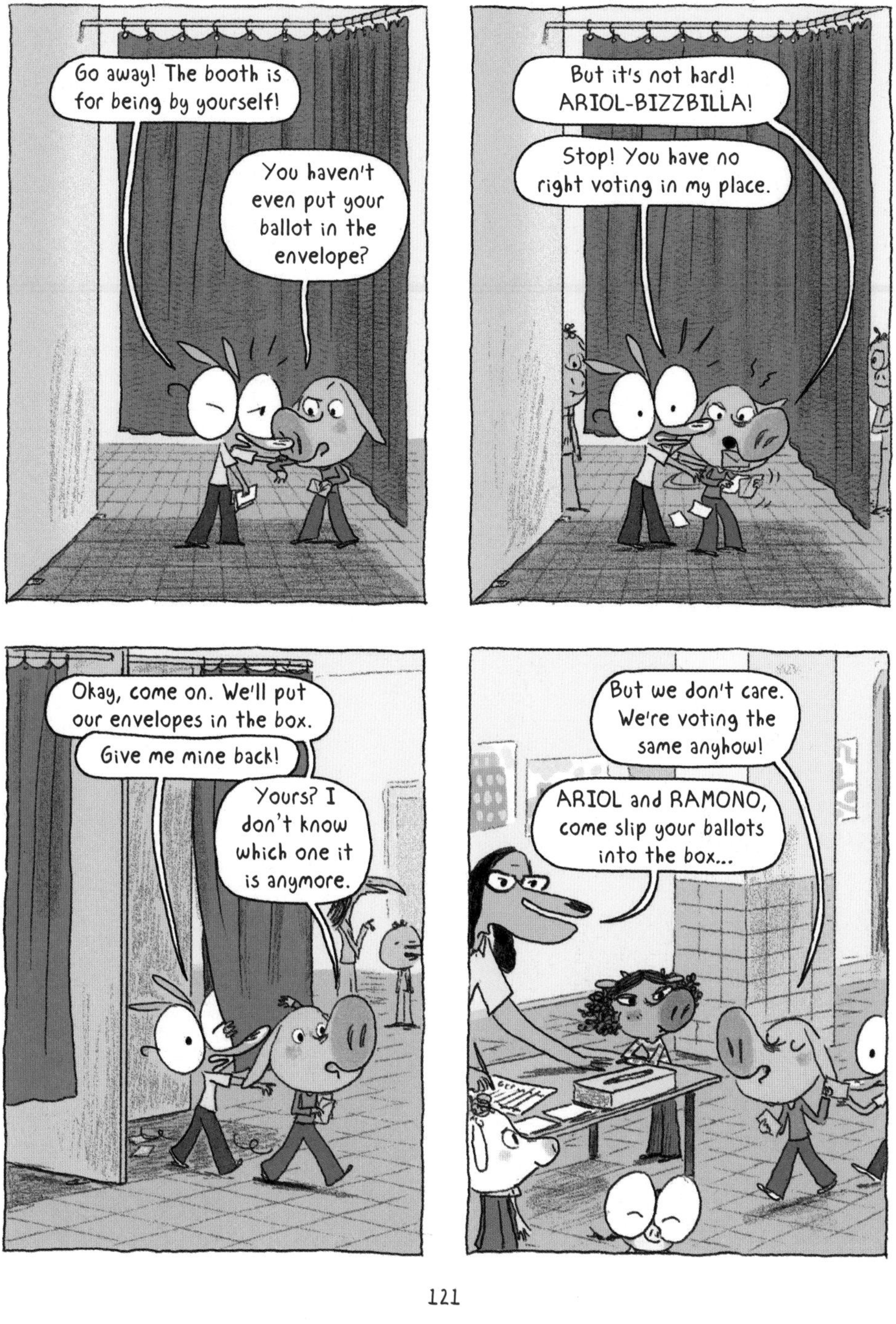
Go away! The booth is for being by yourself!
You haven't even put your ballot in the envelope?
But it's not hard! ARIOL-BIZZBILLA!
Stop! You have no right voting in my place.
Okay, come on. We'll put our envelopes in the box.
Give me mine back!
Yours? I don't know which one it is anymore.
But we don't care. We're voting the same anyhow!
ARIOL and RAMONO, come slip your ballots into the box...

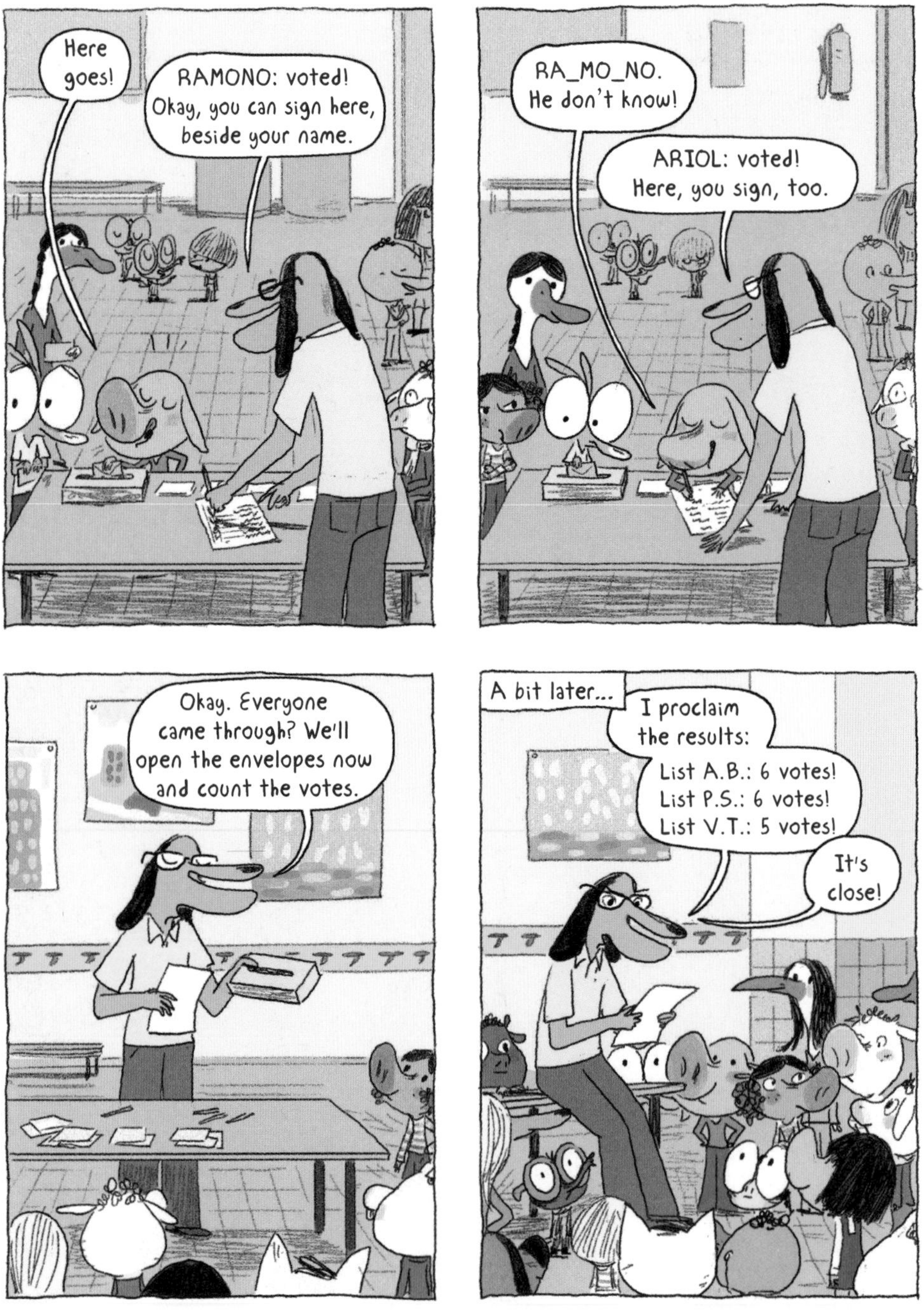
Here goes!
RAMONO: voted! Okay, you can sign here, beside your name.
RA_MO_NO. He don't know!
ARIOL: voted! Here, you sign, too.
Okay. Everyone came through? We'll open the envelopes now and count the votes.
A bit later...
I proclaim the results:
List A.B.: 6 votes!
List P.S.: 6 votes!
List V.T.: 5 votes!
It's close!

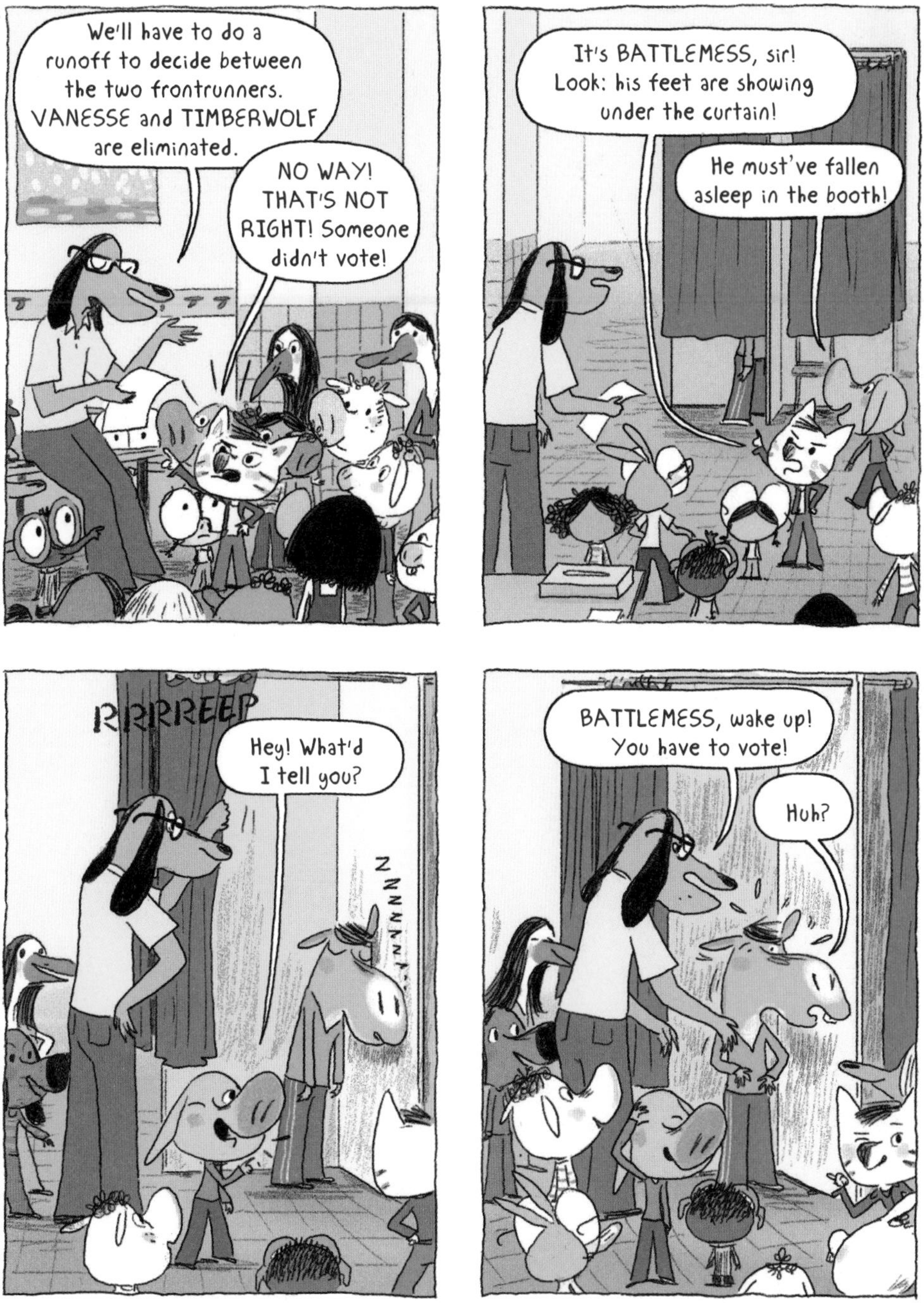
We'll have to do a runoff to decide between the two frontrunners. VANESSE and TIMBERWOLF are eliminated.
NO WAY! THAT'S NOT RIGHT! Someone didn't vote!
It's BATTLEMESS, sir! Look: his feet are showing under the curtain!
He must've fallen asleep in the booth!
RRRREEP
Hey! What'd I tell you?
BATTLEMESS, wake up! You have to vote!
Huh?

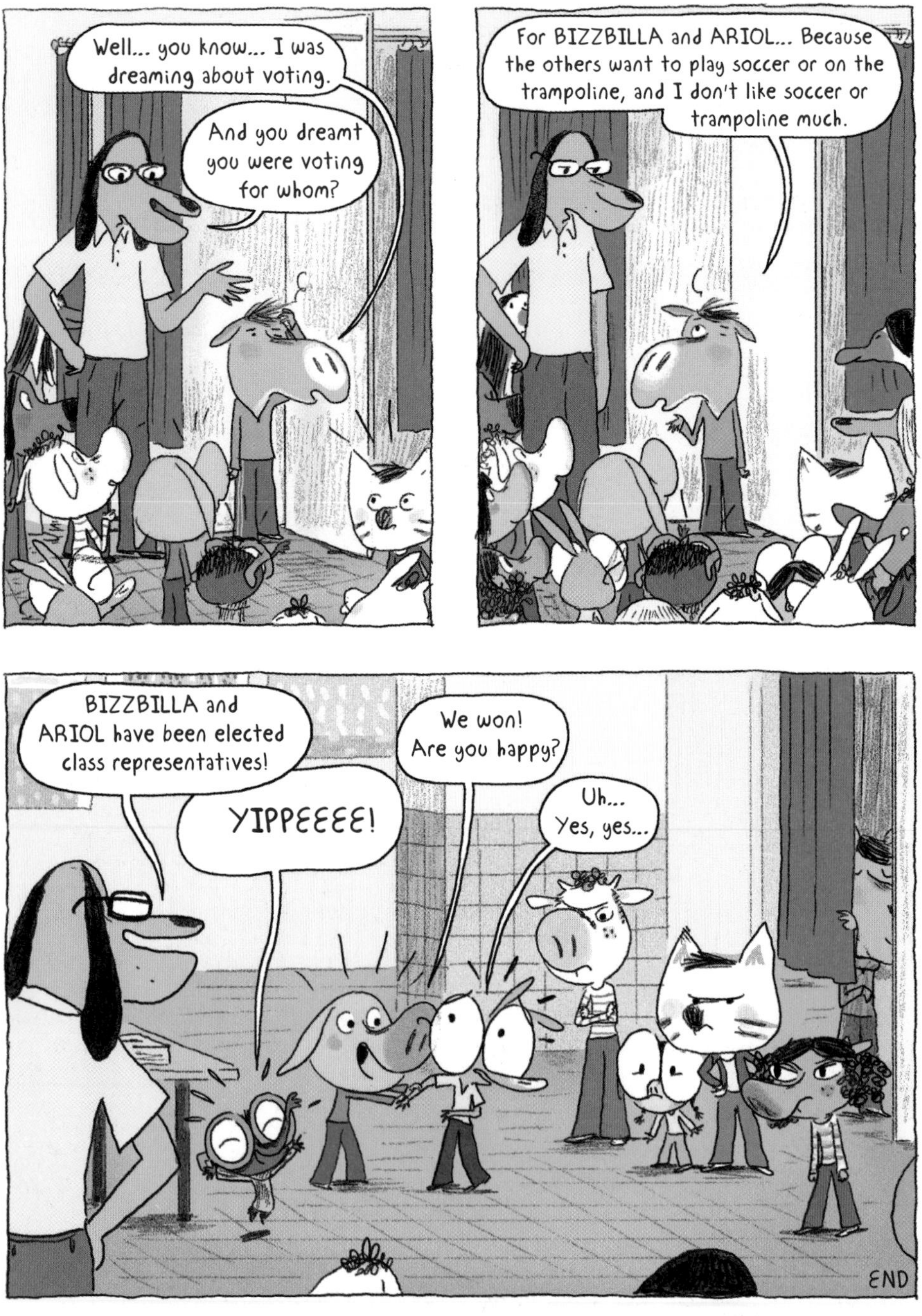
Well... you know... I was dreaming about voting.
And you dreamt you were voting for whom?
For BIZZBILLA and ARIOL... Because the others want to play soccer or on the trampoline, and I don't like soccer or trampoline much.
BIZZBILLA and ARIOL have been elected class representatives!
YIPPEEEE!
We won! Are you happy?
Uh... Yes, yes...
END

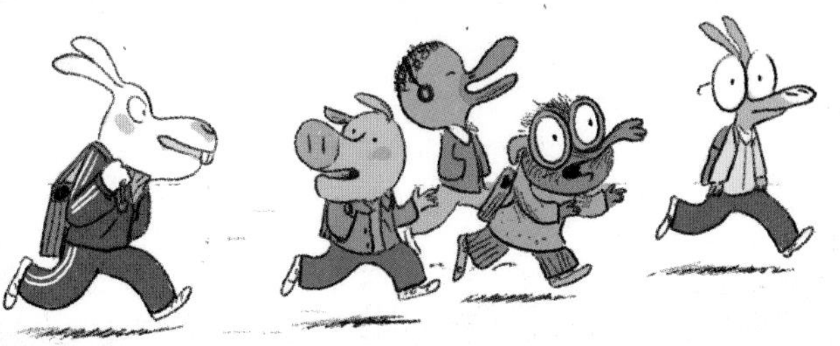

WATCH OUT FOR PAPERCUTZ™

Considering the title of this particular ARIOL graphic novel, perhaps this column should be called "Watch Out for PaperCATz" instead?!

Welcome to the satisfyingly surreal, yet slightly silly sixth ARIOL graphic novel, by the super-talented team of EMMANUEL GUIBERT and MARC BOUTAVANT, from Papercutz, those hard-working souls dedicated to publishing great graphic novels for all ages. I'm JIM SALICRUP, Editor-in-Chief and President of the Thunder Horse Fan Club, New York City Chapter. I'm back again with an ARIOL thought or two, and a suggestion...

POESY DOCTOROW posted another review of ARIOL– you can watch it here: www.youtube.com/watch?v=hkhw3vJmoCI. But just to be clear, you don't need a famous author as a father to post your reviews of ARIOL online. We'd love to see YOU post your own video review of ARIOL on YouTube. Just be sure to tell us about it so we can let everyone else know about it. Oh, and thanks again, POESY!

As I write this column, the USA has just had another Election Day, and I can't help wishing I could've voted for BIZZBELLA and ARIOL! (But I hope the folks I did vote for are able to help make the world a little better place.)

The stories "Vote for ARIOL" and "THE ELECTION" can be seen as just one big twenty-page story. So could "Mrs. SAPOLIN's Pies" and "DON OLIO and his Rhythms." But imagine an ARIOL graphic novel with just one big ARIOL story in it... Wouldn't that be great? Well, you don't have to imagine it– EMMANUEL GUIBERT and MARC BOUTAVANT have created just such an ARIOL graphic novel! It's called "Where's Petula?" and PAPERCUTZ will be publishing it very soon! You certainly won't want to miss the longest ARIOL adventure ever!

For everyone who enjoys ARIOL graphic novels (that includes YOU, right?), there's another PAPERCUTZ graphic novel series, you may also love: ERNEST & REBECCA. When we first meet REBECCA in ERNEST & REBECCA #1 "My Best Friend is a Germ," she is only six and a half years old, but there's a lot going on in her world. Her parents are on the verge of breaking up, so they're fighting often, which is not fun. Her older sister is becoming a teenager, so she doesn't want to play with REBECCA. And REBECCA has been getting sick. All these factors combined have made REBECCA very lonely, but suddenly a friendly super-powered germ named ERNEST appears and becomes her new best friend. Now it may sound kind of silly, but who would've guessed a series about a blue donkey and his pig friend could be so good? So may we suggest checking out ERNEST & REBECCA? If you wind up liking it as much as we do, you'll want to thank us! (For more on ERNEST & REBECCA, check out the PAPERCUTZ website.)

Finally, THANK YOU for picking up ARIOL! It's great that so many people are discovering this series. There's nothing more heartbreaking than to publish a great series and have no one know it exists. So again, THANK YOU so much!

Thanks,

Jim

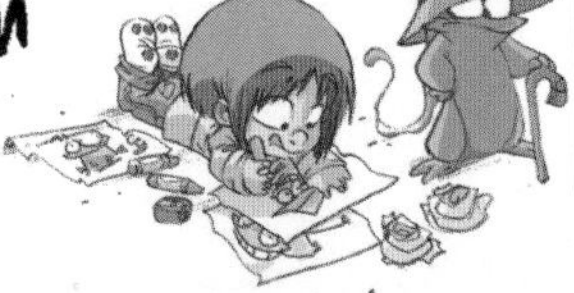

STAY IN TOUCH!

EMAIL:	salicrup@papercutz.com
WEB:	papercutz.com
TWITTER:	@papercutzgn
FACEBOOK:	PAPERCUTZGRAPHICNOVELS
REGULAR MAIL:	Papercutz, 160 Broadway, Suite 700, East Wing, New York, NY 10038

Other Great Titles From PAPERCUTZ™

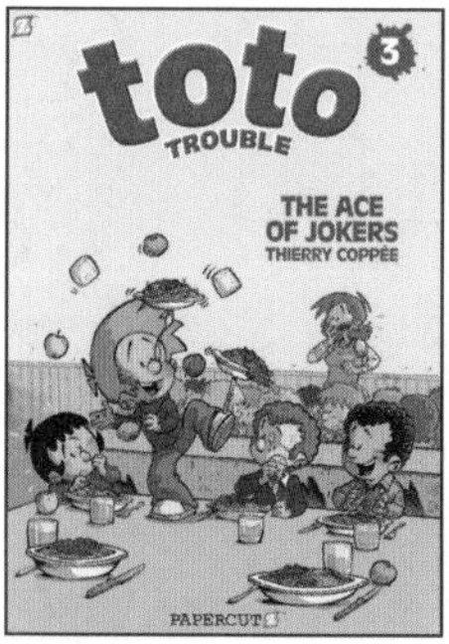
toto
TROUBLE
3
THE ACE OF JOKERS
THIERRY COPPÉE
PAPERCUTZ

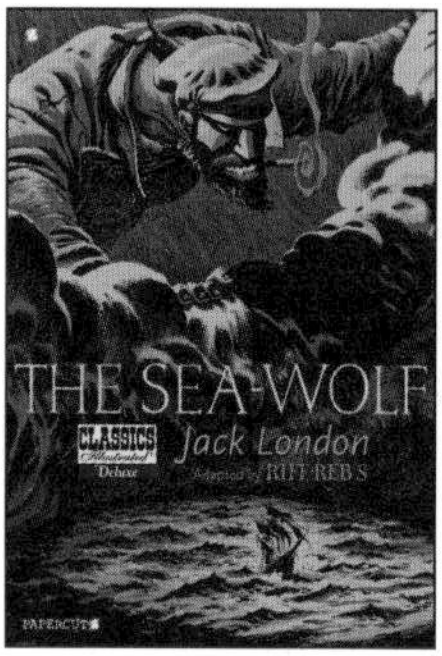
THE SEA-WOLF
CLASSICS Illustrated Deluxe
Jack London
PAPERCUTZ

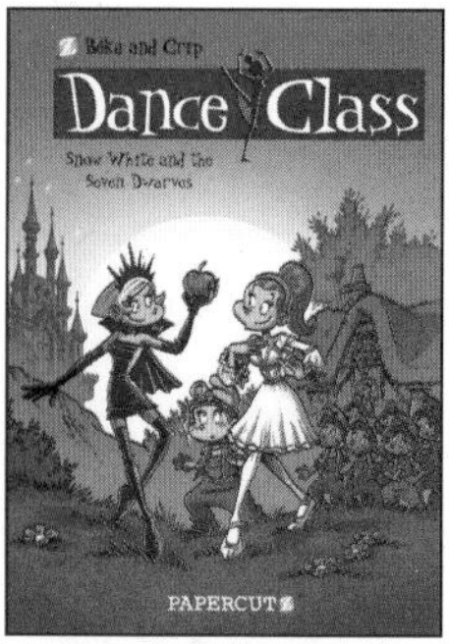
Dance Class
Snow White and the Seven Dwarves
PAPERCUTZ

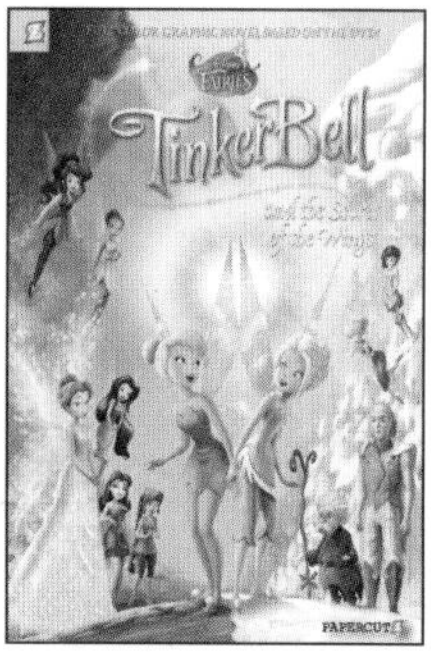
TinkerBell
PAPERCUTZ

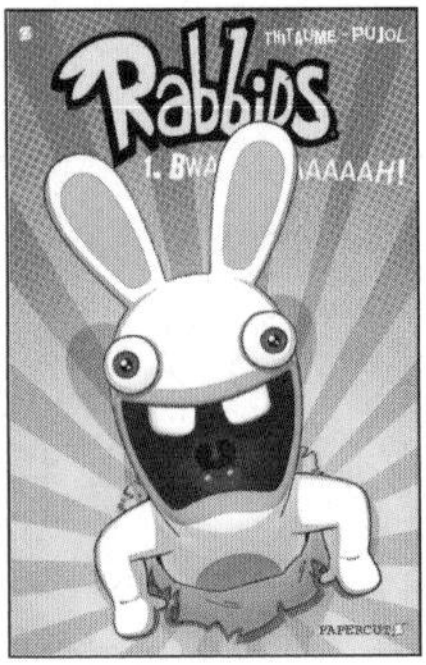
Rabbids
PAPERCUTZ

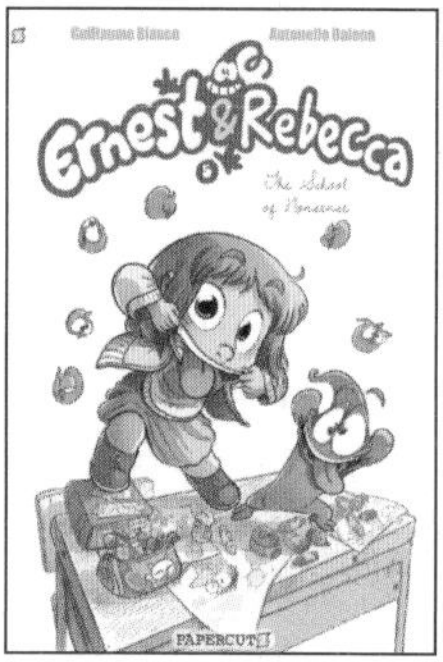
Ernest & Rebecca
The School of Nonsense
PAPERCUTZ

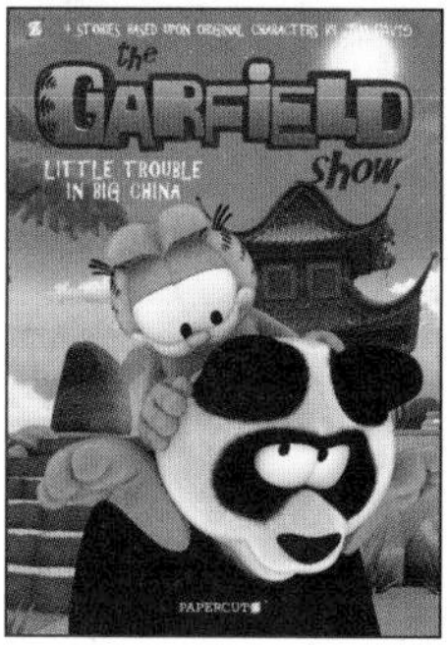
the GARFIELD show
LITTLE TROUBLE IN BIG CHINA
PAPERCUTZ

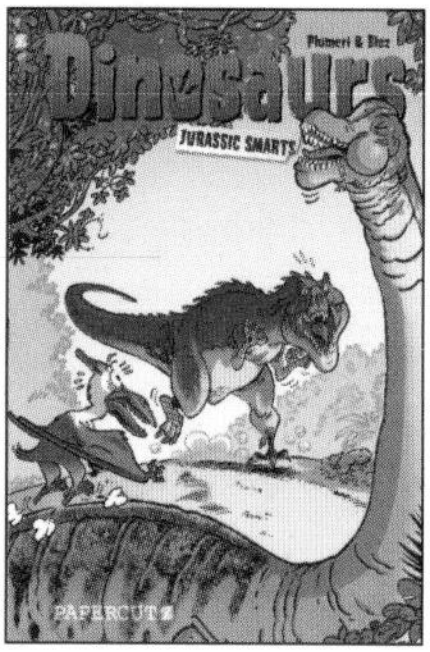
Dinosaurs
JURASSIC SMARTS
PAPERCUTZ

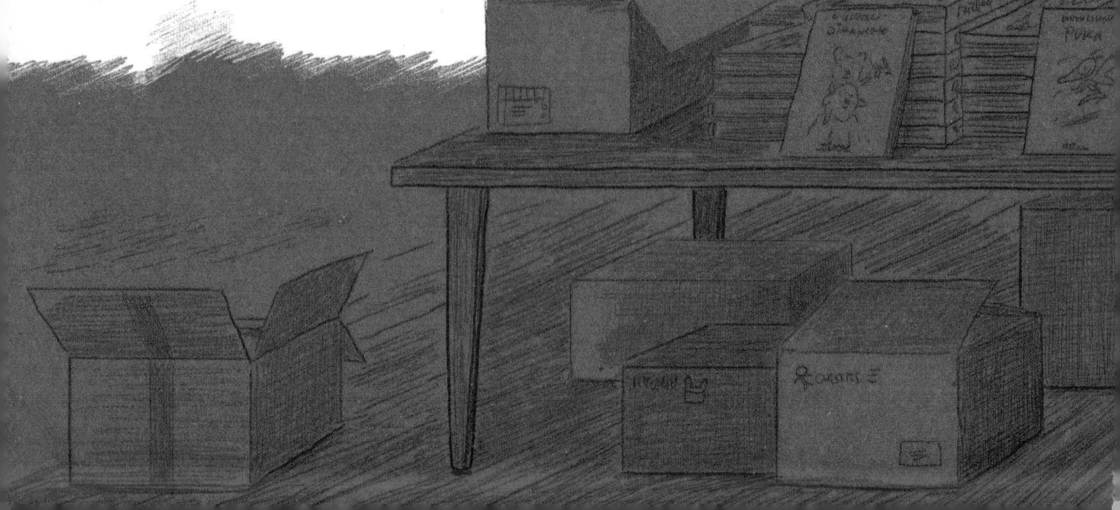